What readers are saying...

Michelle, age 14
I think that the Elsie stories are the most wonderful books that I have ever read, apart from the Bible. These books have affected me by helping my faith to grow stronger.

Elizabeth, age 13
The books made me think about how I can live my life for God and that it is possible to have a very strong relationship with him even when you're very young.

Alyssa, age 12
The Elsie books have changed my life! I feel much closer to God! I want to try to be just like Elsie! It has really changed my attitude.

Kelly, age 11
The books helped me get deeper in my faith, and helped me deal with everyday problems. I feel if I didn't have the books, I wouldn't be half as close to God.

Beth, age 10
Ever since I started reading these books I feel like they have inspired me and I have been trying to be like Elsie. I have been going to church forever, but when I sat down and listened I understood it better than I ever did before. I feel like I am finally beginning to relate to the Bible.

Elsie's
Endless
Wait

Elsie's Endless Wait

BOOK ONE

of the
*A Life of Faith:
Elsie Dinsmore*
Series

Based on the beloved books by
Martha Finley

MCP
Mission City Press

Franklin, Tennessee

Book One of the *A Life of Faith: Elsie Dinsmore* Series

Elsie's Endless Wait
Copyright © 1999, Mission City Press, Inc. All Rights Reserved.

Published by Mission City Press, Inc.

This book is based on the bestselling literary classic *Elsie Dinsmore* written by Martha Finley and first published in 1868 by Dodd, Mead & Company.

Cover & Interior Design: Richmond & Williams, Nashville, Tennessee
Cover Photography: Michelle Grisco Photography, West Covina, California
Interior Typesetting: BookSetters, White House, Tennessee

Special Thanks to Glen Eyrie Castle and Conference Center, Colorado Springs, Colorado, for Photo Shoot Locations

Unless otherwise indicated, all Scripture references are from the Holy Bible, New International Version (NIV). Copyright © 1973, 1978, 1984 by International Bible Society. Used by permission of Zondervan Publishing House, Grand Rapids, MI. All rights reserved.

Elsie Dinsmore and *A Life of Faith* are trademarks of Mission City Press, Inc.

For more information, write to Mission City Press P.O. Box 681913, Franklin, Tennessee 37068-1913

ISBN: 1-928749-01-1

Printed in the United States of America

DEDICATION

This book is
dedicated to
the memory of
MARTHA FINLEY

*May the rich legacy of
pure and simple devotion to Christ
that she introduced through
Elsie Dinsmore in 1868
live on in our day and
in generations to come.*

— FOREWORD —

*I*n this book, the first of the *A Life of Faith: Elsie Dinsmore* Series, you are about to take a trip back in time and to revisit the enduring truths of Christian living. Your journey will begin more than 150 years ago in the American South, two decades before the War Between the States.

At the prosperous plantation of Roselands, you will meet a little girl named Elsie Dinsmore who has never known the love of a parent. You will share Elsie's trials as she deals with resentful and jealous family members, yearns to know and be loved by the father she has never seen, and struggles to find happiness in the face of rejection. From infancy, Elsie has been raised to follow the Bible in every way, including strict observation of the Sabbath, regular prayer and Bible studies, and willing obedience of Jesus' command to love and do good with no expectation of reward. But her unswerving dedication to her Christian principles often causes trouble in the Dinsmore household. With only her loving and faithful nursemaid to rely on, Elsie turns for comfort, guidance, and hope to her little Bible and to Jesus, her closest and truest friend.

Elsie is not perfect by any means, but once you know this extraordinary character, you will find it hard to forget her. So gentle in heart and spirit, yet so strong when the principles of her faith are challenged — Elsie is a nineteenth century child with the power to inspire and uplift people of any era.

Elsie's Endless Wait

Elsie Dinsmore made her first appearance in 1868, and her creator, Martha Finley (1828-1909), eventually wrote twenty-eight novels about the life and times of Elsie. For almost forty years, legions of dedicated readers eagerly welcomed each new Elsie book and treasured them for their enchanting central character and her pure and simple devotion to Christ. But with the arrival of the twentieth century, the popularity of the series faded, and Elsie was nearly forgotten. Now, almost a century after Miss Finley's death, interest in the adventures of her charming Christian heroine has been revived.

Mission City Press is very proud to continue Miss Finley's commitment to Christian faith and the Christian heart by re-introducing Elsie Dinsmore for a new generation and generations to come. It is our hope that you will not only enjoy every one of Elsie's adventures but will also find in them, as we have, a source of spiritual inspiration that is ageless.

This version is a careful adaptation of the *Elsie Dinsmore* series, faithful to the original yet rewritten for modern readers. Since every effort has been made to preserve the nineteenth century flavor of Miss Finley's original text, some terms and customs may require explanation and historical context. The following brief overview of some of the differences between Elsie's era and modern times will, it is hoped, add to the reader's appreciation of the story.

✑ WELCOME TO ELSIE'S WORLD ✑

In the 1830s, when Elsie was born, the family was the fundamental unit of society, just as it is now, but couples married at earlier ages and large families were common.

Foreword

Several generations often lived together, and members of a single household might include grandparents and great-grandparents, aunts, uncles, and cousins as well as immediate family. Children were expected to respect the full authority of their parents and to obey all their elders.

Life expectancy was much shorter than it is today. Because medical knowledge was limited and modern methods of treatment such as antibiotics had not been discovered, virtually every illness in a family was regarded as a serious threat. Childhood diseases that are easily prevented or cured today were especially feared by parents in the nineteenth century.

Apart from trains and steamboats, there were no motorized forms of transportation in Elsie's day, and few paved roads outside large cities. People depended on horses, carriages, and their own feet to take them from place to place. Schools were scarce in the rural South, and children were usually educated at home; wealthy families frequently employed live-in governesses to teach, although teenage boys were sometimes sent to boarding schools. Children learned many of their lessons by rote, or exact memorization, and perfection was expected in their oral recitations of these daily assignments. Even very young children memorized lengthy Biblical passages. This explains Elsie's ability to quote the Scriptures. The Bible was an important part of the total educational process in many families. It was used to teach spelling, grammar, and composition, as well as lessons in morality and proper conduct.

In the 1800s, people had no radios or televisions, no films or videos or audio recordings, no computers and no telephones. In this era, reading and letter-writing were the primary media for communicating news, entertainment, and learning. Letter-writing was considered an art, newspapers flourished, and books were prized possessions even in the poorest homes. Visiting was also an important means of bridging the great distances between isolated farms and plantations. Wealthy homes were often full of guests whose stays extended from overnight to days, weeks, even months. In our story, friends and business associates join the Dinsmore family at mealtime, and in the Old South (indeed, in many parts of the South today), the main meal of the day, served at noon or one o'clock, was called "dinner." The lighter evening meal was "supper."

The Dinsmores are fortunate to live near a church which they can attend each week. But in more remote areas, Christian worship was observed at home, and families welcomed the occasional visit of clergymen, sometimes called "circuit riders," who traveled the countryside on horseback. Plantation-owners were expected to attend to the spiritual needs of their slaves and sometimes employed clergy to conduct services.

At the time this book begins, slavery was an accepted economic and social reality in the Antebellum South. Well-to-do planters with large estates, such as the senior Mr. Horace Dinsmore, "owned" many African-American slaves who were regarded as private property. The workers who plowed and planted and harvested the crops were the "field slaves," while "house servants" tended to the needs of the owner, his family, and the large plantation houses.

A master could do much as he pleased to discipline his slaves and could sell his slaves at any time, often separating families in the process. Although the planter's control was nearly absolute, the law regulated the master-slave relationship to some extent. For example, it was illegal to teach a slave to read and write, so the character of Aunt Chloe, who is Elsie's nursemaid, possesses a knowledge of Scripture learned by memorizing what she heard from Christian masters.

While many Southerners and Southern churches abhorred slavery and sought to abolish its practice, the right to own slaves was not officially ended in all the United States until the 1865 ratification of the Eighteenth Amendment to the Constitution.

Although Martha Finley wrote about the South, she never lived in the region or experienced slavery directly. She did, however, hold a firm belief in the importance of unity and equality among all people and all parts of her native land, and she wrote poignantly, in the preface to a later Elsie book, of "this great, grand, glorious old Union . . . . " She issued a plea to her readers and fellow countrymen to "forget all bitterness, and live henceforth in love, harmony, and mutual helpfulness."

DINSMORE FAMILY TREE

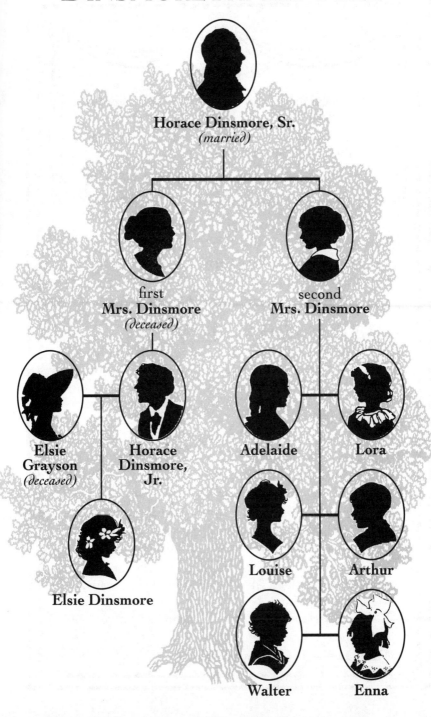

Horace Dinsmore, Sr.
(married)

first
Mrs. Dinsmore
(deceased)

second
Mrs. Dinsmore

**Elsie
Grayson**
(deceased)

**Horace
Dinsmore,
Jr.**

Adelaide

Lora

Elsie Dinsmore

Louise

Arthur

Walter

Enna

SETTING

*R*oselands, a cotton plantation near a coastal city in the Old South during the early 1840s, some years prior to the American Civil War and the abolition of slavery.

CHARACTERS

∾ The Dinsmore Household ∾

Mr. Horace Dinsmore, Sr. — The owner and master of Roselands plantation; Elsie's grandfather.

Mrs. Dinsmore — Mr. Dinsmore's second wife and mother of six children:

Adelaide — Age 16	**Lora** — Age 14
Louise — Age 12	**Arthur** — Age 10
Walter — Age 8	**Enna** — Age 6

Mr. Horace Dinsmore, Jr. — Age 26: The only son of Horace Dinsmore, Sr., and his first wife, who died when Horace was a small boy. Once married to Elsie Grayson of New Orleans, Horace is a lawyer by training.

Elsie Dinsmore — Age 8: The daughter of Horace Dinsmore, Jr., and Elsie Grayson, who died shortly after Elsie's birth. Born in New Orleans, Elsie has lived at Roselands since she was four years old.

Miss Rose Allison — Age 17: Daughter of the Allisons of Philadelphia. She visits Roselands and becomes a close friend of Adelaide Dinsmore and Elsie.

Mrs. Murray — A Scots Presbyterian woman of deep Christian faith. Mrs. Murray was housekeeper to Elsie's guardian in New Orleans. She accompanied Elsie to Roselands but is now living in her native Scotland.

Miss Day — The children's teacher.

Slaves of
Roselands Plantation

Aunt Chloe — The middle-aged nursemaid who has cared for Elsie since birth and taught her in the Christian faith.

Pompey — The chief house servant at Roselands and a special friend of Elsie's.

Jim — A young slave who works in the stables and frequently "babysits" the young Dinsmore children during their outings.

Aunt Phoebe — The Roselands cook and mother of Jim.

Ajax — An expert horseman and the Roselands carriage driver.

Fanny — A chambermaid.

The Travillas
of Ion Plantation

Edward Travilla — Owner of Ion and friend since boyhood of Horace Dinsmore, Jr.

Mrs. Travilla — Widowed mother of Edward, dedicated Christian, and caring friend to Elsie.

The Carringtons
of Ashlands Plantation

Mr. and Mrs. Carrington — Old friends of the Dinsmore family, owners of Ashlands plantation, and parents of five children including:
Lucy and Herbert — Age 8, twin sister and brother; Elsie's playmates.

CHAPTER

1

Trouble in the Schoolroom

*"It is better, if it is God's will,
to suffer for doing good
than for doing evil."*

1 PETER 3:17

Trouble in the Schoolroom

*T*he schoolroom at Roselands was a very pleasant room. True, its ceiling was lower than in the rest of the large plantation house. But the schoolroom was in the wing built in the days before the Revolutionary War, while the main portion of the house was not more than thirty years old. The effect of the low ceiling was offset by tall windows that reached to the floor and opened onto a sunny veranda. The veranda overlooked a lovely flower garden, and the vista beyond offered shade trees, thick woods, and acre upon acre of farm fields. In this rich Southern earth, cotton was grown and picked to be shipped to mills in all parts of the world.

Roselands was the estate of Mr. Horace Dinsmore, Sr., and his house — surrounded by its many outbuildings, stables, gardens, orchards and, at a distance, the living quarters of the slaves — was the hub of all activity on the vast plantation.

On the warm, fall morning when this story begins, the activity in the Roselands schoolroom included lessons in history and geography, English literature and French grammar, arithmetic and penmanship. Six Dinsmore children of varying ages labored at their neat rosewood desks under the sharp eye and quick tongue of Miss Day, the governess.

Miss Day was giving a lesson to six-year-old Enna, the youngest of the group, and Miss Day's patience was wearing thin. The spoiled pet of both her father and her mother, Enna was a willful girl who often pushed her teacher to the limits.

Elsie's Endless Wait

"There!" exclaimed Miss Day as she shut the book and impatiently tossed it onto the desk. "I might as well try to teach old Bruno, for your dog would learn about as fast as you, Enna."

With a pout on her pretty face, Enna walked away, muttering under her breath that she would "tell Mamma."

Looking at her watch, Miss Day announced, "Young ladies and gentlemen, I will leave you to your studies for an hour. Then I will return to hear your recitations. Those of you who have done your work properly will be permitted to ride with me to the fair this afternoon."

"Oh, that will be jolly!" exclaimed Arthur, a bright ten-year-old with a love of mischief.

"Hush!" Miss Day said sternly. "I don't want to hear any more outbursts from you, Arthur. And remember, you won't go to the fair unless you have learned your lessons thoroughly."

Looking to Louise, who was twelve, and fourteen-year-old Lora, Miss Day instructed, "Girls, your French lessons must be perfect, and your English lessons as well."

Alone at a desk near one of the windows, a little girl of eight was bent over her slate and gave every appearance of industry. To her, Miss Day barked, "Elsie, every figure of that arithmetic problem must be correct, and your geography lesson must be recited perfectly, and you must write a page in your copybook without a single blot of ink."

"Yes, ma'am," the girl replied meekly. For an instant, Elsie raised her soft hazel eyes to her teacher, then immediately dropped her gaze back to the numbers chalked on her slate writing tablet.

Miss Day issued her final command to a shy boy of eight who was working quietly at his desk: "Walter, if you miss one word of your spelling, you will stay at home and learn the whole lesson again. And all of you are to remain in this room until I return."

"Unless Mamma interferes, as she's sure to do," Arthur said in a low voice as Miss Day's quick steps retreated down the hall.

For perhaps ten minutes, all was quiet in the schoolroom. Each child seemed absorbed in study until Arthur jumped up and threw his book across the room.

"I know my lessons," he exclaimed, "and even if I didn't, I wouldn't study another bit for old Day — or Night, either!"

"Do be quiet, Arthur," his sister Louise begged. "I can't study when you make so much racket."

Silenced, Arthur tiptoed across the room and crept up behind Elsie. Taking a feather from his pocket, he tickled it at the back of her neck. She jumped in surprise, then pleaded with Arthur to stop.

"But it pleases me to bother you," Arthur said, and he tickled her once more.

With all the persuasion she could muster, Elsie asked him again, "Please leave me alone, or I'll never get this problem done."

"All this time on one little problem?" Arthur replied with a sneering laugh. "You ought to be ashamed, Elsie Dinsmore. Why, I could have done it a half a dozen times before now."

"Well, I've been over it and over it," Elsie said sadly, "and there are still two numbers that won't come out right."

"How do you know they're not right, little miss?" Arthur asked, grabbing at her curls as he spoke.

"Please don't pull my hair!" she cried. Then she explained that she had the correct answer, so she knew that her answer was wrong.

"Then why not just write down the right numbers?" Arthur asked. "That's what I'd do."

"But that wouldn't be honest."

"Nonsense! Nobody will know if you cheat a little."

"It would be like telling a lie," Elsie said firmly, then sighed and put aside her slate. "But I'll never get it right with you bothering me."

Elsie tried to turn her attention to her geography book, but Arthur would not stop his persecutions. He tickled her, pulled at her hair, flipped the book out of her hands, and kept up his incessant chatter and questions. On the verge of tears, Elsie begged him once again to leave her to her lessons.

"Take your book out on the veranda, Elsie, and study there," said Louise. "I'll call you when Miss Day comes back."

But Elsie did not budge from her desk. "I can't go outside because Miss Day said we must stay in this room, so that would be disobeying," she explained with despair.

Giving up on the geography, she took her copybook and pen and ink from her desk. She dipped her pen into the ink and very carefully formed every letter on the clean, white paper. But Arthur stood over her as she wrote, criticizing every letter she made. At last, he jogged her elbow, and all the ink in her pen dropped onto the paper, making a large black blot.

It was too much, and Elsie burst into tears. "Now I won't get to ride to the fair! Miss Day will never let me go! And I wanted so much to see the beautiful flowers."

Trouble in the Schoolroom

Arthur, who was not always as hateful as he seemed, felt suddenly guilty about the mischief he had caused. "Never mind, Elsie. I can fix it," he said. "I'll just tear out this page with the ink stain, and you can start again on the next page. I won't bother you anymore, and I can help with your arithmetic problem, too."

Elsie smiled at him through her tears. "That's kind of you, Arthur, but I can't tear out the page or let you do my problem. That would be deceitful."

Arthur didn't expect his offer to be refused. He drew himself up and tossed his head. "Very well, little miss," he said with his usual smugness. "If you won't let me help, then it's your own fault if you have to stay home."

Louise was also astounded. "Elsie, I have no patience with you," the older girl exclaimed. "You always raise such ridiculous scruples. I won't pity you at all if you have to stay home."

Elsie said nothing. Brushing away her tears, she returned to her writing, and though she took great pains with every letter, she thought sadly, "It's no use. That ugly ink blot spoils it all."

When she finally finished the page, it looked very neat except for the blot. Then she returned to the arithmetic problem on her slate. Patiently, she went over every number, trying to find her mistake. But there was not enough time left, and she was so upset by Arthur's teasing that she couldn't concentrate on the work.

The hour was up, and Miss Day returned. Still, Elsie thought she might be able to complete her assignments, if only Miss Day would call on the other children first. Perhaps Arthur would explain about the ink blot, and everything would be alright after all.

Elsie's Endless Wait

As soon as the teacher had taken her seat, however, she called, "Elsie, come here. Bring your book and recite your geography lesson for me, and I want to see your copybook and your slate."

Although trembling with fear, Elsie recited quite well, for she had studied her geography before coming to the school-room that morning. But her recitation was not perfect, and with a frown, the teacher handed back the textbook. Miss Day was always more severe with Elsie than any of her other pupils — for reasons that will soon become clear.

Noting the two incorrect numbers in Elsie's arithmetic problem, Miss Day put down the girl's slate and opened the copybook. "You careless, disobedient child!" she shouted. "Didn't I tell you not to blot your book? There will be no ride for you today. You have failed in everything. Go back to your seat! Correct that problem and do the next one. Then write another page in your copybook. And mind, if there is a blot on the page, you will not get your dinner today!"

Arthur, who pretended to be studying at his desk, had watched Elsie throughout this scene, and his conscience clearly troubled him. But when Elsie looked at him imploringly as she returned to her desk, he turned his face away and whispered to himself, "It's her own fault. She wouldn't let me help, so it's her own fault."

Glancing up again, he saw that his sister Lora was staring at him, and her eyes blazed with scorn and contempt.

"Miss Day," Lora said indignantly, "since Arthur won't speak up, I have to tell you that it's all his fault that Elsie failed her lessons. She tried her very best, but he was teasing her constantly, and he also made her spill the ink on her copybook. She was too honorable to tear out the page or let him do her arithmetic, which he said he would do."

8

Trouble in the Schoolroom

"Is this so, Arthur?" Miss Day demanded angrily.

The boy hung his head but didn't reply.

"Alright then," Miss Day said, "you will stay at home as well."

Lora was amazed. "Surely you won't punish Elsie now that I've told you it wasn't her fault."

Miss Day only turned her haughty gaze on Lora, and with ice in her voice, she said, "Understand this, Miss Lora. I will not be dictated to by any of my pupils."

Lora bit her lip, but she said nothing more.

As the other children recited their lessons, Elsie sat at her desk and struggled with the feelings of anger and indignation that were boiling inside her. Although she possessed a gentle and quiet spirit, Elsie was not perfect, and she often had to do fierce battle with her naturally quick temper. But because she seldom displayed her anger to others, it was commonly said within the family that Elsie had no spirit.

The other children had just finished their lessons when the door opened and a tall woman dressed in elegant riding clothes entered the schoolroom.

"Through yet, Miss Day?" Mrs. Dinsmore asked.

"Yes, madam, we are just done."

"Well, I hope your pupils have all done well and are ready to accompany us on the ride to the fair." Perhaps it was the sound of Elsie's sniffling that attracted Mrs. Dinsmore's attention at that moment. "What is the matter with Elsie?" she inquired of the teacher.

"She failed in all her lessons, and I've told her that she must stay home today," Miss Day replied, her anger rising again. "And since Miss Lora tells me that Arthur was partly to blame, I've forbidden him to come with us, too."

Elsie's Endless Wait

"Excuse me for correcting you," Lora said indignantly to her teacher. "I did not say 'partly,' because I'm sure it was *entirely* Arthur's fault."

Miss Day didn't have a chance to reply, as Mrs. Dinsmore addressed her daughter curtly, "Hush, Lora. How can you be sure of such a thing? Miss Day, I must beg you to excuse Arthur this time, for I have my heart set on his coming with us today. He's mischievous, I know, but he's just a child, and you shouldn't be too hard on him."

Miss Day's back stiffened, but she spoke with strained courtesy: "Very well, madam. You, of course, have the right to control your own children."

As Mrs. Dinsmore turned to leave, Lora spoke up again: "Mamma, won't Elsie be allowed to go?"

"Elsie is not my child, and I have nothing to say about it," Mrs. Dinsmore said with a condescending air. "Miss Day knows all the circumstances, and she is better able than I to decide whether Elsie deserves her punishment."

When her mother had gone, Lora turned to the teacher. "You will let Elsie go, won't you, Miss Day?"

Her anger now doubled by the insult from Mrs. Dinsmore, Miss Day replied, "I've already told you, Miss Lora, that I will not be dictated to. I've said that Elsie must stay at home, and I will not break my word."

"Why do you concern yourself with Elsie's troubles?" Louise whispered to her sister as Lora returned to her seat. "Elsie is so full of silly principles that I have no pity for her."

Meanwhile, Miss Day had crossed the room to stand over Elsie's desk. "Didn't I tell you to learn that lesson over?" the teacher asked. "Why are you sitting here doing nothing?"

The little girl held her head in her hands as she fought to overcome her feelings. She didn't dare to speak because her anger might show in her words, so she brushed at her tears and opened her book. But Miss Day would not be satisfied. She was angry too, at Mrs. Dinsmore's interference and at the knowledge that she herself was acting unfairly. But Miss Day, unlike Elsie, could not keep her anger hidden. She was determined to vent her displeasure, and Elsie was, as usual, her innocent target.

"Why don't you speak?" Miss Day demanded, and she grabbed Elsie by the arm and shook the girl roughly. "Answer me this instant! Why have you been idling all morning, you lazy girl?"

"I haven't been idling," Elsie protested quickly. "I tried hard to do my work, and you're punishing me when I don't deserve it."

"How dare you? There!" Miss Day shouted, smacking Elsie hard on the ear. "Take that for your impertinence!"

Elsie wanted to shout her own harsh reply, but she restrained herself. Looking at her book, she tried to study, but her ear ached painfully and hot tears came so fast that she could not see the page.

It was at that moment that one of the house servants came to the door and announced that the carriage was ready, and Miss Day, followed by Lora, Louise, and the younger children, hurried from the schoolroom. Elsie, at last, was alone.

Putting aside her geography book, she opened her desk and took out her pocket Bible. The little book showed all the marks of frequent use. Elsie turned its pages deliberately and soon found the passage she sought. Fighting back her tears, she read to herself:

Elsie's Endless Wait

"'For it is commendable if a man bears up under the pain of unjust suffering because he is conscious of God. But how is it to your credit if you receive a beating for doing wrong and endure it? But if you suffer for doing good and you endure it, this is commendable before God. To this you were called, because Christ suffered for you, leaving you an example, that you should follow in His steps.'"

Now her tears came again. "I haven't done it," she sobbed, "I didn't endure it. I'm afraid I'm not following in His steps very well."

"My dear child, what is the matter?" asked a gentle voice, and a soft hand was laid on Elsie's shoulder.

The little girl looked up into the pleasant face of a young woman. "Miss Allison!" Elsie said in surprise. "I thought I was all alone."

"You were, my dear, till this moment," soothed Rose Allison, a recently arrived guest in the Dinsmore home. She drew up a chair and sat close beside Elsie. "I was on the veranda when I heard sobbing, and I came in to see if I could help. Won't you tell me the cause of your distress?"

The young woman's voice was full of kindness, but Elsie couldn't answer; her tears choked her and made speaking impossible.

So Rose went on, "I think I understand. Everyone has gone to the fair, and they've left you at home. Perhaps you have to memorize a lesson that you failed to recite."

The young woman's sweet voice and touch calmed Elsie a little, and she was able to answer, "Yes, ma'am, but being left is not the worst." Then her voice failed her again, and she could only point to the words she had been reading in her Bible.

With a fresh burst of tears, she sobbed out her misery. "I — I didn't do it! I didn't bear it patiently. They weren't fair, and I was punished when I wasn't to blame. Then I — I got angry. I'm afraid that I'll never be like Jesus. Never!"

Rose Allison, who had been at Roselands for just a few days, was extremely surprised by the child's great emotion. A devoted Christian herself, Rose was pained by the Dinsmore family's apparent disregard for the teachings of God's Word. She hadn't known the family before her visit, but her father was an old friend of Mr. Dinsmore's. As a kindness, Mr. Dinsmore had prevailed on Mr. Allison to allow Rose, who had been ill that year, to travel from her home in Philadelphia. She was spending the winter at Roselands where she could regain her strength in the warmth of the Southern climate. Although she was enjoying her visit and feeling much better, she had been struck by the family's lack of devotion. But until now, she had not spoken with Elsie.

Rose wrapped her arm around the child's waist. "My poor Elsie," she said. "That is your name, isn't it?"

"Yes, ma'am. Elsie Dinsmore."

"Well, Elsie, as you probably know, becoming like Jesus is the work of a lifetime, and we all stumble along the way. But Jesus understands, dear."

"Yes ma'am," Elsie said. "I know He does, but I'm so sorry that I've grieved Him and displeased Him. I do love Him, and I want so much to be like Him."

Rose stroked Elsie's hair and spoke tenderly, "But remember Elsie, God's love for us is *far* greater than we could ever imagine and it doesn't depend on our goodness, because none of us can be good enough on our own. It is

Jesus' righteousness that is credited to our account. You must have patience, little one. His Holy Spirit in you will bring about the purity of heart you desire."

Elsie was silent for a few moments as she thought about what the young woman had said. Then she brightened. "Thank you, Miss Allison," she said sincerely.

"And thank you, Elsie," Rose said with a little laugh, "for I'm very glad to find another person in this place who loves Jesus and is trying to do His will. I love Him too, so we will love each other."

Elsie was overjoyed. "Oh, I'm so glad," she said, "for no one loves me but my Aunt Chloe."

"Who is that?" Rose asked.

"My nursemaid," Elsie replied. "Aunt Chloe has always taken care of me. Have you seen her in the house?"

Rose considered. "Perhaps," she said thoughtfully. "I've met a number of nice servant women since I came here. But tell me, Elsie, who taught you about Jesus, and how long have you loved Him?"

"Ever since I can remember," Elsie said. "It was Aunt Chloe who told me how He suffered and died on the cross for us. She talked to me about Him just as soon as I was old enough to understand. Then she'd tell me about my own mother and how she loved Jesus and had gone to be with Him in heaven when I was just a week old. When my mother was dying, she put me into Chloe's arms and said, 'Take my dear baby and love her and care for her just as you did me. And be sure to teach her to love God.'"

Elsie drew from the bodice of her dress a gold chain from which hung a miniature portrait set in a golden locket. It was the picture of a beautiful young girl, no more than fifteen or sixteen years old. She had the same hazel eyes and brown curls that Elsie possessed, and the same regular features, fine complexion, and sweet smile.

"This is my mother," Elsie said softly as she placed the miniature in Rose's hand.

The young woman gazed at the portrait admiringly, then she turned to Elsie in puzzlement. "I don't understand," Rose said. "Are you not the sister of Enna and the other children? Is Mrs. Dinsmore not your mother?"

"She is their mother, but not mine," Elsie replied. "My father, Horace Dinsmore, Jr., is their brother, so all the other children are my aunts and uncles."

"Indeed," Rose mused. "And your father is away, isn't he?"

"Yes, ma'am. He's in Europe. He has been away since before I was born, and I've never seen him. Oh, I do wish he'd come home! I want to see him so much! Do you think he would love me, Miss Allison? Do you think he would put me on his knee and hug me the way Grandpa hugs Enna?"

"I'm sure he would, my dear. How could he help loving his own little girl?" said Rose, and she gently kissed Elsie's cheek.

Then she stood, picking up the little Bible and turning its pages. "I must go now and let you learn your lesson," she said. "But perhaps you'd like to come to my room in the mornings and evenings and read your Bible to me."

"Oh, yes, ma'am," Elsie exclaimed, and her eyes sparkled with delight. "I love reading the Bible best of anything! Aunt Chloe has always taught me that I must 'hide the Word in my heart.'"

"And have you memorized all of your verses by heart?" Rose inquired.

"Not all of them," Elsie said honestly. "But I've memorized many beautiful passages."

"Can you recite something for me?" Rose asked, for she could see that their discussion of God's Word greatly cheered the child.

Elsie thought for a few moments, then said: "Yes, ma'am. These verses from Colossians are some of my favorites." She quoted carefully: "'Therefore, as God's chosen people, holy and dearly loved, clothe yourselves with compassion, kindness, humility, gentleness and patience. Bear with each other and forgive whatever grievances you may have against one another. Forgive as the Lord forgave you. And over all these virtues put on love, which binds them all together in perfect unity.'"

"That is excellent, Elsie!" Rose said, smiling brightly. "And why do you like those verses?"

"Because they're so clear to me, Miss Allison. I sometimes have trouble understanding what I read in the Scriptures."

"Then perhaps I can help you. If you like, we can study God's Word together," Rose said.

"Oh, how kind you are," Elsie replied happily. "I would like that very much."

"Then please come and visit with me this evening," Rose said, and putting the little Bible into the child's hand, she kissed Elsie once again before she left.

⌒

Returning to her own room, Rose found Adelaide Dinsmore, the eldest of the Dinsmore daughters. Adelaide was nearly Rose's age, and the two young women had become friends. Now she was seated on the sofa and working busily on some embroidery.

"I'm glad to see that you're making yourself at home," Adelaide said as Rose entered. "Where have you been for so long?"

"I was in the schoolroom, talking with little Elsie. I thought she was your sister, but she tells me she is not."

"No, she's my brother Horace's child," Adelaide replied. "I thought you knew, but since you don't, I may as well tell you the whole story.

"Horace was a wild boy, pampered and spoiled and used to having his own way. When he was seventeen, he insisted on going to New Orleans to spend some time with a schoolmate. While he was there, he met a very beautiful girl and fell desperately in love with her. Her name was Elsie Grayson, and she was a year or two younger than he — an orphan and very wealthy. Horace knew that the families would object to their marrying because of their ages, so he persuaded the girl to elope and marry in secret. They had been married for several months before any of their friends suspected it."

Adelaide paused to thread a new strand of silk through her needle; then she continued her story: "When the news finally reached Papa, well, you can imagine how angry he was, and only in part because Horace and his bride were so young. You see, old Mr. Grayson was a tradesman and had made all his money in business, so my father didn't consider the daughter to be quite my brother's equal. Papa made Horace come home and then sent him away to college in the North. My brother studied law, and he's been traveling abroad ever since."

"But what about his wife?" Rose asked. "Elsie's mother?"

Elsie's Endless Wait

"I was just coming to her," said Adelaide. "Since her parents were dead, she had a guardian, and he was just as opposed to the marriage as Papa was. She was made to believe that Horace would never return to her. All his letters were intercepted, and finally she was told that he had died. As Aunt Chloe says, the girl 'grew thin and pale and weak and melancholy,' and she died when little Elsie wasn't quite a week old.

"We'd never met Horace's wife, and when she died, it seemed right that little Elsie stay on in the guardian's house. She was cared for by Aunt Chloe, who had been her mother's nursemaid, and by the housekeeper there, a Scotswoman named Mrs. Murray."

Adelaide looked up from her embroidery, and Rose could see that her face had become serious. "It was about four years ago that the guardian died," Adelaide continued, "and little Elsie, Aunt Chloe, and Mrs. Murray came to live with us. Horace never comes home, and he doesn't seem to care for his child. He never mentions her in his letters except in connection with business affairs. He's never even seen Elsie. Of course, I haven't spoken to my brother in many years, but I believe he must associate his child with the loss of his wife, for he did love Elsie's mother with all his heart. Perhaps that is the reason he has stayed away from his daughter."

"But she's such a dear little girl," Rose said. "I'm sure he'd love her if he could only meet her."

"Yes," Adelaide agreed, "she is dear enough, and I often feel sorry for her loneliness. When she came here, you see, she had never been around other children, and it has been difficult for her. I must admit that my brothers and sisters have not always been welcoming, but the truth is, I think we are all a little jealous of her. You've seen that she's very beautiful, and she is also heiress to an immense fortune. I have often heard Mamma fret that someday Elsie will quite eclipse my younger sisters."

Rose was confused by Adelaide's last statement. "Why would your mother feel jealous, " she asked, "when little Elsie is her own granddaughter?"

"But that's not the case," Adelaide explained, "for Horace is not my mother's son. His own mother died when he was quite young, and he was seven or eight when my mother married Papa, and" — she lowered her voice and her eyes — "I don't believe Mamma was ever very fond of him."

Both young women sat quietly for several minutes as Rose pondered this new information. "No wonder the little girl longs so for her father's love," she thought to herself, "and carries such grief for the mother she never knew." Adelaide's recounting of Elsie's lonely birth and her sad position among the Dinsmores perhaps explained, as well, the unusual maturity that Rose had sensed in the child. "God," Rose thought, "may be her only true friend."

At last Adelaide spoke again. "Elsie is an odd child, and I don't really understand her. She is so meek and patient that she will virtually allow the other children to trample her. Her meekness provokes my Papa, and he says she is no Dinsmore because she doesn't know how to stand up for herself. Yet Elsie does have a temper, I know. Ever so often it shows itself, but just for an instant. Then she grieves over it as if she had committed some crime, whereas the rest of us think nothing of getting angry a dozen times a day. And then she is always poring over that little Bible of hers, though what she finds so interesting I can't say. To me, it's the dullest of books."

"How strange," Rose said in surprise. "I'd rather give up all other books than the Bible. The Word of God is more precious to me than gold!"

Now it was Adelaide's turn to be astonished. "Do you *really* love the Bible so? Will you tell me why?"

"For its great and precious promises, Adelaide, and for its teachings about holy living. It offers inner peace and pardon from sin and eternal life," Rose said. "The Bible brings me the glad news of salvation offered as a free, unmerited gift. It tells me that Jesus died to save sinners such as me and that through Him, I am reconciled to God."

Adelaide could hear the deep emotion in her friend's voice as Rose went on, "I often find that my feelings and thoughts are not what they should be, and the blessed Bible tells me how my heart and mind can be renewed. When I find myself utterly unable to keep God's holy law, the Bible tells me of One who kept it for me, and who willingly suffered for my sins," Rose said with a solemn passion that made her seem much older than her seventeen years.

Both women sat silently for a time. Then Adelaide's face clouded, and she said a little sternly, "You talk as if you were a great sinner, Rose, but I don't believe it. It's only your humility that makes you think like that. Why, what have you ever done? If you were a thief or a murderer or guilty of some terrible crime, I could understand your saying such things about yourself. Excuse me for this, Rose, but your language seems absurd for a refined, intelligent, and amiable young lady."

Gently, Rose responded to her friend's complaint. "'Man looks at the outward appearance, but God looks at the heart,'" she quoted. Then she explained, "From my earliest existence, God has required the undivided love of my whole heart, soul, strength, and mind; yet until the last two years,

I was in rebellion against Him, not allowing Him to govern my life. For all my life, He has showered blessings on me. He has given me life and health, strength and friends — everything necessary for happiness. But I gave back nothing but ingratitude and rebellion. All that time I rejected His offers of pardon and reconciliation and resisted all the efforts of God's Holy Spirit to draw me to Him."

Rose's voice quivered, and her eyes brimmed with tears. "Can you not now see me as a sinner?"

Adelaide moved closer to her friend's side and put her arm around Rose's shoulders. "Don't think of these things, dear Rose," she gently admonished. "Religion is too gloomy for one as young as you."

"True religion is not gloomy at all," Rose answered, hugging Adelaide in return. "I never knew what true happiness was until I found Jesus. My sins often make me sad, but my faith in Him? Never."

CHAPTER

Someone To Talk To

"The purposes of a man's heart are deep waters, but a man of understanding draws them out."

PROVERBS 20:5

When Rose Allison had left the schoolroom, Elsie got up from her desk and knelt down with her Bible before her. In her own simple words, she poured out her story to the dear Savior she loved so well, confessing that when she had done right and suffered for it, she had not endured the injustice. Earnestly, she prayed to be made like the meek and lowly Jesus, and as she prayed, her tears fell on the pages of her Bible. But when she stood again, Elsie's load of sorrow was gone, and as always, her heart was light with a sweet sense of peace and pardon.

She went back to her work with renewed diligence and faithfully completed all her assignments. When Miss Day returned from the fair, Elsie was able to recite her geography lesson without a single mistake. Her arithmetic problems were solved correctly, and the writing in her copybook was neat and careful.

But Miss Day, who had been in an ill-tempered mood all day, now seemed angry that Elsie did not give her another excuse for criticism. The governess handed the copybook back to the child and remarked sarcastically, "I see that you can do your duties well enough when you choose."

The injustice of Miss Day's words struck Elsie, and she wanted to protest that she had tried just as hard that morning. But she remembered her earlier, rash words and what they had cost her. Instead of defending herself, she meekly said, "I'm sorry I didn't do better this morning, though I really did try. I'm still more sorry for the disrespectful remark I made, and I ask your pardon."

"You ought to be sorry," replied Miss Day sharply, "and I hope you really are. You were very impertinent, and you deserved a more severe punishment than you received. Now go, and never let me hear anything like that from you again."

Elsie's eyes filled with tears again, but remembering how Jesus made no reply in the face of his accusers, she said nothing to Miss Day's hateful remarks. She simply put away her books and slate and left the schoolroom.

That evening, Rose was alone in her bedroom, thinking of her home and family so far away in the North, when she heard a gentle rapping at her door.

"Come in, darling," Rose greeted Elsie. "I'm so glad to see you."

Rose pointed to an ottoman, and Elsie, who had brought her little Bible, took her seat. "I may stay with you for half an hour; then Aunt Chloe is coming to put me to bed," she said.

Rose smiled. "It will be a pleasant half hour for us both."

Rose took her own Bible, and they read a chapter together, stopping now and then for Rose to give explanations. Then they knelt, and Rose offered a prayer for the teachings of the Spirit and for God's blessing on themselves and all their loved ones.

When they had risen, Rose folded the child in her arms and proclaimed gaily, "How I love you already, little Elsie. How glad I am that you love Jesus as I do and want to study His Word and pray."

"I'm not the only one," Elsie said with great seriousness. "Aunt Chloe loves Him too, very dearly."

"Then I must love her as well, for I have a special love for all who love my Savior."

With that, Rose sat down and put Elsie on her knee. Like old friends, they talked of the joys and challenges of Christian living and of the "race," as Paul the Apostle called it, that they were running and the "prize" they hoped to gain. They felt like pilgrims on the same path, and it was pleasant to walk awhile together.

A knock at the door interrupted their conversation, and a handsome, middle-aged black woman entered. She was extremely neat in her black dress, starched white apron, and turban-like headdress, and with a slight bow, she asked, "Is my little Elsie ready for bed now?"

"Yes, Aunt Chloe," said Elsie, running to her nursemaid's side, "but first I want to introduce you to Miss Allison."

Rose greeted her new guest warmly and took her hand. "How do you do, Aunt Chloe? I'm very glad to know you, since Elsie tells me you are a servant of the same Master I love and serve."

"Indeed I am, Miss Allison," Chloe said, grasping Rose's small hand in her two strong ones. "I love my precious Savior with all my heart."

"Then we are united through our faith in Him," Rose replied warmly. "For the Bible tells us that for all who love Him, there is neither Jew nor Greek, slave nor free, male nor female — we are all one in Christ."

Rose pressed Chloe's hands warmly, and between the two women — the one free and the other slave — the barriers of race and position melted away in the power of their shared faith.

Then reaching down, Chloe took Elsie's hand. "Good night now, Miss Allison. It's time I put this child to bed."

"Good night then, and please come again," Rose said. "And good night to you, little Elsie," she added, hugging the child again.

"What a blessed young lady," Chloe declared as she prepared Elsie for bedtime.

"Oh, Aunt Chloe, she's so good and kind, and she loves Jesus and loves to talk about Him," Elsie said happily.

"She reminds me of your mother, though she is not as beautiful. I think there never was a lady so beautiful as your mother."

Chloe brushed a tear from her eye as Elsie lifted the gold-framed miniature, which she wore day and night, and gave it a kiss. Then she slipped the chain inside her white nightdress. Chloe brushed back Elsie's hair and arranged the nightcap that protected Elsie's curls while she slept. "There now, darling," the nursemaid said, "you're ready for bed."

"Not quite yet, Aunt Chloe." Elsie knelt beside her bed and offered her evening prayer. Then she got her little Bible and began reading aloud from it as Chloe prepared herself for bed, removing her head scarf and replacing it with her own thick nightcap. Chloe, who was never willing to leave her charge for long, slept on a cot in one corner of the room.

When Elsie had finished her reading, she got into her bed, and Chloe tucked the covers securely around her.

"Please wake me early, Aunt Chloe, because I have a lesson to learn before breakfast."

"I will, darling," Chloe said as she snuffed out the light.

 28

Someone To Talk To

Rose Allison was an early riser and always spent an hour or two reading before the family gathered for breakfast at eight o'clock. She had asked Elsie to join her at seven-thirty, and punctually at that time, she heard the child's gentle tap on her door.

Elsie, looking as bright as the morning, carried her Bible and a bouquet of fresh flowers, which she presented to Rose with a graceful curtsy.

"I gathered these for you because I know you love flowers," Elsie said.

"Thank you, darling. They're lovely," Rose said, rewarding Elsie with a hug. "Now we can have our time together before breakfast."

The half hour passed so quickly that both were surprised when the breakfast bell rang.

This was the first of many happy mornings for Elsie. Rose spent the fall and winter with the Dinsmores, and most mornings and evenings she and Elsie read and prayed together. Rose was often amazed at the depth of the little girl's faith in God and knowledge of divine things, but Elsie had received the best of teaching. Chloe, though not formally educated, was an earnest Christian, and she had, from the beginning, endeavored to teach Elsie about Jesus. For most of that time, Chloe had been assisted in her mission by Mrs. Murray, the Scottish Presbyterian woman who had accompanied them to Roselands. It had only been a few months before that Mrs. Murray had suddenly been summoned home to Scotland. An intelligent and pious woman, Mrs. Murray had carefully instructed Elsie, and her and

Elsie's Endless Wait

Chloe's efforts to bring Elsie to a saving knowledge of Christ had been blessed.

Young as Elsie was, she already had a well-developed Christian character. Though not remarkably precocious in other respects, she seemed to have very clear and correct views on her duty to God and her neighbor. She was truthful in both word and deed, very strict in her observation of the Sabbath — unlike the rest of the Dinsmore family — diligent in her studies, respectful to her elders, polite and kind to everyone. She was gentle, sweet-tempered, patient, and forgiving to a remarkable degree.

It was natural that Rose Allison should become strongly attached to Elsie and that the child would return this affection. Elsie felt deeply the lack of sympathy and love in the Dinsmore household, and before Rose came, she had only Chloe, who deeply loved the child.

True, Adelaide often treated Elsie affectionately, but they were far apart in age and Adelaide had little time to spend with her young niece. Lora, who had a strong sense of justice, occasionally intervened and took Elsie's side when she was unfairly accused. But none of the Dinsmores seemed to really care for her, and Elsie was often lonely and sad. Her grandfather, Horace Dinsmore, Sr., treated her with complete neglect and usually spoke of her as "old Grayson's grandchild." Mrs. Dinsmore genuinely disliked her, as the child of the stepson for whom she had no fondness and as a future rival to her own daughters. The younger children, following the example of their parents, usually neglected Elsie and sometimes mistreated her. Miss Day, knowing that there was no danger her employers would object, vented on Elsie the spite she dared not show her other pupils. Again and again, Elsie was made to give up her playthings to Enna, and sometimes to

Arthur and Walter. This treatment often caused Elsie to struggle with her temper; had she possessed less of a meek and gentle spirit, her life might have been wretched indeed.

But in spite of it all, Elsie was the happiest person in the family, for she had peace in her heart and felt the joy which the Savior gives to His own. She constantly took her sorrows and troubles to Him, and the coldness and neglect of the others only drove her closer to her Heavenly Friend. While she had His love, she could not be unhappy, and her trials seemed to make her naturally amiable character even more lovely.

Still, she thought constantly of her absent father, and she longed intensely for his return. Day and night, she dreamed that he had come home, had taken her to his heart and called her his "own precious child" and his "precious little Elsie," just as her grandfather often spoke to Enna. But from month to month, year to year, her father's return was delayed, and her heart grew weary with its almost hopeless waiting.

There were pleasant times, however, and on the morning of her first session with Rose, Elsie got an unexpected surprise. When she and Rose entered the breakfast room, Adelaide called them aside.

"Elsie," her aunt began, "the fair isn't over yet, you know, and Miss Allison and I plan to ride there this afternoon. If you are a good girl in school this morning, you may go with us."

Elsie eyes glowed with happiness, and she clapped her hands in delight. "Oh, thank you, Aunt Adelaide. How kind you are!"

Miss Day, who overheard Adelaide's promise, frowned. Her immediate instinct was to reprove Elsie for her noisy outburst, but the governess was somewhat awed by Adelaide, and so she said nothing.

Elsie's Endless Wait

At that moment Mrs. Dinsmore entered, and Elsie instantly fell silent. She could rarely utter a word in her step-grandmother's presence without being scolded and told that "children should be seen and not heard" — even though Mrs. Dinsmore's own children were always allowed to talk as much as they pleased. But the entire family was silent that morning. Miss Day seemed cross, and Mrs. Dinsmore, complaining of a headache, was moody and taciturn. Mr. Dinsmore retreated behind his newspaper and said nothing. So Elsie was relieved when the meal concluded. She hurried to the schoolroom and began her lessons before the other children arrived.

She had been working on her arithmetic problems for about a half hour when the door opened and, to Elsie's dismay, Arthur entered. The boy did not begin his usual teasing and tormenting, however. Instead, he sat at his desk and rested his head on his hand in a dejected manner. Naturally Elsie wondered what was bothering her uncle, and she stole glances at him every now and then. Finally, she asked, "What's the matter, Arthur?"

"Nothing," he said gruffly and then turned his back on her.

Elsie said no more and returned to her studies. By the time the school day began, Elsie was so thoroughly prepared that Miss Day had no excuse for finding fault. Elsie's lessons were all completed on schedule, and she joined Adelaide and Rose for the promised ride to the fair.

They returned to Roselands about an hour before supper, and with time to herself, Elsie decided to finish a drawing that she had left in her school desk. While she was getting it and hunting for a pencil, she heard voices coming from the veranda. She recognized them as Lora's and Arthur's, but she paid no attention to their conversation until her own name was mentioned.

"Elsie is the only person who can help you," Lora was saying.

"She has plenty of money, and you know that she is generous. But if I were you, I'd be ashamed to ask her, after the way you treated her yesterday."

"I wish I hadn't teased her," Arthur agreed, "but it's so much fun that I can't help myself."

"Well, I know that I wouldn't ask a favor of anybody whom I had treated so meanly," Lora said finally, and Elsie heard footsteps as the older girl walked away.

Elsie worked at her drawing, but her thoughts were of Arthur. What was it that he wanted? Was this an opportunity for her to return good for evil? She was hesitant to speak to him, but when she heard a deep sigh from the veranda, she left her drawing and went outside. Arthur was leaning against the railing; his head was bent and his eyes fixed on the ground. Without thinking, Elsie went to him, laid her hand on his shoulder, and asked if there was anything she could do to help.

"No — yes —" he answered haltingly. "I don't like to ask after — after —"

"Oh, never mind yesterday," Elsie said quickly. "I don't care about that now. I went to the fair today, and it was even better because I went with Aunt Adelaide and Miss Allison. So tell me what you want."

Encouraged, Arthur explained, "I saw a beautiful model of a ship when we were in the city yesterday, and I've set my heart on having it. It only costs five dollars, but my pocket money's all gone, and Papa won't give me a cent of allowance until next month. By that time, the ship will be gone because it's so beautiful someone is sure to buy it."

Elsie's Endless Wait

"Won't your mother buy it for you?" Elsie inquired.

"I asked, but she said she can't spare the money right now. It's so near the end of the month that we've all spent our allowances. Except Louise, but she says she won't lend money to a spendthrift like me."

Elsie took out her little purse and seemed ready to give it to Arthur. But she hesitated a moment, then returned it to her pocket. "Five dollars is a lot of money for a little girl like me," she said with a small smile. "I have to think about it, Arthur."

"I'm not asking you to *give* me money," Arthur contended. "I'll pay it back in two weeks."

Elsie only said, "Let me think about it until tomorrow morning," and she turned away from her disconsolate uncle. Arthur glanced at her retreating figure, and one angry word slipped from his lips: "Stingy."

But Elsie was still smiling as she ran down to the kitchen in search of Pompey, who was one of her special friends among the household servants. Finding him at last, she asked, "Pompey, are you going into the city tonight?"

"I am, Miss Elsie. I have some errands to do for Mrs. Dinsmore and the family, so I'll be leaving in about ten minutes. Is there something you want, eh?"

Elsie moved close and put her purse in Pompey's hand. Whispering, she told the old man about Arthur's wish and asked if he would take the money, and a half-dollar for his trouble, and purchase the coveted toy. And could he keep it secret from the others?

"I sure can do that," Pompey replied, a broad grin lighting his face. "I'll do this business just right for you."

When the supper bell rang, Elsie hurried to the dining room. Arthur sat across from her at the table, but when she smiled at him, he only averted his eyes, and his face darkened with an angry scowl.

When Elsie retired to her room after her evening hour with Rose, Chloe pointed to an item on the mantle. It was the model ship.

"Arthur was right," Elsie exclaimed with delight. "It's a beauty! He's going to be so pleased. Aunt Chloe, could you take it to the schoolroom and put it on Arthur's desk? And be sure no one sees you?"

"I can try, darling," Chloe said, carefully taking the beautifully crafted little boat into her hand.

"Wait a minute," Elsie said with excitement. She took a notecard from her table and wrote on it: "A present to Arthur, from his niece, Elsie."

"There," she said, placing the card on the deck of the little model. "Now please, Aunt Chloe, check the hallway to be sure no one is there."

Chloe opened the bedroom door, and with exaggerated caution, she looked up and down the empty hall. "Coast is clear," she said. "All the children are in bed, I expect." Then taking a candle in her other hand, she disappeared out the door. A few minutes later, she returned, assuring Elsie that the task had been completed and "nobody's the wiser."

Elsie went to bed very happy that night, anticipating Arthur's pleasure.

On her way to breakfast the next morning, she was surprised by two hands seizing her around the waist. It was Arthur, who had just run in from the garden.

"Thank you, Elsie! You really are a good girl," he said, a huge smile filling his face. "The ship sails so well. I've been trying her on the pond. But it mustn't be a present. You have to let me pay you back."

"No, that would spoil my fun," Elsie insisted. "It's a gift, and you're welcome to it. Besides, my allowance is so large that I usually have more money than I can spend."

"I wish that were my problem," Arthur laughed. Then his smile vanished, and he said gently, "I'm sorry I teased you, Elsie. I won't do it again soon."

Arthur kept his word, and for many weeks, Elsie was able to complete her lessons with no annoyance from him. Miss Day, however, was often unreasonable and demanding. Scarcely a day went by that Elsie wasn't expected to give up her toys or inconvenience herself just to please Enna or Walter or someone else in the family. But still, the entire winter was unusually happy; Rose Allison's love and constant kindness, and her ability to draw out the thoughts and feelings in Elsie's heart, warmed the little girl's life like sunshine. Besides, Elsie had learned how to yield readily to others, and when she experienced some unjust or unkind treatment, she would go to her Bible. Her communings with her beloved Savior made everything right again, and she would emerge as serenely happy as if nothing had happened. Her attitude bewildered the family. Her grandfather would sometimes contemplate her behavior when she graciously gave up her wishes to Enna. Then he'd shake his head and say to himself, "That girl's no Dinsmore, or she'd stand up for her rights better than that. She can't be Horace's child, for it never was easy to impose on him. He was a boy of spirit, not like this child."

Even Adelaide had remarked to Rose that Elsie was a "strange" child. "I'm often surprised to see how sweetly she gives in to all of us," Adelaide observed. "Really, she has a lovely temperament. I envy her, for it was always hard for me to give up my own way or forgive those who teased me."

"I don't think it has been easy for Elsie either," Rose said. "But the Bible tells us that it is to a person's glory to overlook an offense. I think her sweet disposition is the fruit of a work of grace in her heart. It is 'the unfading beauty of a gentle and quiet spirit' which God alone can bestow."

"I wish I had that," Adelaide sighed.

"You only have to go to the right source, dear Adelaide," Rose replied kindly.

"And yet," Adelaide went on, "I must say that sometimes I think, as Papa says, that there is something mean-spirited and cowardly in always giving up to others."

"It would be cowardly and wrong to give up *principle*," Rose said, "but surely it is noble and generous to give up our own wishes to another, when no principle is involved."

"Of course, you're right," Adelaide mused. "And now that I think of it, although Elsie gives in on her wishes readily enough, I've never known her to sacrifice principle. On the contrary, she has made Mamma very angry several times by refusing to play with Enna on the Sabbath or to lie to Papa about Arthur's misdeeds. Elsie is certainly very different from the rest of us, and if it's godliness that makes her what she is, then I think godliness is a lovely thing."

Elsie spent her mornings in the schoolroom, and in the afternoons, she walked or went riding, sometimes with her young aunts and uncles and sometimes with Jim, one of the younger slaves and an excellent horseman, who was assigned to watch over her on her rides. There was always company at Roselands in the evening, but she usually preferred sitting with Aunt Chloe by the fire in her bedroom to joining the guests in the parlor or playing with the other children in the sitting room or the playroom. When she had no lessons to learn, she often read aloud to Chloe, and the Bible was the book they both preferred. Sometimes Elsie would pull her little stool close by Chloe's side, put her head on the nursemaid's lap, and ask, "Please, Aunt Chloe, tell me about my mother."

Then, for the hundredth time or more, Chloe would recount the life and death of her "dear young mistress," as she called Elsie's mother. She would speak of the first Elsie's beauty, her goodness, and the sorrows she suffered during the last year of her short life. The story never lost its charms for little Elsie, and Chloe never tired of telling it. As Chloe spoke, Elsie would gaze at the miniature portrait of her mother, and when the story was finished, Elsie would say, "Now, tell me about Papa."

But about young Horace Dinsmore, Chloe had little information. She had known him only as a lively and hand-some stranger whom she had seen occasionally during a few months and who had stolen the sunshine from her mistress, leaving her to die alone. Yet Chloe did not blame him when speaking to his child; her mistress had said that Horace did not desert her and their child of his own free choice. And even though Chloe could not believe him entirely blameless, she breathed no hint of her feeling to Elsie. Chloe was a sen-sible woman, and she knew that it would be hurtful to make her young charge think ill of her remaining parent.

Sometimes Elsie would ask if her Papa loved Jesus, and with a doubtful shake of her head, Chloe would say, "I don't know, darling, but I pray for him every day."

"So do I," Elsie would sigh. "How I wish he would come home."

Someone To Talk To

And thus the winter glided away, and spring came, and with it the time approached when Rose Allison was to return to her family in Philadelphia. Her departure was scheduled for the second of April, and it was now the last day of March. For a number of weeks, Elsie had devoted all her spare time to knitting a purse; she wanted to give Rose something made with her own hands because she knew Rose would prize such a gift more than something more costly.

Elsie was in her room with Chloe. She had been knitting, and suddenly she held up the purse. "See!" she exclaimed. "It's all done except for putting on the tassel. Isn't it pretty, Aunt Chloe? Do you think Miss Allison will be pleased?"

It was, Chloe agreed, a very pretty purse, beautifully knit in crimson and gold, and she was sure Miss Allison would be delighted. They were admiring the purse when Enna opened the door and came in. Although Elsie tried to conceal the purse in her pocket, it was too late. Enna had seen it, and she ran to Elsie, crying, "Just give that to me, Elsie!"

When Elsie refused, explaining that it was a gift for Miss Allison, Enna raised her voice even more and demanded, "Give it to me now, or I'll go and tell Mamma!"

"I'll let you hold it for a few moments, if you promise not to soil it," Elsie said gently. "And if you like, I'll get more silk and beads and make you a purse just like it. But I can't give it to you because then I wouldn't have time to make another one for Miss Allison."

But Enna was adamant: "I want that now, and I want it to keep!" She tried to snatch the purse from Elsie's hand, but Elsie held it up out of the screaming child's reach. Finally Enna gave up and ran crying from the room.

Chloe locked the door, remarking that it was a pity they had forgotten to lock it earlier. "I'm afraid Miss Enna will get her mother to make you give it up," she said sadly.

Elsie went back to her work, but her eyes were full of tears and her hands trembled with agitation.

Chloe's fears were well founded, of course, and it was not very long before they heard hasty steps in the hallway and the rattling of the doorknob. When the door refused to open, Mrs. Dinsmore's booming voice commanded, "Open this door immediately!"

Chloe looked at Elsie. Tearfully, the little girl slipped the purse into her pocket again and lifted her heart in a quick prayer for patience and meekness, for she knew she would need both.

Chloe slowly unlocked the door, and Mrs. Dinsmore entered, with a sobbing Enna hanging onto her hand. The woman's face was flushed a bright red, and she spoke angrily to Elsie. "What is the meaning of this, you little good-for-nothing? Why are you always tormenting my poor Enna? Where is the pitiful thing that this fuss is all about? Let me see it at once!"

Elsie took the purse from her pocket. Her voice trembled as she said, "It's the purse I was making for Miss Allison. I'll make one just like it for Enna, but I cannot give her this one."

"You *can* not? You *will* not is what you mean. But I say you *shall*, and I am mistress in this house. Give it to Enna this instant. I will not have her crying her eyes out just to humor you in your whims. There are plenty of more handsome purses in the city, and if you are too mean to give this one to Enna, then I will buy you another one tomorrow."

"But that wouldn't be my work," Elsie protested, still holding the purse to herself. "This is."

"Nonsense! What difference will it make to Rose anyway?" With those words, Mrs. Dinsmore grabbed the purse from Elsie and gave it to Enna. "There, my little one," she said in a cooing tone to her blubbering child. "It's yours now. Elsie is a naughty, mean, stingy girl, but she won't plague you when your mother is about."

Enna threw a look of spiteful triumph at Elsie and then ran from the room with her prize. Her mother followed, as Elsie collapsed on Chloe's lap and cried bitterly. Chloe had to call on all her faith in God to hold down the anger and indignation she felt. She let Elsie sob for a few minutes, soothing her only with silent caresses, and allowed her own fury to subside. Then she said, "Never mind, child. You just go into the city tomorrow and buy the prettiest purse you can find for Miss Allison."

But Elsie shook her head. "I wanted it to be my own work," she sobbed, "and now there's no time."

Chloe had a sudden thought. "I'll tell you what, pet. Remember the purse you were knitting for your father? The one Mrs. Dinsmore wouldn't send for you? Well, you can get that finished for Miss Allison, then knit another for your Papa before he comes home."

Elsie raised eyes full of relief, though they clouded almost at once. "But I don't have any beads to finish it, and Miss Rose leaves the day after tomorrow."

Chloe, however, would not be discouraged. "Pompey is going into the city this very afternoon," she said, "so we'll ask him to buy the beads. Then you can finish the purse by tomorrow evening and give it to Miss Allison before she leaves. It's going to be just fine."

"You're right, Aunt Chloe," Elsie said excitedly. "Thank you for thinking of it."

She went to her bureau and unlocked a drawer from which she carefully withdrew a purse of gold and blue beads — quite as handsome as the one taken from her — and she rolled it in a piece of tissue paper. She handed the small bundle to Chloe, who hurried away in search of Pompey. But Pompey informed her that with all his other errands, he wouldn't have time to attend to Elsie's needs. Chloe, who knew that Pompey was very fond of the child, believed him and didn't push the request. What could she do?

"I'll go myself, " she suddenly decided. "I'll ride with you, Pompey, and get the beads and silk myself."

She checked first that Elsie would not need her that afternoon, for Chloe was Elsie's servant only, with responsibilities for no one else in the family. Then she joined Pompey for the trip to the city. But it was late before they returned, and Elsie spent the evening alone in her room. She didn't even have her hour with Rose, who remained with the guests in the parlor that night.

At ˋst, Chloe was back, with all the things Elsie needed. She wanted to begin her work immediately, but before she could start, a servant came to the door with a note. It was from Rose Allison.

"Dear Elsie," the note began. "I am very sorry that we cannot have our reading together this evening, but be sure to come early in the morning. It will be our last opportunity, for I have another disappointment for you. I had not expected to leave until the day after tomorrow, but I've just learned that the ship will sail a day sooner, and therefore I am obliged to begin my journey tomorrow. Your friend, Rose."

Elsie dropped the note on the floor and burst into tears. "Oh, no! Dear Miss Allison is going home tomorrow," she sobbed. But she soon stopped her crying, dried her tears, and gathered the items Chloe had brought from the city.

"I must finish the work tonight," she said firmly, and she set about her task. And though she did not sleep many hours that night, Elsie arrived at Rose's door at precisely seven-thirty the next morning.

Rose clasped the child in her arms as Elsie sobbed, "Dear, dear, Miss Rose, what shall I do without you?"

"You have a better Friend, Elsie, one who said 'I will never leave you nor forsake you,'" Rose whispered.

"And He is your friend, too," Elsie said as she wiped her tears. "Don't you think He will bring us together again some day?"

"I hope so indeed. And we must keep very close to Him, Elsie. We must commune with Him, and study His Word, and try always to do His will. If we have the assurance that our dear Friend is with us — that we have His presence and His love — we shall be supremely happy even though separated from our earthly friends. I know you have peculiar trials, little one, and you often feel the lack of sympathy and love here. But you will always find them in Jesus."

With this reassurance, Elsie and Rose shared their last morning of reading and prayer. Rose read the fourteenth chapter of John, a part of the Savior's touching farewell to His disciples. Then they knelt to pray, although Elsie's heart was so full that she could only listen.

"We will hope to meet again before very long," Rose said when her prayer was ended. "Who knows? Your father may come home and bring you to see me someday. He likes to travel, so it seems a good possibility."

Smiling now, Elsie said, "That would be wonderful!" Then she added, with a deep sigh, "But sometimes it seems that my Papa will never come home."

Cheerfully, Rose said, "Well, we can hope. And even though we must be separated for a time, we can still meet in spirit at the mercy-seat. Let's agree to do it every morning at this hour, shall we?"

The idea was a happy one for Elsie, and she eagerly assented.

"And I will write to you, dear," Rose continued. "I will write while I am traveling, if I can, so you will receive my letter a week from now. Then you must write to me. Will you?"

"If you won't care about my mistakes, Miss Rose," Elsie replied a little self-consciously. "I can't ask Miss Day to correct my letter because I don't want her to read it. But I will be so glad to get yours. I've never had a letter in my whole life."

"I won't care at all about mistakes," Rose assured, "and no one will see your letters except me. I don't want Miss Day reading them either."

Rose reached to hug Elsie once more, and the girl's hand went into her pocket, bringing out the finished gold and blue purse. "It's all my own work because I thought you would value it more," Elsie said shyly.

"And indeed I shall!" Rose said. "It's a beautiful purse in itself, but I will value it ten times more because it is your gift and the work of your hands." She hugged her little friend close, and Elsie, so unused to praise for her accomplishments, felt a kind of warmth she had hardly ever known.

They had only a few more minutes together, for immediately after breakfast, Rose's carriage arrived. The family, who had all come to care for their visitor and would miss her presence in their house, gathered at the door to bid her farewell. One by one, they said their good-byes, and Elsie was the last. Rose kissed the child tenderly, and choking back her tears, she said, "God bless and keep you, my poor little darling, my dear little Elsie."

Elsie simply could not speak, and when the carriage had rolled out of sight, she ran to her room, locked the door, and cried out her grief. She had learned to love Rose completely and to depend on her new friend without reservation. Parting, with no certainty of ever meeting again, was one of the hardest trials the child had ever endured.

CHAPTER

3

An Unexpected Homecoming

"Hope deferred makes the heart sick, but a longing fulfilled is a tree of life."

PROVERBS 13:12

An Unexpected Homecoming

It had been a week since Rose Allison's departure — a lonely week for Elsie — and at the breakfast table, Adelaide voiced the little girl's own thoughts. "I think we ought to hear from Rose soon," Adelaide said. "She promised to write during her journey."

Almost in answer to her words, Pompey entered the room, carrying the mail bag which he brought from the city every morning. He handed the bag to Mr. Dinsmore as Mrs. Dinsmore remarked, with some irritation, "You're late this morning, Pompey."

"Yes, ma'am," replied the old servant, smiling sweetly. "The horses were very lazy today. I expect they have spring fever."

"Do hurry, Papa," Adelaide said impatiently, "and see if there isn't something from Rose."

"Have patience, young lady," her father replied as he opened the bag and very deliberately adjusted his spectacles before sorting through the family's letters. "Yes, there is a letter here for you, and one for Elsie, too."

He tossed the letters across the table, and Elsie, being excused, eagerly grabbed hers and ran up to her room. It was like a feast for her — the first letter she had ever received — and from such a dear friend. For the moment at least, it gave her almost as much pleasure as Rose's presence would have.

Elsie had just finished reading the letter through and was beginning to read it again when she heard Adelaide calling. The next moment, her aunt entered the room.

"I suppose you've read your letter," Adelaide said, and a strange smile played on her mouth, "but now I have another piece of news for you. Can you guess it?"

49

Elsie's Endless Wait

"Is Miss Rose coming back?" Elsie ventured hopefully.

"What a silly guess," Adelaide said. "No, little Elsie, it's even more exciting. My brother — your Papa Horace — has actually sailed for America and is coming directly home."

Elsie jumped up, and her heart beat wildly. "Is it really true, Aunt Adelaide?" she asked. "Is he really coming? Will he be here soon?"

"He has really started at last," Adelaide assured, "but I don't know how soon he will be here." As she turned to leave, she added, "I've told you all that I know for the moment."

Elsie clapped her hands together and dropped down onto the sofa. The letter from Rose, so highly prized a few moments before, drifted unnoticed to the floor. The child's thoughts were now far away, imagining the father she didn't know as he crossed the ocean for home. She tried to picture how he would look, how he would speak, and how he would feel about her.

"Oh, will he love me?" she asked herself aloud. "Will he let me love him? Will he take me in his arms and call me his own darling child?"

But there was no one to answer her anxious questions. She would just have to wait and let the slow wheel of time turn until her father's longed-for, and somehow frightful, arrival.

In the schoolroom, Elsie recited her lessons indifferently until Miss Day sternly remarked that receiving letters did not seem to agree with her pupil. Elsie must do better, Miss Day said, if she wished to please her Papa when he came. For once, Miss Day's observation struck just the right chord; Elsie was extremely anxious to please her father and to gain his affection and approval. She turned her whole attention to her studies with such determination that Miss Day could find no more cause for complaint.

⁓

But what, indeed, did the father expect of his daughter? Horace Dinsmore, Jr., was, like his father, an upright and moral man who paid outward respect to the forms of religion but cared nothing for the vital power of godliness. Horace trusted his own morality entirely, and he regarded most Christians as hypocrites and deceivers. He had been told of his little Elsie's Christian devotion, and though he didn't acknowledge it even to himself, this information had prejudiced him against his child.

Also, like all the Dinsmores, he had a great deal of family pride. Although his wife's father, Mr. Grayson, had been a man of sterling worth — intelligent, honest, pious, and very wealthy at his death — he had begun life as a poor boy and made his fortune in business. For this reason, all the Dinsmores spoke of Horace's marriage to his beautiful heiress as a step down. Even Horace himself had come to regard his marriage as a boyish folly of which he was now ashamed. So often in his letters had Mr. Dinsmore referred to Elsie as "old Grayson's grandchild" that Horace had come to think of her as a kind of disgrace, especially because she was always described to him as disagreeable and troublesome.

Horace had loved his young wife with genuine passion and mourned her death bitterly. But distance and the passage of so much time had dimmed his memory of her, and he seldom thought of her now except in connection with the child, the child for whom, in his secret heart, he harbored a feeling of dislike.

At Roselands, scarcely anything was spoken or thought about outside of Horace's anticipated return, and for Elsie especially, the time crawled by. At last a letter came from Horace saying that he would arrive the next day.

"Oh, Aunt Chloe," said Elsie, jumping up and down and clapping her hands at the news. "Just think! Papa will be here tomorrow morning."

Then her wild delight turned sober, and concern clouded her face as the torturing question came again into her mind: *Will he love me?* She stood still now, as Chloe changed her from a riding outfit to a dress and smoothed her curls. Looking into the somber little face, Chloe couldn't resist hugging her little charge and pressing a gentle kiss on her brow.

It was at this moment that an unusual sense of activity seemed to fill the house. Elsie jumped, and the color rushed to her face as she listened intently. She heard the sound of running feet in the hall, and suddenly her door was flung open. "He's here!" Walter shouted as he grabbed her hand and pulled her from the room and down the stairs. But as they approached the parlor door, Elsie begged Walter to stop. She leaned against the wall, and her heart beat so fast she could scarcely breathe. This was the moment she had prayed for; yet she was unprepared and filled with fears she could not comprehend.

"Are you sick?" Walter asked, but not waiting for a reply, he pushed the door open and dragged her inside. Elsie was so overwrought that she almost fainted. The room seemed to spin, and for an instant, she hardly knew where she was.

Then a strange voice asked, "And who is this?" She looked up and saw a man — very handsome and youthful looking, in spite of his heavy, dark beard and mustache.

"Is this great girl *my* child?" Horace asked. "Why it's enough to make a man feel old." Then he took her hand, stooped, and kissed her coldly on the lips.

Elsie was shaking violently, and the power of her feelings made her incapable of speech. Her hand, still in his, was cold and clammy.

Horace searched her face, then dropped her hand. "I'm not an ogre," he said in a voice that betrayed his annoyance. "You need not be afraid of me. Alright, you may go. I won't keep you in terror any longer."

Dismissed, Elsie could only run back to her room where she fell onto the bed and wept as she never had before. For as long as she could remember, she had longed for this hour, yet the disappointment was so deep that it seemed her heart would break. Not even Chloe — who was in the kitchen, rejoicing in the assumption that her young charge was supremely happy at this moment — was there to offer comfort. Alone, Elsie wept as if she might weep her life away.

"Oh, Papa! Papa! You don't love me! Oh, Mamma, I wish I could be with you. There's no one here to love me, and I'm so lonely!"

This was how Chloe found her an hour later, still sobbing out her broken cries of anguish. Chloe understood at once how her child was suffering. She raised Elsie in her arms and cradled her feverish head, smoothing back the tear-sodden curls and bathing the child's swollen eyes and throbbing temples.

Elsie's Endless Wait

"My poor baby," she soothed. "You know your Aunt Chloe loves you better than life. And did you forget your Almighty Friend who loves you and says 'I will never leave you nor forsake you'? He sticks to us 'closer than a brother,' my precious child. Jesus' love is better than any other love, and I know you have His love."

"Then ask Him to take me to Himself, and to Mamma. I'm so lonely, and I want to die!"

"Hush, darling, hush now. I could never ask that. It would break my heart. You mean the world to me, and you know we must all wait for the Lord's time."

"Then ask Him to help me be patient," Elsie begged. "And ask Him to make my father love me."

"I will, darling, I will," Chloe said through her own tears. "And don't you be discouraged right away. I'm sure your Papa will love you once he comes to know you."

That evening, when the family gathered for supper, there was an empty chair at the table, and Adelaide sent one of the servants to find Elsie. When the woman returned, it was with the news that Elsie had a bad headache and didn't want to eat. Horace overheard the message, and he asked his sister, "Is she subject to such attacks? I hope she isn't a sickly child."

"Not really," Adelaide replied dryly. She had observed Horace's meeting with his child, and she felt really sorry for Elsie's evident disappointment. "I imagine that excessive crying has brought this on."

Horace flushed deeply, and in a caustic tone that betrayed his displeasure, he said, "So the return of a parent is a cause for grief, is it? I didn't expect my presence to be so distressing for my only child. I had no idea she disliked me so."

An Unexpected Homecoming

"She doesn't," Adelaide said, her own temper rising. "She has been looking forward to your return for as long as I've known her."

"That's hard to believe," Horace retorted, "given her conduct toward me today."

Adelaide could see that Horace was determined to misconstrue Elsie's behavior. She was afraid that any defense of the child would only increase his sour mood, so she said no more.

Upstairs in her bedroom, Elsie finally fell asleep, but not before she had turned in her sadness to Him who said, "I have loved you with an everlasting love." At least she had the sweet assurance of His love and favor.

<hr/>

The next morning Elsie came to breakfast in a state of hope and fear; she wanted, yet dreaded, meeting her father. But when she entered the dining room, he was not there.

"Your Papa isn't coming down this morning," Adelaide told her kindly. "He is very tired from his long journey. I'm sorry, but you may not see him at all today, for we expect a good deal of company this afternoon and tonight."

Disappointed once again, Elsie found it impossible to concentrate on her lessons. Every time the door opened, she jumped nervously and looked up, hoping it was her father. But Horace did not come to her, and that evening, the children were sent to dine in the playroom because there were so many guests for supper. Just as Adelaide had predicted, Elsie didn't see her father at all that day.

The next morning, however, the children were to breakfast with the adults because all the guests, except one gentleman, had departed. Elsie went early into the breakfast room, and to her surprise, she found her father alone, reading the morning newspaper.

He looked up, and she said in a trembling voice, "Good morning, Papa." The greeting made Horace start, for he had never before been addressed as "Papa," and it sounded strange to his ears. He regarded his child with curiosity and almost reached out to her. But instead of extending his hand, he simply said, "Good morning, Elsie," and returned to his paper.

Elsie remained in the middle of the room; she didn't dare to approach him, however much she wanted to. While she stood there, not knowing what to do, the door swung open, and Enna, looking rosy and happy, ran in and rushed to her brother. She climbed on his knee, put her chubby arms around his neck, and pleaded for a kiss.

"You shall have it, little pet," Horace laughed. Tossing down his paper, he hugged Enna warmly. "*You* are not afraid of me, are you?" he asked playfully, and added pointedly, "or sorry that I have come home?"

"No, indeed," Enna said.

Horace glanced at Elsie to see her reaction. Her eyes had filled with tears, and she could not stop herself thinking that Enna had taken her place and was receiving the love that should be hers. Horace read her reaction correctly, although he misunderstood its source. "She's jealous," he thought. "I cannot tolerate jealous people." He gave her a look that clearly displayed his displeasure, and Elsie, cut to the quick, had to leave the room to hide her tears.

"I am envious," she thought. "I'm jealous of Enna. Oh, how awful of me!" Silently she prayed, "Dear Savior, help me! Take away these terrible feelings."

An Unexpected Homecoming

Despite her youth, Elsie was beginning to learn how to control her own emotions, and in a few moments, she had recovered her composure so that she could return to the breakfast room and take her place at the table. Her sweet face was sad indeed and showed the traces of tears, but it was also calm and peaceful.

Her father took no notice of her, and she didn't trust herself to look at him. The servants filled her plate, and she ate in silence. To her great relief, the others were too busy talking and eating to pay attention to her, and she failed to see how often the visitor who was seated nearly opposite her fixed his eyes on her pale face.

When she had left the room, the visitor asked, "Is that one of your sisters, Horace?"

"No," said Horace, flushing slightly. "She is my daughter."

"Ah! I'd almost forgotten that you have a child," the man said. "Well, you have no reason to be ashamed of her. She is perfectly lovely. Sweetest little face I ever saw."

Anxious to change the subject, Horace suggested to his friend that they call for their horses and take a ride around the property. The subject of Elsie was dropped, and the two men left together.

Several hours later, Elsie was practicing at the piano in the music room when she felt suddenly that she was not alone. Turning around, she recognized her father's friend as Edward Travilla, the owner of a neighboring plantation.

"Excuse me for interrupting," he said and bowed politely. "I heard the sound of the piano. I am very fond of music, so I ventured in."

Elsie was timid with outsiders, but she was also very polite, so she welcomed the guest. "Won't you take a seat, sir? I'm afraid my music won't give you any pleasure. I'm only learning and cannot play very well yet."

Edward thanked her and took a seat near her side. "Will you do me a favor and repeat the song I heard you singing a few minutes ago?"

Though her cheeks were burning and her voice trembled at first, Elsie complied, and as she proceeded, her voice grew strong and steady. She had quite a nice voice for a girl her age, and she also had musical talent, which had been well cultivated by good teachers and diligent practice. Her music was simple, but her performance was very good.

Edward thanked her heartily and complimented both her playing and her singing. Then he asked for another song and another, and they chatted genially until Elsie lost all sense of embarrassment,

"I think your name is Elsie, isn't it?" Edward asked.

"Yes, sir. Elsie Dinsmore."

"And you are the daughter of my friend Horace Dinsmore?"

"Yes, sir."

"Your father has been gone for a long time, so I suppose you must have forgotten him."

"Oh, no, sir. I couldn't have forgotten him because I'd never seen him."

"Indeed," Edward remarked in surprise. "Then, since he is a stranger to you, I suppose you can't have much affection for him."

Elsie looked into his face, her hazel eyes very round, and said with astonishment, "Not love Papa? My own Papa who has no other child but me? Oh, Mr. Travilla, how could you think that?"

An Unexpected Homecoming

"I see I was mistaken," he said with a smile. "I see you care very much for your Papa. But do you think he loves you?"

To the gentleman's great dismay, Elsie dropped her face into her hands and burst into a torrent of tears. Trying to comfort her as best he could, Edward patted her quaking shoulder and said, "My poor child, forgive me. I am very, very sorry for my silly question. But trust me, dear girl, that whether your father loves you now or not, I know he will quite soon."

When Elsie had dried her tears and closed the piano, Edward invited her to take a little walk with him in the garden. He felt very sorry for the pain his thoughtless remark had inflicted, and the little girl interested him, so he did his best to entertain her as they walked. He talked to her about the plants and flowers. He told her about the foreign lands he had visited, and he related stories of his travels, deliberately choosing incidents in which her father had also played a part.

He discovered that Elsie was far from a dull companion. With a natural love of reading and ready access to her grandfather's well-stocked library, Elsie had read more books, and with more thought, than most children her age. The intelligence of her questions and conversation surprised and pleased Edward Travilla.

When the dinner bell rang, he escorted Elsie to the table and seated her at his side. Never was any great lady more carefully waited on than was Elsie at this meal. There were several more gentleman guests present who attended to the older women, so Edward felt at liberty to devote his attention to Elsie, talking to her — and making her talk.

Now and then, Elsie stole a glance at Mrs. Dinsmore, and to her great relief, the woman was too occupied to notice her. Once Elsie glanced at her father, and when their eyes met, his held an expression that was both curious and amused — a look she could not interpret. But since she saw no displeasure there, her heart grew light and her face glowed with happiness.

Later, in the drawing room, as Horace and his old friend talked alone, Edward said, "Really, Horace, your daughter is remarkably intelligent, as well as remarkably pretty. And I've discovered that she has a good deal of musical talent."

"Has she?" Horace replied. "Perhaps it's a pity she doesn't belong to you, my friend, instead of me, for you seem to appreciate her so much more highly."

"I wish she did," Edward said. "But seriously, Horace, you ought to love that child. She certainly loves you devotedly."

Surprised by his friend's assessment, Horace asked, "How do you know?"

"It was clear from what I saw and heard this morning. Horace, she would value a kind word from you more than the richest jewel."

"I doubt that," Horace said, but there was a hint of a question in his words. He turned to the window, and suddenly, without explanation to his friend, he left the room, for he had seen Elsie come out onto the portico. She was dressed in her riding clothes, and Jim, who usually accompanied her when she rode by herself, was bringing up her horse.

Horace approached his daughter and asked, "Are you going for a ride, Elsie?"

"Yes, Papa," she said and looked shyly into his face.

Horace leaned down and lifted her into his arms. Then he placed her in the saddle, saying to the boy, "Now, Jim, you must take good care of my little girl."

An Unexpected Homecoming

This time, the tears that came to Elsie's eyes were for joy. "He called me *his* little girl," she murmured to herself as she rode away, "and he told Jim to take good care of me. I'm sure he will love me soon, just as Mr. Travilla said he would."

From the portico, Horace watched his daughter as she rode down the long avenue that led from the house. He didn't notice Edward Travilla, who had come out to join him.

"How well she sits her horse," Edward said.

"Yes, she does," Horace replied in an absent way. He was thinking of a time some eight or nine years before when he had assisted another Elsie to mount her horse and had ridden for hours at her side. For the rest of that afternoon, memories came flooding into his mind, and in his heart, a feeling of tenderness began to grow for the child of the wife who had been so dear to him. When he saw little Elsie returning up the driveway, he hurried outside again, lifted her from the horse, and asked if she had enjoyed her ride.

"Oh, yes, Papa. It was very pleasant."

He looked into her beaming face, and without thinking, he kissed his child warmly. "I think I will ride with you one of these days," he said. "Would you like that?"

"Oh, very much, Papa. So very much."

Horace smiled at his daughter's earnestness and watched her as she raced away to her room to change her clothes and tell Chloe of her happiness.

Alas, the moment was like a transient gleam of sunshine that lighted her path briefly, then disappeared behind gathering clouds.

Elsie's Endless Wait

More company came to Roselands, and the drawing room was filled with guests that evening. Though Elsie was there, her father was too busy with his guests to give her even a glance. She sat alone and unnoticed in a corner and watched her father's every move. Her ears strained to catch his words. Then Edward Travilla, who had been talking with a group on the opposite side of the room, disengaged himself and came toward Elsie. Taking her hand, he led her to the center table where a pleasant-looking, elderly lady was examining some engravings that Horace had brought home from Europe.

"Mother," said Edward, "this is my friend Elsie."

"I am so glad to see you, my dear," the lady said, giving Elsie a kiss.

Edward set a chair for Elsie close to his mother, and he sat on the child's other side. He began to explain the engravings, and since he attached a clever anecdote to each, Elsie was thoroughly entertained and quite forgot to look for her father.

Suddenly, Edward laid down the engraving he was describing and said, "Miss Elsie, I want my mother to hear you play and sing. Will you do me the favor of repeating the song I admired so much this morning?"

Elsie blushed brightly and exclaimed, "I couldn't play or sing for so many people, Mr. Travilla. Please excuse me."

But from behind her, Horace's voice commanded, "Go immediately, and do as the gentleman requests."

His voice was stern, and Elsie saw that his face was even more so. Trembling, she rose to obey, but Edward, who could see her distress, said kindly, "Never mind, Miss Elsie. I withdraw my request."

"But I do not withdraw my command," her father said. "Go at once, Elsie, and do as I say."

She went, and Edward, silently scolding himself for causing her trouble, placed her sheet of music on the piano and whispered encouragingly in her ear, "Have confidence in yourself, Miss Elsie. That is all that is necessary for your success."

But Elsie was shattered by her father's attitude, and she could not control the tears that welled in her eyes. She could barely see the notes and words, and she blundered badly as she attempted to play the prelude. Her mistakes only increased her misery and embarrassment.

"Never mind the prelude," Edward said in an effort to help. "You can just begin the song."

But it was no use. Before she could get through the first verse, she broke into tears. Her father, looking mortified, came up behind her and spoke in low, hard tones, "Elsie, I am ashamed of you. Go to your room and to bed immediately."

Again she obeyed, and again, she cried herself to sleep.

The next morning, Elsie learned that Edward Travilla and his mother had returned to their home. Elsie was very sorry that she hadn't said good-bye to her new friends, and for the next few days, her sorrow increased, for her father's cold manner had returned. He scarcely ever spoke to her, and to make matters worse, her young aunts and uncles ridiculed her for the failed attempt to play at the party.

Even Miss Day, who seemed unusually cross, taunted her. Elsie tried to pay attention to her lessons, but she was so troubled and depressed that she failed repeatedly and was in constant disgrace with Miss Day, who threatened to go to her father. When Miss Day saw how this threat terrified Elsie, the governess used it all the more.

But what chiefly occupied Elsie's thoughts was how to gain her father's love. She tried every way she could to win his affection. She cheerfully obeyed his every order and tried to anticipate and fulfill his wishes. But he seldom seemed to notice her except for commands and rebukes, while he lavished attention on his sister Enna. Elsie could only watch them in silence until her feelings overwhelmed her and she rushed away to cry in secret and to pray for her father's love. She never complained, not even to Chloe, but the anxious nursemaid clearly saw that her beloved child was very unhappy.

"Maybe you should be more like Enna," Chloe suggested. "Be merry and run and jump on your Papa's knee. I think he'll like you better for it."

But the very thought terrified Elsie. "I can't do that," she said mournfully. "I don't dare."

So as Elsie grew increasingly pale and melancholy, Chloe's heart ached, and she, too, shed many secret tears.

CHAPTER

New Rules

"Children, obey your parents in everything, for this pleases the Lord."

COLOSSIANS 3:20

New Rules

So things went for about a week, until the morning when Elsie entered the breakfast room to be greeted by her father with an unusually pleasant "Good morning, Elsie." Then he took her hand and led her to the seat beside his at the table. Elsie, so used to being ignored, nearly glowed with pleasure.

There were several guests present, and Elsie waited patiently while they and the older members of the family were served. When her turn came, her grandfather asked, "Have some bacon, Elsie?"

But before she could answer, her father said, "None for Elsie. Once a day is often enough for a child to eat meat. She may have it for dinner at mid-day, but never at breakfast or supper."

Old Mr. Dinsmore laughed, "Really, Horace, where did you get such a notion? I always allowed you to eat whatever you pleased, and I never saw it hurt you. But, of course, you must manage your child in your own way."

When hot cakes were passed, Horace again said none for Elsie. Instead he placed a slice of bread on her plate and explained, "I don't approve of hot cakes and rolls and muffins for children, so you must eat only cold bread."

And as old Pompey was about to set a cup of coffee down for Elsie, Horace intervened again. "Take the coffee away, please," Horace said, "and bring Elsie a tumbler of milk. Or would you prefer water, Elsie?"

"Milk, please, Papa," the little girl replied with a small sigh. She was very fond of coffee, and it was not easy to give up.

Elsie's Endless Wait

Horace spooned a serving of stewed fruit onto her plate, and Pompey returned with her milk. "There," her father said. "You have your breakfast. In England, children are not allowed to eat butter until they are ten or twelve years old, and I think it's an excellent plan to make them grow rosy and healthy. I have neglected my little girl for too long," he added, smiling and laying his hand on her head for a moment. "But I intend to take good care of you now."

Whatever the cause for this change in him, his words and his manner were more than enough to reconcile Elsie to her meager meal, and she ate with relish. But the meager fare became a constant, and Elsie often looked longingly at the hot buttered rolls and cups of coffee enjoyed by the others. She tried to content herself with the assurance that her Papa was doing what was best for her and to remind herself that Jesus would be pleased with her obedience, but it was not so easy to understand these new rules.

One morning as he read in the drawing room, Horace overheard Arthur teasing Elsie as usual. "Isn't it great to have your Papa home?" the boy was saying snippily. "And how pleasant for you to live on bread and water, eh!"

"I don't live on bread and water," Elsie replied indignantly.

"Papa allows me as much milk and cream and fruit as I want. I can have eggs and cheese and honey and anything else except meat and hot cakes and butter and coffee. And I wouldn't trade any of those things for a father who loves me. Besides, Papa says I can have all the meat I want for dinner."

Arthur became even more scornful. "That's nothing," he mocked. "And I wouldn't give much for all the love *you* get from him."

The last Horace heard was what sounded like a sob, and he went to the window in time to catch a glimpse of Elsie running down the garden path.

Horace found Arthur just outside, leaning lazily against one of the pillars on the portico, "What do you mean, sir, teasing Elsie in that manner?" Horace demanded.

"I only wanted to have a little fun," Arthur replied sullenly.

"Well, I don't approve of that kind of fun, and you will leave the child alone in the future," Horace commanded.

Returning to the drawing room, Horace picked up his newspaper again, but it no longer held his interest. He kept hearing that little sob and seeing his child running from his brother's hateful taunts. When the ringing of the school bell broke into his thoughts, he tossed his paper down, took a card from his pocket, jotted a few words on it, and called a servant to take the note to Miss Day.

When the note was delivered, Miss Day looked at it and said to Elsie, "Your father wants you. You may go."

With some trepidation, Elsie left the schoolroom and hurried to find her father. Fanny, one of the housekeeping servants, directed her to the drawing room.

When Elsie entered, Horace smiled and held out his hand to her. "Come here, Daughter," he said, and her little heart thrilled, for he had never called her "Daughter" before. She stood at his side, and he took her hand in one of his, placed his other hand gently on her head, and looked deeply into her eyes.

"You've been crying" he said in a gently reproving tone. "I'm afraid you do a good deal more crying than is good for you. It is a very babyish habit, and you must try to break yourself of it."

She flushed, and in spite of herself, her eyes filled.

But Horace stroked her hair softly and said, "Don't begin it again. I have good news for you. I plan to drive over to Ion today, to see Mr. Travilla and his mother, and I would like you to go with me."

"Oh, thank you, Papa," she said eagerly.

"There are no little folks there, but I can see you want to go. Now run along and ask Aunt Chloe to get you ready, and tell her to dress you nicely. The carriage will be here for us in half an hour."

Elsie bounded away, and at the specified time, she came back, looking so pretty that her father gazed at her in proud delight and gave her a kiss as he lifted her into the carriage.

"Have you ever been to Ion?" he asked as the coachman guided the horses on their journey,

"No, sir, but I've heard Aunt Adelaide say it's a very lovely place."

"So it is, though not as pretty as Roselands," Horace said. "Edward Travilla and I have been friends since our boyhood, and I spent many happy days at Ion — long before I ever thought of you."

He smiled and patted her cheek.

"Tell me about those times, please, Papa," Elsie asked. "It seems so strange that you were ever a little boy, and I was nowhere."

Horace laughed and then said thoughtfully, "It seems just a short time ago, to me, that I was no older than you are now."

But instead of telling her more, Horace lapsed into silence. They drove on without speaking for some time, until Elsie spotted a squirrel darting up a tree, and she exclaimed, "Did you see that squirrel? Look, Papa, he's perched on that branch."

The coach moved on, and the squirrel was out of sight, but Elsie's outburst, far from annoying her father, reminded him of a day he had once spent hunting squirrels in those very woods. He gave Elsie a very animated account, including the moment when one of his companions accidentally fired his hunting rifle, and the bullet missed Horace by a hair's breadth.

"I felt like fainting when I realized how near I'd come to death," he concluded.

"Oh, Papa, how good God was to save you. If you'd been killed, I could never have had you for my father."

"Perhaps you would have had a better one, Elsie," he said.

Elsie was about to protest, but just then the carriage turned into a broad, tree-lined drive, and Horace cheerfully announced, "There it is, Elsie dear. There is Ion."

In another few minutes, they were alighting from the carriage, and Edward Travilla was greeting them. "Why, Horace, you've brought my little friend Elsie. This is really good of you," he said with genuine delight. The men shook hands enthusiastically, and Edward planted a little kiss on Elsie's cheek. Then he led them inside. "My mother will be so happy to see you both," he said, "and she seems to have taken a special fancy to Miss Elsie."

Mrs. Travilla's greeting was no less cordial, though somewhat less boisterous, than her son's, and she made Elsie feel at home immediately. When the men had left to tour the plantation, the woman and the girl spent an enjoyable morning together in Mrs. Travilla's room. They chatted, and Elsie helped Mrs. Travilla with some garments she was making for the field hands. Elsie soon learned that Mrs. Travilla was a devoted Christian — a tie that drew them closer. Mrs. Travilla was also a discerning woman; she had known Horace nearly all his life, and she already had some notion of the difficulties of Elsie's situation. Without alluding to anything specific, she nevertheless gave the little girl some excellent advice, for which Elsie was truly grateful.

Several hours had passed when Edward returned. "Come, Elsie. I want you to see my garden and hothouse. Will you come, Mother? We have just enough time before dinner."

"No, Edward, I have some things to attend to. So you do the honors," Mrs. Travilla replied.

"Where's Papa?" Elsie asked.

"In the library looking over some new books. Your father has always cared for books more than anything."

As they walked through the garden, Edward asked, "Well, what do you think of our flowers?"

"They're really beautiful," Elsie said. "And you have so many kinds. That's a lovely cape-jasmine, and look! There's a cactus I've never seen before. Mr. Travilla, I think you have more beautiful flowers than we have at Roselands," Elsie declared. Her admiration greatly pleased Edward, for he took intense pride in his garden.

At dinner, Elsie sat beside her father.

"I hope she hasn't given you any trouble," Horace said to Mrs. Travilla.

"On the contrary," the old lady laughed. "We have had a grand time together, and I hope you will bring her to see me again very soon."

After dinner, they all adjourned to the veranda where thick trees shaded the house from the day's heat and a small stone fountain bubbled gaily. But the adults' conversation soon bored Elsie, and she slipped away to the library. A book on the table caught her eye, and she settled on a comfortable sofa in the corner of the room. Soon she was lost to everything around her as she read.

"So here you are, Miss Elsie," came Edward's pleasant voice. "We've been wondering where you were these last two hours. I should have guessed you are a bookworm like your father."

He sat beside her and took the book from her hands. "You can finish that later. I want you to talk to me."

"But Papa will be leaving soon, and it's such a good book," she said.

"No, he won't come to take you away. I've made a bargain to keep you here," he said gravely. "You see, we think there are more than enough children at Roselands without you, and so your Papa has given you to me."

"You're only joking, Mr. Travilla."

"Not at all." he continued with great seriousness. "Can't you see I'm in earnest?"

Although Elsie was teased often enough by her aunts and uncles and should have recognized Travilla's jesting, her father's affection was too fragile and her fear of losing him too strong. At the thought of leaving him, she felt panic overtake her, and with a little cry of alarm, she ran to the veranda and into her father's arms. Clinging to him as if for dear life, she sobbed, "Oh, Papa! Please don't give me away. I'll be good! I'll do everything you say! I'll —"

"Why Elsie, what do you mean?" Horace asked in perplexity. Then he saw Edward standing in the doorway, a sheepish look on his face.

"Mr. Travilla says that you've given me to him," Elsie went on in great fright.

Elsie's Endless Wait

"Nonsense, Elsie," her father said. "How can you believe that I'd ever give you away? Why, I'd rather sacrifice everything I have than part with you."

Elsie looked up and searched his face. What she saw there brought reassurance, and sighing deeply, she laid her head on his shoulder and said, "I am so glad, Papa."

At this point, Edward came forward and patted her shoulder. "I must say, Miss Elsie, that I hardly feel complimented. I'm vain enough to think I'd be the better — or at least the more indulgent — father. Won't you try me for a month, if your Papa consents?"

Elsie shook her head.

"I'll let you have your own way in everything," Edward urged again.

"I don't want my own way, Mr. Travilla. I know that it isn't always the best," Elsie said decisively, making Horace laugh and run his hand over her curly head.

"And I thought you liked me," Edward said in mock disappointment.

"I do like you, Mr. Travilla. Very much. I'm sure you'd be kind, and I'd love you, but never as much as I love my Papa. You're not my Papa, and never could be, even if he did give me away."

Horace laughed again and said to his friend, "I think you'd better give up, Edward. It seems I have to keep her after all, for she clings to me like a morning glory vine."

"Well, Elsie, will you at least come play a little for me at the piano?" Edward asked. But Elsie still clutched her father, until he loosened her grip and said in his forceful way, "Go on now, Elsie, and do as you are requested."

She rose instantly to obey. (Later Edward would complain to his mother, "I wish that Horace didn't always second my requests with his commands. The child should be allowed to comply of her own will.")

Elsie sang and played until supper time, and afterward she sat quietly while her elders talked.

On the drive home to Roselands, Horace asked if she had enjoyed the day.

"Yes Papa, very much, except . . . . "

"Except what?" he asked, smiling down at her.

"Except when Mr. Travilla frightened me so."

"And do you really love your own Papa best? Are you sure you wouldn't exchange me for another?"

"Oh, no, Papa. Not for anybody in the world."

Horace didn't reply, though a gratified smile settled on his face, and they rode the rest of the way in a comfortable silence.

When they reached Roselands, Elsie kissed her father good night, and ran up the stairs to tell Chloe about her day.

"What a very pleasant visit we had," she said excitedly. "Papa was so kind, and so were Mr. Travilla and his mother."

"I'm glad, darling, and I hope you're going to have many more such days," Chloe said. As she undressed the child and prepared her for bed, Elsie regaled her nursemaid with a minute-by-minute account of everything that had occurred at Ion, even the terrible fright Edward Travilla had given her and its happy resolution.

"Well, you are mighty happy yourself, little girl," Chloe said.

"I am," Elsie agreed, "because I think my Papa is beginning to love me a little, and I hope he will soon love me very much."

Elsie's Endless Wait

The next afternoon, Elsie was returning from her walk when she met her father coming down the driveway. But instead of greeting her, Horace said sternly, "Elsie, I've forbidden you to walk out alone. Are you disobeying?"

"No, sir," she answered meekly. "I was with Aunt Adelaide and Louise until about five minutes ago. They said I was so near home I could come alone. They were going to make a call on a friend and didn't want me along."

Horace was somewhat mollified and took her hand. "How far have you been?" he asked.

"We went down the river bank to the big spring. I think it's about a mile that way, but we took a shorter way back, across the fields and through the meadow."

"The meadow?" Horace said, and he tightened his hold on her hand. "You are never to go into the meadow again, Elsie, unless you have my express permission."

"Why, Papa?" Elsie asked in some surprise.

"Because I forbid it," he said, "and that's enough for you to know. All you have to do is obey. You need never again ask why when I give you an order."

Elsie's eyes filled and a big tear rolled down her cheek. "I didn't mean to be naughty," she said, "and I'll try never to ask why again."

"Another thing, Elsie, you cry too easily. It's entirely too babyish for a girl your age. You must quit it."

"I'll try," she promised. She wiped her eyes and made a great effort to control her feelings.

As they approached the house, a little girl about Elsie's age came rushing out to meet them. "Oh, Elsie," she said excitedly. "I'm so glad you've come. We've been here a whole hour — Mamma and Herbert and I — and I've been looking for you all the time."

"How do you do, Miss Lucy Carrington?" Horace said. "I see you can talk as fast as ever." He laughed and held out his hand.

Lucy shook it and replied with a little pout, "To be sure, Mr. Dinsmore, it hasn't been more than two weeks since you were at our house, and I wouldn't forget how to talk in just that short time." Then she turned to Elsie, clasping her friend around the waist. "We've come to stay for a week," she chattered, "and won't we have a fine time together?"

Elsie finally had a chance to speak, "I am glad you've come," she said sincerely.

"Is your father here, Miss Lucy?" Horace asked.

"Yes, sir, but he's going home tonight, and then he'll come back for us next week."

"Then I must go in and see him. Elsie, will you entertain Lucy?"

As her father walked away, Elsie suggested that the girls go to her room to play.

"Oh, yes, but won't you speak to Mamma first?" Lucy asked. "And Herbert, too? You're such a favorite with both of them. They're still in the dressing room because Mamma is not very well, and she's feeling tired from the ride."

Lucy led the way to her mother's room, babbling all the time. When they entered, Mrs. Carrington rose from the sofa and hugged Elsie close. "Elsie dear, how are you? I'm so glad to see you. I suppose you are very happy now that your father has come home. I remember how you always looked forward to his return, constantly talking of it and longing for it."

Elsie wasn't sure what to say. Her father's return had not been as happy as she had always anticipated, but she didn't want to discuss it with Mrs. Carrington.

Luckily she didn't have to reply, because Herbert, Lucy's twin brother, came in at that moment and grabbed Elsie's hand. "I'm ever so glad to see you again, Elsie," he said, giving her hand a hearty squeeze. Elsie liked Herbert and felt sorry for him; he had suffered for several years from a hip condition that made him weak and sickly.

"Herbert always says that no one can tell such beautiful stories as Elsie," Mrs. Carrington chirped happily. "And no one except his mother and his nurse were so kind to him when he was bedridden here for so many weeks last year. Herbert has missed you very much, Elsie dear."

"How is your hip now, Herbert?" Elsie asked.

"Much better," the boy said cheerfully, though Elsie thought he looked very pale. "Sometimes I can take long walks now, but I can't run and leap like other boys. I still limp."

They all talked for awhile longer, then Elsie retreated to her room to dress for supper.

At the evening meal, Lucy, who was seated next to Elsie, took her third or fourth muffin and said, "These muffins are delicious! Don't you like them, Elsie?"

"Very much," Elsie said cheerfully.

"Then why are you eating cold bread? And you don't have any butter." Lucy turned to old Pompey and asked him to bring butter, but Elsie stopped him and then informed her friend, "I'm just fine, Lucy. And Papa doesn't allow me to eat hot breads or butter."

At this, Lucy's eyes opened wide, and she drew in her breath sharply. "I'm glad my Papa doesn't try that on me," she said. "Why, I'd make such a fuss he'd have to let me eat what I want."

"Elsie knows better than that," said Horace, who had been listening to the girls' conversation. "She would be sent from the table and punished for her naughtiness."

"I wouldn't do it anyway," Elsie said.

In an unusually kind voice, Horace replied, "No, Daughter, I don't believe you would."

The days of the Carringtons' visit passed very pleasantly. Lucy attended classes with Elsie in the mornings, though Herbert stayed with his mother. But in the afternoons, they all went out together, walking or riding. And if the weather was too warm, they played together on the veranda and then took their ride after sundown.

One afternoon, all the children were taking a walk — Arthur and Walter running far ahead because they would not accommodate Herbert's slow pace — when Herbert asked to stop and rest for awhile. "I want to try out my new bow, and you girls can pick up my arrows."

"Thank you, sir," Lucy laughed. "Elsie can chase your arrows if she likes, but I plan to take a nap. This soft grass will make an elegant couch." And she dropped onto the ground and was soon slumbering soundly, or pretending to be. Herbert shot his arrows here and there, and Elsie ran to retrieve them until she was hot and breathless.

"I have to rest," she said, sitting down beside Herbert. "What if I tell you a story?"

Elsie's Endless Wait

"Please do," said Herbert, laying down his bow. "You know how much I like your stories."

When she had finished her tale, Herbert took his bow again and sent an arrow sailing into the meadow.

"See how far it went!" he shouted happily. "Will you get it for me, Elsie?"

"This is this last time," she said, getting up reluctantly. Then she ran to where the arrow lay in the meadow, forgetting entirely her father's prohibition. She didn't remember until she had given the arrow to Herbert, and then in agitation, she exclaimed, "Oh, Herbert, I have to go home as fast as I can! I've forgotten! How could I forget? Oh, what will Papa say?"

"What on earth's the matter?" Herbert demanded anxiously, for Elsie's obvious distress alarmed him.

"Never mind," Elsie said, although she was crying now. "Look, the boys are coming back. They'll take care of you, and I must go."

She ran as fast as she could back to the house, sobbing all the way, and when she saw one of the servants, she asked where her father could be found.

"He's in the house," the servant answered, "but I don't know exactly where."

Before another word could be said, Elsie rushed inside and hurried from room to room. But Horace was not in the drawing room or the library. He wasn't in his own rooms. Elsie was just asking Fanny, the chambermaid, for help when her father's voice came from the veranda. "I'm here, Elsie," he called. "What do you want?"

Running outside, Elsie stopped when she saw her father, then approached him timidly. "I have to tell you something," she said, unable to control the quiver in her voice.

Horace could see that her face was flushed and tear-streaked. He took her hand and asked again, "What is it, Elsie? Are you sick? Have you hurt yourself?"

"No, sir, but — oh, Papa! I've been very naughty. I disobeyed you and went into the meadow!" With that, she burst into tears.

"How is that possible? Would you dare do what I positively forbade the other day?" Horace asked in his most severe voice.

"I didn't mean to disobey, Papa. I forgot you had forbidden me to go into the meadow."

"That is no excuse, no excuse at all. If your memory is so poor, I must find a way to strengthen it," he said.

He paused for a moment, looking at his sobbing, trembling child, then slightly softening his tone, he asked for an explanation.

"Tell me the whole story," he said, "so I may understand how to punish you."

Elsie gave him all the details of what had happened, and when he perceived that she really had forgotten and that her confession had been entirely voluntary, he relented. "Well, Daughter, I won't be very hard on you this time," he said calmly. "You seem very penitent, and you've made a full confession. But you must obey me, or next time you won't escape so easily. I do not take forgetfulness as an excuse. Now, go to Aunt Chloe and tell her to put you to bed immediately."

"But it's only the middle of the afternoon," she said.

"And that is your punishment. You are to stay in bed till tomorrow morning."

"But what will Lucy and Herbert think when they return and I'm not here?"

"You should have thought of that before you disobeyed," he said, a bit of gravity coming back into his voice. "Tell Chloe that you may have bread or crackers for dinner, but nothing more."

Elsie looked into his face. She seemed to want to speak but was afraid.

"Do you have something else to say?" he asked encouragingly.

"Yes, Papa. I'm so sorry for what I did. Will you forgive me, Papa? I won't be able to sleep if you're still angry with me."

Her sadness touched him more than he expected, and Horace said gently, "I do forgive you, Elsie. I am not at all angry with you now, so you can sleep in peace. Now good night, my child." And he kissed her lightly on her brow.

"Good night, Papa," she said with a little smile, "and I hope I'll never be so naughty again."

With his forgiveness, she went to her punishment. But once again, she found comfort in the pages of her worn Bible. She searched for some time before finding the verse she wanted in the twelfth chapter of Hebrews: "No discipline seems pleasant at the time, but painful. Later on, however, it produces a harvest of righteousness and peace for those who have been trained by it." Elsie recited the verse over and over to herself until she felt her hope renewed.

She rose early the next day and had learned all her lessons before breakfast. When she came down the stairs, she could see through the open front door that her father and several of the field hands were standing outside, gathered around some object on the ground.

"Come here, Elsie," her father said when she walked out onto the portico steps. He held out his hand, and she ran to him. He led her a few steps forward and pointed down. A large rattlesnake lay almost at their feet. The snake didn't seem to move, but it was ferocious looking nonetheless.

Elsie immediately jumped back and screamed, "Oh, Papa!"

"It's dead," he said, "and can't hurt you now. The men killed it in the meadow. Do you understand now why I forbade you to go there?"

Squeezing his hand tightly as she realized the danger, Elsie almost whispered, "I do, Papa. I might have lost my life by disobeying. Oh, how good God was to protect me."

Gently, her father said, "After this, I hope you always know that I have good reasons for my commands, even though I may not explain them to you."

"Yes, sir, I think I will," she said, still staring at the dead snake and imagining the possible consequences of her misbehavior.

At breakfast, Lucy finally got her chance to whisper to Elsie, "Where were you last night? I couldn't find you, and your Papa wouldn't tell me where you were, though I'm sure he knew."

Elsie blushed deeply. "I'll tell you later," she said quickly.

When the meal was ended, Lucy grabbed Elsie's waist, pulled her toward the veranda, and then said impatiently, "Now, tell me what happened. You promised."

Elsie's blush returned, climbing to the roots of her hair. "I was in bed," she said meekly.

"Before five o'clock!" Lucy exclaimed. "Whatever for?"

"Papa sent me," Elsie said with an effort, "because I was naughty and disobeyed him."

Lucy, who was always more full of curiosity than sentiment, demanded brightly, "Tell me what you did."

Shamed to recall her behavior, Elsie slowly explained, "Papa had forbidden me to go into the meadow, and I forgot all about it. I ran there to get Herbert's arrow."

"That's all?" Lucy declared in astonishment. "My Papa wouldn't punish me for something like that. He might scold me if I did it on purpose, but if I told him I'd forgotten, he'd just look at me a little sternly and say, 'You must remember better next time, my girl.'"

"My Papa says that forgetting is no excuse. He says that I must remember his commands, and if I forget, he has to punish me so I will remember better," Elsie said.

"He must be very strict, and I'm glad he's not my father," Lucy replied in a voice full of self-satisfaction.

But before Elsie could respond, Adelaide came to the door and called, "Hurry, girls. We are starting out in half an hour."

The whole family and their guests were going up the river for a picnic. They had been planning this excursion for several days, and the children were all looking forward to it a great deal.

"Did Papa say I can go?" Elsie asked, for she was not sure her punishment was ended.

"I presume you can, Elsie," her aunt said good-naturedly. "He never said you couldn't. But you girls must hurry now and dress, or you'll be late."

Just then, the library door opened, and Horace came out.

New Rules

"Horace," his sister inquired, "Elsie is to go on the picnic, of course?"

"I don't see why you assume so, Adelaide," he replied dryly. "No, Elsie is to stay at home and attend to her lessons as usual."

Elsie's disappointment was sharp and showed in her face, but she didn't say a word and turned to go upstairs. Lucy, throwing a look of angry indignation at Horace, ran after her friend, and once they were in Elsie's room, Lucy declared, "It's not fair, and if I were you, I'd go on the picnic just to spite him!"

"I wouldn't do that," Elsie protested. "I must obey my father. God says so. And I couldn't go even if I tried, for Papa would know it and he'd stop me."

"Then you have to coax him," Lucy went on. "I'll come with you, and we'll talk to him together."

Elsie shook her head. "My father never breaks his word. Nothing would convince him after he has said I can't go." She was trying hard not to cry, but the tears came to her eyes as she told Lucy, "You have to go dress now, or you'll be too late."

Turning, but hesitant to leave her friend, Lucy said, "Alright, I'll go, but I won't enjoy myself without you."

Downstairs, Adelaide was just as indignant as little Lucy. "Why can't the child go with us?" she demanded of her brother. "I can't conceive of a reason you might have for keeping her here, and she is terribly disappointed. Indeed, Horace, I sometimes think you take pleasure in thwarting that child."

"So you think I'm a tyrant," he said sharply. "But I beg you to let me manage my child in my own way. And I have no obligation to explain my reasons to you or anyone else."

But Adelaide could not let the matter rest. "Well, if you didn't intend to let her go, you should have said so and not let the child build up her hopes. It's cruel."

His face now red with anger, Horace said, "Until this morning, Adelaide, I did intend to let her go on the picnic, and I intended to go myself. But I've just learned that I must meet a gentleman on an important business matter. You know as well as I how often accidents occur during these pleasure parties, and I'm not willing to send Elsie unless I am there to watch over her. Believe it or not, it's concern for her safety, not cruelty, that leads me to keep her at home."

His explanation just made Adelaide more impatient. "Honestly, Horace, you have such strange notions about that child. The rest of us will take care of her."

"No," he said adamantly. "If there's an accident, you will have enough to do taking care of yourselves. I won't trust Elsie with the group since I can't be there myself."

Seeing that her brother was determined to have his way, Adelaide gave up her attempt to dissuade him and excused herself. Elsie's disappointment was, of course, enormous, and for a good while, rebellion boiled inside her. She tried to put the feeling away, but it was strong. She couldn't imagine why her father refused to let her go on the picnic, except for yesterday's disobedience. It was unjust, she thought, to punish her twice, especially as she had confessed freely to him. It was a pity she hadn't heard his explanation to her Aunt Adelaide, for then she could have been content. But Elsie, though she sincerely desired to do right, was not perfect, and she had already forgotten the lesson of the rattlesnake.

Sadly, she watched the picnickers depart, all in the highest spirits, but she was surprised to discover that her father wasn't going with them. In a way, this helped reconcile her to her own fate. She didn't expect to see him that day, but it comforted her to know that he wanted her at home because he was there himself. Perhaps it was a selfish love, but it was better than none. (These were not Elsie's exact thoughts, of course. She would never have thought of calling her father selfish. Her feelings were not so defined as she watched him help the ladies into their carriage and then return to the house. What she felt was a troubling mixture of anger, disappointment, and confusion about her father's actions.)

It was a terrible morning for Elsie. Miss Day was in a dreadful mood. The teacher was secretly mortified that she had not been invited on the picnic, and her private misery made her more difficult and unreasonable than ever. Her incessant fault-finding and scolding were almost more than Elsie could bear, but at last the lessons came to an end, and Elsie was excused from the schoolroom. At dinner, there were only Elsie, her father, and the gentleman who had come to do business. The guest was not the kind of man who cared to notice children, so he and Horace discussed politics and business and paid no attention to Elsie.

She was very glad when her father finally excused her, but as she was leaving the dining room, he called her back. He explained that he had planned to ride with her that afternoon but could not do so after all. Jim would accompany her instead. Her father spoke so kindly that Elsie regretted her rebellious feelings. If they had been alone, she would have asked his forgiveness.

When Chloe was dressing Elsie for her ride, the little girl suddenly asked, "Is Pompey going into the city today?"

"Yes, darling, he's leaving pretty soon now."

Elsie's Endless Wait

"Then please do a favor for me, Aunt Chloe. Take some money from my purse and ask him to buy me a pound of the nicest candy he can find. I haven't had any candy for a long time, and I saw what they had bought for the picnic, and it looked so good."

When the Dinsmores and the Carringtons returned from their outing just before supper time, Lucy rushed to Elsie's room to tell her all about their delightful day. She gave every detail of their sports and entertainments, interrupting herself now and then to lament Elsie's absence as the only dark cloud over her pleasure. She repeated her assertion that Elsie's father was very unkind, and as she chattered, Elsie felt her own resentments rising again. She said nothing but allowed her friend to accuse her father of cruelty and injustice without any protest.

Lucy continued her narrative during supper, in a slightly more subdued tone, and Elsie asked questions until her father turned to her and said in his stern way, "Be quiet, Elsie. You are talking entirely too much for a child your age. Don't let me hear another word from you until you've left the table."

Elsie flushed hotly under his rebuke, but she uttered not a sound.

When they were excused, Lucy grabbed her friend and said, "Let's go into the garden and finish our talk. Your father can't hear us there."

"Papa only stopped us because we were talking too much at the table," Elsie apologized. "I'm sure he doesn't mind your telling me about your day." Then she lowered her voice to almost a whisper, "But please, Lucy, don't say again that you think Papa was unkind. I'm sure he knows best, and I never should have listened to any unkind words about him."

New Rules

"Never mind then," Lucy said with good humor, and they skipped together down the path. "I won't say another word. But I do think he's cross, and I wish you were my sister and had my kind, good Papa for your own."

Elsie sighed. "I'd like to be your sister, but I wouldn't like to give up my Papa, for I love him so much."

"That's funny, when he's so cross to you!" Lucy exclaimed.

Elsie put her hand over Lucy's mouth, and Lucy pushed it away. "Excuse me. I forgot. I won't say it again," she laughed.

While the girls were in the garden, Fanny, the chambermaid, came onto the veranda where Horace was sitting and smoking a cigar. The young woman, who carried a small bundle, inquired if he had seen Elsie.

"What do you want with her?" he asked.

"Only to give her this package that Pompey brought from the city."

"Well, you can leave it with me," Horace said.

Meanwhile Elsie and Lucy had returned to the house and finding Pompey in the hallway, Elsie asked if he had gotten the candy. He told her he had brought some very delicious treats and given them to Fanny to deliver. Fanny, who had just come their way, said that Elsie's father had the candy, and at this news, Elsie turned away in disappointment.

Lucy, who wanted to see her friend happy, as well as to enjoy a share of the sweets, said, "Go ask him for it, won't you?"

But Elsie just sighed, "I think I'd rather do without."

Lucy, however, was persistent, and she coaxed Elsie for some time. But when Elsie still refused to approach her father, Lucy volunteered to go herself.

Elsie's Endless Wait

Elsie agreed, and Lucy, trembling a little in spite of her boastful claim that she was not afraid, found Horace on the veranda. Putting on a great show of confidence, she said, "Mr. Dinsmore, sir, will you please give me Elsie's candy? She wants it."

"Did Elsie send you?" he asked coldly.

Somewhat frightened by his manner, Lucy said yes.

"Then, Miss Lucy, please tell Elsie to come directly to me."

Elsie received this message with fearful uncertainty. But as she had no other choice, she went immediately to her father.

"Did you want me, Papa?"

"Yes, Elsie. I wish to know why you sent another person for what you want instead of coming to me yourself. It displeases me very much, and you will never get anything you ask for in this way."

Elsie hung her head and said nothing.

"Are you going to answer me?" he demanded. "Why did you send Lucy instead of coming yourself?"

"I was afraid," she said in the softest whisper.

"Afraid? Afraid of what?" he asked, and she could hear the displeasure growing in his voice.

"Afraid of you, Papa," she replied in a voice so low he could barely understand the words.

His anger rose, and he exclaimed, "If I were a drunken brute, if I were in the habit of beating you, there might be some reason for your fear. But as it is, I can see no excuse for it at all, and I am hurt and disappointed."

"I'm sorry, Papa," she said. "I won't do it again."

Then after a moment's pause, she said in a hesitating way, "Papa, may I have my candy, if you please?"

"You may not. And understand that I forbid you to buy or eat anything of the kind again without my express permission."

Elsie's eyes filled, and she choked down a sob as she slowly returned to Lucy. The two little girls sat close together on the steps of the portico.

"Have you got the candy?" Lucy asked eagerly.

Elsie shook her head.

Indignantly, Lucy raved, "It's a shame. He is just as cross as he can be! Why, he's a tyrant! That's what he is, a hateful, old tyrant! And I wouldn't care a cent for him, if I were you! I'm glad he's not my father!"

Elsie merely sighed and said, "I'm afraid he doesn't love me much. He hardly ever lets me have anything or go anywhere I want."

"Well, never you mind," Lucy said. "I'll send to the city tomorrow for *two* pounds of candy, and then we'll have a real feast!"

Sadder still, Elsie said, "Thank you, Lucy, but Papa has forbidden me to eat anything of the sort without his permission."

"He doesn't have to know about it," Lucy encouraged.

But Elsie shook her head again. "You're kind, but I can't disobey Papa, even if he never knows, because that would be disobeying God, and He would know."

Frustrated, Lucy could only lament, "You are very strange, Elsie."

To make matters worse, Horace approached the girls at that moment. From the doorway, he called, "Elsie, what are you doing out there? Haven't I told you not to go out in the night air?"

"I didn't know you meant the doorstep, Papa. I thought you meant the garden," she replied as she rose to go inside.

But Horace would not let her pass. "I see you intend to travel at the very edge of disobedience," he said harshly.

"Go straight to your room and have Chloe put you to bed."

Elsie silently obeyed, and Lucy started to follow, but Horace stopped her. "She is to go alone, if you please, Lucy," he said. And so the little girl, with a frown and a pout, turned on her heel and went to her mother in the drawing room.

Horace walked out onto the steps of the portico where he could watch the moon that was just rising above the tree-tops. But he was not to have this moment alone. From the shadow of a tree near the steps, Arthur sauntered forward and came to Horace's side.

"Elsie thinks you're a tyrant," Arthur began in a voice thick with snide conceit. "She says you never let her have anything or go anywhere and that you're always punishing her. She and Lucy had a fine time out here, talking about how badly you treat her and making plans to have candy behind your back."

"Arthur, I don't believe Elsie would deliberately plot to disobey me. And whatever faults she may have, I know she is above the meanness of telling tales," Horace replied. Then without a look at his younger brother, Horace turned and went into the house, leaving the crestfallen Arthur to creep away.

Chloe was not in the bedroom, for she hadn't expected to be needed so early and was down in the kitchen enjoying a chat. Elsie had to ring for her, and while the child waited, she reviewed in her mind the happenings of the day. She always did this before bed, but rarely was her retrospect so painful. Her tender conscience told her that she had more than once indulged in wrongful feelings toward her father. She had allowed Lucy to speak disrespectfully of him, and by her silence, she'd given the remarks her own tacit approval. Worse, she had complained about him herself.

Tearfully, she murmured to herself, "How soon I forgot the lesson Papa taught me this morning and my promise to trust him without knowing his reasons. How can he love me when I'm so rebellious?"

"What's the trouble, darling?" Chloe asked as she came in. She took Elsie on her lap, cradling the child's head as she said, "I can't bear seeing you so upset."

"I've been so bad today, Aunt Chloe. I'm afraid I'll never be as good as Papa wants me to be. I know he's disappointed with me because I disobeyed him today," Elsie said, as her tears rolled down her cheeks.

"Then you must go to the throne of grace and tell the Lord Jesus about your troubles," Chloe said. "Remember what the Bible tells us: 'If anybody does sin, we have one who speaks to the Father in our defense — Jesus Christ the Righteous One.' Speak to Jesus, darling, and ask Him to help you trust your Papa and obey him even when you don't understand his reasons."

"You're right, Aunt Chloe. Jesus will forgive me and give me right thoughts and feelings," Elsie proclaimed. Then she wrapped her arms around her nursemaid's neck for a loving embrace.

She told Chloe of her father's directions and began to prepare for bed. She had stopped crying, but her face was still sad and troubled. When she was in her nightdress, with her hair brushed and tucked in her nightcap, Elsie took her little Bible and in a trembling voice, read from the twelfth chapter of Proverbs: "Whoever loves discipline loves knowledge, but he who hates correction is stupid."

"I must learn to be grateful for Papa's correction," she told herself, "but Jesus will have to help me." Sighing, she knelt by her bed and prayed. Chloe, watching her little girl, was filled with compassion, and she gave the child every assurance of her own love before tucking her into bed.

But for the next half hour, Elsie shifted and tossed.

"What makes you so restless tonight?" Chloe finally inquired.

"Oh, Aunt Chloe, do you think Papa might come and see me? There's something I must tell him. Would you go and see if he is busy? Don't disturb him if he is, but if not, will you ask him to come see me for just one minute?"

Chloe was not gone long, and she returned with the news that Horace was indeed busy with the guests. "You just go on to sleep, darling," the nurse soothed, "and you can tell your father all about it in the morning."

There was nothing left to try, and Elsie finally cried herself to sleep.

The next morning Lucy was at Elsie's door bright and early. "I was in a hurry to see you, Elsie," she explained. "This is our final day here, you know. Wasn't it too bad your father sent you to bed so early last night?"

"Papa has a right to send me to bed whenever he pleases. I was naughty and deserved to be punished, and besides, it wasn't much earlier than my usual bedtime."

"You, naughty?" Lucy exclaimed. "Mamma often says she wishes I were half as good as you."

Elsie said nothing, for her thoughts were far away. She was thinking of what she had wanted to tell her father and gathering the courage to approach him this morning. "If I can get close to him when no one is near, and if he speaks kindly to me, then I can do it," she mumbled to herself.

"Can't you hurry, Aunt Chloe?" Lucy asked impatiently. "I want to run in the garden before breakfast."

Chloe, who had just re-tied Elsie's sash for the third time and smoothed the child's curls, laughed and said, "We're done now, but Elsie's Papa is very particular."

"He always wants me to look very nice and neat," Elsie explained. "When I go downstairs in the morning, he looks me over from head to toe. If anything is wrong, he's sure to notice and send me back to have it put right."

"You girls run along now and have a pleasant time before the bell rings," Chloe said as she tied the ribbon of Elsie's hat. "There, you look as sweet and fresh as a moss rosebud."

The girls skipped hand-in-hand out of the house and played in the garden until it was almost time for breakfast. Then Elsie went back to her room so Chloe could brush her hair smooth again. She had just rejoined Lucy in the front hall when they saw a carriage driving up to the front door.

"That's my Papa!" Lucy cried joyfully, and she ran straight to the arms of the gentleman who alighted from the carriage, receiving such hugs and kisses as Elsie had always longed for. Lucy was the Carringtons' only daughter and the apple of her father's eye, and Elsie watched this reunion with a strange ache in her heart.

But Mr. Carrington soon set Lucy down and turned to Elsie, taking her hand and giving her a warm kiss. "How are you this morning?" he asked her. "I'm afraid you can hardly welcome me, as I will be taking Lucy home. Have you two had a good time together?"

"Yes, sir, we have, and I hope you'll let Lucy come again soon."

"I certainly shall, but the visits mustn't be all on one side. I'll talk to your father and perhaps persuade him to let you return with us to Ashlands today."

"How wonderful!" Lucy said, clapping her hands. "Do you think he will let you, Elsie?"

"I don't know," Elsie said doubtfully. "I'm afraid not."

"Then you should coax him, as I coax my Papa."

Elsie simply shook her head, and they went to the breakfast room. Her father was there, but when she spoke to him, his reply was so cold and distant that she dared not say anything else. Horace hadn't intended to be influenced by Arthur's malicious tales, but unconsciously, he was. His attitude to his daughter this morning was colder than it had been in a long time.

~~~

After breakfast, Lucy reminded Elsie of her promise to show some beautiful shells her father had collected during his travels. The shells were kept in a curio cabinet in a small room off the library. Elsie knew that the items in this room, most of them belonging to her father, were rare and costly, and she was very careful of them.

But the girls were followed into the little room by Arthur, Walter, and Enna. Elsie, terrified of an accident, begged them to leave, but Arthur, declaring that he had as much right to be there as she, refused to budge. Instead, he gave Elsie a hard shove. Clutching at a small table to keep herself from falling, she dislodged a fine, old china vase that Horace prized dearly. It fell with a loud crash and shattered around their feet.

"Look what you've done!" Arthur shouted, and Horace, hearing the noise and the children's agitated voices, was soon on the scene.

"Who did this?" he demanded, looking from one child to the next.

"It was Elsie," Arthur said. "She threw it down and broke it."

Horace was angrier than Elsie had ever seen him. "You troublesome, careless child!" he yelled. "Go to your room immediately, and stay there till I send for you. And remember, if you ever come in here again without my permission, I promise you will regret it."

Elsie fairly flew from the room and up the stairs, and Horace rushed the other children out, slamming the door behind them.

In the hallway, Lucy turned angrily on Arthur. "How dare you blame it on Elsie? It was all your fault, and you know it, Arthur Dinsmore!"

"I didn't touch that old vase, and I'm not taking the blame, little miss," Arthur said threateningly. But coward that he was, he was all the while backing away from Lucy, with Walter and Enna close at his side.

For some time, Lucy was left to debate with herself: Did she have the courage to face Elsie's father and tell him what had really happened? At length, she resolved her dilemma in favor of her friend. Squaring her shoulders and holding her head high, she went back down the passage to the library. Horace was writing when she entered, and he looked up with an expression of surprise and not a little impatience.

"What do you want, Lucy?" he asked. "Speak up, for I am very busy."

Elsie's Endless Wait

"I just wanted to tell you," Lucy said boldly, "what really happened to the vase. Elsie was not at all to blame. It was Arthur. He pushed her hard and made her fall against the table, and that's how the vase fell."

"And why did he push her?"

"Because Elsie had asked him and Walter and Enna to leave. She was afraid they might do some mischief, and she was right."

Horace sat still for a moment, his pen suspended above his paper and his face clouded. But soon he turned to Lucy and said quite pleasantly, "Thank you very much, Miss Lucy, for your information. I would be very sorry to have punished Elsie unjustly. Will you do me the favor of telling her that her Papa says she need not stay in her room any longer?"

Lucy beamed with joy and relief, and she rushed away to her friend's room. Elsie was sobbing miserably when Lucy entered and delivered the good news. "So you don't have to cry or feel sorry for yourself now," Lucy concluded. "Dry your eyes, and we'll go down to the garden and enjoy ourselves."

Elsie was very grateful to Lucy and glad her father knew now that she wasn't to blame for breaking the vase. But his angry words had hurt her deeply, and though she tried to forget the incident and enter happily into Lucy's games, it would be a long time before the hurt was healed.

The girls played for much of the morning, then joined Mrs. Carrington in the drawing room. Herbert, who had not felt well enough to go outside, lay on the sofa with his head in his mother's lap. Horace and Mr. Carrington sat not far away, talking.

Lucy ran to her father and sat on his knee. Elsie, stopping first to say something to Herbert, nervously approached her own Papa and, with her eyes down, said softly, "I'm sorry about the vase, Papa."

Taking her hand, he drew her close and leaned forward to whisper in her ear, "Never mind that, Daughter. We'll forget about the vase. And I am very sorry that I spoke to you so harshly, since Lucy tells me you were not at fault."

His words brought great relief, but before Elsie could respond, Mrs. Carrington called out, "Elsie, we want to take you home with us to spend a week. Will you go?"

"I'd like to very much, ma'am, if Papa agrees," said Elsie, and she looked a little wistfully at her father.

"What do you say, Mr. Dinsmore?" Mrs. Carrington inquired. "I hope you have no objection." Then Mr. Carrington added, "By all means, you must let her come, Dinsmore. You can surely spare her for a week, and with Lucy's governess — a superior teacher, by the way — she can keep up with her lessons."

Horace looked grave, and before he said anything, Elsie guessed from his expression what his answer would be. Horace had several times noticed Lucy's disrespectful looks at him, and remembering the conversation reported by Arthur, he had decided that the less Elsie saw of Lucy, the better.

"Thank you both for your kind courtesy to my daughter," he said politely, "but while I appreciate your invitation, I must beg to decline. Home, I think, is the best place for Elsie at present."

With good humor, Mrs. Carrington said, "I suppose we should hardly expect you to spare her so soon after your return, but I am sorry. Elsie is such a good child, and I am always glad to have Lucy and Herbert with her."

"Perhaps you think better of her than she deserves," Horace said. "I find that Elsie is sometimes naughty and needs correction, just as other children. I think it best to keep her under my eye," he concluded, casting a serious look at his daughter.

Elsie flushed hotly and struggled not to cry. Fortunately the dinner ball rang, and Horace led her to the table. But she couldn't help thinking to herself how naughty her father would judge her if he knew about her thoughts and feelings of the day before.

As the Carringtons prepared to depart, Lucy retired upstairs to put on her bonnet. Elsie was ready to follow, but Horace took her hand and held her back. "Lucy will be down in a minute," he said. He did not let go of her hand, even when Lucy came back, and he didn't leave her side as the girls said their good-byes.

But as Horace was talking to Mr. Carrington, Lucy ventured to say under her breath, "I think he's mean not to let you visit."

In equally low tones, Elsie protested, "I'm sure Papa knows best, and I have been naughty. But I'd dearly love to go with you."

Horace didn't loosen his hold on Elsie's hand until the Carringtons' carriage had disappeared down the drive. Then he told her to come to him in the library in a half-hour's time. Seeing that he had frightened her, he added, "Don't be afraid. I'm not going to hurt you."

Elsie tried not to be afraid, but she had to wonder what he wanted, and despite her best efforts, she trembled a bit when she approached the library. He was alone there, sitting at a table covered with papers and writing material. Elsie saw his account book, and beside it a pile of bank notes and gold and silver coins.

"Come here, Elsie," he said, motioning her to the table. "I have your month's allowance. Your grandfather paid it to you in the past, but of course, it is my responsibility now. You have been receiving eight dollars, but now it will be ten."

He counted the money carefully and laid it before her. "From now on, I will require a strict accounting of everything you spend," he continued. "I want you to learn to keep accounts, for someday you will have a great deal of money to take care of. I've prepared an account book for you, so you can do it easily. Every time you spend or give away money, write it here as soon as you can. Be particular about doing it, so you don't forget anything. At the end of each month, you must bring your account book to me and let me see how much you have spent and what your remaining balance is. If you can't make it square, then you will lose part or all of your next month's allowance, according to the delinquent amount. Do you understand?"

"Yes, sir."

"Very good. Now, let's see how much you can remember of your last month's expenditures. Take your book and write down everything you remember spending."

Elsie had a good memory, and she was able to recall almost every penny. She wrote each number down, then added all the numbers in the column correctly.

"That was very well done," her father said with approval as he looked over the figures. "Let's see. A half a dollar for candy. Remember that you are not to buy candy anymore, not as a matter of economy, but because I think it injurious. I want you to grow up strong and healthy."

Suddenly, he closed the account book and asked her, "Were you very anxious to go to Ashlands?"

"I would have liked to go, Papa, if you'd been willing," she said meekly.

"I'm afraid Lucy isn't a good companion for you. I think she puts bad notions in your head," he said seriously.

Elsie flushed, and she was about to make her confession when the door opened and her grandfather entered. She kept silent.

"Doesn't Lucy sometimes say naughty things to you?" Horace asked in a low voice, so his father would not overhear.

"Yes, sir," Elsie replied.

"I thought as much. I shall keep you two apart as often as possible, and I hope there will be no grumbling from you."

"No, sir."

Then he put the allowance money in her hand and dismissed her. After she left, he sat and quietly contemplated. The list of Elsie's expenditures had consisted almost entirely of gifts for others, especially the servants. There were some beads and sewing silks for making a purse and a few drawing things, but with the exception of the candy, she had bought nothing else for herself.

"What a dear, unselfish, generous little thing," Horace thought. But he had not yet rid himself entirely of his old prejudices against his child. "I must not leap to conclusions," he told himself. "I can't judge from one month alone. She seems submissive, but perhaps that is for effect. I overheard her speaking to Lucy, but she may have suspected that I was listening. Perhaps she really does think I am a tyrant, and she obeys out of fear, not love."

This last thought — which, had he known, expressed his own fears more than his child's — came strongly and drove away the tenderness that had been warming his feeling.

New Rules

When he next met Elsie, his manner was as cold and withdrawn as ever, and Elsie could not bring herself to tell him what was in her heart.

CHAPTER

5

Gold Watch Mischief

"A wise man fears the Lord and shuns evil, but a fool is hotheaded and reckless."

PROVERBS 14:16

Gold Watch Mischief

One hot afternoon, in the week after the Carringtons' visit, Arthur, Elsie, Walter, and Enna had just set out for a walk when Elsie spotted an object that instantly sent a cold chill through her. Catching the light of the sun, the object glittered brilliantly — a gold chain dangling from the pocket of Arthur's jacket.

Elsie immediately recognized it, for there was only one such heavy gold chain within Roselands. Taking her young uncle by the elbow, she whispered urgently, "Arthur! How could you take Grandpa's gold pocket watch? Please, put it back now. You're sure to break it otherwise."

Arthur jerked his arm from her grasp. "Hold your tongue, Elsie," he hissed at her. "I can do exactly as I want."

"But Arthur, you know that Grandpa would never let you take his watch. He's told us all how very valuable it is. He paid a lot of money for it, and he says it's worth even more than he paid."

Arthur turned on her. "If this watch is such a prize, then Papa shouldn't leave it lying around on his table." The boy leered hatefully into her worried face. "I'll just teach the old man a lesson, I will. It's about time he learned to be more careful with his things."

Elsie pleaded once more, "Please, take it back now, Arthur. If anything happens to that watch. . . . You know how angry Grandpa will be. Then he'll ask us all what happened, and you know I can't lie to him. He'll ask me if you took the watch, and I can't say no."

"Oh, you're a great little tattletale, Elsie Dinsmore," Arthur snarled. "But if you ever tell on me, I'll make you pay. Believe me, Elsie. You *will* be sorry."

His threat issued, Arthur ran ahead, down the dusty drive, with Walter and Enna trying to keep pace. But Elsie lingered behind them. She walked slowly, but her mind was in a whirl. What should she do? Arthur would pay no attention to her, and all the adults in the household were away, so there was no authority to whom she could appeal for help. Perhaps she should just turn around and go back to the house then and there. If she were not present when the inevitable disaster happened, then she could not be a witness to it. But her father had firmly told her to stay with the other children that afternoon. Besides, she had already seen Grandpa's watch in Arthur's jacket. Even if nothing too terrible happened to the watch, she still knew that Arthur had taken it.

Unhappily she quickened her steps to catch up with the other children. Then another idea struck her. There was a faint hope that she could convince Arthur not to do anything that would endanger the watch. He might even let her take charge of it while he played. Ordinarily, Elsie would have been too afraid even to touch her grandfather's valuable possession, but if she could protect it from Arthur, then she would gladly be responsible.

Their play that afternoon was far from pleasant for Elsie. When the boys weren't running her breathless, then Arthur was up to some antic that made her tremble for the safety of the watch. Though she asked him to let her guard it while he romped and tumbled, Arthur merely answered back with jeers and taunts.

"I'll do just as I please," he laughed at her. "I will not be ruled by *you*, Elsie."

Then it happened. Arthur was scrambling up a tree when his jacket snagged on a limb. As Arthur tugged to release the cloth, his pocket was up-ended, and the precious watch fell, like a golden spark, to the hard ground. It hit with a thud and a sharp crack.

Elsie screamed, and Arthur, now pale with fear, clattered down from the tree and stumbled to where the watch lay.

Its crystal was shattered, and each broken bit of glass flashed at them in the sunlight. Gingerly, Arthur picked up the watch, and they all saw that its case was badly dented. They knew that it was damaged inside, too, for the delicate, little hands no longer moved.

Walter shouted at his brother, "Now see what you've done, Arthur!"

Enna whined, "What will Papa do?"

Elsie could only stare at the terrible mess that Arthur held in his shaking hand.

"All of you, hush!" the boy finally exclaimed. His voice quivered, but whether from fright or rage, it was impossible to say.

He glared at each of them in turn. "If any of you dares to tell about this," he said with defiance, "I'll make you sorry to the last day of your life. I promise I will. Do you understand?"

The smaller children cowered in silence, but Elsie spoke up. "Grandpa will know that *somebody* did it," she said. "He will blame somebody, and Arthur, you can't let an innocent person be punished for what you did."

"I don't care who gets punished!" Arthur exploded. "Just so Papa doesn't find out that I did it."

He turned on Elsie, narrowing his eyes to thin, dark slits. "Remember this," he said in a low and nasty voice. "If you dare to tell on me, little Elsie, I *will* make you pay."

Elsie stood firm. "I won't say anything, Arthur, unless an innocent person is blamed or I'm made to speak. But I won't lie for you then. I'll tell the truth."

Suddenly, Arthur put up his tight fists and lunged at the girl, but Elsie was too quick for him. She darted behind the tree, and before Arthur could grab for her again, she fled, running as fast as she could up the long, dusty driveway. The angry boy pursued, but before catching up to her, he apparently thought better of creating more trouble for himself. He quit the chase, and Elsie escaped into the safe haven of the house.

Careful not to be observed by any of the servants, Arthur managed to restore the pitifully damaged watch to its place on his father's table. Then he, Walter, and Enna gathered what courage they could to await their father's coming.

Arthur was not yet finished with his schemes. When he had calmed himself, he approached his little brother and took him aside. "I say, Wally," Arthur began in a voice as soft as butter. "You know my new riding whip?"

"Of course," said the smaller boy with interest.

"If I should give my new whip to you," Arthur asked, "what would you give to me in return?"

Walter's face lit up with his excitement. "Anything I've got," he almost shouted. Then his face fell. "You're just teasing me again. You'll never give me that whip."

"But I will give it to you," Arthur said agreeably, "if you'll be a good fellow and do what I tell you."

"What's that?"

"All you must do is to tell Papa that Jim broke the watch."

Astonished, Walter protested, "But Jim didn't do it! He wasn't even watching us. He was at the stables all afternoon."

"So what of it?" Arthur demanded with impatience. "Papa doesn't know where Jim was. He's just a slave anyhow. What do you care about him?"

"But I do care, and Jim will be punished," Walter said, "and I don't want to tell such a big lie."

"Then you won't get the whip. But if you don't do as I ask," Arthur went on, his voice becoming low and cold, "then I'm sure you will see a ghost one night very soon. There's one who comes to me sometimes, and I will send it to you."

The little boy cried out, "Oh, please don't do that, Arthur. I'm so afraid of ghosts." As he spoke, Walter looked nervously over his shoulder, half-expecting the dreaded haunt to appear at that very instant.

"If you don't do as I say, then I'll have the ghost come to your room tonight. Is that what you want me to do, Wally?" Arthur peered down at the terrified child, then he went on speaking even more softly, "You are a small boy yet, Wally. It would be easy for the ghost to carry you off. We'll probably never see you again."

Walter's eyes grew round, and his mouth fell open. Words tumbled out in a cascade of terror: "Don't, Arthur! Please don't send the ghost! I'll say anything you want me to say."

Arthur smiled. "That's a good boy, Wally. I knew I could trust you."

Arthur's terrible threat proved even more effective with little Enna, and she quickly promised to speak against Jim rather than face a ghostly visitor in the night.

Arthur could not try his tricks on Elsie. On returning to the house, she had gone directly to her room. For the remainder of the afternoon, she sat there in a state of terrible anticipation, waiting for the sound of footsteps that would signal a summons from her grandfather.

But the footsteps never came, and finally the dinner bell rang. When Elsie had nervously come downstairs and entered the dining room, she discovered, to her great relief, that her grandfather and Mrs. Dinsmore had still not arrived back at Roselands.

As Elsie slipped into the seat beside her father, Horace scrutinized his daughter's face. "You look pale," he said. "Are you well?"

"Yes, Papa, quite well."

Though Horace continued to study her with concern, he said no more, and when the evening meal was done, Elsie hurried back to her room.

It was not long before the elder Mr. Dinsmore and his wife returned. For once, they had brought no late-night visitors. They had not been in the house more than a few minutes when Mr. Dinsmore went to get his watch.

Grabbing up his shattered treasure, Mr. Dinsmore stormed into the drawing room. His suspicions had fallen immediately on Arthur, whose talent for mischief was well established at Roselands, and flushed with rage, the old man demanded, "Where is Arthur? Where is that young scoundrel?" Holding the battered watch out for all to see, he thundered, "This is some of *his* work, I've no doubt!"

In her smoothest tone, Mrs. Dinsmore said, "My dear, how can you say so? Do you have any proof? It's simply not fair to blame my poor boy for everything that goes wrong."

"He gets no more blame than he deserves," replied her furious husband. Bellowing, he called, "Arthur! Arthur, where are you?"

"He's in the garden, I think," said Horace. "I saw him walking there a few moments ago."

Mr. Dinsmore instantly sent one of the servants to bring Arthur inside. A second servant was dispatched to find the overseer of the plantation, and a third was ordered to assemble all the household and stables servants.

"I'll sift to the bottom of this," Mr. Dinsmore exclaimed, "and child or servant, the guilty person *will* suffer."

The old man was angrily walking the room when Arthur appeared. "How dare you meddle with my watch?" Mr. Dinsmore demanded of his son.

Arthur responded boldly. "I didn't, sir. I never touched it."

"There, my dear, I told you so," Mrs. Dinsmore declared in triumph.

"I don't believe him," said Mr. Dinsmore, then he turned his fiery eyes on his son. "Arthur, if you are guilty, as I strongly suspect, you had better confess at once, before I find the truth in some other way."

"I didn't do it, sir," Arthur lied. "It was Jim. Walter and Enna saw him, too. We all saw the watch fall from Jim's pocket when he was up a tree. He cried like anything when he found it broken, and said he didn't mean any harm. Jim said he only wanted to wear your watch for a little while and then put it back all safe. But now you'd find out and have him whipped."

"If what you say is true," the old man shouted, seeking out Jim's face among the servants gathered near the door, "I'll have him whipped and send him to work with the slaves in the fields. No such meddlers will stay in my house!"

Mr. Dinsmore looked at Enna. "What do you know about it?" he asked.

Glancing uneasily around the room, the little girl blushed and said, "It's true, Papa. I saw Jim do it."

"And you, Walter, did you see it, too?'

"Yes, Papa," the boy replied reluctantly. "But please don't punish Jim. I'm sure he didn't mean to break it."

"Hold your tongue!" the old man shouted with fury. "He *will* be punished!" Without asking any questions of Jim or hearing the young man's protests, Mr. Dinsmore pointed a shaking finger at the accused and ordered the overseer to "take him out now and give him a punishment that he will never forget!"

Alone in her bedroom, Elsie could hear nothing of the commotion below. She was trying to learn a lesson for the next day but found it very difficult to concentrate her thoughts. Suddenly, Aunt Chloe entered. She was clearly upset and held her apron to her weeping eyes.

"Oh, Aunt Chloe," Elsie said, "what's the matter?" In her alarm, Elsie dropped her book and ran to her nurse. "Has anything happened to you?"

"Not to me, little darling," Chloe sobbed. "It's Jim. He broke your Grandpa's gold watch, and now he's going to be whipped. Aunt Phoebe is crying fit to break her heart about her son, because —"

Elsie could hear no more. She ran into the hall, nearly colliding with her father. Bursting into tears, she exclaimed, "Papa! Oh, Papa! Don't let them whip poor Jim!"

"I cannot interfere," Horace said, trying to calm his distraught child. "Jim has done wrong and must be punished."

"But Jim didn't break the watch! I know he didn't because I saw it all!"

Much surprised, Horace asked, "Then who did break the watch, Elsie? It couldn't have been you, could it?"

"No, Papa! Not me. I never touched the watch. Please don't make me tell tales," she cried in great distress, "but it was not Jim! Please, Papa, stop them now, before he is whipped!"

Horace called out urgently to Aunt Chloe, "Go and tell my father to delay the punishment until I can speak to him. Tell him I will be down in a few minutes. Hurry!"

As the old nursemaid hastened down the stairs, Horace took Elsie's hand and led her back into her room. Drawing her to his side, he said, "If you want to save Jim, then Elsie, you must tell me all that you know."

The little girl pleaded again, "Don't make me tell tales, Papa. It's so mean. Isn't it enough for me to tell you that Jim didn't do it?"

"No, Elsie. It is necessary that you tell me all you know." He saw the tears flowing from her eyes, and he continued, speaking very kindly, "I would naturally be ashamed of you if, in ordinary circumstances, you were willing to tell tales on other people. But now it is the only way to save Jim. Unless you tell all you know, Jim will be severely punished and then sent away from this house. You understand how that will hurt his poor mother. Elsie, I think it would be wicked to let an innocent person suffer when you can prevent it. And as your father, I instruct you that you must obey me and tell the full truth now."

Elsie understood everything that her father was saying, and although reluctant, she did tell the whole story, her simple and straightforward words confirming her truthfulness for him.

The moment she finished, Horace took her hand and led her to the door. "You must repeat this story to your grandfather," he said.

Elsie pulled at his hand, wanting to retreat into her room. "Please, don't make me do it, Papa," she begged.

Sternly, Horace replied, "You must, my daughter," and he guided his child into the presence of her grandfather.

Except for Walter, the family were still gathered in the drawing room. Mr. Dinsmore, disturbed and angry, paced the room and cast occasional, mistrusting glances at Arthur. The boy, who had guessed the meaning of Aunt Chloe's message from Horace, was now the picture of guilt.

Walter had crept away from the scene. Crying over Jim's fate and his own lack of courage, the little boy told himself that he would make it up to Jim somehow — even if it cost a month's worth of allowance.

With Elsie's hand firmly in his own, Horace entered the drawing room and announced to his father, "I have another witness, sir. Elsie was there when your watch was broken."

"Then maybe I'll get the truth now," the old man exclaimed.

"It wasn't Jim, Grandpa. But please don't make me say who it was," Elsie cried.

Her father tightened his hold on her hand, and commanded, "Elsie! The whole truth now."

Elsie clung to his side and just caught a threatening look from Arthur. Horace, sensing her terror, also looked at Arthur and returned the boy's malicious gaze with his own hard stare.

Mr. Dinsmore addressed Elsie, "If you don't tell me what you know, child, then I can't let Jim off. Come now, Elsie. No one will hurt you for speaking the truth."

Sobbing, she blurted out, "I'll tell you, Grandpa, but please don't be angry with Arthur! Forgive him this time, and he won't meddle anymore. I'm sure he didn't mean to break your watch."

Mr. Dinsmore was at his younger son's side in an instant. He seized the boy by the shoulder and raged, "I knew it had to be you!" Holding Arthur securely, he turned back to Elsie. "Let's have the rest of the story, little girl," he demanded.

When she had finished, Arthur began to plead for his father's forgiveness.

"Forgive you?" the old man spluttered. "I'll forgive you — after you have had a good spanking and a week of solitary confinement with nothing but bread and water!"

He was about to drag Arthur from the room when Elsie rushed to his side. "Please, don't punish him, Grandpa! He won't do it again, will you Arthur? And let me pay for the watch. I *want* to pay for it."

"I don't care about the money," her grandfather replied, a hint of contempt in his voice. "And where would you get that kind of money?"

"But I'm rich, aren't I?" she said softly. "Didn't my mother leave me a great deal of money?"

Her father gently took her to his chair. He sat down and held her before him. "No, Elsie," he explained. "Until you come of age many years from now, you have only what I choose to give you."

"Then please, give me the money for the watch, Papa."

"I can't do that, Elsie. Arthur must take the penalty for his own wrongdoing," Horace said firmly. "That is what your grandfather cares about, not the money."

At this point, the elder Mr. Dinsmore harshly dragged Arthur from the room — but not before the boy had shot a burning look of hatred and defiance at Elsie. She felt his intensity so deeply that she could hardly stand. Her father, seeing the exchange that had just taken place, steadied her and said soothingly, "Don't be afraid, Daughter. I will protect you."

It seemed to Elsie that her father was, at long last, about to lift her onto his knee, as he so often did with Enna, and to hug her close to him. But at that moment, a servant entered to announce the arrival of visitors, and Elsie was dismissed to her room.

As Elsie reluctantly left her father to his guests, she saw Mrs. Dinsmore, who plowed down the hallway like a massive ship in a storm; her face was grim and full of fury. Wanting to avoid any meeting with the woman, Elsie ran up the stairs to find solitude in her own quiet bedroom. But the room wasn't empty. Chloe awaited her. Aunt Phoebe was there too, and the woman's fervent expressions of gratitude made Elsie forget for the time that she wouldn't see her father again that night.

There was a knock at the door, and Jim put his head in. Elsie invited him inside and received his grateful thanks as well. Jim explained that he had been so astounded by the unexpected charges against him that he'd been unable to speak up in his own defense. Besides, Mr. Dinsmore had refused to listen to his protests of innocence. If it hadn't been for Elsie, well, no one wanted to contemplate what might have happened.

When Jim and his mother had gone and Chloe had settled down to her knitting, Elsie at last had time to think again of all that had happened. She remembered the understanding and kindness of her father that night, his loving words, and his protection and care. Bedtime came, and although she retired at precisely the time her father dictated, Elsie lay awake for some time, imagining — as she had done so often before — a future in which her father would truly love her as much as she loved him.

At breakfast the next morning, she greeted Horace with an eager yet shy, "Good morning, Papa."

His response was both serious and absent-minded. Immediately beginning a business conversation with his father, Horace paid no further heed to his child, except to supervise the food that she was allowed to eat. When the meal was done, Elsie lingered at the table, hoping for her father's attention. But beyond a brief glance in her direction, there was none. Horace informed his father that he would be riding to Ion, to see Mr. Travilla, and probably would not return before night. Sadly disappointed, Elsie returned to her room to prepare for her morning lessons.

For awhile, Elsie enjoyed complete freedom from Arthur's torments. Even when his punishment was ended, Arthur was much too afraid of his brother Horace to openly bother Elsie in any way. In secret, however, he nursed his desire for revenge.

Aunt Adelaide was always kind; Lora still stood up for Elsie when she saw an injustice; and Elsie's grandfather was nice enough in his gruff fashion. But the rest of the family did little to make her feel comfortable. Mrs. Dinsmore remained extremely angry with her because of Arthur's disgrace, and when Horace was not around, the woman treated Elsie most unpleasantly. The younger children were unusually cold and distant. Even her father, though careful to see that all her wants were met, seldom seemed to take much notice of her, unless to chide her for some fault. Nothing she did was too trifling to escape his eye.

One day, when Horace had sent Elsie to her room for some small thing, Adelaide said to him, "You seem to expect that child to be a great deal more perfect than any grown person I know. She is not even nine years old, yet you want her to understand all the rules of etiquette."

"If you please," he responded haughtily, "I would like to manage my own child as I see proper, without any interference."

Adelaide answered him calmly. "I had no intention of interfering. But really, Horace, you have no idea how eagle-eyed you are for any fault in Elsie, nor any idea how stern your tone is when you correct her. Remember that you have not been a father to her for more than a few months, and until you came home, she had never had a real parent before. But I've known Elsie for more than four years now; I've seen how sensitive she is and also how much she wants to do right and to please you. I'm sure that a gentle reproof would be just as effective and not hurt her feelings so."

"Enough!" Horace exclaimed impatiently. "Perhaps if I were ten years younger than you, instead of the other way round, you might be right to advise and direct me. But as it is, I regard your words as simply impertinent." With that, he angrily left the room.

Adelaide watched him depart and thought to herself, "I am glad you have no authority over me, dear brother."

All that Adelaide said was true; still, Elsie never complained or blamed her father. Indeed, in her heart she blamed herself for his cool aloofness. His many reproofs only made her more timid and sensitive, and she tended increasingly to distance herself from him. She seldom ventured to speak or even move in his presence, and she was far too young to understand that her behavior flowed naturally from his. As for Horace, he could plainly see that Elsie feared him. But prideful as he was, he was unable to admit the wisdom of Adelaide's words, so he attributed his daughter's reticence solely to her lack of love for him. And in this way, both father and daughter continued to walk their separate paths.

CHAPTER

Bird on
the Wing

"Are not two sparrows sold for a penny?
Yet not one of them will fall to the ground
apart from the will of your Father.
And even the very hairs of your head
are all numbered.
So don't be afraid; you are worth
more than many sparrows."

MATTHEW 10:29 – 30

Bird on the Wing

It was the Sabbath morning, and Adelaide, Lora, and Enna were already in the carriage. Elsie stood on the portico steps, waiting for her father, and watched as the horses, two young steeds purchased by Horace only a few days before, stamped and tossed their heads.

As Horace came out, he remarked to Ajax, the coachman, "I didn't intend to harness that pair today. Where are the old bays?"

"Old Kate has a lame foot, sir, and your father said these youngsters have to be put to use sooner or later. I reckoned I might as well take them out today."

Horace, glancing first at the horses and then at Elsie, asked, "Are you sure you can hold them in?"

Smiling broadly with self-confidence, Ajax said, "I've driven these horses twice already, and they went splendidly. I reckon I can hold them in good as anything, sir."

Still uneasy, in spite of Ajax's assurance, Horace turned to his daughter. For a moment, he considered keeping her home from church that day, but he realized what disappointment this would cause her, so he lifted her into the carriage, and ordering Ajax to proceed with caution, Horace climbed in and sat beside his child.

"Change seats with me, Elsie," Enna said, sounding very much like her mother. "I want to sit next to my brother."

But Horace, putting his hand on Elsie's shoulder, said, "No, Enna. Elsie's place is beside me."

Enna started to pout. Horace, however, turned his attention to Adelaide who asked him a little anxiously, "Do you think there's any danger of the horses bolting?" She had seen Horace's concern, and she also realized that they were moving unusually fast.

"The horses are young, but Ajax is an excellent driver," Horace replied evasively. "Besides, I wouldn't have brought Elsie if I believed we were in any danger."

And in truth, their journey to church was uneventful. On the ride home, however, the horses took fright, and the carriage careered down a hillside at a frightful speed. Elsie thought they were going very fast, but she didn't suspect any danger until her father lifted her from her seat and placed her between his knees, holding her very tightly as if afraid that she might be snatched from his grasp. Elsie saw that his face was very pale and his eyes were fixed on her.

She whispered, "Don't worry, Papa. God will take care of us."

"I'd give all I'm worth to have you safe at home," he said hoarsely and held her even closer to him.

As their speed increased, the carriage bounced and shuddered and seemed ready to tip over at any second, an outcome they had little hope of surviving. Lora was leaning back in her seat, white with terror. Adelaide clutched Enna to her, and the little girl sobbed bitterly. But even in the face of death, Elsie remembered that they were in their Heavenly Father's hands. Her faith was strong, and she put her trust in Jesus.

As Ajax struggled to regain control over the charging horses, a large and powerful man, who happened to be walking down the road, heard a roaring, thudding sound behind him; he turned to see the galloping horses and imperiled carriage. Without a thought to his own danger, the man planted himself in the middle of the road, and as the horses neared, he reached out and grabbed their bridle — a sudden check that caused the horses to rear excitedly and then halt.

"Thank God, we're saved!" Horace exclaimed. He threw open the carriage door and leaped to the ground, lifting Elsie out first and then his sisters. They were near the entrance to Roselands, and they all preferred walking the rest of the way to returning to the carriage. As Adelaide led her sisters to the house, Horace, keeping Elsie at his side, remained some time, thanking and talking with the man who had, at the risk of his own life, saved theirs. Although Horace insisted the man accept a handsome reward, he knew it could never be enough for the courageous rescue.

Ajax guided the horses back to the stable as Horace and Elsie walked slowly up the drive. Neither spoke a word until they reached the house; then Horace bent and kissed his child and asked if she had recovered from her fright.

"Yes, Papa," she said softly. "I knew that God would take care of us."

"That He did," Horace replied, very seriously. "Now go upstairs and tell Chloe to get you ready for dinner."

Later that afternoon, Elsie was alone in her room when Lora surprised her by entering. It was seldom that the older girls chose to visit their young niece.

Lora still looked a little pale, and more thoughtful than Elsie could remember. Lora didn't say anything at first, then suddenly she burst out, "Oh, Elsie! I can't help thinking, what if we'd all been killed? Where would we all be now? Where would I be? I believe you would have gone straight to heaven, but I? I would be like the rich man the minister talked about this morning, lifting up my eyes in torment."

Lora covered her eyes and a shudder ran through her. Then she said, "We were all so afraid, but you, Elsie. What kept you from being afraid?"

"I was thinking of a Bible verse I know. 'Even though I walk through the valley of the shadow of death, I will fear no evil, for you are with me.' God said for us not to be afraid because He is with us. I knew that Jesus was there with me, and if I were killed, I'd wake up again in His arms. That's why I wasn't so afraid."

"I'd give anything to feel as you do," Lora sighed. "But didn't you feel afraid for the rest of us? I'm sure you must know that even though we go to church and study the Bible sometimes, we are not very good Christians and don't even pretend to be."

Elsie blushed and looked down. "It happened so quickly I only had time to think of Papa and myself. I've prayed so much for Papa, and I was sure God would spare him. It was selfish, I know, and I can't tell you how thankful I was that we were all spared."

"You did nothing wrong," Lora maintained. "And we haven't given you much reason to care what becomes of us. But Elsie, can you tell me how to be a true Christian? I want to try very hard and never rest until I am one."

Elsie was overjoyed, and she picked up her little Bible. "Let me show you Jesus' words," she said, finding the verse she wanted. "'For everyone who asks, receives; he who seeks, finds; and to him who knocks, the door will be opened.' That must encourage you.

"And see this verse: 'You will seek me and find me when you seek me with all your heart.' Oh, dear Lora, all you have to do is seek Him. The Bible promises that if you seek the Lord with all your heart, you will find Him."

"Yes," Lora said a little doubtfully, "but how do I seek Him, and what must I do to be saved?"

Elsie, who knew the Bible more thoroughly than most children her age, recalled the answer that Paul the Apostle gave to the jailer: "'Believe in the Lord Jesus Christ, and you will be saved.'" She turned to the tenth chapter of the book of Romans and read aloud: "'If you confess with your mouth, 'Jesus is Lord,' and believe in your heart that God raised Him from the dead, you will be saved.'

"You see, Lora," said Elsie, "you simply have to believe in Jesus. But you must believe with your heart — not just your mind."

"But how do I get rid of my sins? How do I make myself pleasing in the sight of God?" Lora asked eagerly.

Elsie turned to the book of First John. "See what it says here, Lora?" she asked. "'The blood of Jesus Christ, His Son, purifies us from all sin.' Jesus has already done all that is necessary. We have nothing to do but to believe in Him and accept His offer of forgiveness of sins and eternal life. Just accept them as free gifts, and then love and trust Him."

"But surely I must *do* something?" Lora asked.

Elsie thought carefully. "Well," she replied, "God says, 'Give me your heart.' You can do that. You can invite Him to come live in your heart. You can tell Him how much you need Him. And the Bible says, 'If we confess our sins, He is faithful and just and will forgive us our sins and purify us from all unrighteousness.' So you can tell Jesus your sins and ask Him to forgive them. You can ask Him to teach you to be sorry for your sins and give you a desire to be like Him — loving and kind and forgiving. Of course, we can't be like Him without the help of His Holy Spirit. But we can always get that help if we ask.

"Oh, Lora, don't be afraid to ask. Don't be afraid to come to Jesus. But you must come humbly, for the Bible says 'God opposes the proud, but gives grace to the humble.' He won't turn away anyone who comes to Him humbly, seeking to be saved."

For the rest of the afternoon, Lora stayed with Elsie, asking questions and reading from the Scriptures. Elsie explained that being a Christian meant having Jesus in your heart, not just attending church and reading the Bible. Then they sang a hymn together, and Elsie talked about her own peace and joy in believing in Jesus. "Oh, how good of God to make being saved so easy that anyone can do it — even children like us," she exclaimed.

When the supper bell rang, Elsie went to join the others with a new sense of happiness. Besides the joy of her conversation with Lora, she also remembered her father's deep concern for her during their perilous ride. "Surely he does love me," she murmured to herself.

When Horace met her at the table and asked with a smile, "How is my little daughter this evening?" her cheeks glowed, and she wanted to throw her arms around him and tell him how much she loved him. That was impossible for her, with all the family gathered around, so she simply returned his smile and said, "I'm very well, thank you, Papa."

But once again her joy was short-lived, and before the week was out, she was again in sad disgrace.

It was a bright afternoon several days later, and Elsie was walking alone in the garden when she heard a fluttering noise coming from a nearby arbor. Hurrying toward the source of the sound, she discovered an up-turned glass vase in which a beautiful hummingbird was imprisoned. Struggling to escape, the tiny bird fluttered and beat its fragile wings against the glass, causing the noise Elsie had heard.

Always tenderhearted, Elsie could never bare to see any living creature in distress. She knew that Arthur was often guilty of torturing insects and small birds — she'd several times endured his wrath to intervene on behalf of his small victims — so she instantly assumed that this was his handiwork. The desire to release the terrified bird overwhelmed her, and without a moment's hesitation or reflection, she lifted the glass, and the bird flew free.

Only then did she consider how angry Arthur would be, and the prospect caused a little shiver to pass through her. But it was too late now, and after all, she didn't really fear any consequences since she was sure her father would approve of her action. She'd often enough heard Horace reprove his brother for his cruel practices.

The day was very hot, and Elsie retreated to the veranda off the drawing room on the east side of the house, where a canopy of trees and vines provided cooling shade. Arthur, Walter, and Enna were just inside, enjoying a lively game of jacks, and Louise was stretched languidly on the couch, engrossed in her latest novel.

Elsie, taking up a book of her own, wondered why Arthur didn't go to check on his captive bird, but she soon forgot all about her uncle as she buried herself in the adventures of the Swiss Family Robinson.

The players were just finishing their jacks game when Horace suddenly burst into the room and demanded, in a voice full of rage, to know who had been in the garden and released the hummingbird he had taken such pains to capture. It was one of a rare species, he said, and an important addition to his collection.

Elsie was terribly frightened and would have been glad to sink through the floor at that moment. She dropped her book, and her face turned pale and flushed in turns as she struggled to choke out a confession, as her conscience told her she must.

Her father's attention was focused not on her, but on Arthur. "I presume it was you," Horace was saying angrily, "and if I'm right, you should prepare yourself for punishment as severe as your last."

"I didn't do any such thing," Arthur replied with fierce indignation.

"Of course, you'll deny it," Horace went on, "but we all know that your word is good for nothing."

At that moment, a small voice interrupted the brothers' angry exchange.

"Arthur didn't do it, Papa. It was I."

"You?" her father exclaimed, turning on her an expression that oddly mixed anger and astonishment. "You, Elsie? Can this be possible?"

Covering her face with her hands, Elsie burst into tears.

"Come here to me this instant," Horace commanded. He took a seat on the settee that Louise had abandoned. "Tell me what you mean by meddling in my affairs."

"Please, please, don't be so angry, Papa," she sobbed, moving to him. "I didn't know it was your bird. I didn't mean to be naughty."

"You never *mean* to be naughty," he said. "Your misbehavior always seems to be by accident. But I find you are a very troublesome and mischievous child. Remember the valuable vase you broke the other day, and now you've caused the loss of a rare specimen that I spent a great deal of time to procure. Really, Elsie, I'm tempted to administer a very strong punishment. Tell me why you did it. Was it pure love of mischief?"

"No, sir," Elsie said in a whisper. "I was sorry for the little bird. I thought Arthur put it there to torture it, so I let it go. I didn't mean to do wrong, Papa, really I didn't," she pleaded, her tears falling faster than ever.

"You had no business to meddle, no matter who put it there," he said. "Now, show me which hand did it."

Elsie held out her right hand, and Horace took it in his. He could feel her trembling, and when he looked into her face, he saw her fear and pain. The evidence of her sorrow relaxed his anger, and the stern expression faded from his face. He was tempted at that instant to forgive her entirely. But the loss of the rare bird was extremely upsetting, and his anger flared again. She must be punished, he decided, but not with physical pain. He freed his hand from hers and began to reach into his pocket.

"Watch out, Elsie," Louise laughed maliciously. "He's reaching for his knife. I expect he wants to cut off your hand."

"Hush, Louise," her brother said sharply. "I'd as soon cut off my own hand as my child's. You should never speak anything but truth, especially to children."

"I think it's sometimes good to frighten them a little," Louise replied defensively. "And I thought that's what you intended to do."

"Never," Horace said firmly. "That is a very bad approach, and one I'll never adopt. Elsie will learn in time, if she doesn't know now, that I never utter a threat which I do not intend to carry out. And I never break my word."

While remonstrating with his sister, Horace had taken a linen handkerchief from his pocket. Lifting Elsie's hand again, he said to her, "I shall wrap up this hand, for those who do not use their hands aright should be deprived of their use. There!" He finished knotting the handkerchief, making sure it was not too tight. "Now go to your room and stay there till supper." He gave her a little pat on the back and sent her off.

Elsie felt deeply humiliated, so Arthur's nasty laugh and Enna's smug little smirk added nothing to her suffering. Her father's punishment, which was indeed mild, had wounded her more than the most severe chastisement, because the mere knowledge of his displeasure was the worst pain she could endure.

Walter, whose heart was much kinder than his brother's or sister's, was touched by Elsie's distress, and he ran after her when she had left the room. "Never mind, Elsie," he said sincerely. "I'm so very sorry for you, and I don't think you were the least bit naughty."

She thanked him, for she was deeply grateful for his concern. Then she hurried to her room. Alone, she sat by the window, and through her tears, she tormented herself with questions. "Why am I so naughty? How can I be good so that Papa will love me?" And she raised an earnest prayer for help to do right and for the wisdom to understand how to gain her father's love.

When the supper bell rang an hour later, Elsie jumped up, but then she sat down again. Better to have no supper, she decided, than to show her handkerchief-bound hand and tear-swollen eyes at the table. It was not long, however, before a servant came to her door with a message from her father; she was to come down to the dining room immediately.

When she took her seat beside him at the table, Horace turned hard eyes on her. "Didn't you hear the bell?" he inquired.

"Yes, sir."

"Remember, Elsie, that you are to come as soon as you hear the bell, unless you are directed otherwise or you are sick. The next time you're late, I will send you away without your meal."

"But I don't want to eat," she said softly.

"Nevertheless, you will have your supper tonight, and there will be no pouting or sulking." His voice was low, but clearly irritated as he added, "Stop that crying at once." He spread some preserves on a slice of bread and laid it on her plate, and repeated, "Stop crying, or I'll take you from the table, and you will be very sorry."

Elsie was struggling valiantly to choke back her tears when her grandfather addressed her. "Why is your hand bandaged, little girl?" he asked. "Have you been hurt?"

Elsie's face flushed, but she said nothing.

"You must speak when you are spoken to," her father commanded. "Answer your grandfather's question now."

"Papa tied it because I was naughty," she said, a sob escaping with her words.

Horace made a move as if to take her away from the table, but Elsie begged him, "Please, don't, Papa. I'll be good."

"Then no more crying," he said. "This is shameful behavior for a girl of nearly nine. It would be bad enough for a child of Enna's age." He took a fresh handkerchief from his pocket and wiped her eyes. "Now eat your supper at once, and don't make me have to correct you again."

Elsie tried to eat her bread and jam, but it was almost impossible. Struggling as hard as she could to stifle her tears and sobs, she could not swallow and felt as if she might suffocate. She knew that her father was watching her closely, and she sensed that everyone else was looking at her. "If they would just forget about me," she thought.

It was at that moment that Adelaide, who had watched the whole scene, addressed a question to Horace and adroitly set the whole table talking about something else. How grateful Elsie was to her aunt for this time to regain her composure.

When they rose from the table, Elsie timidly asked if she might go to her room.

"No, child," her father said. Taking her left hand, he led her to the veranda. Horace settled in a comfortable chair and lit a cigar. He told Elsie to get his book from the drawing room; then he had her draw a stool close to his chair and sit beside him.

"Do not move from that stool. Let's see if I can keep you out of mischief for an hour or two," he said, and he began reading to himself.

"May I get a book to read, Papa?"

"You may not. Do just as I tell you, nothing more and nothing less."

Elsie took her seat on the stool and tried to amuse herself with her own thoughts. She watched her father's face as he read. "How handsome my Papa is," she thought. But her sadness came back to her again as she tried to decide how she could please him and win his love. More than anything, she wanted only to climb on his knee, hug him, and tell him how sorry she was about the bird. In her imagination, she could see him returning her affection with his own hugs and smiles.

A cry from Enna broke into her dream, and without thinking, Elsie jumped up from the stool. "Papa," she exclaimed, "there's a carriage coming up the drive. If it's visitors, please let me go to my room!"

"Why do you wish to go?" he asked coolly.

Elsie blushed and hung her head. "Because I don't want them to see me, Papa," she answered.

"You are not usually so afraid of strangers," he observed.

"But they will see that my hand is tied and ask me why. Oh, please let me go, Papa, before they get here," she pleaded desperately.

"No, you must stay, if only to punish you for leaving your seat without my permission. You must learn to obey me at all times, Elsie, and under all circumstances. Now sit down, and don't move again until I say you may."

Elsie sat quickly, but two hot tears dropped on her cheeks.

"You need not cry," her father said. "The visitor is only an old gentlemen here to see your grandfather on business. He never notices children, so he's not likely to ask you any questions. I really hope, Elsie, that you will learn to save your tears for an occasion that requires them."

Her father was right. The old gentleman paid no attention to her, and her relief was so great that, for once, she scarcely noticed Horace's rebuke. A half hour at least passed in silence, and Elsie grew so weary that without intending to, she laid her head on her father's knee and slept.

His voice seemed to come to her from far away. "You may go to bed now, Elsie, if you like."

She stood up slowly and was turning to go, but she hesitated.

"Do you have something else to say?" Horace asked.

"Yes, Papa. I'm sorry I was naughty today. Will you forgive me?" Her words were spoken softly, but she managed not to cry again.

Horace responded sternly, "In the future, will you try not to meddle in the affairs of others and not to sulk and pout when you are punished?"

"I will try to be a good girl always," she promised.

"Then I forgive you," he said, and he carefully untied the handkerchief and removed it from her hand.

But she still lingered, hoping for some token of his forgiveness. Sensing what she wanted, Horace considered what to do. With a hint of impatience, he said at last, "No, Elsie, I will not kiss you good night. You have been entirely too naughty. Now go straight to your room at once."

Could she *ever* win her father's love? The wait seemed endless at times. In her bed that night, Elsie searched her little Bible for words of hope. And she found them in the promise of God's eternal love: "For I am convinced that neither death nor life, neither angels nor demons, neither the present nor the future, nor any powers, neither height nor depth, nor anything else in all creation, will be able to separate us from the love of God that is in Christ Jesus our Lord." Whatever else happened to her, God's love would be with her always.

CHAPTER

A Terrible Injustice

*"Consider it pure joy, my brothers, whenever you
face trials of many kinds, because you
know that the testing of your faith
develops perseverance.
Perseverance must finish its work
so that you may be mature
and complete, not lacking
anything."*

JAMES 1:2 – 4

A Terrible Injustice

*E*ach month, Miss Day presented the parents with reports on the conduct and recitations of her pupils. Horace Dinsmore had received one such report since his return to Roselands. It had been most satisfactory, as Elsie was usually a diligent scholar who tried to carry her religious principles into her studies as in everything else. As much as Miss Day looked for faults, Elsie's work rarely gave her good excuses.

Horace had pronounced the first report quite good. "I'm glad to see that my daughter is industrious and well-behaved," he had told Miss Day, "for I want her to grow into an intelligent and amiable woman."

Now the time for the second report arrived, and Elsie knew it would not be as the first. The warm weather of the last month had distracted her, and more seriously, she had often been too depressed and anxious to concentrate fully on her lessons. Arthur had become more annoying than ever; in the schoolroom he was forever shaking Elsie's chair and jogging her elbow when she was writing. Her copybook was very messy as a result, and Miss Day's report on her work had never been so bad. With secret satisfaction, the governess presented the report to Horace, together with a long list of complaints about the child's idleness and inattention.

"Send her to my room immediately," Horace said angrily.

Elsie was still in the schoolroom, putting her desk in order, when Miss Day brought the message. With a hateful smile, she said, "Elsie, your father wishes to see you this moment. He is waiting in his room."

Elsie's Endless Wait

The look on Miss Day's face told Elsie what to expect, and for several moments, the little girl was quite unable to move.

"I advise you to go quickly," said Miss Day, "for the longer you wait, the worse it will be, I have no doubt."

As the teacher spoke, Elsie heard her father's voice calling her name; struggling to control her fear and trembling, she hurried to obey.

The door to Horace's room was open, and Elsie walked slowly in. "Did you call me, Papa?" she asked.

"Come here to me," he said. He was sitting with her copybook and the report in hand, and she could both see and hear his reproachful attitude. But Horace could see as well, and the terror in Elsie's face touched him. Less sternly he asked, "Can you tell me how it happens that your teacher has brought me so bad a report of your conduct and lessons? She says you have been very idle, and this report tells the same story. Your copybook is really shameful."

Elsie could answer only with tears, which seemed to irritate him. "When I ask a question," he said, "I require an answer at once."

"Oh, Papa. I — I *couldn't* study! I'm very sorry. I'll do better. Please don't be angry with me, Papa!"

"I am angry with you. Very angry, indeed. And strongly inclined to punish you. You couldn't study, eh? For what reason? Were you not well?"

"I don't know, sir."

"You don't know? Well, you could not have been very ill without knowing it, and you seem to have no other excuse. However, I will not punish you this time, as you seem to be truly sorry and have promised to do better. But do not let me see this kind of report again or hear such reports of your idleness, unless you wish to be severely punished. I warn you, Elsie, that unless your next copybook is much improved, I will certainly punish you."

As he spoke, he leafed through the pages of her writing book. "There are a number of pages here that look quite well done," he noted in a slightly milder tone. "They show what you can do, if you choose. There is an old saying, 'A bird that *can* sing and *won't* sing must be *made* to sing.'"

Elsie started to speak, but he commanded her to be quiet. "Not a word. Just go now." Then he leaned back in his easy chair and began to read his newspaper.

But Elsie, though dismissed, lingered in his room. This was the first time she had ever entered his room, and it should have been a happy occasion. She felt she couldn't leave without some word of kindness from her Papa. But when Horace finally saw her standing there, he only said, "I gave you permission to go, Elsie. Go at once."

So she sought solitude in her own room, and again and again she reproached herself for her failures during the last month. Then she had a thought which added greatly to her misery. Arthur! He was sure to continue his persecutions, and how could she possibly make her copybook more presentable if he would not let her alone? Miss Day usually left the schoolroom during the writing hour, and the older girls were often absent, too. With no one around but the little children, Arthur had ample opportunities to torment her and ruin her work. Elsie didn't tell tales; besides, she could never have sought help from the adults. Arthur was his mother's great favorite, and telling on him would have brought a great deal of trouble to Elsie herself. She wondered if she might persuade her uncle to give her some peace, but that course seemed hopeless.

Elsie's Endless Wait

In desperation, she took her trouble to her Heavenly Father and asked for His help. She was still on her knees when someone knocked on the door. Elsie opened it to find her Aunt Adelaide.

"I'm writing to Rose," Adelaide said cheerfully. "Would you like to write a little note to her? I can enclose it in my letter." But as she spoke, she saw Elsie's tear-stained face and worried expression. "Whatever is the matter, child?" she asked, taking Elsie's hand and drawing her close.

With a great many tears, Elsie sobbed out the whole story, including her father's threat and her fear that she could not, because of Arthur's endless teasing, do well enough to avoid the punishment.

Adelaide's sympathies were fully enlisted, and wiping the child's tears away, she said reassuringly, "Never mind about Arthur, dear. From now on, I will take my book or needlework to the schoolroom every day, and I'll sit there through the writing hour. That will take care of Arthur. But why didn't you tell all this to your father?"

"I don't want to tattle, Aunt Adelaide, and it would make your mother so angry with me. Besides, I can't tell Papa anything."

"I understand," Adelaide comforted, and to herself, she said, "It's no wonder the child can't talk to him. Horace is strangely stern with her, and I mean to give him a good talking to!"

Leaving Elsie with a warm kiss, Adelaide had every intention of finding her brother and carrying out her mission. But he had gone out, and when he returned, brought several gentlemen with him. It was some time before she had the opportunity to get Horace alone, and by then, her resolve had disappeared.

144

Still, Adelaide's promise had come like an answer to Elsie's prayer, and when her aunt left her room, Elsie's heart was greatly lifted. Locking her door against any surprise intrusion by Enna, Elsie went to her bureau, unlocked a drawer, and removed the purse she was knitting for her father, to replace the one she'd given to Rose Allison. Elsie had started this project even before Horace's return, and now it was nearly finished. How many of her hopes and fears were woven into its bright gold and blue beads!

With her aunt's kind promise fresh in her mind, Elsie settled into her sewing chair and began to work. Her little fingers moved briskly, and the bright, shining needles glanced in and out. As she knitted, her thoughts moved equally swiftly: "No wonder Papa is vexed with me. I've never had such a bad report. What's come over me? It seems I can't study. Maybe I need a holiday. Could it be laziness? If it is, I should be punished. I *will* try harder next month. It's only a month, after all, and then June will be over. Miss Day will go North, and she won't return till August or maybe September, and we'll have a long summer holiday. And this month won't be so hard. No classes on Saturday. That means no class tomorrow, so I can finish this purse. I wonder if Papa will be pleased." She sighed deeply. "I've disappointed him twice this week — the bird and now my bad report. But I will do better next month, especially with Aunt Adelaide's help."

Her thoughts ran on in this way. "I wonder how we will spend our vacation? I went to Ashlands last summer, and then the Carringtons came here, and poor Herbert had such a dreadful time with his hip. How thankful I am not to be lame and always to be so healthy. But Papa probably won't let me go to Ashlands this year, or ask them here. He thinks Lucy isn't a suitable companion, and I was very naughty when she was here. Have I been more naughty than I ever was before he came home? I wonder if he will punish me severely? I wonder what that means?"

At that, a new and horrible thought struck her, and she dropped her work. "He can't mean *that*! He wouldn't send me away! It would break my heart! I must be very, very good, so that I never deserve a severe punishment; then it makes no difference what he means."

Elsie had heard vague stories about naughty children who were sent away by their parents. She had heard of schools where children actually lived, separated from their families and their homes. In her imagination, this was the most terrible thing that could happen to a child. What if this were the severe punishment her Papa had threatened? The thought of it made her tremble with fear. For all her troubles, she could not bear to be separated from her dear father when she had so recently found him. At the thought of losing him again, she became more determined than ever to do her best to please her Papa and to win his love.

The next day, when she had put the final touches on the beaded purse, she asked Aunt Chloe if her father was at home.

"No, darling," the nurse replied. "He rode out earlier with some gentlemen."

Elsie neatly put away her knitting things and took a piece of notepaper from her desk. Then she wrote, in her very best hand: "A present for my dear Papa, from his little daughter, Elsie." Carefully she pinned the note to the purse and carried it to her father's room. Fearing that he might have returned, she rapped gently at the door, but as there was no answer, she went in. She was about to place the gift on her father's dressing table when his voice startled her.

"What are you doing in my room without my permission?" he demanded.

Elsie quaked and tried to hold back tears as she silently put the purse in his hand. He looked at the present, then at his daughter.

"I made it for you, Papa," she said softly. "Please take it."

"It is really very pretty, " he said, examining the beaded purse closely. "Is this possibly your work? Of course it is. I had no idea you have so much taste and skill. Thank you, Daughter. I'll be happy to take it, and I will use it with great pleasure."

He had taken her hand as he spoke, and now he lifted her onto his knee and asked, "Elsie, my child, why do you always seem so afraid of me? I don't like it."

With a sudden impulse, she threw her arms around his neck and kissed his cheek. Dropping her head onto his shoulder, she sobbed, "Oh, Papa, I love you so very dearly! Won't you love me? I know I've been naughty, but I will try to be good."

For the first time since they had met, Horace folded his child in his arms and kissed her with all the tenderness of a loving parent.

"But I do love you, my little Daughter," he said softly.

So great was Elsie's happiness that she did not try to stop her tears.

"Why are you crying, dear?" Horace asked.

"Because I'm so very happy!"

"Then if you care so much for my love, you mustn't tremble and turn pale whenever I speak to you. I'm not a cruel tyrant, you know."

"It's only because you look so stern. I can't bear to have you so angry with me," she said and added, "but I'm not afraid of you now."

He hugged her again, and as they sat there together, they heard the supper bell. "Now go into my dressing room and wash your face," Horace instructed, "and we'll go down together."

There were several visitors at the table that evening, and the conversation centered on the adults, but every now and then, Horace bestowed a loving look on his daughter, and he carefully attended to all her needs. She was happier than she had ever been.

~~~

Things proceeded this way for some time. Elsie did not see as much of her father as she wished, because he was often away on business and he frequently brought guests home on his return. But whenever he saw her, he showed great kindness, and she gradually began to overcome her fear of him. She looked forward to the time when he would have more leisure for her, but she was genuinely happy even so. With her mind now at ease, she could concentrate on her lessons. Adelaide faithfully kept her promise, coming to the schoolroom every day. With Arthur unable to annoy her, Elsie progressed well with her writing; her copybook showed marked improvement in her penmanship. There was not a single blot on any page, and she was actually anticipating with pleasure the next report to her father.

But there came a morning when Miss Day was in her very worst humor — peevish, fretful, irritable, and unreasonable to the extreme. As usual, Elsie took the brunt of her bad temper. Miss Day found fault with everything Elsie did; she scolded and shook the little girl, refused to explain the method of solving a very difficult arithmetic problem, and wouldn't allow the girl to ask help of anyone else. Then she punished Elsie when the problem was done incorrectly. Elsie struggled to hold back her tears but at last she began to cry, and Miss Day derided her as a baby for shedding tears and a dunce for not understanding the arithmetic.

Elsie bore it all without answering back, but her patience only provoked Miss Day all the more. Finally, when Elsie came up to recite her last lesson, Miss Day deliberately put her questions in the most perplexing way and then didn't allow the child to answer. Throwing down the textbook, Miss Day angrily scolded Elsie and marked down the lesson as a complete failure.

Poor Elsie could take no more. She protested, "I *did* know my lesson Miss Day, every word of it. But you didn't ask your questions as usual or give me time to answer."

"I say you did not know it, and you failed," Miss Day angrily replied. "Now sit down and learn every word of it over again."

But Elsie did not sit down. "I do know it if you will hear me right," she cried indignantly, "and it is unjust of you to mark it a failure."

Miss Day was furious. "Impudent girl!" she screamed. "How dare you contradict me? I'm taking you to your father right now!"

Seizing Elsie by the arm, the teacher dragged her from the room and into the hallway.

"Please don't tell Papa!" Elsie begged, but Miss Day only pushed her to Horace's door. It was open, and he was inside working at his writing desk.

"What is all this?" he asked as they entered.

"Elsie has been very impertinent, sir," Miss Day said. "She accused me of being unjust, and she contradicted me."

Horace was frowning darkly now. "Is this true, Elsie? Did you contradict your teacher?"

"Yes, sir," she said softly.

"Then I certainly must punish you." He picked up a small ruler from his desk and took Elsie's hand as if he meant to strike it.

"Oh, no, Papa!" she cried in alarm. But he put the ruler down and said, "I shall punish you by depriving you of your play today and giving you only bread and water for your dinner." He pointed to a stool in the corner of his large room. "Sit down there and do not move."

Then with a dismissive wave of his hand at Miss Day, he said, "I think she will never do the like again."

Soon after, the dinner bell rang, and Horace left, and after a little time had passed, old Pompey came up the stairs carrying a tray with a tumbler of water and a slice of bread on a plate.

"This isn't much of a meal, Miss Elsie," he said as he put the tray down beside her. "Mr. Dinsmore says it's all you can have, but if you say so, I'll ask Phoebe to send up something more for you before your father comes back."

"That's kind of you, Pompey, but I can't disobey Papa," Elsie said, "and I'm really not hungry at all."

Pompey lingered a bit, hesitant to leave her alone, but Elsie told him to go back to the dining room where he might be needed.

When her father returned, the glass of water and piece of bread lay uneaten on the tray.

"What is the meaning of this?" he demanded. "Why haven't you eaten what I sent to you?"

"I'm not hungry, Papa."

A *Terrible Injustice*

"That's nothing but stubbornness, Elsie, and temper. Take that bread and eat it now. You will eat every crumb and drink every drop of your water."

She obeyed instantly. As he watched, she took a bite of bread, but hard as she tried, she simply could not swallow it. "I can't," she said. "It chokes me."

"You will obey me," he said coldly. "Take some water to wash it down."

She saw that it was no use to protest, and at length every crumb of bread and every drop of water was gone.

His severity in no way diminished, Horace said, "Never dare show me such temper again, Elsie. You won't escape so easily next time. You are to obey me always. Do you understand?"

She knew that his words were unfair — it had not been temper — but Elsie was too fearful now to speak in her own defense. As the tears gathered in her eyes, Horace told her that she was to stay in his room until he returned.

Timidly she asked, "May I have my lesson books, Papa?"

"You may. I'll have them brought to you."

"And my Bible?"

"Yes, yes," he said impatiently as he left the room and shut the door on her.

When he returned to the drawing room, Adelaide asked him what troubled Elsie.

"She has been impertinent to the governess, and I've confined her to my room for the rest of the day," he said with impatience.

"Are you so sure, Horace, that Elsie was to blame?" Adelaide asked as gently as she could. "From what Lora has told me, I believe that Miss Day is often cruelly unfair to your daughter — more than to any of the others."

Horace looked at his sister in surprise. "Are you certain of that?"

"I am. And it is a fact that Miss Day sometimes mistreats her."

Horace colored deeply. "I will not allow that," he said heatedly. But after a moment's thought, he added, "I think you are wrong in this instance, however. Elsie herself acknowledged that she had been impertinent. However severe you think I am, I didn't condemn her without a hearing."

"Believe me, Horace, if she was impertinent, it was after serious provocation. Her acknowledgment is no proof at all, to my mind, for Elsie is so sensitive she'd think herself impertinent simply because Miss Day said so."

"Surely not," he said incredulously. "Elsie does not lack sense."

But Adelaide's words troubled him, and he was half-inclined to go back upstairs and question his child more closely. He considered this, then gave up the idea, telling himself, "If she refuses to be frank with me and speak up for herself, she deserves her punishment. And there was that stubbornness about eating." Horace was very proud, and he did not like to admit, especially to himself, that he may have punished his child unjustly.

It was almost supper time when Horace finally returned to his room, but Elsie didn't hear him enter. He saw that she had not moved from the stool and sat bent over her little Bible. When he came close, she looked up with a start. "Papa," she said, "will you forgive me?"

"Certainly I will, if you are really sorry." He leaned over and kissed her, a cold and dutiful kiss. "Now go let Aunt Chloe dress you for supper."

But Elsie's punishment was not truly over, for she continued to struggle with herself. She was particularly distressed about her bad mark that day and how it would appear on her monthly report. Yet it had not been her fault, and again and again she determined to tell her father what had really happened. Again and again, however, she failed to summon the courage to approach him, and the days passed without her speaking to her father — until it was too late.

CHAPTER

8

Arthur's Scheme

"For God will bring every deed into judgment, including every hidden thing, whether it is good or evil."

ECCLESIASTES 12:14

Arthur's Scheme

*I*t was Friday, and Miss Day's reports were to be presented on the next morning. School was over, but Elsie remained alone in the classroom to arrange her books and her writing and drawing materials. When she had finished, she took her report book from the desk and looked over her marks for the last month. As her eye stopped on the one bad mark, she lamented yet again that she had never told her father the whole story of what had occurred. Her copybook, however, gave her complete satisfaction, for every page showed painstaking care and clear improvement. And not a single ink blot marred any of its pages.

"This will surely please Papa," she said to herself. "How good Aunt Adelaide was to come sit with me!"

Then she replaced the copybook and locked her desk securely. She went to her room and placed her desk key in its habitual place on the mantel.

That afternoon, when Elsie and the others had gone out for their walk, Arthur found himself alone in the house with nothing to do. Having gorged himself on candies a few days before, he still felt too sick for his usual activities and lounged lazily in the children's playroom. Although Arthur was not generally fond of reading, he decided to amuse himself with a book he had seen Elsie reading that morning. It was her book, of course, and she was not there to give it to him. But Arthur had very little respect for property rights, except his own.

With Elsie out and Chloe in the kitchen, Arthur felt certain no one would stop him from taking the book, and he went to Elsie's room. It was lying on the mantel, beside Elsie's desk key. Catching sight of the key, Arthur couldn't suppress a squeal of delight, for he knew exactly which lock the key fit. In an instant, he conceived a plan for the revenge he'd been seeking ever since the affair of his father's gold watch.

His hand reached for the key, but he hesitated. He had to think this through to avoid any chance of detection.

He wanted to deface Elsie's copybook, but Adelaide would testify to the girl's neatness, for his eldest sister had been in the schoolroom every day at writing hour. Adelaide, however, had just left to visit a friend and would be gone from Roselands for several weeks, so she posed no danger. Miss Day, to be sure, well knew the appearance of Elsie's book, but she was even less likely to interfere, and Arthur knew of no one else who could speak up for Elsie.

He decided to run the risk, and he grabbed the key. Checking the hallway to be sure no servants might see him, he hurried to the schoolroom. Almost giddy with glee, he unlocked Elsie's desk and took out her copybook. Using her own pen and ink, he proceeded to blot nearly every page. Some pages got big, black ink drops; others, two or three splatters. He also scribbled between the lines and in the margins so Elsie's work would appear as ugly as possible.

He knew that Horace was sure to be very angry with Elsie, and that thought pleased him mightily, but bad as Arthur was, it must be said that he was unaware of Horace's threatened punishment. The mischief did not take long to accomplish, though Arthur was frightened several times by the sounds of footsteps outside the schoolroom door. No one came in, however, and when the book was thoroughly ruined, he carefully replaced it, wiped the pen and replaced it too, and locked Elsie's desk. Then he rushed back to Elsie's room, put the key in its place on the mantel, and took the book that had been his original objective.

In all this, he had been seen by no one, and back in the playroom, he settled on a couch to read. But he could think of nothing except his vengeful act and its probable consequences. Now that it was too late, he experienced some doubts; yet he never for a single moment considered confessing and saving Elsie from blame. Then another thought struck him: he had Elsie's book, so it was obvious he had been into her room. That would raise suspicions. He jumped up, intending to take the book back, but at that moment, he heard Elsie's voice from the hall. "Well," he thought to himself, "I'll just bluff it out."

Elsie didn't notice the guilty look on his face when she entered. "I'm looking for the book I was reading. I thought it was in my room," she said, searching likely places. Then she saw it in Arthur's hands. "Oh, you have it! You can keep it, Arthur," she said, "and I'll finish it another time."

But Arthur tossed the book to her. "Take it back," he said roughly. "I don't like it. 'Tisn't any fun."

"I think it's very interesting, and you're welcome to read it," Elsie said politely. "But if you don't want to, I will take it."

The next morning was the last day of the school term, and the writing hour was omitted, so Elsie had no reason to open her copybook. As soon as the children had finished their brief exercises, Miss Day announced, "Young ladies and gentlemen, this is the regular day for your reports, and they are all prepared. Elsie, here is yours. Now take it and your copybook directly to your father."

Elsie obeyed. She was very conscious of the one bad mark in her report, but her copybook had been written with such care and effort that she hoped her father would not be seriously displeased. Neither she nor anyone else except Arthur knew what had been done to her careful penmanship.

She found her father in his room and handed him the report. With a slight frown, he remarked, "There is one very bad mark here for recitation. But as all the other marks are remarkably good, I will excuse it."

Then he took the copybook. He opened to the first page, and to Elsie's surprise, he threw her a look of great displeasure. His face darkened as he leafed through the rest of the pages. Finally, he said, his voice low and edged with anger, "I see I shall have to keep my promise, Elsie."

"What, Papa?" she asked, turning pale with fear.

"What!" he shouted. "You ask what! Didn't I tell you positively that I would punish you if your copybook did not present a better appearance this month?"

"But it does, Papa! I tried so hard, and there are no blots in it."

"No blots?" He thrust the book under her face. "What do you call these?"

Elsie gazed at the pages of her book in unfeigned astonishment. At first, she could hardly believe the book was really hers. Then she turned to her father and said earnestly, "I didn't do that, Papa."

"Then who did?"

"I don't know, Papa."

"I must get to the bottom of this business," he declared, "and if it isn't your fault, you won't be punished. But if you are telling a falsehood, Elsie, you shall be punished more severely than if you'd admitted your fault."

Taking her hand, he led her to the classroom where the other children were waiting to meet with their parents. Horace pushed the open copybook at the teacher and asked, "Elsie says these blots are not her work. Can you tell me whose they are?"

"Elsie *generally* tells the truth," Miss Day said smoothly, "but I must say that in this instance, I think she has not. Her desk has a good lock, and she keeps the key, so no one else could have gotten at her copybook."

Horace turned back to his daughter. "Have you ever left your desk unlocked," he asked "or left your key lying about?"

"No, sir, I'm sure I haven't," she answered quickly, though her voice trembled and her face had grown very pale.

"Then I am certain you have told me a falsehood, for the evidence is clear that this must be your work. Come with me." His face was almost as pale as hers, from rage rather than fear, and grabbing her hand again, he dragged her from the room. "I'll teach you to tell the truth to me at least."

Lora, who was just coming back to the schoolroom, heard Horace's angry words. She knew Elsie would never tell a falsehood, and as she looked around the room, her eyes fell on Arthur's guilty face. She hastily crossed to his desk and whispered, "I know that you had a hand in this, Arthur. You'd better confess it quickly, or Horace will half-kill Elsie."

"You don't know anything," Arthur replied.

"Oh, yes, I do," Lora persisted, "and if you don't speak up at once, I will save Elsie myself and find proof of your guilt later. It would be better for you to confess."

Arthur shoved his sister and shouted angrily, "Go away! I have nothing to confess."

Seeing that Arthur could not be moved, Lora rushed to Horace's room and banged the door open without a thought of knocking. She was just in time, for Horace's hand was raised, and he was just about to administer the first spanking of poor Elsie's life. The look he cast at his sister burned with fury, but she took no notice. Instead, Lora cried urgently, "Don't punish Elsie, for I'm sure she's innocent!"

Horace stayed his hand and demanded, "How do you know? What is your proof? Tell me, for I want to be convinced."

Elsie stood rigid at his side, too terrified even to cry.

"In the first place," Lora began, "there is Elsie's established character for truthfulness. In all the time she has been with us, she has always been perfectly truthful in word and deed. And what motive would she have for spoiling her own book? She knew that your punishment was certain to be very severe. Horace, I'm sure Arthur is at the bottom of this. He won't confess, but he doesn't deny it. And I saw Elsie's book just yesterday. It was neat and well written and had absolutely no blots."

Horace's expression changed dramatically as Lora spoke, and he found himself trembling at the thought of what he might have done if his sister had not intervened. "Thank you," he said softly when she finished. "Thank you, dear Lora, for stopping me before I punished Elsie unfairly. I need no more than your word to establish her innocence."

Lora, deeply relieved that she had prevented an injustice, quietly left the room as Horace was taking Elsie into his arms. "My poor child," he said. "My poor little Daughter, I have been terribly unjust to you."

Elsie hardly knew what to reply. "You thought I deserved it, Papa."

"And you have every reason to be angry with me," he continued, his voice strained with emotion. "I love you very much, Elsie, even when I seem cold and stern. And I am more thankful than words can express that I haven't punished you wrongly. I could never forgive myself if I had done that, and I think you have reason now to hate me for what I have done."

This idea struck Elsie like a bolt, and she sobbed, "Oh, Papa, I could never hate you. Never! Never!"

"There, there. Don't cry anymore, dear Daughter," he said, attempting to soothe both her and himself. "Adelaide tells me that perhaps you were not to blame for being impertinent to Miss Day the other day. I want you to tell me all the circumstances now. I won't encourage you to find faults with your teacher, but I also have no intention of allowing you to be mistreated."

"Aunt Lora was there, and she can tell you what happened."

"I want the story from *you*, Elsie. I want to know exactly what passed between you and Miss Day, as best you can remember."

For all her desire to defend herself, Elsie was extremely reluctant to speak against another. She was careful to tell the truth without casting blame on Miss Day, but as she spoke, her father grew increasingly incensed.

"Elsie," he said at last, "if I'd known all this at the time, I would not have punished you. Why didn't you tell me that you were ill treated?"

"But you didn't ask, Papa."

"I asked if it was true that you contradicted Miss Day."

"Yes, sir, and that was true."

"But you should have told me the whole story, though I understand now that I frightened you with my sternness. Well, Daughter," he said gently, "I will endeavor to be less stern in the future, and you must try to be less timid with me."

"I will try, Papa, but I can't help being afraid when you are so angry with me."

Elsie and Horace sat together for a long time, and Elsie talked with him more freely than she had ever done. She spoke about her sorrows and her joys. She told him about Rose Allison and the many happy hours they had spent together in Bible study and prayer. She described how sad she felt when her dear friend went away, and she told him about the wonderful letters she received from Rose. Horace was both pleased by and interested in his child's conversation, and he encouraged her with occasional questions and words of approval. While she was talking, he noticed the gold chain around her neck. "What is this?" he asked.

Gently, Elsie took out the miniature, and Horace needed no explanation to recognize the beautiful face in the portrait. The sight took him back many years, to the few short months he had shared with his wife. Looking from the portrait to his child, he said, as if addressing someone else in the room, "Yes, she is very much like — the same features, the same expression, complexion, hair, and all. She'll be the very counterpart someday."

Elsie caught part of his words, "Am I like Mamma?" she asked him.

"Yes, you are, darling, very much indeed."

"And you loved Mamma?"

"Very dearly."

"Then tell me about her, please," she begged.

"But I haven't much to tell," he sighed. "We knew each other such a short time before we were torn apart. And now we can never meet again on this earth."

"But we may meet her again in heaven, Papa," Elsie said with certainty, "for she loved Jesus, and if we love Him, we will go to heaven when we die. Do you love Jesus, Papa?"

This question greatly concerned Elsie, but instead of answering her, Horace asked, "Do you, Elsie?"

"Oh, yes, sir! Very much. I love Him even better than I love you, my own dear father."

He searched her little face. "How do you know that?" he wondered.

"Just as I know I love you," she responded with evident surprise. "I love to talk of Jesus. I love to tell Him all my troubles, and ask Him to forgive my sins and make me holy. It means so much to know that He loves me and always will, even if no one else does."

Horace set her down from his lap and said, "It's almost dinner time. Go now, and get ready, dear Daughter."

"Are you displeased, Papa?" she asked a little anxiously.

"Not at all, dear," he replied with a gentle laugh. "I thought we might ride together this afternoon. What do you say?"

At her eager response, he again told her to prepare for dinner, but before she could leave, he asked one question more: "Do you remember where you put your desk key yesterday? Did you take it when you went riding?"

"No, sir. I left it on the mantel in my room and —"

She stopped suddenly, but her father instructed her to continue. "I don't want you to express any suspicions," he assured her, "but I must have all the facts you can furnish. Was Aunt Chloe in your room while you were out?"

"No, sir. She was in the kitchen with Aunt Phoebe until I came back."

"Do you know if anyone else entered your room?"

"I don't *know*, sir, but I think Arthur must have been there, because when I came home, he was reading a book I'd left on the mantel."

"Ah, ha!" her father said, and nodded with satisfaction. "Now I see. Elsie, go on to your dinner, and I'll join you shortly."

But Elsie, who did not fully understand the implications of her father's questions, lingered a moment, and when her father looked at her inquiringly, she said, "Please don't be too angry with him, Papa. I don't think Arthur meant to take my book without permission."

"Don't worry, Daughter, I won't hurt him."

It so happened that the elder Mr. Dinsmore and his wife were visiting some friends in the city, and Horace was acting as head of the household in his father's absence. Though Arthur's father was expected back that evening, his mother would be away for several days, and Arthur was beginning to worry very much about the consequences of his actions — not without reason. His brother's wrath was fully aroused, and Horace was determined that this time, his younger brother would not escape punishment for his misdeeds.

Arthur was seated at the table when Horace entered the dining room.

"Step into the library a moment," Horace said to the boy. "I have something to say to you."

Arthur didn't move, but answered back, "I don't want to hear it."

Without raising his voice even a fraction, Horace said, "I'm sure you don't, sir, but that makes no difference. Walk into the library at once."

Under his breath Arthur muttered something about doing as he pleased, but he was too intimidated by Horace's determined look and forceful manner to disobey. Reluctantly he stood up and slowly followed his brother.

In the library, with the door closed, Horace said evenly, "Now tell me how you came to meddle with Elsie's copybook."

Arthur's denial was hot with false indignation, but Horace simply went on, "It's useless for you to deny it, Arthur, for I know it all. You went to Elsie's room yesterday, when she was out and Aunt Chloe was in the kitchen. You took her desk key from the mantel and went to the schoolroom and did your mischief, hoping to get her in trouble. When you had returned the key, you thought you had escaped detection. And I very nearly gave my innocent child the spanking you deserve."

Arthur looked up in amazement. "Who told you?" he demanded. "No one saw me!" Then catching himself, he said quickly, "I tell you I didn't do it. I don't know anything about it."

Suddenly, Horace revealed his anger, taking Arthur by the collar and shaking him. "How dare you repeat your falsehood?"

"Let me go," Arthur whined. "I want my dinner."

"You will get no dinner, sir," Horace replied. "I am locking you in your room until our father returns. And if he doesn't punish you as you deserve, I will. I intend that you receive your just deserts at least once in your miserable life. I know you did this in revenge for the watch business, but I give you fair warning — if you even attempt to harm my child in any way, you will regret it."

Arthur seemed to want to protest, but the look in Horace's eyes told him it was useless. He fell into a sullen whimpering: "You wouldn't treat me like this if Mamma were here."

"But she is not here, and even if she were, she could not save you this time," Horace answered. He had by now hauled Arthur up the stairs and to his bedroom. Horace pushed the boy inside, locked the door, and pocketed the key.

If Arthur expected sympathy from his father, he was sadly disappointed. Mr. Dinsmore took great pride in Horace and trusted his judgment in almost everything. Besides, the older man had a strong sense of justice, and he hated any mean and underhanded behavior. So when the older man returned and Horace had reported on his brother's latest activities, Arthur received a punishment which he truly never forgot.

CHAPTER

9

A Matter of Conscience

*"Judge for yourselves whether
it is right in God's sight
to obey you rather
than God."*

ACTS 4:19

A Matter of Conscience

*H*appy days had come for little Elsie. Her father treated her with the most loving affection and kept her with him as much as possible. He took her wherever he went — riding, walking, on visits to the neighboring plantations. She was much admired for her beauty and sweet disposition, but even with this new attention, she lost none of her natural modesty. She felt grateful for all the kindness she received from others, but her happiest hours were spent at home with her father. She could sit for hours with him, talking or reading. He helped with her studies and taught her some botany and geology on their walks. He helped with her drawing. He sang with her when she played piano, bought her stacks of new sheet music, and hired the best music masters to instruct her. In short, Horace took a lively interest in all she did and gave her the most tender care. He was extremely proud of her, and flattered by the praise of others.

Everyone could see the change in Elsie herself. Her eyes became bright with happiness, and her face lost its pensive expression, becoming as rosy and merry as Enna's.

During their summer holiday, Horace took his daughter traveling, and they stayed at several fashionable resorts. Elsie, who had not traveled anywhere since arriving at Roselands, enjoyed every minute of their trip. They were gone from July until September, and Elsie was rested and ready to resume her studies. But she was not sorry to learn that Miss Day had been delayed in the North for a few weeks and the start of school was to be postponed.

Elsie's Endless Wait

Adelaide was delighted by the changes she saw in Elsie on the day that the child and her father returned home. The family was gathered in the drawing room, and Elsie was entertaining her younger aunts and uncles with stories of her holiday.

"It's good to see how entirely she seems to have overcome her fear of her father," Lora agreed, watching as Elsie ran confidently to Horace and appeared to be asking him for something. With his permission, she displayed a richly bound book of engravings acquired on the journey.

She had, indeed, lost her fear and could now talk to Horace as freely as Enna ever did. And during all their time together, he had never had occasion to scold her or use a single harsh word.

On the first Sabbath afternoon after their return, Elsie was alone in her room. She had asked not to accompany her father on his ride; instead, she spent the time with her favorite books — the Bible, her hymnbook, and *Pilgrim's Progress* — and in self-reflection. She had just opened the Bible to the story of Elijah, which she promised to read to Chloe later, when she heard a rattling at her locked door.

"Open this door right now, Elsie Dinsmore!" Enna shouted imperiously. "I want in!"

Elsie sighed, realizing that this was the end of her nice afternoon, but she opened the door and asked pleasantly, "What do you want, Enna?"

"I want to come in," Enna declared in a saucy little voice, "and I want you to tell me a story. Mamma says you must, because I have a cold and can't go out."

A Matter of Conscience

"Well, I'm going to read a beautiful story to Aunt Chloe when she comes back, and you're welcome to stay and listen."

"No!" Enna cried. "I don't want it read." She flounced across the room and took her seat in a delicate rosewood rocking chair that Horace had recently given to his daughter. With her sharp little thumbnail, she began to scratch on the arm of the chair "Please don't do that to my new chair," Elsie said in alarm. "It's a gift from Papa, and I don't want it spoiled."

"Who cares for your old chair," Enna said scornfully and dug another gouge into the wood. "You're a little old maid — so particular about your things. That's what Mamma says. Now, tell me a story."

"If you stop scratching the chair," Elsie said with remarkable patience, "I can tell you about Elijah on Mount Carmel, or Belshazzar's feast, or the children in the fiery furnace. . . ."

"No! None of your old Bible stories. I want to hear the pretty fairy tale that Herbert Carrington likes so much."

"But I can't tell that one today," Elsie said firmly. "I can tell any story that's suitable for the Sabbath and honors God, but not fairy tales. I can tell it to you tomorrow if you wait."

"I want it now!" Enna shouted. "If you don't do what I want, I'll tell Mamma on you!"

With that, the little girl jumped from the chair and dashed out of the room, and it was not many minutes later when a servant came to summon Elsie.

Mrs. Dinsmore began chiding Elsie the moment she walked into her room: "Aren't you ashamed of yourself, Elsie? Why do you refuse Enna so small a favor, especially when the poor child isn't well? I believe you are the most selfish girl I've ever seen."

173

Elsie tried to explain: "I offered to tell a Bible story or anything suitable for the Sabbath. But it would be wrong to tell a fairy tale today, for the Bible tells us to 'observe the Sabbath day by keeping it holy.'"

"Nonsense! A fairy tale is no more harmful today than any other day," Mrs. Dinsmore said angrily.

At her side, Enna sobbed and whined, "I want a pretty fairy tale. Make her tell me the fairy tale, Mamma!"

Enna's wailing and her mother's scolding had apparently disturbed the elder Mr. Dinsmore, who came charging in from the adjoining room. From his puffy red eyes and tousled hair, Elsie thought he must have been napping, and he was in no mood to listen to a quarrel.

"What's all this fuss?" he roared.

"Nothing," said his wife, whose voice had suddenly grown sweet, "except that Enna is not well enough to go out and wants a fairy tale to help pass the time. And your granddaughter" — she stared pointedly at Elsie — "is too lazy or willful to tell it."

Mr. Dinsmore turned on Elsie. "Is that so? Well, there's an old saying, little girl. 'A bird that *can* sing and *won't* sing must be *made* to sing.'"

Elsie, who knew the meaning of the saying all too well, started to speak, but Mrs. Dinsmore cut her off. "The child pretends it is all on account of conscientious scruples. She says it isn't fit for the Sabbath. I don't care what that Mrs. Murray taught her. *I* say it is a great impertinence for a child of Elsie's age to set her opinion against yours and mine. I know very well it's just an excuse because she doesn't choose to oblige."

"Of course, it's an excuse," Mr. Dinsmore said hotly. Though by nature a just man, he also had a quick and often unreasonable temper, like all the Dinsmores.

A Matter of Conscience

Elsie spoke up, "No, Grandpa. It's not an excuse — "

"How dare you contradict me, you impudent little girl!" Catching her by the arm, he set her down hard on a chair. "Now, little miss," he shouted, "don't move from that chair till your father comes home. Then we'll see what he thinks of such impertinence. If he doesn't give you the punishment you deserve, I miss my guess."

"Please, Grandpa, I — "

Again he stopped her. "Hold your tongue, girl!" he bellowed. "And not another word until your father comes."

For the next half hour — and a very long one it seemed — Elsie sat in silence, wishing for, yet dreading, her father's return. Would he punish her as her grandfather seemed to wish? Or would he listen patiently to her side of the story? Might she be punished in either case? A few months before, she would have been certain of serious chastisement. And even now, though she trusted her father's love beyond a doubt, she also knew that Horace was a strict disciplinarian who never excused her faults.

At last she heard the sound of his steps in the hall, and her heart beat faster as he entered the room and addressed his father, "You wanted to see me, sir?"

"I want you to attend to this girl," Mr. Dinsmore said gruffly, nodding his head toward Elsie. "She has been very impertinent to me."

Horace's expression was of complete amazement, and he turned to her with such grave eyes that her tears immediately began to flow.

"It is hard to believe," Horace said, "that my little Elsie could be guilty of such conduct. If she has been, she must be punished, for I cannot allow this kind of behavior. Elsie, go to my dressing room and stay there until I come to you."

"Papa, I — "

"Hush!" he commanded with some of the old sternness. Sobbing, Elsie instantly obeyed.

Horace took a seat and turned to his father. "Now, sir, if you please, I'd like to hear the whole story," he said calmly. "Precisely what has Elsie done and said? What was the provocation, for that must be taken into account if I am to do her justice."

"If you do her justice, you'll spank her well," Mr. Dinsmore grumbled.

Horace colored deeply, for he strongly resented interference in his management of his child. But he calmed himself and asked again for the details. Mr. Dinsmore deferred to his wife, and she painted as bleak a picture as she could against Elsie. She was, however, obliged to state that it was Elsie's refusal to humor Enna and to tell a fairy story on the Sabbath that started the whole upset. This admission vexed Horace immensely, and he informed his stepmother that, while he did not always approve of Elsie's strict notions on such matters, his daughter was not to be made a slave to Enna's whims. If Elsie chose to tell Enna a story — or do anything for her — he had no objection. But never was Elsie to be forced, and Enna must understand that she had no right to Elsie's favors.

His father, hearing the whole story for the first time, agreed.

"You are right there, Horace," he said, "but that doesn't excuse Elsie's impertinence to me. I have to agree with my wife that it is a great piece of impudence to set her opinions against ours. Besides, she contradicted me flatly."

He then related the exact words of his exchange with Elsie. But he changed the tone of her words, and omitted the fact that he had interrupted her before she could complete a

sentence. From this recounting, Horace received the erro-
neous impression that Elsie had been very disrespectful, and
he left the room with every intention of giving her a severe
punishment indeed. But as he walked slowly to his room, his
anger began to cool, and he determined that, to be fair, he
must hear her side of the story before he condemned her.

When he entered his room, Elsie could see that his face
was sad and serious, but there was little sternness in it. He
sat beside her on the couch and hugged her gently. Finally,
he said, "I am very sorry to hear so bad an account of your
behavior. I don't want to punish you."

Elsie didn't say anything, but he could feel her shaking as
she cried.

"I won't condemn you unheard," he said gently. "Now tell
me how you came to be impertinent to your grandfather."

"I didn't mean to be saucy," she managed to say.

"Then stop crying and tell me everything that happened.
I want to know what words passed between you and Enna,
as well as Mrs. Dinsmore and your grandfather. I know I
can trust you to tell the truth and not to use a falsehood to
save yourself from punishment."

"Thank you for saying that, Papa," Elsie said, smiling up
at him. "I will try to tell you just what happened."

Carefully, she repeated everything that had occurred,
word-for-word when she could. Her account sounded very
different from her grandfather's, and she added that she had
tried to explain to Mr. Dinsmore that it was not unwilling-
ness to oblige Enna, but fear of doing wrong that led her to
refuse to tell the fairy story.

"Was I very naughty?" she asked when she had finished.

"So much depends on the tone," her father said honestly.
"If you spoke to your grandfather as you did in repeating

your words just now, then no, I don't think you were impertinent. But you must always treat your grandfather with respect. And understand that to him there is something quite unseemly about a little girl setting her opinion against that of her elders. You must never do that with me."

Elsie hung her head and asked, "Are you going to punish me, Papa?"

"Yes," he said, "but first I'm going to take you downstairs to ask your grandfather's pardon. I know you don't want to do it, but you must."

"I'll do whatever you want, Papa, but please tell me what to say."

"You must say 'Grandpa, I did not intend to be disrespectful, and I'm very sorry for whatever seemed impertinent in my words or tones. Will you please forgive me, and I will try always to be respectful in the future.' You can say all of that with truth, can't you?"

"Yes sir, because I am sorry and I do intend to be respectful to Grandpa always."

When they went to his father's room, Horace said, "Elsie has come to beg your pardon, sir."

Mr. Dinsmore, casting a triumphant look at his wife, said, "That's as it should be. I told the girl you wouldn't support any such impertinence."

"I will never support her in wrongdoing," Horace replied, a marked tone of displeasure in his voice, "but neither will I allow her to be imposed upon. Now speak, Elsie, what I told you to say."

When Elsie had sobbed out her apology, Mr. Dinsmore said coldly, "Yes, I must forgive you, girl, but I hope your father won't let you off without a proper punishment."

"I will attend to that," Horace replied in a tone as frosty as his father's. "I certainly intend to punish her *as she deserves*."

He had laid special stress on those final words, and Elsie totally misunderstood his meaning. She trembled so with fear that he had to carry her back to his room. When they were out of anyone's hearing, he wiped her tears away and said with a smile, "Don't be so afraid, Elsie. I'm not going to be severe."

She looked at him in glad surprise.

"I said I would punish you as you deserve, so I intend to keep you here with me until your bedtime. You can't go down to supper, and I'm going to give you a long lesson that you must be able to recite perfectly before you go to bed."

Elsie worried for a moment that the lesson might be something inappropriate for the Sabbath, but she relaxed when her father took his Bible and pointed to the thirteenth and fourteenth chapters of John.

"But that won't be a real punishment, Papa," she laughed. "I love these chapters, and I've read them so often I almost know all the words already."

Pretending to be very stern, Horace said, "Hush! Don't tell me my punishments are *no* punishments. Now take your book to that seat by the window and learn what I tell you."

Horace took up a newspaper, but in fact he spent most of his time looking at his child as she diligently studied the holy book. It struck him with great force how important she was to him, and he wondered how he could ever have been harsh with her.

When the supper bell rang, Horace got up to leave. "I'll send some supper up to you, and I want you to eat it," he said at the door.

"Will it be bread and water, Papa?" she asked with a smile.

"Wait and see," he laughed.

The tray of food that Pompey soon brought to Elsie was a far cry from the fare provided during her last imprisonment. Elsie was truly astonished when she saw a plate of hot, buttered muffins, a large piece of broiled chicken, a cup of jelly, and another cup filled to the brim with steaming coffee.

"I reckon you have been a very nice girl today," Pompey said as he set the tray down, "or else your Papa thinks you're a little sick."

As Elsie put away her book and began to eat, Pompey told her, "Just ring the bell if you want something more, and I'll fetch it for you. Your father told me so himself."

Elsie certainly enjoyed every crumb of her supper, and when Horace returned, she thanked him graciously. "But I thought you didn't allow me such things," she commented.

Playfully, he said, "Don't you know, Daughter, that I am absolute monarch of this small kingdom and you are not to question my decrees?"

His tone then became more serious, "I do not allow it as a rule, because I do not think it for your good. But this once, I don't think it will hurt. I know that you don't presume on favors, Elsie, and I wanted to indulge you a bit. I think you were made to suffer more than you deserved this afternoon."

His words were very tender, and before he went on, he kissed her gently on the forehead.

180

"Don't think, though, that I'm excusing you for impertinence. I am not. But what you had to endure from Enna's insolence — it will stop, for I will not have it."

"I don't mind it much, Papa," Elsie responded. "I'm used to it, for Enna has always treated me that way."

"And why did I never hear this before?" he asked, his temper rising. "It's abominable! Not to be endured! And I shall see that Miss Enna is made to understand that *my* daughter is fully her equal in every respect and to be treated as such."

Elsie, who was somewhat frightened at his vehemence, made no reply, and her father continued in a somewhat softer tone, "I have no doubt your grandfather and his wife would have liked me to force you to give in to Enna's whim. But you are to use your own judgment wherever Enna is concerned. If I had bidden you to tell her that story, well, that would have been a different matter. You are never to set your will, or your opinion of right and wrong, against mine, Elsie, for I won't allow it. I don't altogether like some of these strict notions of yours, and I give you fair warning — should they ever come into conflict with my wishes and commands, you are to give them up.

"But don't look so alarmed, Elsie," he added very kindly. "I hope that will never happen."

Her face was very serious as she lay her hand on his shoulder and said, "Oh, Papa! Please don't ever ask me to do anything wrong. It would break my heart."

"Elsie dear, I never want you to do wrong. On the contrary, I want you always to do right. But *I* must be the judge of what is right and wrong for you. Remember that you are only a little girl and not yet capable of judging for yourself. As long as you obey your father without hesitation, there will be no problem."

His tone was kind but firm, and Elsie had a strange sense as he spoke, as if she were in the shadow of some great, impending trouble. But with some effort, she managed to banish this feeling of foreboding and enjoy her present blessings. She knew that her father loved her dearly, and he was not requiring her to do anything against her conscience. Perhaps he never would. God could incline his heart to respect her principles. Or if the dreaded trial should happen, He would give her His wisdom and strength to bear it, for she remembered His promise, "And God is faithful; He will not let you be tempted beyond what you can bear. But when you are tempted, He will also provide a way out so that you can stand up under it."

"What are you thinking about?" Horace asked her at length.

"A good many things, Papa. I was thinking of what you said and how glad I am to know that you truly love me. And I was asking God to help us both to do His will. And I thought that I might be able to always do what you bid, without disobeying Him. May I say my lesson now? I think I know it perfectly."

"Of course," he said in an abstracted way.

Elsie brought the Bible to him and drew up a stool for herself beside his chair. With her arm over his knee, she began to repeat with great feeling the chapters she had learned — the touching description of the Last Supper and Jesus' farewell to His sorrowing disciples.

"Isn't it beautiful, Papa?" she asked when she had finished her recitation. "'Having loved His own who were in the world, he now showed them the full extent of His love,'" she quoted again.

"It seems so strange that Jesus could be so thoughtful of them when all the time He knew the dreadful death He was going to die. And He knew they were all going to run away and leave Him to His enemies. It's so sweet to know that Jesus is so loving and that He loves me and will love me forever."

"But do you think you are good enough for Jesus to love you?" Horace asked.

"I know I'm not at all good, Papa," she said with grave seriousness. "My thoughts and feelings are often wrong, and Jesus knows all about it. But that doesn't keep Him from loving me because it was sinners He died to save. How good and kind He is. And who could help loving Him?"

She looked up into her father's eyes, and Horace was surprised to see sadness there as she went on, "I used to feel so lonely sometimes, Papa, that I thought my heart would really break. I think I would have died if I had not had Jesus to love me."

Her words moved Horace deeply, and he asked, "When were you so lonely and sad, darling?"

"Sometimes when you were away and I'd never seen you, I used to think of you and my heart would ache to see you and have you hold me and call me Daughter, as you do now." She paused and had to struggle to keep back her tears. Then she said, "But when you came home, Papa, and I saw you didn't love me — oh, that was the worst. I just wanted to die and go to Jesus and to Mamma."

She broke into tears, and Horace lifted her to his lap, hugging her close. "It was very, very cruel of me," he said, his own voice choking with emotion. "I don't know how I could close my heart like that. But I had been much prejudiced and led to believe that you feared and disliked me as a cruel tyrant."

Elsie's Endless Wait

Elsie was amazed at this admission. "How could you think that, Papa? I've *always* loved you, ever since I can remember."

Later, in her own room, Elsie thought seriously of everything that had happened that day and everything her father had said. In her prayers, she expressed many thanks to the Lord that her father had learned to love her. Then she added a fervent petition that her father would come to love Jesus and would never bid her to break any of God's commands. But the gray shadow of foreboding had not vanished entirely, and storm clouds were already gathering in the distance.

CHAPTER

10

Elsie's Sabbath Day Choice

*"If you keep your feet from breaking the Sabbath
and from doing as you please on my holy day,
if you call the Sabbath a delight and the
Lord's holy day honorable, and if you
honor it by not going your own way
and not doing as you please or
speaking idle words, then you will
find your joy in the Lord...."*

ISAIAH 58:13–14

Elsie's Sabbath Day Choice

*O*n a Sabbath day some weeks later, quite a few guests had dined at Roselands and were gathered in the drawing room. The gentlemen were laughing and joking, talking of politics, and conversing with the ladies, and everyone was in high spirits.

Adelaide, noticing that one of the men was glancing about the room in an attitude of disappointment, said, "May I ask what you are searching for, Mr. Eversham?"

"Yes, Miss Adelaide. I was looking for little Elsie. Edward Travilla has given me such a glowing account of her musical talent that I hoped to hear her sing and play."

"And so you shall, Eversham," said Horace, who had overheard his guest's request. He crossed the room to summon a servant, but he was stopped by a hand on his arm.

"You'd better not send for her," Mrs. Dinsmore whispered.

"May I ask why not?" he inquired in a tone of annoyance.

"Because she will not sing," his stepmother replied coolly.

"Pardon me, madam, but I think she will, if I bid it."

Though Horace was becoming heated at the woman's words, Mrs. Dinsmore maintained her cool, haughty manner as she said, "No, she will not. She will tell you she is wiser than her father and that it will be a sin to obey you. Believe me, Horace, she will defy your authority. You had better take my advice and leave her alone. Save yourself from the embarrassment."

Horace, biting his lip to control his anger, replied, "Thank you, madam, but I believe this lies solely in your imagination. I'm at a loss to understand you, for Elsie has never shown the slightest resistance to my authority."

With a slight arch of her eyebrow, Mrs. Dinsmore left him, and Horace gave the bell rope a hard pull. A servant appeared and was sent to summon Elsie. Horace joined a group around the piano, where Adelaide had just begun to play.

Though outwardly calm, Horace was already having doubts about his action. He had never understood the full depth of his child's convictions, and in his desire to display Elsie's talents, he had forgotten her conscientious scruples about the observance of the Sabbath. But he saw clearly that there would be a struggle, for on a point of principle, Elsie would be as unyielding as he. Though he felt sure Elsie would obey him in the end, he might have avoided the conflict but for his pride. He had gone too far to retreat, and perhaps, he told himself, it was just as well that this inevitable struggle should take place here and now.

When the servant came to her room with her father's message, Elsie immediately sensed what was about to occur. Elsie had been taught since her earliest days that the Sabbath is a day to rest and honor God by focusing on Him. With alarm now, she said to herself, "Papa wants me to do something that is not right on the Sabbath." Though she hoped that she was wrong, she nevertheless knelt quickly and prayed to the Lord for the strength to do right.

Elsie's Sabbath Day Choice

When she entered the drawing room, her father greeted her affectionately, but Elsie turned pale as he led her to the piano where Adelaide had just finished playing. He selected a piece of music that Elsie had learned during their holiday and handed it to her. "My friends are anxious to hear you play and sing," he said, "and I think this song will be perfect."

In almost a whisper, she said, "Won't tomorrow do, Papa?"

From the corner of his eye, Horace caught the smug expression of Mrs. Dinsmore as he replied to Elsie, "Certainly not, Daughter. You know this piece very well without more practice."

"That's not the reason," the little girl said. "But you know today is the holy Sabbath."

"What of it, child?" he asked, struggling to keep his voice mild. "I consider this song perfectly proper to be sung today. That should satisfy you that you are not doing wrong. Remember what I told you a few weeks ago. Now, sit down and sing."

"Oh, Papa, I can't sing it today! Please let me wait until tomorrow!"

But in his most stern manner, Horace commanded Elsie to sit and perform. She complied to the extent of taking the stool, but with her eyes full of tears, she again refused to sing. "I can't, Papa! I can't break the Sabbath," she cried in heartfelt agony.

"You must," he said as he placed the music before her. "I've told you it will not be breaking the Sabbath, and you must let me be the judge."

At this point, several of the guests urged Horace to let the matter go. Adelaide good-naturedly said, "Let me play it, Horace. I think I can do it almost as well as Elsie."

189

Horace could not be swayed. "I have given my child a command, and it must be obeyed," he said sternly. "She may not set her opinion of right and wrong against mine."

But Elsie, tears streaming down her face, made no move to obey her father. An uncomfortable silence settled on everyone for a few moments, until Horace finally said, "You shall sit here until you obey me, Elsie, no matter how long it takes."

"Yes, Papa," she replied, her words barely audible, and with relief, the guests drifted away from the scene.

Horace went to join a group of the men when Mrs. Dinsmore halted him with a remark. "I told you," she said in a low, self-satisfied tone, "how it would end."

"But it hasn't ended," Horace snapped, "and before it does, Elsie will know who has the stronger will."

Though none of the guests talked to her, Elsie felt that they were all looking at her, and the embarrassment was hard to bear. She was deeply troubled, too, by the thought that her father's displeasure would lead to the withdrawal of his affection entirely. As the time passed, she became extremely uncomfortable on the little seat of the music stool. It was an unusually warm fall afternoon, and the sultry heat of the drawing room caused her head to throb. Feeling that she might faint, she leaned forward and rested her head on the piano.

She had sat this way for almost two hours, when Edward Travilla came to her side. "I'm so sorry for you, my little friend," he said gently, "but I advise you to submit to your father. You can never conquer him, for I've never known a more determined man. Won't you sing the song? It will only take a few minutes, and your trouble will be over."

Elsie's Sabbath Day Choice

Elsie raised her tear-stained face. "But, Mr. Travilla, I don't want to conquer my father," she said earnestly. "I want to obey him in everything and honor him as the Bible tells me. But I can't disobey God, even to please my Papa."

"But, Elsie, would it really be disobeying God? Is there any verse in the Bible that says you must not sing songs on Sunday?"

"The Bible says to keep the Sabbath *holy*. It says that we are not to do as we please or go our own way or speak idle words. We're to rest from our work and honor God by giving all our attention to Him. We're to study the Bible, or worship and praise Him. But, Mr. Travilla, there's not a word of praise in that song. Not one word about God or heaven. I wish it were a song of praise; then I could obey my father."

Seeing that he could not convince the child, in spite of her obvious desire to please her father, Edward approached his friend. "Horace," he said, "I'm convinced that Elsie is entirely conscientious. Won't you give in to her in this instance?"

"Never!" Horace replied with some consternation. "This is the first time she has rebelled against my authority, and if she succeeds, she will expect to have her way always. I must subdue her now, whatever the cost."

The elder Mr. Dinsmore added his hearty agreement. "Quite right," he said. "Let her know from the start that you are the master."

"But I have to question a parent's right to coerce a child to act against her conscience," Edward contended, then added in a lowered voice. "You know, my friend, that this is no rebellion against you but entirely a matter of faith."

"Nonsense!" Horace replied harshly, but in truth this battle of wills with his daughter was wearing him down

191

almost as much as his poor child. "Elsie must learn to let me be the judge in these matters for many years to come."

Edward Travilla was not the only guest discomforted by Horace's strong discipline. At the moment, Mr. Eversham, who was feeling regret and responsibility for what had happened, was asking Adelaide if she might tell him how to repair the situation. But Adelaide could only shake her head sadly. "There's no moving my brother," she said, "and as for Elsie, I doubt any power on earth can make her do what she considers wrong."

"But where did she get such odd notions?" Eversham asked.

"Partly from the Scottish lady who cared for her for many years," Adelaide explained, "and partly from her Bible study. She is forever reading her Bible. I think it would break the child's heart to do anything that she sincerely believes would betray her faith."

"Then I can do nothing," Mr. Eversham said with a sigh.

Another hour dragged by, and when the supper bell rang, Horace went to his daughter and asked her once more to sing the song. She again refused.

"Very well," he said in a voice that no longer held any anger. "You know I cannot break my word. You must stay here until you obey, and you cannot eat until you do. Your obstinacy is causing great pain for us both."

After supper, the guests moved to the veranda where the breeze was cool, and Elsie was left alone in the darkening drawing room. The air inside the room seemed to draw close around her, and at times she could barely get her breath. Her whole body ached, and the pain pounded in her head. Her thoughts began to wander, and she forgot where she was. Her head seemed to spin, and everything swirled in confusion until she finally lost all consciousness.

Horace, Edward, and several others were talking just outside the drawing room when a sudden noise as of something falling startled them. Edward rushed inside, and seeing a small bundle by the piano, he rushed to Elsie.

"A light, quick!" he shouted as he raised the child. "She's fainted."

One of the men found a lamp and brought it close. In the light, they could see Elsie's deathly pale face and a stream of blood from a gash on her temple. She was a pitiable sight — her hair, face, and neat white dress covered with blood.

"Horace, you're a brute!" Edward said as he gently laid the child on a sofa. Horace bent over his little girl, but he was too anguished to make a reply.

Fortunately, there was a physician among the guests, and he hurried to treat Elsie's wound and give her restoring medication. But it was some time before she returned to consciousness, and her father was all this while terrified that she might die. But when her eyes at last opened, she gazed at Horace and asked, "Are you angry with me, Papa?"

"No, no, my darling child," he murmured. "Not at all."

"But what happened?" she asked in bewilderment. "What did I do?"

"Not a thing," he assured. "You were ill, but you are better now, so don't think any more about it."

The doctor said Elsie should be put to bed at once, and Horace tenderly cradled her in his arms and carried her upstairs.

"There's blood on my dress, Papa," Elsie said weakly.

"You fell and hurt your head, but you will be fine now."

"Oh! I remember," she moaned.

 193

Horace helped Chloe, who was steady as a rock even at the sight of so much blood, and they prepared Elsie for bed.

"Are you hungry, darling?" Horace asked.

"No, Papa, I just want to sleep."

So Horace carried her to the bed and was about to tuck her in when Elsie suddenly cried, "My prayers, Papa!"

"Not tonight, dear. You're too weak.

"Please, Papa. I can't sleep otherwise."

So he helped her to her knees and listened as she spoke. To his surprise, he heard his own name mentioned more than once, coupled with a request that he should come to love Jesus.

When Elsie was at last wrapped in her covers, he asked, "Why did you pray that I might love Jesus?"

"Because I want you to be happy, and I want you to go to heaven, Papa."

"And what makes you think I don't love Him?"

"Don't be angry, Papa, but you know what Jesus says: 'Whoever has my commands and obeys them, he is the one who loves me.'" As Horace leaned down to kiss her good night, Elsie threw her arms around his neck and whispered, "I love you very, very much."

"Better than anyone else?" he asked with a smile.

"I love Jesus best, and you next."

When she woke the next morning, Elsie felt nearly as good as ever. After her bath, Chloe carefully brushed her hair so the curls concealed the bandage on her temple, and except for a slight paleness, there was nothing about Elsie's appearance to betray the accident.

She was reading her morning Bible chapter when her father came in and sat down beside her. "You look very pretty this morning," he said, winning a sweet smile. "How do you feel?"

"Fine, Papa."

"Do you know that you came very near dying last night?"

Elsie's face showed obvious disbelief, and Horace explained, in a voice that trembled with emotion, "The doctor says that if the wound had been half an inch nearer your eye.... Well, I might have lost my little girl."

Elsie said nothing for a few moments, then she asked, very softly, "Would you have been very sorry?"

"Oh, Elsie," he said, almost overcome by her question. "You are more precious to me than all my wealth, all my friends, and all my family. I would rather part with everything else than lose you."

She lapsed into silence again until he inquired what was on her mind now.

"I was just wondering whether I was ready to go to heaven, Papa. I think I was. I know I love Jesus, and I know Mamma would be glad to see me. Don't you think she would?"

"I can't spare you yet," he said, trying to keep his emotions under control, "and I think she loves me too well to wish it, dearest child."

Elsie continued to consider these things solemnly that morning, and as there was no school and her father was called into a business discussion, she retreated to the garden to read her Bible. She had been alone there for some time when she heard someone approaching. It was Edward Travilla.

He saw how intent she looked, and sitting beside her, he glanced at the book she held.

"What can you be reading that affects you so?" he asked.

"Oh, Mr. Travilla, doesn't it make your heart ache to read how our dear Savior was so abused, and then to know it was all because of our sins. Isn't it wonderful to know that we can be saved from the penalty for our sins, and be His friend now, and someday go to heaven?"

Her ideas intrigued him. "Really, Elsie," he said, "you are quite right, but aren't such ideas very serious for a young girl like you?"

"Mr. Travilla," she exclaimed. "These ideas bring me such peace and joy. When I read my Bible like this, I sometimes feel as if Jesus were sitting here beside me, just as you are."

"Can a person really be that close to God?" he asked half-jokingly.

"Oh yes, sir. Our dear Savior wants all His children to draw near to Him. You only have to *want* to spend time with Him, for He is always ready and waiting with His love," she replied.

"And how did you come to have such a close relationship with Jesus?"

"Aunt Chloe and Mrs. Murray taught me from the Bible, Mr. Travilla, that everyone who calls on the name of the Lord will be saved. I was just a little girl when I asked Him to forgive my sins and come into my heart."

"Then perhaps you know these words," he said and quoted, "'For God so loved the world that He gave His one and only Son, that whoever believes in Him shall not perish but have eternal life. For God did not send His Son into the world to condemn the world, but to save the world through Him.'"

Elsie nodded, for she knew the verses well.

Elsie's Sabbath Day Choice

Edward, who found himself curious about the depth of the child's faith, went on, "Do you think it is necessary for a person to ask in order to be saved, my little friend? What of a person who simply leads an honest, upright, and moral life? Cannot that person be saved?"

Elsie thought for several moments, then said slowly, "I know that the Bible teaches that there is not a person on earth who always does right and never sins. The Bible says it is by *grace* that we are saved, through our faith in Jesus — not by our good deeds. I don't think we could ever be perfect enough to win God's love and forgiveness. But we don't have to be perfect, because God gives us His gifts freely. The Bible says that we only have to believe with our hearts and confess with our mouths that Jesus Christ is Lord, that He died for our sins and rose from the dead. Do you remember, Mr. Travilla, that the Bible tells us that to enter the Kingdom of God we must be 'born again'?"

"And do you know what is meant by being born again?"

"It means that when we accept Jesus' death on the cross as payment for our sins," Elsie explained as carefully as she could, "then God's Holy Spirit comes to live in us and changes our hearts. We are born into a new life. That's the life of the Spirit, Mr. Travilla. And our change of heart makes us want to honor Jesus and be like Him and please Him in every way — not because we have to, but because we love Him and *want* to do it."

As Edward looked into Elsie's solemn little face, he suddenly remembered something else Jesus had said: "I praise you, Father, Lord of heaven and earth, because you have hidden these things from the wise and learned, and revealed them to little children." It was now obvious to Edward that the child had been very well taught, but he marveled that her acceptance of these great Bible truths was so natural. "No wonder," he thought to himself, "that Jesus spoke of the need to have 'faith as a little child.'"

Suddenly Edward saw tears welling in Elsie's bright eyes, and in an attempt to jolly her out of this serious mood, he said teasingly, "Well, my little friend, let us hope that everyone will repent and believe before they die."

But Elsie heard nothing humorous in his comment. She looked at him and asked, "Do you know how near I came to death last night? Then you know there can never be time enough, Mr. Travilla."

Edward, still wondering at this child's unusual spiritual maturity, quoted, more to himself than his little companion, "Blessed are the pure in heart for they shall see God."

Realizing that the morning was almost over and they would soon be expected for dinner, Edward hurriedly walked Elsie back to the house where the guests were gathered in the drawing room. When Horace saw his daughter enter the room, he asked her to sing, and Elsie obliged with enthusiasm. Her performance made her father very proud indeed.

For all his outward reserve, the events of the previous day had greatly deepened Horace's tender feelings for his daughter. His one desire now was to protect her from all dangers and to save her from the unhappiness of so many children who were raised without discipline. His own brother Arthur, not yet in his teens, was already a liar and a sneak. Horace would never let such a fate befall his beloved child. In their short time together, she had become more important to him than his own life.

Looking into Elsie's lovely face, so much like his lost wife's, he wondered how he could ever have been prejudiced against her or doubted her love for him. One thing he would never forget, and that was how close he had been to losing his precious little Elsie forever.

As Elsie began to sing another cheerful song for her father, Edward, standing somewhat apart from the group around the piano, regarded his old friend closely. Although he often disagreed with Horace's stern methods, he knew that Horace only wanted what was best for the child and had come to love Elsie as much as she loved him.

"But his love may not be enough," Edward thought, "for I fear Horace still does not share the deeper love that is Elsie's first loyalty. Can he ever understand how God's love sustained her through all those lonely years when her earthly father was absent? I wonder what their future will be. Can their happiness survive another clash between Horace's pride and Elsie's faith?"

Edward was so deep in his musings that he failed to notice when Adelaide came to stand at his side.

"Why, Mr. Travilla," she said brightly, "what makes you look so gloomy on this happy day?"

Quickly recalling himself to the present, Edward replied with a smile, "Not gloomy at all, Miss Dinsmore. It is only that the sight of your brother and your niece reminded me of some words of Scripture I learned many years ago."

Adelaide followed Edward's gaze to Elsie's shining face. "And will you share those words with me, Mr. Travilla?" she asked.

Edward began to speak with an intensity that surprised Adelaide. "'Let the little children come to me,'" he quoted, "'and do not hinder them, for the Kingdom of God belongs to such as these.'"

Are Elsie's troubles *really* over?
Will her father *ever* understand her and the deep faith that guides her?
Can she find love at Roselands?

Elsie's story continues in:

ELSIE'S IMPOSSIBLE CHOICE

Book Two of the
*A Life of Faith:
Elsie Dinsmore* Series

Available at your local bookstore

Collect all of our Elsie Dinsmore books and companion products!

A Life of Faith: Elsie Dinsmore

* Now Available as a Dramatized Audiobook!

Check out
www.alifeoffaith.com

- Get news about Elsie and her cousin Millie
- Find out more about the 19th century world they live in
- Learn to live a life of faith like they do
- Learn how they overcome the difficulties we all face in life
- Find out about Elsie and Millie products
- Join our girls' club

A Life of Faith: Elsie Dinsmore
"It's Like Having a Best Friend From Another Time"

Collect all of our Millie products!

A Life of Faith: Millie Keith Series

* Now Available as a Dramatized Audiobook!

— ABOUT THE AUTHOR —

*M*artha Finley was born on April 26, 1828, in Chillicothe, Ohio. Her mother died when Martha was quite young, and James Finley, her father, soon remarried. Martha's stepmother, Mary Finley, was a kind and caring woman who always nurtured Martha's desire to learn and supported her ambition to become a writer.

James Finley, a doctor and devout Christian, moved his family to South Bend, Indiana, in the mid-1830s. It was a large family: Martha had three older sisters and a younger brother who were eventually joined by two half-sisters and a half-brother. The Finleys were of Scotch-Irish heritage, with deep roots in the Presbyterian Church. Martha's grandfather, Samuel Finley, served in the Revolutionary War and the War of 1812 and was a personal friend of President George Washington. A great-uncle, also named Samuel Finley, had served as president of Princeton Theological Seminary in New Jersey.

Martha was well educated for a girl of her times and spent a year at a boarding school in Philadelphia. After her father's death in 1851, she began her teaching career in Indiana. She later lived with an elder sister in New York City, where Martha continued teaching and began writing stories for Sunday school children. She then joined her widowed stepmother in Philadelphia, where her early stories were first published by the Presbyterian Publication Board. She lived and taught for two years at a private academy in Phoenixville, Pennsylvania — until the school was closed in

1860, just before the outbreak of the War Between the States.

Determined to become a full-time writer, Martha returned to Philadelphia. Even though she sold several stories (some written under the pen name of "Martha Farquharson"), her first efforts at novel-writing were not successful. But during a period of recuperation from a fall, she crafted the basics of a book that would make her one of the country's best known and most beloved novelists.

Three years after Martha began writing *Elsie Dinsmore*, the story of the lonely little Southern girl was accepted by the New York firm of Dodd Mead. The publishers divided the original manuscript into two complete books; they also honored Martha's request that pansies (flowers, Martha explained, that symbolized "thoughts of you") be printed on the books' covers. Released in 1868, *Elsie Dinsmore* became the publisher's best-selling book that year, launching a series that sold millions of copies at home and abroad.

The Elsie stories eventually expanded to twenty-eight volumes and included the lives of Elsie's children and grandchildren. Miss Finley published her final Elsie novel in 1905. Four years later, she died less than three months before her eighty-second birthday. She is buried in Elkton, Maryland, where she lived for more than thirty years in the house she built with proceeds from her writing career. Her large estate, carefully managed by her youngest brother, Charles, was left to family members and charities.

Martha Finley was a remarkable woman who lived a quiet Christian life; yet through her many writings, she affected the lives of several generations of Americans for the better. She never married, never had children, yet she left behind a unique legacy of faith.

Beloved Literary Characters
Come to Life!

*E*lsie Dinsmore and Millie Keith are now available as lovely designer dolls from Mission City Press.

*M*ade of soft-molded vinyl, these beautiful, fully jointed 18¾" dolls come dressed in historically accurate clothing and accessories. They wonderfully reflect the biblical virtues that readers have come to know and love about Elsie and Millie.

For more information, visit www.alifeoffaith.com or check with your local Christian retailer.

A Life of Faith Products from Mission City Press

"It's like Having a Best Friend from Another Time"

Also by Peter Godwin

Mukiwa:
A White Boy in Africa

Wild at Heart:
Man and Beast in Southern Africa
(PHOTOGRAPHS BY CHRIS JOHNS, FOREWORD BY NELSON MANDELA)

The Three of Us: A New Life in New York
(WRITTEN WITH JOANNA COLES)

"Rhodesians Never Die":
The Impact of War and Political Change
on White Rhodesia, c. 1970–1980
(WRITTEN WITH IAN HANCOCK)

WHEN A CROCODILE
EATS THE SUN

WHEN A CROCODILE
EATS THE SUN

A MEMOIR OF AFRICA

Peter Godwin

LITTLE, BROWN AND COMPANY
New York • Boston • London

Little, Brown and Company
Hachette Book Group USA
237 Park Avenue, New York, NY 10169
Visit our Web site at www.HachetteBookGroupUSA.com

First U.S. Edition: April 2007
First Published in South Africa in 2006 by Picador Africa

All photographs from the Godwin Family collection. Used by permission.
Map by George W. Ward

Library of Congress Cataloging-in-Publication Data
Godwin, Peter.
When a crocodile eats the sun : a memoir of Africa / Peter Godwin. — 1st ed.
        p.   cm.
ISBN 978-0-316-15894-7
    1. Godwin, Peter.   2. Godwin, Peter—Family.   3. Zimbabwe—
History—1980- —Biography.   4. Family secrets—Zimbabwe—Case studies.
5. Fathers and sons—Zimbabwe—Case studies.   6. Harare (Zimbabwe)—
Biography.   7. Whites—Zimbabwe—Biography.   8. Journalists—Biography.
9. Godwin, Peter—Travel—Africa, Southern.   10. Africa, Southern—
Description and travel.   I. Title.
DT2999.G63A3 2007
968.9105'1092—DC22   2006027973
[B]

10 9 8 7 6 5 4 3 2 1

Q-FF
Book design by Meryl Sussman Levavi
Printed in the United States of America

IN MEMORY OF GEORGE GODWIN

For the next generation
Hugo, Thomas, Holly, and Xanthe

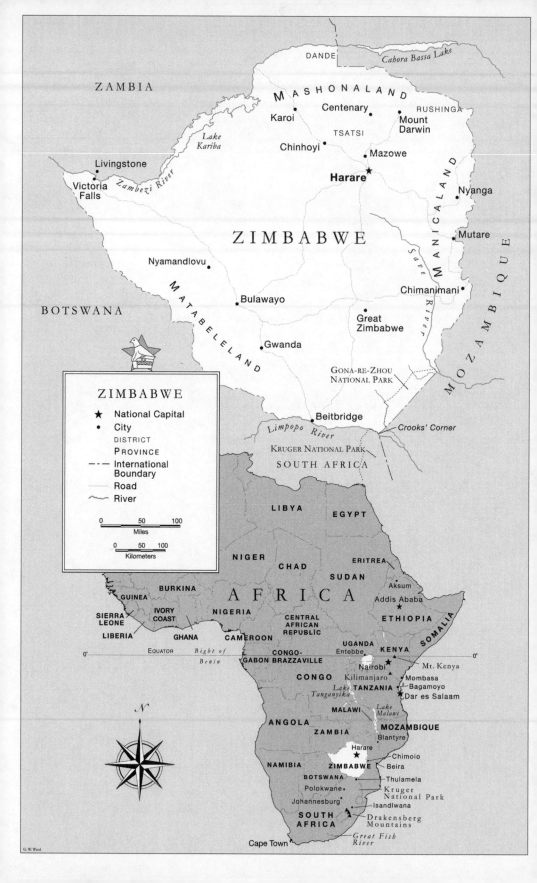

ZAMBIA

DANDE

Cahora Bassa Lake

M A S H O N A L A N D

Centenary •

Karoi •

RUSHINGA

Mount
Darwin •

TSATSI

*Lake
Kariba*

Chinhoyi •

• Mazowe

M A N I C A L A N D

Livingstone •

Zambezi River

Harare ★

• Nyanga

Victoria
Falls

Z I M B A B W E

• Mutare

Nyamandlovu •

Save

Chimanimani •

M A T A B E L E L A N D

• Bulawayo

River

M O Z A M B I Q U E

BOTSWANA

Great
Zimbabwe •

• Gwanda

GONA-RE-ZHOU
NATIONAL PARK

ZIMBABWE

★ National Capital

• City

DISTRICT

PROVINCE

—·— International
Boundary

········· Road

——— River

• Beitbridge

Limpopo River

Crooks' Corner

KRUGER NATIONAL PARK

SOUTH AFRICA

0	50	100

Miles

0	50	100

Kilometers

LIBYA

EGYPT

NIGER

CHAD

SUDAN

ERITREA

A F R I C A

• Aksum

GUINEA

BURKINA

NIGERIA

CENTRAL
AFRICAN
REPUBLIC

Addis Ababa ★

SIERRA
LEONE

IVORY
COAST

ETHIOPIA

SOMALIA

LIBERIA

GHANA

CAMEROON

UGANDA

KENYA

0°

EQUATOR *Bight of
Benin*

CONGO-
BRAZZAVILLE

Entebbe •

GABON

Mt. Kenya

0°

Nairobi •

CONGO

Kilimanjaro

Mombasa

*Lake
Tanganyika*

TANZANIA

• Bagamoyo
★ Dar es Salaam

MALAWI

*Lake
Malawi*

ANGOLA

ZAMBIA

MOZAMBIQUE

Blantyre •

Harare ★

Chimoio •

NAMIBIA

ZIMBABWE

Beira •

BOTSWANA

Thulamela •

Polokwane •

Kruger
National Park

Johannesburg •

Isandlwana

SOUTH
AFRICA

Drakensberg
Mountains

Cape Town •

*Great Fish
River*

N

G. W. Ward

*WHEN A CROCODILE
EATS THE SUN*

M Y FATHER IS NOW more than an hour late. We sit on a mossy stone bench under a giant fig tree, waiting for him. We have finished the little Chinese thermos of coffee that my mother prepared, and the sandwiches.

Tapera looks up. The motion pleats the base of his shaven skull into an accordion of glistening brown flesh.

"At last," he says. "He is arrived."

The car, long and low and sinister, glides slowly toward us, only the black roof visible above the reef of elephant grass. It passes us and then backs up into position.

Keith jumps out of the passenger side.

"Sorry we're late," he says. "We were stopped at a police road-block up on Rotten Row. They wanted to check inside. Can you believe it?"

He hands me a clipboard. "Sign here and here."

The driver reaches down to unlatch the tailgate. It opens with a gentle hydraulic sigh. Inside is a steel coffin. Together we slide it out and carry it over to the concrete steps. Keith unlatches the lid to reveal a body tightly bound in a white linen winding-sheet.

"Why don't you take the top," he says.

I ease one hand under the back of my father's head and my other arm under his shoulders, and I give him a last little hug. He is cool and surprisingly soft to my touch. The others arrange themselves along his body, and on Keith's count we lift it out of the coffin.

We shuffle up the concrete stairs that lead to the top of the iron crib. We have woven fresh green branches through its black bars. And on top of the tiers of logs inside it, we have placed a thick bed of pine needles and garnished it with fragrant pine shavings. Upon this bed we lay my father down.

Gently, Tapera lifts Dad's head to place a small eucalyptus log under his neck as a pillow. As he does so the shroud peeks open at a fold, and I get a sudden, shocking glimpse of my father's face. His jaw, grizzled with salt-and-pepper stubble; the little dents on his nose where his glasses rested; his mustache, slightly shaggy and unkempt now; the lines of his brow relaxed at last in death. And then, as his head settles back, the shroud stretches shut again, and he is gone.

Tapera is staggering up the steps with a heavy musasa log. He places it on top of the body.

"Huuuh." My father exhales one last loud breath with the weight of it.

"It is necessary," Tapera says quietly, "to hold the body down in case . . ." He pauses to think if there is a way to say this delicately. "In case it explodes because of the buildup of the gases." He looks unhappily at the ground. "It happens sometimes, you know."

Keith slides the empty coffin back into the hearse and drives away down the lane, where it is soon swallowed up again by the green gullet of grass.

The old black grave digger, Robert, has his hand in front of me now. His palm is yellow and barnacled with calluses. He is offering me a small Bic lighter made of fluorescent blue plastic.

"It is traditional for the son to light the fire," says Tapera, and he nods me forward.

I stroke my father's brow gently through the shroud, kiss his forehead. Then I flick the lighter. It fires up on my third trembling attempt, and I walk slowly around the base of the trolley, lighting the kindling. It crackles and pops as the flames take hold and shiver up the tower of logs to lick at the linen shroud. Quickly, before the cloth burns away to reveal the scorched flesh beneath, Tapera hands me a long metal T-bar and instructs me to place it against the back of the trolley, while he does the same next to me. We both heave at it. For a moment the trolley remains stuck on its rusty rails. Then it groans into motion and squeaks slowly toward the jaws of the old redbrick kiln a few yards away.

"Sorry it's so difficult," says Tapera, breathing heavily with the effort. "The wheel bearings are shot."

The flaming pyre enters the kiln and lurches to rest against the buffers. Robert, the grave digger, clangs shut the cast-iron doors and pulls down the heavy latch to lock them.

We all squint up into the brilliant blue sky to see if the fire is drawing. A plume of milky smoke flows up from the chimney stack, up through the green and red canopy of the overhanging flame tree.

"She is a good fire," says Tapera. "She burns well."

one

July 1996

I AM ON ASSIGNMENT in Zululand for *National Geographic* magazine when I get the news that my father is gravely ill.

It is night, and I am sitting around a fire with Prince Galenja Biyela. I am sitting lower than he is to show due respect. Biyela is ninety-something—he doesn't know exactly—tall and thin and straight backed, with hair and beard quite white. Around his shoulders, he has draped a leopard skin in such a way that the tail lies straight down his chest, like a furry necktie. A yard of mahogany shin gleams between his tattered sneakers and the cuffs of his trousers. His long fingers are closed around the gnarled head of a knobkerrie, a cudgel.

"All is well," he declares.

It is his only English phrase. He speaks in classical Zulu, his words almost Italianate, lubricated by vowels at either end.

His tribal acolytes start chanting his praise names.

"You are the bull that paws the earth," they call.

"Your highness," they sing, "we will bow down to the one who growls."

Prince Biyela's grandfather, Nkosani—the small king—of the Black Mamba regiment, was the hero of Isandlwana, the battle in which the Zulus famously trounced the mighty British Empire in 1879. Tonight, the old prince wishes to revel in the glory days, to relive the humbling of the white man.

He tells me how the British watched in awe as twenty-five thousand Zulu warriors stepped over the skyline and began to advance, chanting all the while, and stopping every so often to stomp the ground in unison, sending a tremor through the earth that could be felt for miles. He tells me how the *impi,* the Zulu regiments, were armed with short stabbing spears, *ixlwa,* a word you pronounce by pulling your tongue off the roof of your mouth, a word that deliberately imitates the sucking sound made by a blade when it's pulled out of human flesh.

As the warriors advanced, he says, their places on the ridge above were taken by thousands of Zulu women, urging on their army in the traditional way by ululating, an eerie high-pitched keening that filled the air.

Biyela tells me how the Black Mamba regiment was cut down by withering gunfire until, he says, after nearly two hours, the force "was as small as a sparrow's kidney," and the remaining men were on their bellies, taking cover. And how his grandfather, Nkosani, seeing what was happening, strode up to the front line, dressed in all his princely paraphernalia—his ostrich plume headdress and his lion claw necklaces—and berated them. Electrified by his example, the young warriors leaped up and again surged forward, overwhelming the men of the British line, even as Nkosani was felled by a British sniper with a single shot to the head.

And in the final stages of the battle, when the handful of surviving British soldiers had run out of bullets, a most unusual event occurred. The moon passed in front of the sun, and the earth grew dark, like night. And the Zulu *impi* stopped their killing while this eclipse took place. But when the light returned, they resumed the bloodletting.

Biyela tells me that night how his grandfather's warriors, having overrun the main British camp, dashed from tent to tent mopping up the stragglers — the cooks and the messengers and the drummer boys — until they crashed into one tent to find a newspaper correspondent sitting at his campaign table, penning his report.

"Just like you are now," he says to me, and his acolytes all laugh until Biyela raises his hand for silence.

"They said to him, '*Hau!* What are you doing in here, sitting at a table? Why aren't you out there fighting?' And this man, he was a local white who could speak some Zulu, he said, 'I am writing a report on the battle, for my people.'

" 'Oh,' they said, 'all right.' And they left him.

"But soon afterward, when they heard that my grandfather Nkosani had been shot, they ran back to the tent and said to the journalist there, 'Now that our *induna* [leader] has been killed, there is no point in making a report anymore,' and with that they killed him."

Biyela's men nod. I keep writing.

At the end, according to the few British soldiers who escaped, the Zulus went mad with bloodlust, killing even the horses and the mules and the oxen. They disemboweled each dead British soldier so that his spirit could escape his body and not haunt his killer. And if an enemy soldier had been seen to be particularly brave, the *impi* cut out his gallbladder and sucked on it, to absorb the dead man's courage, and bellowed, *"Igatla!"*— "I have eaten!"

And that night Biyela tells me how, once the battlefield fell quiet, a great wail was heard from the retinue of the Zulu women, as they mourned their dead. And this wail moved like a ripple through village after village until finally it reached the Zulu capital, Ulundi, fifty miles distant.

And here, Prince Biyela ends his telling, choosing not to dwell on what followed the Zulu victory. For the eclipse of the sun was a bad portent, and it drew down terrible times—the British reinforced and quickly snuffed out the independent Zulu nation. But still their spirit was not entirely doused. Their ferocity was merely curbed, and there was a sullen dignity to their defeat. It is said that before they would sign the surrender proclamation, one old *induna* stood and said to Sir Garnet Wolseley, "Today we will admit that we are your dogs, but you must first write it there, that the other tribes are the fleas on our backs."

Prince Biyela pauses to gulp another shot of the Queen's tears, as the Zulus call Natal gin, and the silence is jarred by a ring tone.

"*uMakhalekhukhwini,*" says one of his acolytes—it means "the screaming in the pocket," Zulu for *cell phone*—and they all grope around in the dark in their jackets and bags. It turns out to be mine. I reach in to cut it off, but it's my parents' number in Zimbabwe, eight hundred miles to the north. They never call just to chat. I excuse myself.

My mother's voice sounds strained. "It's your father," she says. "He's had a heart attack. I think you'd better come home."

two

July 1996

THAT NIGHT I climb up out of the valley to my car, which is
parked on the red-basalt plateau above. Trumpeter hornbills,
disturbed from their sleep, call as I pass by, a sound like an enraged
cat's screech. The hillside is peppered with thorny leafed aloe, a
plant sacred to the Zulu. They dig their graves under aloes because
these succulents are poisonous to hyenas, which might otherwise
dig up the bodies and eat them. Many of the aloes here mark the
graves of Zulu warriors felled at Isandlwana.

From my school days in rural Zimbabwe come fragments of a
gory Kipling poem. It is called "The Hyaenas," and it starts like this:

> *After the burial-parties leave*
> *And the baffled kites have fled*
> *The wise hyaenas come out at eve*
> *To take account of our dead.*
>
> *How he died and why he died*
> *Troubles them not a whit*

They snout the bushes and stones aside
And dig till they come to it.

They are only resolute they shall eat
That they and their mates shall thrive,
And they know that the dead are safer meat
Than the weakest thing alive.

"When I die," I told my mother, after learning the poem at the age of nine or ten, "will you make sure you cremate me?"

"Good heavens, don't be silly," she said brightly. "You're not going to *die*. And anyway, we're going to die before you. But no one's going to die yet. Not for a long, long time, anyway."

But now, this is that long, long time away. And soon, I expect, I will have to foil Kipling's hyenas on my father's behalf.

I drive fast through the night toward Johannesburg, where I will catch the plane home. Along my left flows the dark towering spine of mountains, the range the Zulus call *uKhahlamba,* "the Barrier of the Spears," though in the atlas they bear a more recent Afrikaans name, Drakensberg (Dragon) Mountains. I am familiar with these mountains, with this country. As a boy, growing up in Zimbabwe, I used to come down here occasionally on vacation. The first snow I ever saw was on these peaks, bright white upon these dark spear tips. And I came back here as a foreign correspondent for five years beginning in 1986, covering what turned out to be the death throes of apartheid. Since then, I have been based out of London, though I come back often to Africa, and I know in my bones that I will return here to live one day, that this is still my home. Contemplating my father's death, I realize how seldom we have lived in the same place. How remote I have been from him all my life. I have been a largely absent son, at boarding school from the age of six, then military service, university in England, working abroad.

As I drive, I dial my mother to make sure my father is still alive.

His heart is racing at nearly two hundred beats a minute, she says — that's faster than the pulse of a teenage sprinter, unsustainably high for a man in his seventies. They've tried everything to lower it, but he's just not responding. My mother is a doctor, so she knows about these things.

"Is there anything I can bring?" I ask.

"No," she says. "Just get up here as quickly as you can."

AHEAD OF ME, a golden glow slowly appears. Soon, this sodium dome obscures all but the brightest stars. It is Johannesburg. The sun rising behind me catches on the latticed steel headgear above the gold mines, and shimmers the glass of the high-rise offices in the city center. On my left, from the elevated highway that swoops across the city, I can see Soweto, a township I knew well when it was burning and barricaded. Dawn is heralded there with the switching off of the stadium-style floodlights perched on tall gantries around the township.

The screaming in the pocket starts again.

"He's still hanging on," my mother quickly reassures me. She has called to tell me of a new class of drug she has just heard about, one for exactly this condition. "It's not available here, but it might be in South Africa," she says with a sigh, and that's all it takes. Now I have a task, a way to help my father.

I CHECK INTO the Grace Hotel in northern Johannesburg and sit with the open Yellow Pages, making calls to pharmacies and hospitals. I recruit various friends to help, but we get nowhere. Some say the drug has not been approved yet. Others say it is not yet commercially available. No one in South Africa appears to stock it.

But seven hours later, I am on the way to the airport, and on the seat beside me is a small white insulated box containing rows of precious glass vials. Dozens of phone calls tracked down the new drug at a private clinic in the northern suburbs, where it is being tested as part of a pilot study. In a stroke of serendipity, the pharmacist there happens to be a Zimbabwean, and she has bent the rules to save my father's life.

I am very late for the last flight of the day to Harare, driving feverishly fast, fearless, invincible. I cannot die while my father is on his own deathbed; I am statistically immune. Coming off the highway, I run a red light and accelerate away.

MY FATHER'S EYES are shut. His head, resting on the thin hospital pillow, is monumental, a head fit for Mount Rushmore. He is seventy-two, but his hair is still thick, drawn back off his wide sloping brow in a solid silver spume. Usually tamed by some sort of pomade, it has become unruly, sprouting out in small pewter horns over his ears.

He pants fast and shallow, like a hot hound. The cadence of the electronic heart monitor is all wrong, my mother explains. His pulse rate is still twice what it should be. Nurses pad around us on the chipped linoleum floor in their laceless sneakers. One unbuttons the collar of my father's pajamas so she can get at his heart-monitor connection. The buttons below his wattle open to reveal a ruddy V, tidemark of the sun. It is the tattoo of the *rooinek*, the English who came to Africa, mocked by Boers for our pale skin's propensity to burn in the sun. She buttons him back up and moves to adjust the IV in the vein on the back of his hand, settling his arm on the overdarned bedspread. That arm bears more stigmata of the white man in Africa: solar keratosis lesions that have slowly developed over years of working outdoors under the tropical sun. My father, in his methodical scientific way, had explained that to me, as a child. The rays of the African sun, so directly overhead, pass through less atmosphere and so far less of its dangerous ultraviolet spectrum is filtered out. My sister Georgina and I joke that if you ask Dad the time, he will tell you how a watch works. He knows how everything works, and if it doesn't, he can fix it.

GEORGINA IS TEN years younger than me, with long dark hair, a marble-white complexion that she is careful to keep out of the African sun, a mordant sense of humor, and a twenty-a-day habit. She needs a cigarette now, so we go outside and she lights up a local

Madison. She exhales and looks around the parking lot. "Remember when Dad got caught pissing in a bottle?" she says. He had been parked here, reading a book, waiting for my mother, who works here, and needed to pee. As he had suffered from prostate problems and the nearest lavatory was a fair distance, down several long hospital corridors, he had come equipped with a wide-necked plastic bottle with a screw top for just this purpose. Midstream, there was a tap at the window. He looked up to see a female social worker from the hospital, a friend of ours, who'd wandered over to say hello. Clutching the bottle between his thighs and drawing his book discreetly over it, he rolled down the window and the woman started chatting. Soon the urge to pee became overwhelming—he *had* been interrupted midstream—so he began risking little surreptitious spurts, until finally she departed, just as he was getting cramps in his thighs from clutching the bottle between them.

It feels good to laugh out loud.

The parking lot is baking hot in the afternoon sun and strewn with rubbish: bleached mango pips and corncobs and fibrous pulp of chewed sugarcane. Minibuses jostle for passengers, hawkers ply tiny packets of cookies and half-loaves of bread, and some are boiling up large black pots of *sadza*, cornmeal porridge that is the culinary mainstay of this part of Africa. Rolled-up grass mats stand against the trees; there is a whole community camping out here, the relatives of the sick, of the dying.

A knot of women burst through the glass door behind us. They slump onto the curb, weeping and rocking on their haunches. Some have babies tied to their backs in white crocheted shawls. Their grief is raw and fierce, unmediated. A couple of men in ragged jackets stand by, embarrassed and self-conscious, and a gaggle of bewildered toddlers with mango-smeared mouths look up with wide almond eyes.

Georgina and I move off to stand under a cassia tree. Dad had refused an ambulance, she tells me, so they had reclined a seat in the car and laid him in it to drive to the hospital. On the way, Mum realizes they are about to run out of fuel, so they pull in to a service station to fill up. One by one, the attendant, Mum, Georgina, all feverishly wrestle to get the fuel cap open while Dad lies groaning.

Finally Mum shakes Dad by the shoulder and his eyes open. She tells him that he has to put his collapse on hold. They haul him out and support him as he staggers to the fuel cap, which he quickly undoes in a deft maneuver. Then he collapses back into the car, and the emergency drive resumes.

Though my father's life is clearly at stake, it is a matter of honor that he be treated here at the Parirenyatwa, this cash-strapped government hospital named after the country's first black doctor. To take him to the smarter private hospital would be, my mother insisted, a vote of no confidence in the Parirenyatwa staff. My father agreed entirely. So they had brought him into the emergency department of the Parirenyatwa where the nurses and doctors—my mother's colleagues—rushed to admit him to the coronary care unit. For once, Georgina says, the elevator even worked. But before they would let him into the ward, Dad lay for ages on a gurney in the corridor gasping like a grounded guppy.

When he was finally wheeled in and connected to a cardiac monitor and an IV, my mother asked the nurse, a woman in her late fifties, about the delay. She is an ex-guerrilla, a so-called bush nurse, one of those who at the end of the civil war—the war to end white rule—was inducted, after top-up training, as a full-fledged nurse at the insistence of the new government. She looked at the floor out of embarrassment. But my mother had treated her at the staff clinic on several occasions, and they are friends, and finally the nurse looked up.

"It was the head nurse who made us wait," she said. "She wanted to make sure the ward was clean and tidy and that there was a proper bedspread for Mr. Godwin's bed. But there were no bedspreads in the linen room—they have all been stolen—so we had to go searching in other wards."

So my father nearly died in their pursuit of a bedspread. But now, at least, he has a chance. Now he has the new wonder drug I tracked down in Johannesburg. A drug unavailable to the rest of the patients at the Parirenyatwa. An expensive drug. A First World drug.

I SIT BY DAD's bed, dozing. When I glance up I see his bleached blue eyes looking at me. He attempts a smile that comes out as a lopsided grimace and reaches weakly for my hand.

"Thanks for coming, Pete." It's all he has the strength to croak.

I squeeze his hand.

Pete. He's the only person in the world who still calls me that. Very occasionally, if he's feeling particularly loquacious, he calls me Pedro.

Our uncharacteristic moment of intimacy is interrupted by a sudden roar from a patient across the aisle. My father turns in panic, rattling his IV against its metal stand. Low guttural growls and barks of astonishing power burst up from the pit of his wardmate's stomach. I worry that this tumult could tip Dad's failing heart over the edge. There are no nurses in sight, so I get up to see what I can do. A black man in his twenties is straining to rise from his bed, the sinews in his neck cording with the effort. He looks immensely strong. He sees me and bares his teeth, growls again, and redoubles his attempt to get free, twisting up and dislodging his bedding. He is naked and as well muscled as a Nubian wrestler. His wrists and ankles are bound to the bedstead with an improvised selection of straps and belts.

The nurse appears next to me. "He has come from Ward Twelve, you know, the psych ward. We call him Lion Man." She giggles. "Now his sedative has worn off and we have no more left. We have no budget." She tests his straps then wanders off again.

I return to my father's bedside to report that Lion Man is securely lashed to his bed and cannot escape to tear us limb from limb. Dad rolls his eyes. I do not tell him that Lion Man's sedatives have just run out.

We will bow down to the one who growls, I remember. One of Prince Biyela's praise names. It already seems like months ago.

* * *

MY MOTHER RETURNS with the consulting physician, Dr. Nelson Okwanga. He is a Ugandan. I feel the beginnings of First World panic. I take my mother aside. It is time to assert myself.

"Dad's life's on the line here," I say. "The time for political correctness is over. We must get him the *best* physician."

She narrows her eyes. "Okwanga *is* one of the *very* best," she says. "He qualified in Britain."

Dr. Okwanga bustles about but says little. Then he draws us away from the bedside. In a voice that never rises above a murmur, he says that Dad's condition is no better, that the new drug has not lowered his heart rate yet. He will give it another twelve hours. Then he will have to *reevaluate*—the word is somehow wreathed with menace.

Later my father is wheeled to see the cardiologist. His name is Dr. Hakim. He is from Sudan. I say nothing. Dr. Hakim is meticulously dressed in a charcoal pin-striped suit and oxblood brogues. He makes my father lie on his side and rigs him up to a machine that videos his heart. On the screen is the blurred gray image of one of my father's heart valves. It looks like the key of a clarinet going up and down. Up and down so fast it is shaking itself to pieces. He is literally going to die of a broken heart.

When he is back in bed, I think of that little clarinet key racing away. And I find I am cheering it on, willing it to slow its frenetic, destructive pace. But he continues to weaken. His life hangs now from the merest trembling filament. Or on the whim of a deity. *"As flies to wanton boys are we to the gods. They kill us for their sport."*

Although I went to Mass every day at St. George's, a local Jesuit boarding school, I have not prayed in years. The urge to pray now seems ridiculous, a foul-weather religious conversion, Christian only in a crisis. I know that God, any god, will need something in return, a penance for my secular life. I start silently deal making. If my father survives I will . . . what? What will I do? I could stop running around the world and come home to Africa. Come back and spend some time with my father. Get to know him.

As he lies there, I think how little I really know of my father. I have been conditioned by his manner not to pry. He is emotionally truculent, quick to anger, irascible, rather forbidding really, a remote Victorian paterfamilias. Mum happily talks about personal stuff. Dad does not. He sits aloof from the rest of the family, an inaccessible island with a rocky shoreline. You cannot make landfall on your own. You must first take my mother on board as the pilot to guide you through the treacherous channel. And her MO depends on the nature of the mission.

Sometimes, when we had infuriated him, she was like one of those little grooming fish swimming right up to the great white shark in an apparently suicidal approach and nibbling at the menacing snout. And we would hold our breath, waiting for her to be gobbled up in a flash of fish fangs, but the great white would exhibit some instinctive override, some primal understanding of emotional symbiosis, and would tolerate her proximity. And so the pattern has been established over decades.

I imagine trying to write my father's obituary.

George Godwin, born in 1924 in England to . . .

Where in England? I don't know. I realize I've never seen the inside of his passport. I realize that I know almost nothing about his family. I think his father's name was Morris, a businessman of some sort.

He was educated at . . .

Pass again. He mentioned going to high school at St. Andrews in Scotland, I think.

When World War II was declared . . .

Now I'm on stronger ground.

He joined the British army . . .

But which regiment? An infantry unit, I think . . .

After the war he studied engineering at London University and worked on the team that designed and built the Sunderland flying boat before coming to Africa on a contract in the early 1950s and falling in love with the place. He ran copper mines and timber estates and government transport divisions and ended up writing industrial standards for the Standards Association of Zimbabwe.

He is survived by a wife and two children and was predeceased by a third.

THE THREADBARE RÉSUMÉ is interrupted by my mother. She insists I go home to wash and sleep. She will wait at his bedside. "I'll call you the second there's any change," she promises.

My parents live in Chisipite (in Shona, the local language, it means "spring," after the water source there), an outer suburb of the city, in a rather austere 1950s house, with a Dutch-style mansard roof, in an astonishingly fecund acre of garden. I don't have keys, so at the gate I give a short honk, and Mavis comes jogging down the drive followed by Isaac, the young gardener, and by our Dalmatians. Mavis has been our housekeeper for twenty years. She was divorced by her husband and cast out by her family when her first baby was born dead and she had to have a hysterectomy and became barren. She and Isaac live in separate wings of the small brick staff quarters at the top of the garden.

"Is boss Godwin all right?" she asks through the car window.

"He's alive," I say.

"Oh, praise Jesus!"

"But he's still in a serious condition."

"I have been praying for him," she says. "The Lord will look after him because your father, he is a very good man."

THAT NIGHT, I wander around the house, looking for evidence of the man. The house itself was his choice—none of the rest of us particularly liked it, but he was taken with its location, on the very northern edge of town, close to the bush from which we were returning. It is an odd mélange of styles: imposing wooden beams appear to hold up the living room ceiling, but they are hollow and purely decorative, contributing to the bogus baronial look established by the large fireplace topped with a wide beaten-copper cowl, which my mother has attempted to smother with indoor ivy.

All the portraits that hang on the walls of the living room are, I realize, of my mother's family: miniatures of her great-aunts in

Victorian bustles and elaborate feathered hats; a gilt-framed oil of her great-great-great-uncle as a boy in pastoral England, wearing a gold riding coat over white jodhpurs and sitting astride a white steed, a King Charles spaniel yapping at them from the foreground of the canvas. The mementos too, come from her side: a trumpet-barreled blunderbuss, salvaged by her father, a chaplain in the Royal Navy, from the gore of Gallipoli during World War I. An early eighteenth-century brass-faced, single-hand grandfather clock. A needlepoint sampler by a twelve-year-old girl, Elizabeth, in the year 1850. She has carefully embroidered a prayer: "When I lay me down to sleep, I pray the Lord my soul to keep. If I should die before I wake, I pray the Lord my soul to take."

I flip through the family photo albums. My father was quite a serious photographer once, with his own darkroom, so he was usually the one behind the camera, and there are few pictures of him here. I search in vain for a single picture of us together as adults.

I unlock the garage and browse his "heavy workshop" — tools on boards arranged in ascending order of caliber; screws and bolts of different sizes segregated in their own recycled jam jars; car parts swaddled in burlap sackcloth, bound with twine and neatly labeled.

Next door in his "light workshop" is all his radio equipment. In the old days when he worked on plantations in the eastern highlands, the estate managers used two-way radios to communicate. He made himself into an expert repairman and become a radio ham in the process, rigging up a lofty antenna and chatting to people on other continents via a big single-sideband (SSB) radio transmitter. The tools here are as shiny and delicate as surgical instruments: minute, long-nosed pliers and screwdrivers with heads so small that they look like spikes. Along one bench is a circuit tester he'd built himself.

As I turn to go, I inadvertently nudge some little screws onto the floor. On my hands and knees to retrieve them, I see that there is quite a large storage space down there, concealed by the circuit tester. Mostly, it seems, he uses it to store radio parts. At the back is a flat object about twelve inches by nine, wrapped in a plastic shopping bag. I reach in and peel back the plastic to find a layer of newspaper, tear it back a little, to find another layer, stiff brown paper, which I unfold and try to look inside. It's hard to see from this oblique angle, but I can make out that it's a posed black-and-white photo of three strangers: a middle-aged couple with a young girl of about twelve between them. Then the phone rings, and I rush out to answer it. It's my mother, saying nothing has changed. When I hang up, I feel grubby, prying in Dad's things while he lies dying, so I smooth back the wrapping on the photo and slide it back.

I walk back through to his study where a to-do list in his beautiful sloping handwriting sits on the wide mahogany desk. His silver letter opener and pens are all neatly arranged in an antique brass stand, with cut-glass inkwells that belonged to my mother's father. Two rows of locked filing cabinets flank the desk, and along one wall is a bookcase full of technical journals and alphabetized manuals and reference books on metallurgy and standards. I check the answering machine and hear my father's outgoing message, his voice strong and deliberate, an upper-middle-class British accent, clipped and correct and authoritative, the dialect of command.

I can't help thinking that I'm a disappointment to my father. He is a practical, technocratic, empirical man, a man who makes and runs things, who organizes people—he is a doer. I only describe, criticize, review—I am not really a doer.

"When are you going to get a real job?" he often says, then laughs to signal that this is just a joke, though on one level, of course, it never really is. It's true that I have been through a rather rapid succession of jobs. When I left school, the civil war against white rule—which the black insurgents called the *Chimurenga*, "the struggle"—was still raging, and I was drafted into the security forces. I was fighting on the wrong side of a losing war, but my father felt that it was dishonorable for me to dodge the draft when my turn came, for until then we'd been guarded by other people's sons. White rule had been conceded, anyway, so my father reckoned I would just be helping to hold the line while peace negotiations took place. After a year in uniform I managed to get into Cambridge, but Dad seemed nonplussed—he had suggested I attend the local university and train to be a district commissioner. He bridled when I wanted to major in English or history, so we compromised on law. When I graduated, I moved on to Oxford rather than coming home to face more combat. After a year of course work in international politics, I began research for a doctoral thesis on the war I had just fought in, in a belated effort to understand it.

When peace was declared and Rhodesia became Zimbabwe the next year, I bought an antique army-surplus truck with a few friends and drove it from Oxford to the south of France, where we put it on a ferry to Algiers. We set off across the Sahara Desert and down the African continent, finally reaching my parents' house in Harare, lean, brown, and unkempt, not having slept in beds for nearly a year. I was happy to be back home in the new, multiracial Zimbabwe.

To subsidize my thesis research, I began practicing as a lawyer, and my father basked in my respectability. But my legal career was short-lived. Most of my time was spent helping to defend seven guerrilla officers, all Matabeles, the southern Zimbabwean tribe that was an offshoot of Prince Biyela's Zulu. The officers belonged to the Patriotic Front, one of the two factions that fought against white rule but lost to Robert Mugabe's Zimbabwe African National Union (ZANU) in the country's first universal suffrage elections. Now he accused them of plotting a coup, of committing high treason. After a lengthy trial, we secured their acquittal, but Mugabe immediately ordered them rearrested under the "emergency regulations," draconian laws introduced by the last white prime minister, Ian Smith. So I resigned as a lawyer, to my father's chagrin, and took up freelance journalism, still trying to write up my thesis on the side.

The next year, 1983, I saw what the new government was really made of. Mugabe unleashed his new North Korean–trained Fifth Brigade troops on the civilians of Matabeleland, and I went down to investigate, to discover a full-scale massacre. Even after all these years no one knows the final toll—somewhere between ten and twenty thousand people were killed, possibly more. The sheer scale and ferocity of the killings dwarfed anything that had happened in the independence war, but now there was little outcry and few reprisals from the international community. When my reports ran in the London *Sunday Times,* they brought death threats down on my head and forced me to flee the country just before being declared a foreign spy and an enemy of the state.

I continued as a journalist, assigned by the *Sunday Times* to Eastern Europe and to South Africa. Then I moved to the BBC, based in London, making TV documentaries around the world. I took a sabbatical to write a book, *Mukiwa,* about my African childhood and the independence war and the Matabeleland massacres. And I found I didn't want to go back to the BBC so went freelance instead, still based in London. My father tried, but failed, to mask his puzzlement at my walking away, again, from a full-time job.

For several years after reporting on the Matabeleland massacres, I couldn't go home. But then the two main political parties merged, and the men I had defended in court were absorbed into the new establishment. One of them, Dumiso Dabengwa, became the minister of home affairs, and he saw to it that I could finally come back without being arrested. So for the past few years, I have returned to Harare as often as I can, and whenever I appear my father observes the same ritual.

"Ah, Pete. Would you come here a minute," he calls from his armchair when he has finished his supper of ham-and-cheese sandwiches. I sit on the ancient slipcovered sofa while he asks me where I've been and poses questions I never seem able to answer quite to his satisfaction. These questions are nearly always quantitative; his instinct is to measure. How many people do you think were killed in the Matabeleland massacre? How long will apartheid survive? When will the Berlin Wall fall? What effect will the ivory sales ban have on elephant poaching? Can Cuba survive the end of the Cold War? How dangerous are Eastern Europe's nuclear power plants? Is the rise of Islamic fundamentalism in Indonesia inexorable? As if I really know. I am just a journalist, a hack. I don't have a *real* job.

DR. OKWANGA, NORMALLY quite inscrutable, now looks extremely worried. He sighs and steps away from the bedside and tells my mother that the prognosis is not good at all. As a last resort, he wants to give my father a megadose of the new drug, my new drug, in the hope that this will shock his system into rebooting at a more plausible heart rate. He orders the last six vials to be injected at once.

We watch my father closely, but nothing happens. I sense that he is slipping away. For the first time, my mother begins to lose her composure. She has witnessed many deaths in her long medical career, and I can see she thinks he is lost. Rather than break down in public, she excuses herself to go to the bathroom, and my sister accompanies her.

The nurse pulls the curtain around my father's bed, and I realize that she is preparing for his death, so he can die in private. While I wait for him to go, I look out the window at the treetops over Mazowe Street and then blankly watch the flies battering themselves at the windowpane, trying to escape. *"As flies to wanton boys are we to the gods."* And while I stare, I become aware that the soundscape is changing subtly. It is the rhythm of the cardiac monitor getting slower. His heart is weakening, the thumping of those clarinet keys finally fading. His labored breathing seems to ease a little as his pulse lowers on the way to stopping. I look at his face. Nothing. Then back up at the monitor.

"You still here?"

At the sound of my father's voice, I lurch back in my chair and upset the bedside tray. My father is grinning his lopsided grin. A blush of color is returning to his face.

"Can you help me sit up?"

I prop the pillows behind him.

"What I'd really like is some tea," he says.

The ward nurse goes to get it.

And when Mum and Georgina return from the bathroom, they find Dad sitting up, chatting and drinking tea.

THE WONDER DRUG, it seems, has lived up to its billing. By delivering it, I have actually saved my father's life. I have proved myself as a son.

Soon he is ready to come home.

"You know, I felt you would actually be sorry if I died," he says to me on his last day in the hospital, as though surprised by this discovery.

The nurse, the same one who had tested Lion Man's restraining straps, insists on packing up his clothes and his wash things and his leftover medications. She hums as she works.

"I am so happy for Dr. Godwin," she says to me. "She looks after us very well at the staff clinic when we are sick. I am happy that she will not be a widow, as I am."

She embraces me, and I can see that her eyes are wet.

What my mother does not tell me, at least not until much later, is that among my father's possessions, helpfully assembled by the nursing staff, is my box of wonder drugs. My mother eventually looks inside and notices four of the glass vials are still there—still full. The nurse had misunderstood the doctor's instructions. Instead of administering all six vials in the last megadose, she had injected only two, which is too little to have played any significant role in my father's recovery. And though my mother doesn't tell him this, my father has recovered on his own, spontaneously, unaided by me.

"What did you do about it?" I ask my mother.

"Do? I did nothing," she says.

"But the mistake could easily have killed him."

"Well, she was her family's only breadwinner, and she was about to retire," my mother says. "I didn't want to put her pension at risk."

* * *

So my father survives, and I don't have to seek out an aloe under which to bury him to keep Kipling's hyenas at bay. At least not yet. He can sail on toward the landmarks of old age. And the first of those landmarks is Georgina's wedding the following year.

three

March 1997

I TRAVEL UP FROM Cape Town, where I have been living for the past six months, to be closer to home. With me is Joanna, my English girlfriend, a reporter for the *Guardian,* who has come over from London for the wedding. At home, I find that Dad has shrugged off his brush with mortality and is completely restored to his old bluff, inaccessible self. Our relationship is back in its default of remoteness.

Before the wedding, Joanna and I stay at the Chisipite house. We swim lengths of the pool while Dad fiddles happily with the filter and tests the pH balance of the water, carefully adjusting the ionizer to keep the water sparklingly clear. Though he designed the pool—an irregular curved shape finished in a ceramic mosaic of blues and greens with a vaguely Moorish feel and a stone waterfall at one end—and though he monitors it lovingly, he seldom gets in it himself; he just likes to admire it. The surroundings of the pool are admirable too. It is bordered by agave plants entwined with pink rambling roses reaching out to a small frangipani tree. A mass of blue plumbago grows around the waterfall and up a sturdy aloe plant. The lawn is broken up by an acacia thorn tree, supporting a lilac potato vine and a slender ivory-flowered kapok tree.

GEORGINA'S WEDDING IS scheduled to take place a week before her thirtieth birthday.

"I promised myself I'd get married before I was thirty," she says briskly.

We are having tea in the orchid house of the thatched stone cottage where she lives with her fiancé, in a converted stable block at the bottom of the eight-acre garden of her future in-laws, who occupy the big ship of a house on the crest of the hill overlooking them. Together Georgina and her fiancé, Jeremy, a blond photographer, run a public relations firm that handles hotels and airlines. She has returned to Africa after three years at an English drama school and another two to secure her actor's Equity card. This she did as Georgie Porgie, a clown who performed at children's parties. She also toured with repertory theater groups for a year, principally as the tart in a rather successful farce called *The Tart and the Vicar's Wife*. But she missed Africa. So after six years away, she came back to become something of a celebrity in a somewhat smaller pond.

Back home she helped Jeremy research and write *Mhondoro (The Lion Spirit)*, a play about Ambuya Nehanda, a famous Shona spirit medium who had largely inspired the 1896 uprising—the First *Chimurenga*—against white rule. When Nehanda was executed, she was said to have declared, "My bones will rise again," and one night shortly after her death wild lions were seen trotting through the center of Harare. The lead role of Nehanda was played by Georgina's best friend and colleague at the state broadcaster, ZBC radio, Tsitsi Naledi Vera, and it was the first truly multiracial Zimbabwean drama. Georgina and Tsitsi were also busy writing a soap opera, *Radio Rumpere* ("to break" in Latin), about two girls, best friends who work for a radio station, when one of them gets AIDS. It was supposed to explain cultural differences and challenge racial stereotypes. But they never finished it. Tsitsi suddenly died—officially, from pneumonia.

Later, Georgina was the lead actress in *Strange Bedfellows,* an adaptation by the black Zimbabwean playwright Steven Chifunyise of August Strindberg's *Miss Julie.* Georgina played Sandi Grobelaar, a white Zimbabwean, who complains to Farai, the black servant, "I cannot be held accountable for the sins of my fathers," and eventually snogs him onstage. The play toured through Europe, showcasing the artistic vitality of the new Zimbabwe.

Now Georgina presents the early morning drive-time radio program, *The Good Morning Show,* for ZBC; she reads the TV news and hosts a TV interview program; and she writes a column called "Between the Sheets" about social life in the "low-density" suburbs for the *Northern News,* a monthly newspaper. She wears big hats to open supermarkets, rappels down tall buildings to raise money for the mayor's Christmas Cheer Fund, and produces comedy reviews for Save the Rhino. She emcees the Mr. Iron Man competition, and judges karaoke contests and Elvis look-alike gigs and the "Jacaranda Queen" drag festival. Georgina's approach to these enterprises is cheerfully casual. Her TV interview show is dizzyingly improvised, featuring whatever flotsam washes through town, from Aboriginal Australian didgeridoo players to entire troupes of Congolese *kwasa kwasa* dancers who speak no English. On air she's as relaxed doing horoscopes as she is introducing sporting events for sports she has no idea how to play.

"How's business going?" I ask.

Her ZBC salary is a pittance, but it doesn't really matter. The fact that she is back home, near our parents, as they grow old, is of huge comfort to them and worth any subsidy that might be necessary. Her presence enables my absence.

"It's going OK, I suppose," she says. She lets one of her Dalmatians curl up on her lap.

"We had an incident with a lion cub the other day at Meikles Hotel," says Jeremy as he lowers one of the rolls of plastic sheeting that form the sides of their bush conservatory.

Meikles is one of the oldest hotels in the country, opened in 1915 by a pioneering Scottish trader. The low colonial building has long since been rebuilt as a five-star high-rise, but it is still guarded by its original twin stone lions, who are supposed to roar every time a virgin walks by. (To date they have remained oddly silent.)

"We'd organized a bit of a do," Georgina says, "to promote their refurbishment. They've put in lovely beige carpets with a lion paw-print motif. Anyway, it was a must-be-seen-at event, with the whole press corps in attendance. In one corner we had a harpsichordist, the only one in the country, a sixteen-year-old schoolgirl, and for backup, in the hotel lounge, the British high commissioner's wife on a baby grand playing her repertoire of show tunes. And in keeping with the carpet motif, a tame six-month-old lion cub."

"He was called Hercules," calls Jeremy, from behind a fuchsia orchid he's tenderly spritzing.

"That's right," says Georgina, "and he was fine to begin with, padding around frightening the waiters. But then . . ."

"But then indeed . . ." says Jeremy.

"But then, he came up behind the lady high commissioner as she sat playing, jumped up and put his front paws on her shoulders, and started dry humping her, just like a dog!"

"She was very game about it," says Jeremy, deadheading a rhododendron.

"Yes," says my sister, "she just carried on playing 'Climb Every Mountain,' while Hercules lunged at her back with his engorged pimento. The handler had disappeared, and no one else quite knew what to do. She got halfway through 'Send in the Clowns' before she abandoned the piano and made a dash for the restroom, with Hercules, me, and a stringer from the *Daily Telegraph* in hot pursuit."

"It was good publicity for the hotel," says Jeremy dryly from somewhere behind the plinth of their decorative fountain.

"Yes," says Georgina, "and we did pay her dry-cleaning bill."

She squints at a chip on her fingernail. "By the way, I've block-booked manicures and pedicures for the whole bridal party."

I examine my own nails. They are clipped short and square. "No, I'm fine, thanks," I say.

"Oh, come *on*." She rolls her eyes. "Pamper yourself. I'm getting a full set of acrylic nails. You won't be the only man, you know. Manuel and Jeremy will be there."

"Nah. I'm OK, really."

"I've reserved Esnat to do you," she says.

Esnat is Georgina's Deep Throat in a lurid case that is about to come to trial in Harare. The manicurist's boyfriend, a handsome young policeman, Jefta Dube, was aide-de-camp to Canaan Sodindo Banana, the country's first black president (a largely ceremonial position that disappeared in 1987 when the British-style post of prime minister was abolished in favor of an executive presidency—assumed by Robert Mugabe). Banana is also a Methodist minister who became a liberation theologian and once reworked the Lord's Prayer to include the lines: "Teach us to demand our share of the gold, / And forgive us our docility."

And despite being married with four children, it was rumored that President Banana was partial to men, a somewhat precarious position given that Mugabe had denounced gays as "lower than pigs and dogs," declared them to be "a colonial invention, unknown in African tradition," and passed laws punishing consensual homosexuality with ten years' hard labor.

Jefta Dube was being tried for the murder of a fellow policeman, and though the trial was held in secret, salacious tidbits were beginning to leak. Dube was pleading in mitigation that the president had repeatedly raped him and that finally, when a colleague had taunted him calling him "Banana's girlfriend," he'd snapped and shot the colleague dead.

"She's quite happy to chat to you about the case," Georgina promises.

SOON I AM reclining in a chair at Cleopatra's Beauty Salon in Newlands Shopping Center. It sits above a Greek restaurant and is permeated with the fumes of dolmades and sheftalia and stale retsina.

"Hold out your hand," says Esnat. She is a slender black woman in a white smock with her name embroidered in pink on its breast. She scrabbles around in her tray of utensils, many of which look alarmingly like surgical instruments, selects a metal nail file with a curved point, and begins to scrape back my cuticles. I am just summoning up the courage to ask her about President Banana when the file slips and stabs my thumb.

"I'm so, so sorry," she says, aghast.

She looks over to see if the manageress has noticed.

"That's OK," I say quietly.

But her file has punctured a vein, and my thumb is pumping out blood with each beat of my pulse. It quickly overwhelms her tissue and her paper towel, and soon the salon has come to a standstill to stanch my spurting wound as Esnat writhes with embarrassment.

"I told you I didn't want my nails done," I say to Georgina.

THE DRIVE TO the village of Chimanimani, where the wedding is to be held, is about three hundred miles. Joanna and I have rented a little Nissan in an arresting shade of canary yellow. Its faded blue velour seats are infused with the sour aroma of sweat, and its history of accidents and improvised repairs is manifested in an awkward crablike diagonal trajectory. At the industrial eastern suburb of Msasa we leave the city behind us, and soon the vista is punctuated by huge outcrops of granite boulders, balanced improbably on one another since time prehistoric, and then the central plateau slowly tilts up through some of the country's richest farmlands toward the hazy blue mountains of Nyanga, the roof of Zimbabwe. To either side of the main road stretch tracks that lead to the network of commercial farms, the junctions festooned with clusters of signposts bearing witness to old allegiances and origins, farm names like Tipperary, Tintagel, Grimsby, Saffron Walden.

Until about fifteen years ago, when the war for independence ended, you could only make such journeys in heavily guarded convoys, which were frequently attacked. But today the countryside radiates peace. We stop the car at a rest stop and sit on a concrete bench to eat our picnic on the inverted cement mushroom of a table, in the shade of a musasa tree. The occasional faint chug of a tractor plowing a distant field, and the slow *tuc, tuc, tuc* of a diesel generator come floating across the ridge in little wind-borne swells. And behind this is the background screech of cicadas—the tinnitus of nature.

Abruptly, the cicada screech stops, and the bush is eerily quiet. When I was in the armed forces, lying in ambush, waiting for so long that fear was finally displaced by boredom and fatigue, the sudden hush of the cicadas heralded the possible approach of danger—of guerrillas in a blur of olive fatigues and AK-47s and Chinese stick grenades, of shouts and the rattle of gunfire and the Doppler zinging of ricochets, and the air being sucked out of my chest by the percussion of a grenade exploding; all the orchestrated cacophony of combat, and with it that acute postadrenaline awareness of the exquisite fragility of life itself.

That first moment of silence when cicadas cease feels like nature's herald of danger, even now.

"What's wrong?" asks Joanna, and I almost tell her.

"Nothing. I was just thinking how peaceful it sounds when the cicadas stop."

The cause of the cicadas' silence crests the path into sight: a ragged crocodile of small black children jogging back from school. Joanna takes in their threadbare khaki uniforms and the striped jute book bags bouncing on bony shoulders, and I can see how it must look to her. Even when they whoop and wave and flash bright-toothed smiles as they pass by, she sees ill-fitting, hand-me-down clothes and scuffed shoes or the bare feet of kids who walk miles to and from school each day and go home to thatched huts without indoor plumbing or electricity. But what I see are functioning schools: pens and paper and near-universal education producing

Africa's most literate population. She compares up, to the First World, where privileges are treated as rights. I compare down, to the apocalyptic Africa that presses in around us, where rights are only for the privileged. After covering wars in Mozambique, Angola, Uganda, Somalia, and Sudan, Zimbabwe feels to me like Switzerland.

AFTER FIVE HOURS on the road, just as Joanna is despairing of us ever reaching the fabled Chimanimani, we strain up a final hill to find the quartz amphitheater of the mountains glistening ahead. Soon we are coasting down through timber plantations and orchards and coffee estates to the little village itself.

The Zulu people sometimes call us white ones *inkonjane*, "the swallows," because we arrived from overseas, just as the migrating birds do. If I *were* a swallow, Chimanimani is the place that my avian navigation system would draw me back to. It's my true north, the fixed point by which I situate all other points, the closest place I have to a spiritual home.

Chimani has supplied a seedbed of images in my memory that seem as fresh today as when they first sprouted in my childhood. My mother in her white coat marching down a long line of tribespeople that coiled through the bush, vaccinating arm after arm. Or peering into the chest of a disinterred three-week-old cadaver, her scalpel poised for the autopsy. It was here, in the Biriwiri Valley, that I used to play with the lepers at their colony—who were not infectious, my mother assured me, because they were dry lepers, not wet. Here where I padded around after Albert the Mozambican, our gardener, wrenching weeds out of the rich red African earth and tossing them into his big green wheelbarrow. Here I rode on horseback with Jeremy Watson, my childhood friend, helping to herd the cattle to new grazing grounds. And at night beside the fire, Isaac, the chief herdsman, told us long magical fables about ancestors and demons.

At Silverstream my father ran the heart of the estates, the big factory that pounded away all day and night, extracting tannin (for leather) from the bark of wattle trees, creosoting their trunks and turning them into railway sleepers and telegraph poles and pit props. During the winter, when the cane was harvested and trucked up from the Save River Valley, the factory turned it into brown sugar, and there were African bees everywhere. Dad strode around in his desert boots and shorts and cotton safari jackets, with a slide rule and a packet of Gold Leaf cigarettes in his top pockets, keeping the whole thing going.

It was here at Silverstream that I went in secret with my nanny, Violet, to worship with the Vapostori ("Apostolics"), the African charismatic sect who wear long white robes and become possessed with the spirits of their ancestors. In their bush temple made of logs and mud and thatch, I would dance around the tree trunk in the middle or beat skin-covered drums around the outer circle until I too once spoke in tongues and everyone grew afraid.

It was here between Biriwiri and Skyline Junction, on a road carved into the mountainside, that our next-door neighbor, Oom Piet Oberholzer, was murdered by the Crocodile Gang, in the first guerrilla attack of the war to end white rule. And after he was killed, I was sent away to boarding school. And once Mozambique became independent of Portuguese rule in 1975, and its new Marxist government, Front for the Liberation of Mozambique (FRELIMO), threw its support behind anti-Rhodesian guerrillas, it was here, along this densely forested frontier, that our war was at its worst. One of every six adult male whites in Chimanimani was dead by the end of it, many of their bodies now buried in the little cemetery by the side of road into the village.

And when peace was declared and Robert Mugabe ascended to power, his men took sledgehammers to the pioneer memorial in the center of the village green and smashed it to pieces, and they changed the name from Melsetter, which had been taken from a town in the Scottish Orkney Islands, to Chimanimani, the name of the mountain range, "a space too small to turn around in," because the mountain passes were so winding and narrow and steep.

* * *

THE WEDDING PARTY has taken over the Chimanimani Arms Hotel and the Frog and Fern Bed and Breakfast, Mawenje Lodge, and Heaven Lodge, the backpackers' hostel. Some of us are billeted with friends in the village or on farms. We sit on the lawn of the hotel where we used to sit twenty years before, served tea by the same waiters in the same faded red-baize fezzes, looking out at the towering mountains. Just above us, in the game sanctuary on the side of the hill called Pork Pie, for its shape, a herd of eland graze. They are monumental even from a distance, Africa's biggest antelope, bison big, with great humps at their shoulders, and wattles dangling in loose folds of skin beneath their necks. Sleek, taupe, and plump, they toss their corkscrew horns and swish their tails and chew their cud, mouths flecked with green foam. In this sanctuary they are without predators. We are too high for lion, and they are too big for leopard.

My mother and I stroll across the village to her old clinic, a cluster of rough, round, tin-roofed huts, now closed and replaced by a new one down the valley. It was at this old clinic that as a child I used to mingle with the African patients who congregated on the grass slope, sitting patiently with their bundles, waiting to be treated. This was where I came across Mr. Arrowhead, who had a barbed fishing arrow lodged straight through his head and yet walked and talked still, though not for long. This was where my mother and her black nurse Janet endeavored to blunt the scythe of death that cut through rural African communities — tuberculosis and tetanus, bronchitis and bilharzia, pneumonia, smallpox and malaria. And blunt it they did. Infant mortality fell, life spans rose, the population swelled.

We look at the abandoned clinic in silence, and then my mother sighs, in a way that seems to mean both "Well, fancy that," and "Let's not get maudlin about this." We make our way back to the hotel to find my father alone at a wire-mesh table in the flower garden where the rose blossoms are as big as babies' heads. He half raises a hand and grunts a greeting.

"Where've you two been?"

"Exploring," says Mum. "We need to go for a fitting now. You too."

"Ugh," he says, tossing his head like a horse refusing its harness, "not me."

Georgina has had green vests made for all the men in the wedding party to wear under our tuxedos, but Dad is refusing to wear either the vest or the tuxedo.

"It's ridiculous," he says. "Pretentious."

"Oh, c'mon, Dad. It's what Georgina wants. We're *all* doing it."

"Well, not me," he says crossly. And with an air of finality he lights up a cigarette.

We leave him there at the garden table, gazing up at the mountains, refusing the embrace of his own family.

"His behavior's verging on the surly," I complain to Mum.

"You'll just have to tolerate it," she says mildly.

"I suppose it's because he can't stand all the socializing," I say, "all the rushing around and the prewedding chaos."

"No, it's not that."

"Well, what, then?" I am beginning to get irked at her defense of him.

She pauses and then says quietly, "It's because he's afraid."

"Afraid?"

"He's afraid to enjoy this wedding, to anticipate it, after what happened before Jain's wedding."

Jain is my other sister, my dead sister, older than me by seven years, but forever frozen at twenty-seven, killed just weeks before her own wedding. It was in 1978, during the civil war. She and her fiancé and their best man were traveling back to their home in Shamva in the northeast of the country, when their car ran into an army ambush that was preparing to attack guerrillas in a roadside village. The only survivor was Spence, the best man's fox terrier. Jain was the nurturing one, the glue that held our family together, a grade school teacher, a homebody, the organizer of reunions and Sunday lunches, the keeper of the domestic flame. Her death is the ugly scar that overlays our family's emotional topography, less a scar really than a sore that even after all these years still suppu-rates.

"The wedding's going to go off fine this time," I say to my father later.

"What do you mean?" he says blankly.

"We're all here and we're safe and it's going to be a great wedding."

But he still can't bring himself to acknowledge its lethal prece-dent, let alone discuss it, so it just hangs there full of menace, this grenade of history rolled onto the dance floor of the present, primed to sabotage our family festivities.

"YOU'D BETTER COME and let Jeremy show you around the car," says Georgina.

I am to be the wedding chauffeur, and the car is a 1976 bronze Rolls-Royce Silver Shadow that belongs to the Summerfields, the parents-in-law to be. It is said to be one of only three Rollers in the entire country, two of which are theirs. It sits now in the hotel park-ing lot, looking quite out of place among the beaten-up pickup trucks and the little Japanese compacts. A black gardener with a rag is gingerly polishing the silver Spirit of Ecstasy statuette mounted on the hood.

Looking at it I feel a twinge of unease. "You don't think it might be a little over the top?" I say.

"Over the top?" Georgina frowns. "Why?"

"I dunno. Maybe it's a bit . . . insensitive for us to ride around the African bush in a Roller?"

Georgina rolls her eyes. "Oh, for God's sake! It's an ancient bor-rowed Roller at a wedding, not a fucking Ferrari at a famine."

Jeremy is explaining the foibles of the car's eccentric gear-shift.

"Tell me, then," Georgina lobs from over my shoulder, "would it have worried you if I'd been getting married in England and we drove to the church in a rented Rolls there? Why is it OK to do it there but not here?"

I ignore her as Jeremy moves on to explain the badly adjusted clutch.

"And anyway," she continues, "the black elite here swan around in squadrons of the latest luxury SUVs, each of which is worth ten times this eccentric old thing."

"It's true," says Jeremy ruefully. "We've been trying to sell her for ages, but they're impossible to get spare parts for, so no one wants to buy her."

ON THE DAY of the wedding, I knock on the door of my sister's hotel room. From within, ABBA is blasting. She appears, wearing a dress of cream lace and green chiffon looped at the waist with strings of pearls, and on her head a hooded cape instead of a veil.

"I know green is an unlucky color to get married in, but it's supposed to echo the bucolic venue," she laughs.

My father is waiting for us in the lobby, trussed in a tuxedo, his previous objections notwithstanding. He takes Georgina's arm and escorts her to the car. I slide in behind the ivory wheel and settle back into the age-scored cream-leather seat and drive them slowly down the pitted red-dirt lane around the side of the mountain toward Bridal Veil Falls. It's a dead-end road leading up to the eland sanctuary, its edges lined with dense foliage that teems with morning glories and flame lilies, red-hot pokers and buffalo beans, serrated bracken and perforated elephant ears. The only people we encounter are barefoot Ndau tribespeople who step back into the bush to allow our stately progress and to stare after the Silver Shadow crunching slowly by. Georgina, in her green chiffon hood and pearls, waves with the back of her hand pretending to be the Queen of England, and they return her wave, astonished at this passing specter. She giggles with nerves.

"Stop the car," she says as we near the falls.

"What?"

"Stop the car, I need to pee."

"Can't you hold it?" I ask as I pull over.

She swings out of the car, walks behind a small tree, hoicks up her chiffon frock, and pees, trying to keep the splash from wetting her shoes. Dad and I stand watching a troupe of vervet monkeys scampering in the umbrella trees above us, chattering indignantly at our intrusion. And when Georgina returns, he lights up two cigarettes and gives her one, and they stand smoking in silence.

I get down on my knees and begin picking off the black jacks and burrs that have attached themselves to her dress.

"I can't go through with it," she suddenly blurts above me.

Dad rolls his eyes.

"You have to. Everyone's waiting," I say, rising to my feet. "And we're already late. C'mon. Let's get back in the car."

I take her by the arm toward the open door.

"No." She shrugs off my hand. "I want to call it off."

"Listen." I can hear the panic in my own voice. "Just go through with the ceremony, and if you still feel like this afterward you can get the marriage annulled."

She sighs and throws her cigarette down on the road and twists it out with her shoe.

"*Fodga?*" asks an old Ndau tribesman who has caught up with us. He wants a cigarette.

Dad hands him his unfinished one, and the man immediately takes a drag and exhales twin plumes through his nostrils while he cocks his head to one side and observes us arguing.

"Oh, all right, then," says Georgina. "Let's get it over with."

At Bridal Veil Falls, I open the heavy bronze door and let her out into the enchanted fern-flush glade to greet the congregation gathered on a grassy hummock in the lee of the waterfall.

A string quartet from her old high school is playing, but they are drowned out by a white filigree of water that tumbles a hundred and fifty feet down the cliffside behind them. When Georgina and Jeremy had reconnoitered the venue, it was dry season, and the river was far smaller. Now, as they exchange vows, we can see their lips move but can barely make out their words over the rush of the water.

After the ceremony, we move down to a long trestle table topped in white linen where canapés and Mukuyu brut de brut, a local sparkling wine, are served. A camera crew from ZBC is filming the procession for a little feature to be shown later on the national news, Georgina arm in arm with her maid of honor and best friend, Ellah Wakatama—black and white together, totally at ease, friends since elementary school, Zimbabweans now for nearly twenty years. Race, it seems, is finally losing its headlock on our identities in this little corner of Africa.

four

May 1998

Y OU DRIVE," says Georgina.

I am passing through Harare on my way back to New York, where I have been living for more than a year, since Joanna accepted an assignment there for the *Guardian*. My daughter Holly, from a previous relationship, is nearly four and lives with her mother in London, and now Joanna is pregnant. In order to be able to work in New York, I have begun the lengthy process of applying for permanent residence in the United States, a so-called green card, under the portentous category, "alien of exceptional talent." For this I'm endeavoring to prove that I'm an invaluable cultural asset to America, which, as my father suggests, grinning, "might be a bit of a reach."

This trip to Harare is a personal detour from another *National Geographic* assignment, this time on the last of the San, Africa's aboriginal people. I have been camping with them for weeks out in the Kalahari Desert in Namibia and Botswana, and now I badly need a drink.

The city is somnolent and soggy with a summer downpour in its third straight day, but Georgina is determined to take me out. We're in her Renault Four. It's the car I learned to drive in twenty-five years ago, and it was already old then. The gearshift comes straight out of the dashboard and looks like an umbrella handle. Once behind the wheel I see why she has asked me to drive; the Renault refuses to budge into second or third gear no matter what tactic I try, double declutching and fingertip gentleness or brute force. So we drive through rain-swept Harare alternating from an over-revved first gear to a lurching fourth. The internal fan has also given up, leaving the windshield permanently fogged.

"I just had it serviced," observes Georgina mildly, lighting up another Madison and throwing the scrunched red-and-white packet onto the backseat where it joins dozens like it.

Jeremy is away, running a course training hotel waiters, and all she can find for us to do this wet Monday evening is an Irish-themed event in Avondale at a pub called the Phreckle and Phart. It is not an uplifting occasion. Inside, half a dozen white men and two white women, dressed all in green, are huddled in a corner resolved to get drunk. An up-tempo Irish jig executed on a lone fiddle buzzes out of the faulty overhead speakers.

Georgina brings news of ex-President Banana, who is finally about to go on trial for sodomy. Prurient details have emerged from Jefta Dube: waltzing lessons to Kenny Rogers ballads, with the ex-President Banana holding him so close that he could "feel the stubble on his chin"; Banana's erection digging into his belly; the former president lacing his Fanta with a sleeping potion and him then waking up facedown on the red carpet of the State House library, clad only in his shirt, with the beaming Banana looming over him announcing in a soft voice, "While you were sleeping, we have helped ourselves."

Dube has been telling how he pleaded with Banana to stop the abuse and how Banana refused, pronouncing, "We are the final court of appeal." And how Banana worked his way through the

State House Tornadoes, the soccer team of strapping young men he handpicked for their looks. Dube had appealed to his boss, the commissioner of police, and to the deputy prime minister, only to have them shrug and do nothing. Even Mugabe was informed, but instead of the news sparking his rabid homophobia, he too was strangely acquiescent. Until the day the taunt incited Dube to take fatal action.

"How are things otherwise?" I ask Georgina. I'm feeling a bit out of touch since I moved to America.

"It might still look just about OK from the outside, but I think we've been white-anted," she says.

White ants devour wood from the inside out. A wooden chair or bed may look fine from the outside, but when you sit on it, it will collapse into a heap of dust.

"I'm thinking of leaving ZBC," she continues. "There's so much political interference now, I can't bear reading the news anymore. It's lies, total crap. I'm beginning to feel like such a hypocrite."

One of the white women at the Phreckle and Phart has wandered over to the dais and is tapping the karaoke mike with a long red fingernail. She has bottle green platform sandals, thick green eye shadow, and a big green cardboard shamrock pinned to her green tube top. It soon becomes apparent that she has misjudged the key of "Danny Boy." Her voice breaks into a tragic squawk, and she quickly retreats to a lower octave.

"Oh, God, this is just too depressing. Let's go," Georgina says.

As we try to leave, a terrible commotion begins outside the Phreckle and Phart, a fight between black hookers. They're cursing and slapping and scratching each other in the rain, while their pimps and several customers ineffectually try to pull them apart.

We lurch back through the downpour to Georgina's cottage where I am to stay the night. On the ZTV news black police frogmen with shaved heads are searching inside a bus that has been washed over a low bridge. A survivor is saying that the passengers had all shouted at the driver to stop and asked to be let off if he was going to try to cross. But he suddenly plunged ahead into the torrent regardless. A dozen people are missing, including several babies.

Georgina has to be up again at 4:00 a.m. to go to the radio studios and broadcast *The Good Morning Show*. At 9:15 a.m. she returns, exhausted. "You should go up and say hello to Shaina before you go," she says on her way to bed.

Shaina is Georgina's mother-in-law, a remarkable woman, and one you didn't want to offend. There was a photo on Georgina's corkboard of Shaina as a South African beauty queen, slender and curvy and sexy in her black bathing suit and Miss Port Elizabeth 1952 sash. Before Sunday lunch once, Joanna had made the mistake of trying to compliment Shaina on this photo.

"You looked beautiful then," she said.

"What do you mean 'then,' missy?" said Shaina.

Afterward, Joanna discovered the placement at lunch had been altered. She'd been demoted from the seat of honor next to Shaina and was now at the other end of the table, between toddlers.

Shaina wants to show me her extraordinary hilltop garden with its views out toward the Umwinsidale Hills. She walks me around the effusive beds of well-tended flowers. Hovering in attendance is the gardener, Naison, equipped with fork and trowel, ready to pounce on any weed. Shaina identifies the plants as we walk: cannas, strelitzias, primroses, black-eyed Susans, begonias. And nosing along behind us are two Rhodesian ridgebacks, hackles bristling with russet menace. They stay between Shaina and Naison, always facing Naison and occasionally baring their sharp yellow fangs and growling if he gets too close to her or makes any sudden movement. As we walk, I become aware of a soft hissing sound coming from close by.

"Now this, this is a Java orchid," says Shaina. "It's actually quite rare, and very delicate, hard to grow."

I hear the sound again, "*Ksst, ksssst.*" It's like the sound you would make to provoke a dog, and indeed it's followed by a low bass growl like the grumble of distant thunder. I look up and realize that the *kssst* is coming from Shaina, and that every time she does it, the dogs growl and bare their fangs at Naison's torn trouser legs. Naison stands still but seems oddly unperturbed. Dogs and gardener are performing an old dance, I realize, just going through the motions.

When I ask Shaina about it, she says, "Oh, that. I just don't want them to get *too* used to him. I don't want them to lose *all* their hostility—or else they won't be much good as guard dogs, will they?"

AT HOME MY father sits in the sunporch, drinking weak tea from a chipped pottery mug with "Dad" painted on it in wobbly childish letters by Georgina years ago. He shakes his head and snorts as he reads the *Herald,* the government-owned newspaper—snorts at the distorted, looking-glass world it reflects, as Zimbabwe has been a one-party state for ten years now, and the *Herald* faithfully preaches the word according to the government gospel.

From time to time it all becomes too much for Dad, and he writes a letter to the editor, usually about some very specific falsehood, signing the letter with a pseudonym. Often he's "Rustic Realist." Mostly the letters aren't printed, but he keeps on writing just the same.

I sit down to give him a report on my travels with the Kalahari Bushmen.

"Aren't we supposed to call them the San now?" he asks.

He is right. But much to the consternation of my editors in Washington, all the San I have met in the desert are still demanding to be called Bushmen, a name that Western anthropologists now consider derogatory.

Dad has just retired from the Standards Association of Zimbabwe, a nonprofit institution that devises and administers quality, safety, and management systems for industry, and he is studying to qualify as an independent assessor, the only one in the country. Some of the technical standards he is studying, he wrote himself.

At seventy-three, my mother has tried to retire several times, but there is no one to replace her, so she still works at the hospital. She starts each morning at 6:30, and she sees more than eighty patients a day.

When I visit her at her clinic later, her longtime assistant, Nurse Machire, welcomes me, as she always does, like Odysseus returning to Ithaca. She escorts me through the packed waiting hall to my mother's examining room. Beige manila patient files are piled high on Mum's desk, and behind her on the windowsill is a bright pink ceramic vase full of colorful ceramic flowers. My mother's not usually one for knickknacks, so I gently tease her about it. She picks up the vase and turns it in her hands and wipes it carefully with a paper towel.

"It was given to me by one of my patients," she says, "an operating room nurse."

She sighs and puts it carefully back onto the sill.

"She came to see us years ago with a novel ailment that looked like German measles but wasn't. I thought it might be HIV, but we'd never seen HIV before. It was still so new there was no test for it then. When testing became available a few months later, she was one of the first patients we tested. It came back positive.

"For the first time we had to deal with the problem of how you inform patients they have HIV. It was decided that a panel should do it: a consulting physician, a psychiatrist, and me. The OR nurse was an intelligent woman, and the others talked to her for about fifteen minutes, discussing contraception and the prevention of transmission, and then they left, well satisfied that they'd told her all they could. And she turned to me after they had gone and said, 'What was that all about? What were they trying to tell me?'

"I said, 'You have a new viral disease that may cause you great difficulties in time. And there is no treatment for it yet.'

" 'But I feel better now,' she said.

"I said, 'Good, just enjoy yourself, then, while you feel well. Keep as healthy as you can, eat well, don't get overtired. And I will be at your side.'

"There was no point in spelling it out to her that she had a death sentence and spoiling what life she had left to live. Anyway, she survived nearly ten years, and she gave me this china flower basket as a present just before she died."

My mother's assistant knocks gently on the door to say that the next patient is ready.

"You must remember how many years we weren't even allowed to *talk* about AIDS here," my mother reminds me. "It was all a dreadful secret. Herbert Ushewekunze, the minister of health, issued an edict, a ministerial fatwa, that there was to be absolutely no publicity at all. And later he died of it himself." She shakes her head and reaches for the top patient file. "Why don't you wait for me in the waiting area and then you can drive me home."

I SIT AT the back of the room behind the rows of patients: nurses and orderlies, maintenance men and cooks and cleaners. All of them are black. Two-thirds of them have contracted HIV. In Shona they now call it *mukondombera,* which means "a plague." It has become so common that my mother can usually diagnose someone at the doorway of her examining room. As a patient politely knocks on the metal door frame, she already knows what is wrong.

There are no more consulting physicians and psychiatrists now. And antiretroviral drugs are not yet available, so there is no treatment at all, there is only shame. Shame and its offspring, secrecy. The death notices and the obituaries only mention the opportunistic diseases that actually felled the victims. They never mention that these diseases galloped in through the open gate of a collapsed immune system — collapsed because of AIDS.

And sometimes, especially when it is a man who is infected, my mother says, he has a terrifying hunger for revenge. If he is going to die anyway, then he will infect as many women as he can before he goes, because it is a woman who has done this to him, a woman who has given him this sickness.

There are orphans, so many orphans. In an African society where there has never been much of a need for orphanages or nursing homes because the extended families have always looked after their own, there is suddenly a great need for both. The people in the middle die, leaving the very young and the very old behind. Deep in the bush, whole villages are being found where the eldest person is a twelve-year-old girl. Villages of children, alone. And these children walk miles to fetch the water and collect the firewood and plant the crops and cook their meager food, and sometimes they even try to keep on going to school, all by themselves.

Because it is only blacks who die of this sickness, not whites, some have started to claim that it is a white man's weapon, part of a plan to get rid of blacks. Some claim it has been deliberately concocted in a secret laboratory, by the American CIA.

When Robert Mugabe, resentful at his overshadowing on the African stage by Nelson Mandela, sent thousands of Zimbabwean soldiers to fight rebels in the jungles of the Congo in return for diamonds for himself and his cronies, many of the soldiers came back on leave infected. It was said that whole units came back with the virus, shared among them by the bar girls in the noisy village shebeens; and the camp followers who became their "temporary wives" and even bore their children; and by the timid tribal girls deep in the forest clearings, who the soldiers found on patrol, girls who had never had any money or owned anything like radios or bicycles or flashlights or even shoes, girls who were afraid of men with guns and would sleep with the Zimbabwean soldiers for a pair of plastic shoes molded in China—even if they were the wrong size and hurt their broad, path-worn feet. They could not talk to the soldiers—they had no common tongue. They would just see the gun and the plastic shoes, and they would have to make a choice, and then later they would die in their villages in the clearings deep in the forest. And the soldiers came back home to Zimbabwe, and they passed this disease on to their wives and to their girlfriends.

Week after week after week, there are funerals, so many funerals now.

The population projections have had to be revised. In 1980, at independence, a man might expect to live to sixty and to see his children grow up strong and have children of their own, and if he was fortunate, a man might even live to see his great-grandchildren bring him gourds of beer before he died. But life expectancy dropped to fifty, and now it has collapsed, all the way down to thirty-three. It is hard to comprehend. At thirty-three, just as people should be in their prime, they suddenly sicken and die. And the managers of the mines and the factories and the farms have begun training three people to fill every job, because they know two will not live to do the work.

I can see that my mother is weighed down by the burden of it all. Every day she has to tell dozens of people they have an incurable disease. She sits in her office surrounded by the badges of her profession, her white coat and her stethoscope, and they serve only to mock her inability to heal.

And some of her patients, intelligent, educated, middle-class people, people who drive cars and work on computers and watch TV, they have lost all faith in the Western empirical catechism, and in desperation they go to those who peddle the promise of a cure. Some unscrupulous *ngangas,* traditional herbalists and sorcerers, say they know how to defeat this sickness, for a fee. And they prescribe snuff to be shoved up the vagina, or *muti,* various bogus unguents and ointments made from the ground bones of wild animals.

And worse, some of them have begun saying that the only way for a man to cure himself of this lethal affliction is to have sex with a young virgin, that this will make him clean again. Many young girls are raped by men for this reason, and they too die in their turn, as do the ones who rape them. Some of the unscrupulous *ngangas* fall back on atavistic rites long suppressed by overbearing white district commissioners, instructing their patients to eat the heart of another human, that it will give them the strength to survive.

I think of Prince Biyela's Zulu *impi* cutting out the gallbladder of a brave adversary and sucking on it to ingest his courage, shouting, "*Igatla!*" — "I have eaten!" And I realize that maybe not so much has changed as we all thought, that maybe the whole idea of progress is a paradox, a rocking horse that goes forward and back, forward and back, but stays in the same place, giving only the comforting illusion of motion.

And as I sit there in this waiting room full of dying people, I'm struck by an image of futility from Joseph Conrad's paean to melancholy, *Heart of Darkness*. Sailing toward the African coast for the first time, the narrator, Marlow, sees a French warship shelling the bush:

> *In the immensity of earth, sky and water, there she was, incomprehensible, firing into a continent.* Pop, *would go one of the six-inch guns; a small flame would dart and vanish, a little white smoke would disappear, a tiny projectile would give a feeble screech — and nothing would happen. Nothing could happen.*

But my mother hasn't given up. At seventy-three she still gets up at dawn every morning and comes into the hospital, working on well past her retirement age, paid only her meager government salary, impelled only by her stubborn sense of duty. Even when there is little she can do for them, she has not abandoned her patients. She continues to lob her little shells of compassion, benignly bombarding the mangrove littoral with her good offices.

FOR SOME YEARS now she has also been playing another role: trying to roll back corruption, in a small way, by serving on a medical compensation board, reviewing claims from former guerrillas disabled in the independence war. The compensation fund set up to make grants to them has been ransacked by false claimants, for fictitious injuries. Several perfectly fit cabinet members have qualified as quadriplegics and are being paid for 100 percent disability.

And here it is that my mother comes up against her nemesis. He too is a doctor, Dr. Chenjerai "Hitler" Hunzvi, a prominent member of the War Veterans Association. He has chosen Hitler as his *Chimurenga* name, the deliberately frightening nom de guerre used in the war, though, like many of the most militant, he never actually fought in the independence war himself, sitting it out in the safety of Warsaw, from where he returned only after independence, with a Polish medical degree and a Polish wife. (She didn't last long, fleeing back to Warsaw with their two sons, and describing in her book, *White Slave*, how Hunzvi tortured her.) It is the same diagnosis — polyarthritis — with Hunzvi's signature that my mother finds again and again below many of the false payments. They include his own for being 85 percent disabled. Now the coffers are empty for actual war veterans who really were disabled in combat.

The other doctors who are supposed to be reviewing drop out until there are only two left, my mother and Dr. Edwin Mhazo. Together they sit long hours at the hospital, one white, one black, reexamining claimants and challenging hundreds of bogus physicals, some of them of senior party members and members of Parliament.

When Hitler Hunzvi hears what they are doing, he is furious. He sends word to my mother that he is "coming to sort her out," that she should "beware." He has now been elected leader of the War Veterans Association, and his threats are to be taken seriously. But neither my mother nor Mhazo will back down. And my father waits for her in the hospital parking lot, so that she doesn't have to drive home alone, with Hitler Hunzvi out to "get her."

With the revelation that the compensation fund had been drained, mostly by party fat cats, the war veterans take to the streets, to demonstrate, with a hypocritical Hunzvi at their head. Mugabe concedes immediately. These ex-guerrillas were the backbone of his revolution. And from 1997 he starts putting through what are, by Zimbabwean standards, enormous onetime payments to the fifty thousand war vets, plus generous monthly pensions. Many economists calculate the real collapse of the economy from this moment. The Zimbabwe dollar crashes, never to recover. Mugabe brings Hunzvi into the government; he is too much of a threat outside it.

Later, after my mother does eventually retire, Dr. Mhazo dies very suddenly, under mysterious circumstances. He is perfectly healthy on a Friday, and over the weekend he dies in the hospital of massive organ failure. My mother is deeply suspicious. But she can do nothing.

five

April 2000

FOR THE FIRST YEAR of his life, our new baby, Thomas, seems to absorb all our time. We are exhausted by him, intellectually numbed. When he is nine months old, Joanna and I bring him out to Africa, briefly, to meet my parents. They seem nonplussed at first, Dad in particular. On being presented with his grandson, he lowers his newspaper and makes some baby sounds. When I look again, the paper is back up. Only later when I examine photographs of their encounters do I see that I have somehow missed the glowing smile that my father is bestowing on Thomas as the baby confidently grips his grandfather's russet forearm. It is a smile I have never seen before.

Now I am coming back to Africa on my own, on assignment for the *New York Times Magazine,* after a six-month absence.

The heavyset Congolese businessman sitting next to me on the flight into Harare wears a houndstooth sport coat, a Chanel necktie, a sheen of sweat, and two Rolexes, one on each wrist.

"This one for local time; this one for Washington time," he explains, following my glance. His children are safely in the United States at college, he says. The profits from the cell-phone network deals he's cobbling together are parked securely out of Africa too. He palms some peanuts and chugs some Cape sauvignon blanc and turns to look out the window.

"Africans can't do governments," he suddenly announces. "We are useless at it, disorganized."

I close my newsmagazine and nod noncommittally.

"And our institutions never work because we never pay our dues." He reaches up and presses his bell for more wine.

Recent events in Zimbabwe have strengthened his thesis. As he turns away I look back at my magazine, at a photograph of a white Zimbabwean farmer, a big bear of a man, sporting a bushy beard. His name is Martin Olds, and his body lies as he fell, on his back, beneath a shattered window, arms outstretched. He is barefoot, dressed in dark green shorts and a khaki shirt, his injured right leg bound between two makeshift wooden splints. I examine them closely. Are they baseball bats? No. They're wooden curtain rods, and he has tied them around his broken leg with torn strips of curtain, now bloodied. The bald dome of his head is crisscrossed with red gashes. His position looks oddly like a supine crucifixion, one foot over the other against the pinewood of the curtain rod, arms flung open along a worn wooden broom handle, the horizontal beam of his cross.

Today I am flying into a firestorm. After ten years of one-party rule, President Robert Mugabe has suddenly encountered real opposition. It began as a minor obstacle on the political skyline, an irritating clause in the constitution that limited his term in office. So he has rewritten the constitution to increase his already considerable presidential powers, and reset the presidential clock, another twelve years in office. But his change needed to be ratified by a referendum, and he needed something to sweeten the deal, something to entice the continued loyalty of a threadbare people. So he inserted into the new constitution a law allowing the seizure of commercial farmland and its redistribution to black peasants.

Land is something of a paradox in Africa. It was not always precious. There is, for most societies, a litmus test that shows if there's a
scarcity of land or of people, the wedding test: does the bride come
with a dowry, or must the groom pay a price to the bride's father?
Europe has mostly dowry cultures. In Africa, bride price is the rule.
Fertility is prized above all, because, hard as it is to believe today,
the continent's historic curse was underpopulation, which hinders
centralized rule and state building.

To early white visitors, much of Africa seemed almost empty.
For the most part, "an unpeopled country," said the bellicose explorer and correspondent Henry Morton Stanley as he strolled
through East Africa.

This impression of emptiness was accentuated by the African
system of shifting agriculture. Bush was cleared, land prepared
mostly by hand, crops planted, and rain relied on to water them. No
fertilizer was used other than the ash from the initial burning, and
when the soil became exhausted after two or three seasons, the
farmer simply moved on to a new patch of bush. The idea of land
"ownership" as such was an alien one. A white farmer once told me
of his grandfather going to see a local chief about buying some land.
"Buy land?" said the chief. "You must be crazy. You don't buy the
wind or the water or the trees."

When the first white pioneers trekked up from South Africa
to cross the Limpopo River, it wasn't the land they were interested in but what lay beneath it. They had come to prospect for
gold. The deal they struck with Lobengula, the paramount chief of
the Matabele, and his subject Shona tribes, dwelled exclusively on
mineral rights. Under the Rudd Concession of 1888, emissaries for
Cecil Rhodes's British South Africa Company agreed to pay him
one hundred pounds every lunar month, and give him one thousand Martini-Henry breech-loading rifles, one hundred thousand
rounds of ammunition, and a gunboat on the Zambezi (or, in lieu,
another five hundred pounds, which is what he eventually got), in
return for which he would cede all mineral rights to his territory,
though not the rights to the land itself.

But this proved to be no Eldorado, and following the defeat of Lobengula and the subjugation of the indigenous people, Rhodes granted his pioneers parcels of land to farm, as a sort of consolation prize. Subsequent farmers purchased their land from the British South Africa Company, which was the colonizing authority under a royal charter, but tribal authorities were never compensated. Rhodes created tribal reserves for "natives," of whom there were then estimated to be fewer than six hundred thousand in a country the size of Spain.

Racially based land tenure was later codified under various laws, and population pressure in the so-called Tribal Trust Lands began to grow as the black population increased with their access to Western medicine, with people like my mother carrying out wide-scale vaccinations against killer diseases. By mid-1945, blacks already numbered over four million, and white immigrants were being recruited from a war-ravaged Europe, under the so-called Empire Settlement Scheme, to buy farms in Rhodesia with low-interest loans.

For much of the twentieth century, whites possessed more than half of Rhodesia/Zimbabwe's agricultural land, even though they made up barely 1 percent of the population, and this land disparity was seen as one of the main causes of the country's civil war. But at independence in 1980, when white-dominated Rhodesia became black-ruled Zimbabwe, the new president, Robert Mugabe, at the urging of his ally, President Samora Machel of Mozambique, made racial reconciliation the centerpiece of his policy. Machel rued the economic chaos wrought at his own country's independence when his policy of wholesale nationalization triggered a swift exodus of a quarter of a million Portuguese, after five hundred years of settlement. People like my parents, who had feared that Mugabe, an avowed Marxist, would bustle all whites out of the country, were hugely relieved to find instead that he welcomed them to remain in a tolerant, multiracial Zimbabwe. He appointed a white minister of agriculture and toured the country with him, appealing to white farmers to stay on and contribute to the new country.

And they did. Their produce, in particular tobacco, brought in 40 percent of the country's export earnings; their food crops fed the cities; they employed a quarter of the country's workforce. Zimbabwe became the fastest-growing economy in Africa, and it was the continent's breadbasket, frequently exporting food to neighbors in need.

Robert Mugabe did begin a program of voluntary land redistribution, funded mostly by the British government, and nearly 40 percent of the land held by whites at independence was purchased—at market prices—and transferred into black hands by 2000. But Mugabe's interest in land resettlement waned, and in the past decade his government had allocated an average of only 0.16 percent of his annual budget to land acquisition; the military got over thirty times that amount. And when the British realized that many of the newly acquired farms were being given not to landless peasants, as had been agreed, but as bonbons to Mugabe's political cronies, they froze the remains of the fund. Even then, some 740,000 acres of land acquired for resettlement remained empty and idle.

But Mugabe's neglect of the land question failed to raise any spontaneous clamor from his people, by now the best educated in Africa. Most of them, especially the young, had aspirations to salaried jobs in towns rather than to a life of toiling in the fields. A poll conducted by the Helen Suzman Foundation in early 2000 found that only 9 percent of Zimbabweans saw land redistribution as a priority. By then, according to the Commercial Farmers Union (CFU), 78 percent of white farmers were on property they had purchased *after* independence, only when that land had first been offered to—and turned down by—the government, as was required by law.

Opposition to Mugabe's new constitution came from an eclectic congregation drawn from all points of the political, racial, tribal, and social compass, and it was especially strong in the urban areas, among the black middle class and the trade unions and people like my parents, who had been part of the old white liberal establishment. It also came from white farmers who realized that their land was to be seized. Many joined a new political party, the Movement for Democratic Change (MDC). Its leader, Morgan Tsvangirai, was a former trade union head. The MDC didn't disagree with the idea of land reform—no one did really, not even the white farmers themselves—but Tsvangirai said it had to be done in a planned and orderly way, so that the golden goose of commercial agriculture would not be cooked. Campaigning for the February 2000 constitutional referendum was lively, but the opposition was denied access to the government-controlled radio and TV, and no one thought Mugabe would actually lose. He had never lost at the polls before. So when he did, we were all shocked. I found myself taking a deep breath and thinking, *Now there's really going to be trouble.*

President Mugabe gave a speech after the referendum result saying that he was a democrat and would respect the will of the people. But his face was tight with anger as he said it, and his smile was not a real smile; it was a rictus, a barely suppressed snarl. And he looked over the camera, not into it, over our heads, not into our eyes. And you could see that this was a man fueled by thoughts of revenge, that he was boiling with the public humiliation. How could he, who had liberated his people, now be rejected? How could they be so ungrateful? It couldn't be his own people who had done this (even though 99 percent of the electorate was black); it must have been other people, white people, leading them astray. He would show us. He would show these white people not to meddle in politics. In things that did not concern us. We had broken the unspoken ethnic contract. We had tried to act like citizens, instead of expatriates, here on sufferance.

During the referendum campaign, Mugabe's ruling ZANU-PF party had already taken out race-baiting ads in the *Herald*. Among the local press clippings my father sent me was a full page ad featuring a large photo of an elderly white couple wearing "Vote No" T-shirts. "They are going to vote no," read the caption, "Vote yes." In the news reports, white Zimbabweans were now referred to as the "nonindigenous," "Britain's children," and even simply "the enemy."

"What do you think?" I ask my father.

"Oh, no one takes any notice of it," he says cheerfully. "For God's sake, the war ended twenty years ago. There's no racial animosity these days. I've never felt any. Mugabe's trying to divert attention from his terrible economic mismanagement, but it isn't working."

And indeed in the forthcoming parliamentary election, four months later, Mugabe's ZANU-PF party candidates faced a real opposition — the MDC — which had coalesced around the referendum campaign. And so Mugabe was doing what old generals always do, girding up to fight the last war. Just like Fidel Castro, Mugabe pulled on his old olive green army fatigues, the vestments of a battlefield he had never personally fought on, to emphasize the victories of the past and to distract from the failures of the present. At rallies around the country, he punched the air and ranted anew against an antique and increasingly irrelevant colonialism, now a generation past.

And then he choreographed a crisis. Days after his referendum defeat, people calling themselves "war vets," ex-combatants from the independence war, began arriving on white-owned farms and refusing to leave. The way they pronounced "war vets" was elided so that it sounded like "wovits," which is what my sister and others started to call them. Very few were actual war veterans at all; they were just a ragtag collection of Mugabe supporters and unemployed youths, many of whom were being paid a daily stipend by the ruling party to participate. Hitler Hunzvi was clearly the architect of the campaign — and the wovits arrived in government buses and trucks. When the white farmers complained to the police, the police said it was a "political" matter beyond their jurisdiction.

Still, when the farm killings began, it took my parents by surprise. Suddenly my father wasn't quite so sanguine.

Martin Olds — who I am reading about on the plane — was murdered on April 18. He had farmed in a place called Nyamandlovu. It means "Meat of the Elephant" in Ndebele, the tongue of our southern tribe, the offshoot of Prince Biyela's Zulus. Many down there, Olds among them, had joined the MDC. He was alone when his homestead was attacked. He had sent his teenage daughters and his wife into Bulawayo. The attack came just after first light. It was a hit squad, the locals said, Shona-speaking, from up north. The CFU tried to reconstruct what happened. A hundred men, armed with AK-47s and pangas (machetes), arrive in a fourteen-vehicle convoy. When Olds goes out to speak to them, they shoot at him, so he retreats inside. The men take up six ambush positions around his homestead and open fire. Olds calls the police, pleading for help, but no one comes. He calls his neighbors, who try to help but are forced back with gunfire, as is an ambulance they have requested.

For three desperate hours, the gun battle rages. Olds was once a soldier; he knows how to defend himself. But he is one against a hundred. He is shot in the leg; he ties it with a makeshift splint and fights on. The attackers lob burning Molotov cocktails through the windows. A neighbor flies over the homestead in a little Cessna and sees the house in flames below, sees the gunmen converging on it, but can do nothing to help. And as the house burns, Olds retreats from room to room, finally to the bathroom, where he fills the tub with water, wets his clothes, and prepares to make his final stand. He returns fire until he runs out of bullets, until he is overcome by the smoke and the heat, and then he climbs out the window, hands raised.

He is barely outside before the gunmen converge on him, beat him with shovels and rifle butts, stones and machetes. Then they get into their trucks and drive back north. Those injured in the attack are escorted by police to a nearby hospital where they are treated and released. Police confirm that no arrests have been made.

Surreptitiously the Congolese businessman leans across the empty seat between us to see what I am studying so intently. He sees the picture and raises his eyes to look at me with an expression I cannot quite recognize at first. Then I realize it is pity. He feels sorry for Olds and for me and for our little tribe of white Africans. I feel embarrassed, humiliated, mortified. I am not used to being the one pitied. I am the one who pities others. I casually close the magazine and pretend to look out at the roiling black clouds we are about to penetrate on our way down to land.

It is raining heavily when we disembark at Harare Airport, which is gently atrophying as plans for a new one are pondered. We jog across the tarmac to line up in the immigration shed. The rain drums down on the corrugated-tin roof, making it hard to hear. Strategically positioned pails catch the gushing leaks. Above us an electronic ticker flashes a message from the Zimbabwe Investment Center: "Welcome to the most favorable investment destination on the continent." But when it comes to the telephone number for potential investors to call, the ticker lettering breaks up into a jumble of x's and y's and z's.

When I reach the head of the line, I hand my passport to the black official and greet him in Shona, Zimbabwe's main vernacular. He ripens in smile and demands, "Why don't you stay here? We need people like you."

By "people like you," he means white Zimbabweans. I shrug and feel half pleased, half ashamed. It always has this sweet-and-sour effect on me, this place. Even as it gets poorer, more ramshackle, more dangerous, its slide accentuated for me by my periodic overviews, snapshots separated by absence, I am tempted each time to tear up my return ticket and stay. For whether I like it or not, I am home.

Dad is noticeably more frail; he now has early-stage emphysema. Mum's back hurts constantly, and she thinks she may need it operated on. Mavis, the housekeeper, is aging with them, stooped and slow now, and being kept alive by expensive hypertension drugs that Mum gets her.

The swimming pool lies green and still and opaque, its pump quiet, with a slimy watermark around its rim. Dad has given up. The chemicals, he says, have increased tenfold in price and are often unavailable. Georgina warned me about this, and I e-mailed them to say that I would arrange to have the chemicals delivered monthly to them, via a Web site I have discovered. It is important to keep exercising, I argue.

WHEN A CROCODILE EATS THE SUN • 63

"Please let me help?" I say to my father, but he gets angry.

"It is absolute robbery," he says, "what they're trying to charge. I will have nothing to do with it. We can do quite well without the pool."

"Anyway," says my mother brightly, "we saw a program on ZTV about converting your pool into a fish facility, and we're going to drive into town, to the Ministry of Agriculture, to pick up a pamphlet on how it's done. It's getting increasingly difficult to find fish in the shops, so we'll breed bream for the pot."

I AM SUPPOSED to be writing an article about the attacks on white farms, and my father has carefully clipped articles he thinks will be of relevance and stored them in a box file that he now presents to me. On top of the pile is a piece about David Stevens, the first farmer to die, on April 15, and another prominent member of the MDC. He was abducted from his farm, Arizona, by forty armed men who arrived in a bus. His hands were tied behind his back and he was driven away. White neighbors who came to his aid were shot at and took refuge at the local police station, but the gunmen followed, dragged them out, beat them and tortured them, forcing Stevens to drink diesel oil.

One was witness to Stevens's death: "I saw a man step forward and shoot Dave in the back and then in the face with a shotgun — he literally blew him away," he said.

His widow, Maria, is a friend of ours, so I call her. "I'm also supposed to be writing a piece on . . ." I swallow back my embarrassment. "On all of this," I say. "So you don't have to talk to me if you'd rather not. Or at least not on the record. Or if this isn't a good time . . ."

"Why not?" she says. "They've already killed my husband, what else can they do to me?"

David Stevens came up to Zimbabwe at independence from South Africa because he wanted to live in a free country. Here he met Maria, a Swede, recently arrived as part of a Scandinavian aid program. Now a handsome woman in her late thirties, I visit Maria in her temporary Harare refuge, a suburban house owned by the Swedish Embassy. Her twin twenty-month-old boys crawl restlessly over her.

"They don't really understand that their father has been killed," she says. Her voice is flat. "I don't really know how to explain it to them." She arbitrates a squabble between the boys, and sits one on either thigh.

"We bought our farm from a black man in 1986. It was a run-down overgrown mess," she remembers. "No rivers flowed there. It was called Arizona because it was arid and rocky. Now all the rivers flow. We grew tobacco and corn, and I bred ostriches. We employed seventy-five families. David spoke fluent Shona and was on the local council trying to sort out the roads in the communal area. Eventually he got involved in opposition politics and joined the MDC. There was even an MDC rally held on our farm.

"When the war vets first invaded, we had fairly good relations with them. But then one weekend when I was away they raped a little girl in our compound, and our workers got the hell in with them."

That's when the trouble started. The workers chased the wovits off the farm, and soon they returned with reinforcements and seized Stevens.

"When David was taken away by vets, the last thing he said to me as he left was, 'Don't worry, darling, I'll be safe.' I never saw him alive again. I haven't been back to the farm. The vets have burned down the compound and looted our house. They took the bag in which I had packed all our valuables: birth certificates, passports, jewelry. So now we have nothing." And then she is crying, for the first time this afternoon, and it's her tears that capture her sons' attention as the abstract news of their father's death cannot. On her lap, they finally still; they look up at her in alarm.

"David always said that he was not a hero or a missionary," she says, "that if it got dangerous, we'd leave."

* * *

NEARLY A THOUSAND white-owned farms have now been invaded by the wovits, but the CFU has told their members to sit tight while they negotiate with Mugabe. The CFU has warned the farmers that any of them named in the media will risk being singled out for reprisals by the government. And the wovits themselves are very hostile to strangers coming onto the farms, especially anyone suspected of being from the media. Photographing farmers is hugely problematic; photographing war vets is almost suicidal. Nonetheless, the *New York Times* has sent Antonin Kratochvil, a Czech photographer, now a New York resident, to cover this story with me.

Antonin cuts an unlikely figure here. Corpulent and bearded, he speaks American English with a Czech accent. He usually has a cheroot in the side of his mouth and he laughs constantly, a booming rumble that rises from his belly. He is a tropical Santa, able to suck the tension from a room. His very strangeness makes him a perfect choice. I collect him from the Meikles Hotel, where he stands waiting on the lion paw-print carpet in his sleeveless khaki camera jacket, his little Leica over one shoulder.

WE HAVE FOUND one farmer, Rob Webb, who's willing to talk. He owns Ashford Farm in the Centenary district, a hundred miles north of Harare. The drive takes you through the lands of milk and honey: neatly trammeled fields of corn standing eight feet tall, manicured groves of fruit trees on the vast Mazowe citrus estates, black-headed sheep and plump Hereford cattle shining with good health. In the fields, black workers are stooped over the rich red earth, planting winter wheat. Huge metal irrigation gantries spritz the contoured grooves of the earth with water.

And, periodically, bursts of gaudy bougainvillea mark the houses of white men. Bougainvillea is exotic to Africa, just like the white man. It hails from the rain forest of the Amazon. From the air, you can trace the progress of the European by the bright scarlets, mauves, and pinks of bougainvillea. The corrugated-tin roofs of the homesteads peek through thickets of musasa trees.

On the sides of the road, black men in yellow fatigues try to keep Africa at bay, slashing at the elephant grass that plumes out of the shoulders and threatens to envelop the road completely. Coming in the other direction, straining back up the escarpment toward the capital, Harare, are trucks piled high with bales of golden Virginia tobacco, destined for the auction floors. Zimbabwe is the world's second biggest producer of Virginia tobacco, and the crop provides nearly half of all the country's foreign exchange. Buses too groan up the hills on their way to the capital, their roof racks towering with luggage, ears of corn, bicycles, chicken coops, and the odd hobbled goat.

Centenary farming district has seen more than enough trouble in its half century of white settlement. Originally opened to the white man in 1953, it was apportioned and sold mostly to common-wealth ex-servicemen fresh from World War II. In late 1972, its farms came under guerrilla attack in the first shots of the decisive phase of the Rhodesian civil war.

Ashford is one of the last farms before the earth falls away dra-matically down the escarpment to the great Zambezi River, which is only ten miles away as the fish eagle flies. Just inside the farm gate are dozens of rough grass shelters erected by the "war vets" who have invaded the Webbs' farm. "If they challenge you, say you're a fertilizer salesman," Webb had told me.

The wovits are sitting, sleeping, listening to a radio, washing their pots, sharpening their pangas. They stare at me, and one gets up and walks toward my car. He squints at my license plate and jots it down. Antonin and I wave blithely and drive slowly on, and he makes no move to stop us. At the top of an avenue of flame trees is a lawn of lush Durban grass around a hacienda-style homestead where Rob and Jenny Webb sit on their barred-in veranda. Behind them is a wagon wheel, a common household emblem embedded in walls or gateposts by pioneers when they finally arrived at their des-tination, their trek over.

"Sorry my house is a bit bare," apologizes Jenny. "I stripped it of anything that meant anything to me and sent it to Harare for safe-keeping."

They are a good-looking middle-aged couple, tanned and fit from an outdoor life, surprisingly calm and considered, given their current situation. We sit down at the dining table for lunch, and Jenny reaches to tinkle the bell to summon the cook, and then remembers it is not there. She apologizes for the second-best cutlery we are using too.

Rob slices the rare roast beef. "This place was mostly unpopulated when we arrived," he says. "There were tsetse flies, so no cattle could survive. No cattle, so no people. Whites used to come here to hunt lion, that's all."

His grandfather came out to Africa as a veterinarian with the British cavalry fighting the Boer War. His father served in the police force of old colonial Bechuanaland (now Botswana). Rob's uncle wrote the Kenyan constitution.

After lunch, the Webbs take us for a drive to show us the lay of the land. Rob points to a prominent rock outcrop, Banje Hill, visible across the district. It provided the main navigation point for the guerrillas as they infiltrated the country during the independence war.

"We survived seven years of war," says Jenny. "The roads were land mined, and I was here by myself with the children when the house was attacked." But after the war ended and Mugabe asked white farmers to stay on, the Webbs did.

At its height, Centenary boasted 154 commercial farms, but that is now down to 96. At independence, the eastern area, which abuts a crowded communal land, was handed over for black resettlement.

"We told the government," says Webb, "if you're going to take land, do it in a planned way, rather than just extending subsistence farming."

But as we drive through it, most of the land—once some of the most productive in the country—stands empty of crops, choked with undergrowth. Farms lie abandoned, their buildings stripped of their tin roofs.

"Just look at it," says Webb in dismay. "It's such a terrific waste."

Webb shows me the Farm Development Trust, an old commercial farm converted into a tobacco training center by white farmers. More than a thousand black farmers pass through it every year taking courses to learn how to grow tobacco commercially. "Some of the farmers being trained there are those now invading us," he says. His wife choruses this hymn of despair. "This will never end. If they get more farms, in five years' time when our corn is ten feet tall and theirs is only two feet, they'll come again and say, 'We want your land.'"

Only now does Rob take me on a tour of his own farms—he has three, combined into one unit. Here he grows coffee, paprika, wheat, sugarcane, soybeans, asparagus, tobacco. At his tall brick tobacco barns, workers are busy grading and packing leaves. "There's millions of dollars' worth of tobacco here," he says. "And they've warned me that they'll burn it all down if they lose the elections."

He employs 620 people, and, with their families, some two thousand live on the property. "We run an elementary school for the laborers' children and a fully staffed clinic."

Rob Webb has gone to great lengths to stay on good terms with the ruling party as a political insurance policy for his business. His wife shows me a recent letter of thanks they received from Border Gezi, the local member of Parliament, and one of Mugabe's prominent lieutenants. It is headed in bold type, "Appreciation of corn donation to Muzarabani Constituency," and it acknowledges contributions Webb and his fellow commercial farmers have made to the ruling party. "Rob," it continues, "the people have high regard for you. Please keep up the spirit of togetherness that you have demonstrated. This good work is highly commendable, and as your member of Parliament, I am proud of the cooperation that I have received from you, the commercial farmers."

But this was no use to him when a mob of a hundred people armed with pangas and rocks marched up the drive chanting hostile slogans and beating tom-toms and dancing the *toyi-toyi*, an African war dance.

"They demanded to speak to me, and when I came down, they shouted, 'We have come to take your land—that is what we have been told to do.' "

They pegged land claims on his soybean fields, which were just about to be harvested, and demanded they be plowed immediately. When Rob insisted on reaping his crop first, they tried to set fire to it; only the greenness of the shoots prevented it from catching. Now Webb is combine-harvesting day and night to salvage as much of the crop as he can.

Jenny Webb's mother was ill with cancer and needed to be taken to the hospital. The wovits eventually permitted an ambulance to take her to town, "but they refused to let me go with it," says Jenny. "Three days later my mother died, alone." Her mouth purses with anger.

The farm, a big business built up over decades, is on the verge of collapse. Webb is unable to plant winter wheat, unable to water his soy crop, unable to enter or leave his property without permission. His workers are scared and worried about their future. The occupiers spend much of their time drunk or stoned. They squabble incessantly, contradicting themselves from one day to the next. They live parasitically, depending on the farm for their survival even as they destroy it. Their behavior plays to every colonial prejudice about the chaos and hopelessness of Africa.

"As far as I can see, they're nothing but little warlords," says Rob. "I'm being intimidated every bloody day. I give in to their demands so they won't beat my workers. They constantly demand transport and food. But I've said it has to end. The political commissar of this bunch then threatened to stop all work on my farm, and I finally said, 'OK, fine. Do it.' "

Now he is agonizing over whether to go to England this week

for his son's wedding. He can't stand to miss it, but he's afraid that if he goes the invaders will use his absence to move into his house, and he will lose his farm forever.

Rob wants to go over to check on Peter Hulme, who farms on the Range, which is surrounded by communal lands and resettled areas. A group of 250 wovits has just pegged the whole of the Range and subdivided it into 101 plots of twenty acres each.

Hulme gives us the all clear; his squatters have drifted away for the time being. They have marked their territory, though. On the gate to his homestead is a wooden sign hand-painted with a picture of an AK-47 spitting bullets. Below is written the name of the squatters' leader, his political pedigree, and his new address: "Shack Karai Chiweshe, ex-combatant. Plot Number One."

"They raided my cornfields and my vegetable gardens and chopped down trees across all the exit roads," says Peter Hulme. "We sat in the garden and watched their antics, beating drums and chanting war slogans and threatening us with axes and cudgels and pointing sticks at us as though they were guns, shouting: 'Bang! Bang! You dead.'

"Most of them were local peasant farmers, a lot of them I recognized, people who had worked for me on a contract basis, during harvest time. A lot of them I'd helped over the years. When I've seen them on their own, they say that they were forced to come. Their leader is a chap who still owes me sixteen hundred dollars for fertilizer I lent him last season so he could plant his own land.

"Initially they set up their shelters on my land and then moved onto the next farms. The police then gave me permission to clear the shelters so that I could work on the field, which I did. The squatters were back within three hours—furious—and said that if I didn't rebuild their shelters in six hours I would have to leave forever. So I got my labor force together and we rebuilt their shelters chop-chop.

"My plans?" says Peter, repeating my question. "My plans are to . . ." He trails off. "I have no plans."

"Still," he says, brightening. "It could be worse. Our neighbors' wovits demand supper and beers and sit watching their satellite TV and sleeping in the guest room. You know, the irony is that this farm has been offered to the government twice for resettlement. They turned it down both times."

As we leave, the Agric-Alert radio in Rob Webb's Land Rover splutters to life with a message that a special task force established by the CFU to try to control the outbreaks of violence over land invasions is about to arrive by helicopter. Louis Maltzer, of McClear Farm, is being threatened by a local wovit commandant. Rob is asked to join the delegation to help Maltzer. We decide that I will join him in the guise of a fellow farmer—somewhat unconvincing, I worry, with my New York pallor. Also I am the only white man in long trousers. Antonin doesn't stand a chance, and anyway he won't be able to photograph this, so we drop him back at Ashford Farm with Janey.

The chairman of the task force is a black Jesuit, Father Fidelis Mukonori, Mugabe's confidant (Mugabe was mission educated by Jesuits), who is supposed to be trying to broker peace here. With him are three CFU representatives, a police officer, an army colonel, and a man, I'm told, who is a senior member of the Central Intelligence Organization (CIO). Rob introduces me with a false name, and I move down the delegation shaking hands until I come face-to-face with a farmer I know well, Johnny Heynes, with whom I was at elementary school. Johnny is standing next to the CIO agent, and he starts to greet me by my real name. I cough and frown at him and he gets it and greets me as a stranger.

McClear Farm sits on the very lip of the Zambezi escarpment, the first commercial farm you come to if you walk up from the neighboring tribal lands. Louis Maltzer is waiting at the gate when we arrive. He tells us that his occupiers arrived a few weeks earlier. They felled a huge gum tree across his drive, making it impossible for him to escape. They cut through the fence and came up onto his veranda where they lit a fire and began to drum and dance and chant *"Pasi ne maBhunu!"* which in Shona means "Down with the Boers!"

Today, only a few teenage wovits are around. They seem suddenly small and vulnerable. Father Fidelis tells them they must stay in their own bit of the farm and let Maltzer and his workers get on with farming, and the kids nod emphatically.

But as our convoy drives out, we are intercepted at the farm gate by a battered pickup truck. The door opens and a stout black man jumps out wearing long trousers and flip-flops and a Zimbabwe War Veterans Association T-shirt that strains to encompass his belly. He waddles quickly over to us, losing a flip-flop in his rush and hopping the last few yards. He is Comrade Mavusi, he tells us, "the local commander." He is followed by a group of young men armed with pangas, hunting knives, clubs, hoes, metal staves, and axes. One of them reverently lays the missing flip-flop on the ground, and Mavusi slides his plump foot into it. Alcohol scents his breath. "Why did you invite these people here?" he shouts at Maltzer in English. Before Maltzer can answer, Mavusi turns to Father Fidelis. "Why have you come to interfere with us down here?"

Father Fidelis suggests a meeting the following day to hammer out a modus vivendi between the white farmers and their unwelcome guests. But Comrade Mavusi bridles at this. He has not heard from his superiors about this meeting, he says.

The army colonel signals that he wishes to speak. *Now,* I think. *Now he will assert himself.* But he only points out that a storm is approaching and we are starting to lose the light, and that the task force needs to leave now to fly back to Harare tonight.

"If the farmers try to leave," Mavusi instructs his followers, "chop them with your axes." He has effectively taken us hostage. But his demands are difficult to follow, and they keep changing. Now he seems to want transport and food for two thousand supporters that he has summoned from the Zambezi Valley. If this is not done, his guys will burn the farm, beat the workers, kill Maltzer. Fidelis just agrees to everything so we can get away. But by the time we reach the helicopter landing pad, the pilots are busy tying down the aircraft in the face of the approaching storm. There will be no flight out for the task force tonight.

Maltzer finds us half an hour later at the police station. "It's all very well for you guys to just fly in and out," he says. "I've got to bloody live here, and my farm's going to be in flames if this isn't resolved before you leave."

He is wild-eyed and desperate. The obvious solution—to deploy policemen to safeguard the farm—is, both Maltzer and the local police commander agree, out of the question. As soon as the police leave, the farmer and his workers will pay heavily for their presence.

Antonin and I drive back through the rain to Harare with Johnny Heynes, my old schoolmate, as our passenger. I am shaken by what we've witnessed, astonished at the way the frothing Comrade Mavusi has the confidence of command, that neither police nor army is prepared to contradict him. Afraid too that Maltzer will not survive the night. But Heynes is phlegmatic. This is all just political grandstanding, he says, the mock charge of the elephant, when it sticks out its ears to look bigger and more dangerous, rather than a real charge when its ears are folded flat against its neck to cut wind resistance. It's one of those pieces of bush lore that we were both raised on. It sounds convincing in theory, but things seem rather different when the beast is actually bearing down on you.

It'll all quiet down after the elections, he insists. When the government wins, the wovits will go away. He's been told as much by the president in private, he confides. "And we're telling all our members to sit tight. This madness will pass, Peter. We just have to keep our cool."

six

May 2000

Back in Harare, I phone Maltzer several times a day. For the first two days, his phone just rings and rings. Rob Webb hasn't been able to contact him either. The comrades won't let anyone onto Maltzer's farm. When I call again on the third day, his line is dead.

I put down the phone and walk to the open window of Georgina's room on the nineteenth floor of the Monomotapa Hotel. From the park below comes the clear trilling soprano of Papagena in *The Magic Flute*. Before the aria is completed, it is drowned out by the sound of a police siren wailing up Robert Mugabe Avenue. In a lull, I hear the barking of police dogs nearby. Even as Zimbabwe is gripped with tension, as the farms burn and opposition supporters are attacked, the city is hosting the Harare International Festival of the Arts (HIFA).

The festival is run by Manuel, Jeremy's best man. Georgina and Jeremy's company handles its publicity. In the weeks before this year's event, they have been fielding worried calls from various acts who have been reading about mayhem in Zimbabwe. The fact that a bomb has just been thrown into the offices of the *Daily News,* one of the country's few independent newspapers, just across from the HIFA site, hasn't made it any easier to mollify visiting artists, and several have canceled. There are mixed feelings too about the appropriateness of going ahead with the festival at all.

Downstairs, in a festival marquee, Georgina is showing off her ten-week-old baby girl to a caucus of well-wishers and fans. At a ceremony performed last week by a Buddhist Quaker in their orchid house, she was named Xanthe Naledi Jain. Xanthe means "golden" in Greek; Naledi, which means "star" in Ndebele, is after Georgina's close friend Tsitsi Naledi Vera; and Jain is after our older sister. Georgina finishes feeding Xanthe, redoes her nursing bra, and hands the baby to Auxillia, her aptronymic nanny, who decants Xanthe into an old-fashioned Silver Cross baby carriage and wheels her away through the crowd.

This evening's great attraction is Oliver Mtukudzi, the gravel-voiced singer who holds Zimbabwe in his thrall. He opens his set with one of his current numbers, "Wasakara" ("You Are Worn Out"). The song is a pointed message to the president that it's time for him to move on and let younger men take over. "Wasakara" has just been banned from all ZBC stations. As the band falls silent, the multiracial crowd cheers wildly and ululates. Mtukudzi introduces his band, and when he comes to his two daughters, who are performing as his backup singers, they are greeted by a welter of cat-calls and wolf whistles from admiring males in the audience.

"Give me your farms for them, then," Mtukudzi calls out, a reference to *lobola,* "bride price," still practiced here.

The crowd roars with laughter. And I sit there thinking of Louis Maltzer and wondering what has happened to him.

AFTER THE CONCERT we repair to "Coca-Cola Green," the refreshment area, and I begin drinking Zambezi lagers with Keith Goddard, a friend of Georgina's. He is a small, birdlike white man with long hair, metal-rimmed glasses, and laughing eyes. My sister secretly admits to finding him rather attractive. Not that she would be of romantic interest to him—he is openly gay and heads up a group called Gay and Lesbians of Zimbabwe (GALZ), which the infamously homophobic government keeps trying to shut down. The government's fury has been stoked recently on the streets of London when Peter Tatchell, head of the UK gay rights group OutRage!, tried to perform a citizen's arrest on Robert Mugabe as he arrived to shop at Harrods, but was rebuffed by his bodyguards.

Goddard is regaling me with the tale of his farcical court case, still on appeal, in which he is charged with multiple rapes. Because of his diminutive stature, he has to stand on a box to give evidence. The alleged victim, Vuma, claims that he was raped twice, forced to sleep overnight, and ordered to drink cold coffee and eat burned toast the next morning before being allowed to leave. Given that Vuma is a huge man, and Goddard tiny, the judge expresses some skepticism. Ah, says the prosecutor, but the acts were done at gunpoint. And he presents exhibit A, a pair of plastic water pistols, neon pink and green, in camp retro-futuristic style. They are still sealed in the original plastic wrapping.

Shortly afterward, a reporter from a government paper, the *Sunday Mail,* tries to infiltrate GALZ. He is discovered almost immediately, one of the first cases in history of a straight man being outed. Police harassment of GALZ continues, but its members (at last count there were some four thousand of them, overwhelmingly black) are fearless. Mutual antipathy to Mugabe's policies has made strange bedfellows of GALZ members and the raw-boned white farmers.

Goddard points across the crowd to a young black man. It is his tail from the CIO. The agent acknowledges Goddard with a half wave and turns his attention back to the stage where a black dancer is somehow twitching the hemispheres of her posterior individually to appreciative whistles from the crowd.

The talk that night is full of the rising tempo of the conflict around us. Local real estate agents are reporting a tripling of properties for sale in suburban Harare as the farm invasions cause a ripple of anxiety through the small white community. And feverish rumors are breeding — of internal coups, of a raid by ex-Rhodesian Special Forces to "take Mugabe out," of international rescue contingency plans.

THE NEXT MORNING I phone Rob Webb to ask again about Maltzer.

"He's bolted," says Webb, and he gives me a contact number in Harare. "By the way, we've been ordered to host a ZANU-PF rally this weekend. You might be able to sneak in. But you'd better dress like one of us. Oh, and leave Antonin behind or he'll be dead meat."

I call Maltzer's Harare number, and his wife, Maryanne, answers. Half an hour later, they open the door to me at a tiny borrowed apartment in the Avenues district of central Harare.

"Man, after you left it got really crazy." He sighs. "Mavusi and his gang demanded to move into my father-in-law's cottage and gave us only two hours to move all our things out. And as my son and I tried to drag our belongings out of the house, they kept on dancing around us, brandishing carving knives at us and cracking whips and making death threats. 'We haven't killed any farmers in this area yet,' they said, 'and we think it's time we started.' "

And at that, Maltzer said, something snapped inside him. It felt almost physical. He got his emergency bag and his son and just drove away. Even as they followed, screaming and shouting and warning him not to leave or they would burn everything, kill everyone, never let him back on his farm, he kept going, abandoning everything, everyone.

"I feel terribly worried about the farmworkers," he says now. "I feel a lot of responsibility for them, but I don't know what to do. I don't want to go back. Not after what we've been through.

"We've applied to go to Australia. I've only ever been a farmer, you know. That farm is my life's work. Everything we've got has gone into that farm. I'll be walking away from a three-quarters of a million US dollar investment. But I'll do whatever I have to — sweep streets if necessary—as long as I don't have to put up with this non-sense anymore."

THAT NIGHT, BACK at my parents' home in our converted garage guest room, I draw the batik curtains made by my dead sister and lie on the candlewick bedspread surrounded by the books and LPs of my childhood. I pull the top book off the dusty stack, an illustrated collection of Greek myths. The first story features the Chimera, the fire-breathing monster, part lion, part goat, part serpent—a word that has now taken on the meaning of an impossible, foolish fancy. Maybe this whole country is a chimera: part developed, democratic; part ancient, atavistic, authoritarian, and, in its very conception, a foolish, unworkable contraption destined to split asunder along its very evident seams, a Frankenstein country where the crude sutures are visible to all.

And as I lie there, I hear the convoys going by, straining up Enterprise Road, the trucks full of war vets beating their fists and their knobkerries and their pangas on the metal sides in time with their songs and their slogans. Our Dalmatians stir, creaking their wicker baskets, and they begin to whine and howl at the rhythmic sound of the war vets' beating on their trucks, just as Prince Biyela's Zulus once beat their spears on their cowhide shields in unison to frighten their enemies. Sometimes, when the wind picks up across the silent city, I can even hear snatches of their words: "*Pasi ne maBhunu! Pasi ne maBhunu!*" they chant as they beat the metal sides. "Down with the Boers," they chant as they are carried out to the farms in government trucks.

And I think of Louis Maltzer cornered in his borrowed apartment, broken by intimidation and threats, ready to do anything, to sweep the streets of distant, unknown towns, rather than remain in this mad and dangerous place.

Is this how it ends? Will we be picked off one by one until those who remain just run?

I finally drift off to sleep in the early morning.

* * *

WHEN I AWAKE, sunlight is streaming through the windows, and birds are warbling. The smell of coffee and bacon wafts over from the kitchen, and Mavis is singing a hymn as she hangs up the laundry in the courtyard. The war vets of the night before banging on their trucks seem like nothing more than an unsettling dream.

But then Dad meets me in the main house with a sheaf of phone messages. The war vets have occupied the Rydings, a private elementary school, out in a farming district called Karoi. The students there are mostly farmers' kids, and feelings are running very high. The situation is confused. I need to get there fast. My parents stand at the top of the drive and wave. Antonin is waiting for me at Meikles Hotel, standing on the lion paw-print carpet again, trying to look like a tourist with his battered panama hat, a cheroot in the side of his mouth. Soon we are on the open road once more, driving due west.

THE RYDINGS SCHOOL is housed on an old farm on the outskirts of Karoi. Tobacco barns have been converted into classrooms and dormitories. Their brick walls are covered in ivy and surrounded by lush lawns of broad-bladed kikuyu grass. Today is the first day of the new term, and the school should be teeming with small children, but it is not. The school has asked them to stay away. Instead, the barn of an assembly hall is filled with their parents, some four hundred in all, their faces clenched with tension.

The "war veterans" are demanding half of the small farm on which the school stands. Their behavior, says the chairman of the school board, has been erratic and belligerent. The staff, he announces to the gathered parents, can no longer guarantee the children's safety. It is an emotional meeting, with all the fear and frustration of the past few months boiling over. Many parents, besieged on their own farms, say their children are already at risk. They have been counting on the school as a safe haven for their kids.

"Can you imagine if news gets out that our children are in danger, and two hundred parents come down the road and meet two hundred war vets armed with knobkerries and pangas—there's going to be blood on your hands," says one farmer.

"If our kids are all here, we'll do anything to get them back, and the vets know that," says another.

"We'll be looking at a hostage situation here—that's the threat, the vets would have us by the nuts."

"It's time to make a stand," says one farmer. "This is where the line is drawn."

"They will use you," warns the farmers' security coordinator. "It's a political thing, and it will never end."

"We're actually not in charge of our own destiny here," admits the chairman. "We know how these people operate. We know how they lie. Let's wait until the government people who deal with these idiots tell us it's safe."

At the gazebo pub on the edge of the school grounds the parents gather after the meeting to drink Lion and Zambezi beers and ponder their future. The sky darkens, and a pulsing spray of stars emerges, under a bright crescent moon.

"Godwin?" inquires a young white man in a khaki blouson.

"Yes . . ." I do not recognize him.

"It's me, Simon Tucker. You used to be my prefect at St. George's."

"I hope I didn't beat you," I say, for Tucker has grown into a tough-looking young man.

"No," he laughs. "You were actually OK."

Tucker farms nearby and has had many dealings with the group of men—mostly real war veterans, not just rent-a-mob—now threatening the Rydings School.

"There are about sixty of them," he says. "And they have rival leaders. The first one was a Comrade Peugeot. I rode out to meet them on my motorbike when he first arrived, and we shook hands. He said, 'Fine, we want half the farm,' and he got out a hoe and began marking his half, which included my tobacco crop, still in the field. He agreed to let me grow wheat on 'his land' and wrote a letter to that effect.

"Ten days later, another group came and demanded, 'Why are you plowing in our fields?' I showed them the letter from Comrade Peugeot giving me permission, and they took it away. So I went ahead and fertilized the field and was about to seed it when the vets turned up at the house again. This time the leader was a guy wearing a tree-bark headdress and a black leather jacket, holding a machete. He was shaking with rage. He started poking me in the chest and shouting: 'Tucker, we are going to kill you!' I just said, 'I'll do whatever you want.'

"The vets have been intimidating my labor too. The tractor drivers were told that if they continued to plow they would be tied to their tractors with wire and set afire. Then the vets ransacked the house of one of my guys, a builder, who was quite high up in the local MDC. I took him to the police station to file a complaint, and the police just turned him over to the vets at the ZANU-PF offices, who burned him with cigarettes and beat the soles of his feet.

"They told him they were going to give him forty lashes, 'twenty for you and twenty for your boss'—me—'because he isn't here.' Then the vets had a meeting in the compound and ordered everyone to bring all MDC cards, literature, and T-shirts in, and they publicly burned it. They said, 'If we find any MDC stuff on you after this, we will kill you.' "

I ask Tucker if he thinks it would be possible to meet his vets.

"I dunno. They're very volatile," he says. "The best time to try is first thing in the morning before they're high or stoned, before their blood's up. But you just never know with these guys."

His wife thinks it's a terrible idea.

Antonin and I spend the night at the Twin River Inn, and at dawn the next morning we drive back out to Tucker's farm. On the way we pass a war vets' sign.

"No Go for Whites," Antonin reads in his Czech accent. "Hmm. You sure about this, Peter?" And he grins, game for anything.

By 7:00, we are waiting with Tucker outside the trading store that has become the vets' base camp. A man emerges, red eyed and sleep fugged, and hawks fruitily on the ground. He is Comrade Muroyi (Shona for "wizard"), the base commander, he says, and he is pretty annoyed to see us here.

"Who are these ones?" he asks Tucker roughly.

Tucker answers as we have rehearsed. He says we are from overseas and we have come to look at the land question. He does not actually say we are journalists.

"They should report immediately to ZANU-PF HQ in Karoi," says Muroyi. This quickly mutates from a suggestion into an order, a trip on which we will be escorted by armed vets. Given what happened to Tucker's builder there, it's not really a trip we want to make. But Muroyi clangs on a *simbi,* an iron pipe hanging from a tree branch, which is their call to arms, and he shouts for his comrades to get up. Tucker and I exchange glances, and he rolls his eyes. His wife had been dead right. This was a terrible idea.

Antonin just grins and pretends he can't really understand what's going on, which is not far from the truth, as we are speaking a combination of Shona, English, and Chilapalapa, a bastard translingual patois. He steps over to Comrade Muroyi and offers him one of his dark cheroots. Muroyi has evidently never seen a cheroot. He takes one from the packet, rolls it in his callused fingers, draws it under his nose, intrigued. Antonin flicks his Bic, and Muroyi accepts a light. He inhales deeply and suppresses a cough. He's clearly impressed. His lungs are used to smoking marijuana seeds and stalks rolled in cheap newsprint, and he still feels a kick from the cheroot. These babies are strong.

"Hey, man, have the pack," invites Antonin. "I got more."

Muroyi snatches it, and as he is scrutinizing the raised gold motif, I risk a question. I ask him about himself.

He is a real ex-combatant, he says, not like many of the others. "I went back to stay with my parents after the war, but I am plowing only two acres to support two wives and nine children," he complains.

So why has it taken him twenty years to take this drastic action?

"The government kept promising us land, but we never got

anything, so now we have come to take it for ourselves, it is our spoils of war. The government was not able to give us land before, you know, because of the laws. That's why we have done it for ourselves."

He is joined by another war vet, Comrade Satan, who immediately makes it clear that *he* is actually the base commander by demanding custody of the cheroot pack. Muroyi scowls but hands it over.

Before they can reprise the idea of hauling us off to the party headquarters and torture chambers, I press on with my benign questioning, this time addressing the senior Comrade Satan.

"We will live together with the white farmers," Satan explains. "We will take half of each farm, and we will plant our crops, just like them. And if we need tractors we will borrow them from the farmer, and if we have money we will pay for the use."

Just as he says that a tractor drives past, its trailer piled high with wood.

"One of mine," murmurs Tucker. "They've commandeered it."

At the entrance of their camp I had noticed a fresh grave, and now I ask for a closer look. There is a large cross at the head of the grave, and at its base is arranged an MDC T-shirt with a hole burned out where the wearer's heart would be. On a piece of iron drum they have scrawled the name of the grave's symbolic occupant, the opposition leader: "Morgan Tsvangirai, MDC." Above his name they have painted their rallying call: "War Vets Back to War!" Underneath it is written "He will kill the people."

"MDC, it means Morgan Don't Come . . . again!" yells Comrade Satan, and he and Muroyi and other men who have been filtering in pound their feet on the grave as they begin to dance around it. So far, Antonin has not revealed his camera, but now I ask if he might photograph the grave, and Satan agrees. But just as Antonin lifts his Leica, Satan suddenly shouts, "Wait! Wait!" Antonin whips down the camera, fearing some sudden irrational countermand, and Satan dashes away. Seconds later, he returns with a broad-brimmed felt hat on his head. Around its crown is a leopard skin band and a large label that reads "The mighty denim VOLO — king of all jeans — designed in Korea."

Satisfied now with his attire, Comrade Satan strikes a pose at the graveside looking suitably fierce, clenching his fist to the skies.

"Now," he says to Antonin, "I am ready. You can shoot me."

THE FOLLOWING SATURDAY morning, I am back at Rob Webb's farm, without Antonin, watching from the veranda as thousands of farmworkers converge on the farm school for an enforced political rally. ZANU-PF marshals with clipboards note the size of the farm contingents. The commercial farmers from this entire district and its neighbors have been ordered to attend with all their workers. The penalty for absence no longer needs to be enunciated.

The rally is modeled on what they used to call a *pungwe* in the liberation war, a public working-up of emotion. The warm-up is a series of *pamberis* — "forward withs" — and *pasis* — "down withs." *Pamberis* for the ruling party, its local candidates, Robert Mugabe. *Pasis* for "Rhodesians," "sellouts," and the MDC.

I sit, incognito, among the white farmers, all men; they have left their wives and children behind. There are about a hundred of us, dressed in desert boots and shorts and work shirts and floppy hats. We are perched on wooden schoolchildren's benches, our knees up by our chests. The farmers work hard to keep the scowls off their faces.

"Not all white commercial farmers are bad," says a ruling party official in Shona. "Only those who support the MDC."

From time to time I see ZANU-PF marshals pull someone from the crowd and frog-march them away for "reeducation."

There is a ripple of excitement through the throng of black workers when six youth-league members appear, parading a casket shoulder high. It is another symbolic coffin for the political corpse of MDC leader Morgan Tsvangirai, he of many funerals. Large bundles of MDC T-shirts are lugged in, and the marshals spread them on the dust and spit on them. They load the coffin onto the roof of an old car, which the driver attempts to start. For several minutes, the engine sputters and dies, sputters and dies, while the farmers try not to laugh. Then a phalanx of youth militia pushes the car over the carpet of T-shirts, and a mock mourning cohort ululates and cheers the death of Morgan and his party. The scene is filmed by the cameras of the state-controlled ZTV, the only media allowed here today.

The leader of the local farmers' union, George Stam, is called to the podium.

"With war, there is no progress, no development," he says. "We are now reeducated," he assures Mugabe's men. "And I'd like to thank all those who have made this possible—the farmers, the workers, the war veterans."

It is craven, but the white farmers know he is hamming for their survival, placating, playing for time. And he manages to insert a coded note of protest.

"It is not in our culture to make public statements about whom we support," he says. "But I have asked all my farmers to get their ZANU-PF party cards so there can be no mistake about our intention."

Stam ends with a public plea to the ruling party for protection from the unreasonable wiles of the war vets.

"There is a need to reestablish authority in some places," he says, and the farmers around me almost choke on the understatement.

In the following *pamberis*, a teenage marshal approaches me to inquire why my fist is not reaching high enough, why my cheers seem halfhearted.

"What is your problem?" he demands. "Most other people are doing it. You must too." I shrug. He hisses. "I am not kidding you!" I remain silent, and he points his whip handle at me. "I am watching you."

The local governor, Border Gezi, the party's rising star, takes the mike. A former accounts clerk for the power utility, Gezi has recently converted to the Vapostori faith, now one of Zimbabwe's fastest-growing religions, in order to attract Vapostori support. As is their custom, he now shaves his head and wears a long beard.

This is the man who sent a letter of thanks to Rob Webb for his donations.

"Be warned," Gezi tells the farmers now, "your business is farming and *not politics*."

But he lies. What he really means is that, to have any hope of surviving, the members of this community must not exercise their democratic rights, unless it is to vote and campaign for the ruling party, and that is mandatory.

"There will be many more meetings on your farms," he tells them. "You will be sure to facilitate those."

Most of Gezi's remarks are in Shona, and these sentiments are much more militant than his comments in English, as is the case with Mugabe's speeches too. In Shona he talks frequently of a *hondo*—"a war"—if his aims are frustrated. It's a schizophrenic performance.

At the end of his speech, Gezi starts to dance a traditional jig called the *kongonya*. He stoops forward and then hobbles in little baby steps with one hand on his waist and the other holding the back of his head. And though he is short and very fat, he is oddly nimble.

The smoke from huge cooking fires hangs over the meeting. Cows and cornmeal and chickens and sheep "donated" by the farmers are being prepared for the crowd.

"At least they didn't cook and eat *us*," says the farmer next to me when it is finally all over, and he laughs nervously.

Back at Rob Webb's house, some sixty of Mugabe's men, led by Border Gezi, have arrived for a buffet lunch, serving themselves huge portions of roast chicken, potatoes, asparagus, and gravy, piling it high on Jenny Webb's second-best crockery.

I DRIVE OUT past the rough straw shelters of the vets who occupy the Webb farm. They sit there listlessly, excluded from the festivities up at the big house. Soon I am stuck behind a long column of tractors and trailers packed with farmworkers returning to their farms from the rally. Eventually they draw to one side to let me pass. As I overtake them, I give a wave of thanks, and, mistaking my gesture, they all return the open-palmed sign of the opposition.

I sit with my parents that night, dazed from the driving and the rally, and we watch it on the eight o'clock ZTV news. Not even the lens of the state can disguise the stony faces of the farmers as they are hectored, nor the desultory party chants of the farmworkers press-ganged to attend, nor what looks like a reeducation session from the Cultural Revolution. In the *Sunday Mail* the next day, the front-page headline reads: "Farmers Pledge Their Support for ZANU-PF."

There has been another white farmer murdered too, Alan Dunn. His crime was to defeat a ruling-party candidate for a seat on his local council. He answered his door to five men who knocked him to the ground and pounded him with heavy chains, rocks, and tire irons. His three terrified daughters hid under their beds as he was being killed.

I sit now, on Sunday, at his memorial in Harare. Most of the mourners are elderly, their gray hair and glasses glinting in the afternoon sun. As we wait for the service to begin, two farmers behind me discuss another casualty, John Weekes, a farmer shot in the stomach, who now lies dying in the hospital. "At least he nailed one of the gooks," says one with satisfaction. "They found blood spoor."

A friend and neighbor recalls Dunn's words at a dinner just before his death. "I'm going for it," he had said. "I'm putting in a full set of seedbeds and going for it. This thing will sort itself out."

"Lord, in the midst of our tears and aching hearts," prays the priest, "give us the love and strength to face whatever comes."

He reads from the Gospel of John: "Together we sow and reap a rich harvest . . ." But many of the farmers standing here today, uncomfortable in their mothballed suits, have been prevented by the wovits from planting their winter wheat. Already the alarm is being sounded about the future food shortages this will cause.

"Alan came to Africa with nothing in his pockets," recalls another eulogizer, "and built an empire. We are going to run Alan's farms like they were run before. We will not let these farms go down. We will run them until the girls are old enough to take them over."

Dunn's three tow-haired daughters file up to the altar. Each bears a single sunflower. The youngest girl also clutches a frayed brown teddy bear.

"Death is nothing at all," they declaim together, from Canon Henry Scott Holland's famous sermon, "The King of Terrors," their piping voices wobbling with suppressed sobs. "It does not count. I have only slipped away into the next room. Nothing has happened. Everything remains exactly as it was. I am I, and you are you, and the old life that we lived so fondly together is untouched, unchanged."

But they are wrong. Nothing is as it was. Everything has changed.

seven

June 2000

Soon after Dunn's memorial, a new election banner is
erected over Enterprise Road. VOTE FOR COMRADE STALIN MAU
MAU! it shouts. It is echoed by posters on streetlights and walls
throughout the northern suburbs. The elections are only a few
weeks away.

"Who the hell is Stalin Mau Mau?" I ask Dad. I'm helping him
take our empty bottles back to the bottle return at Bon Marché, the
local supermarket.

"Oh, him," he says dismissively. "His real name is Keen Mar-
shall Charumbira and he's an impresario and boxing promoter—a
sort of Zimbabwean Don King. He's the ZANU-PF parliamentary
candidate for our constituency."

"And the name?"

"Stalin Mau Mau? His *Chimurenga* name, I think."

If I hadn't just spent weeks out on the beleaguered farms, I
would laugh. Stalin Mau Mau. How crude could you get in con-
cocting a cocktail of fear by association? A hybrid that mixes a com-

munist dictator who killed millions in his purges, and the Kikuyu tribal rebellion against British rule in Kenya, where black domestic workers slit the throats of their white employers. This was a particularly frightening chimera for white Zimbabweans.

"I shan't be voting for Mr. Mau Mau," says Dad unnecessarily. Instead he will be voting for Tendai Biti, the MDC candidate, a young black law lecturer at the local university. The MDC is entering candidates for all 120 contested seats in Parliament. They are a mixed slate of academics, trade unionists, businessmen, lawyers. Four are white. One of these, a farmer, Roy Bennett, is running in our old home district of Chimanimani.

"I think I'll go down and take a look," I tell Dad. "See how he's doing."

CHIMANIMANI IS STILL recovering from Cyclone Eline, which has swept away all its bridges, leaving it cut off by road for more than a month. My small rental car labors up the hill from the Biriwiri Valley, now the sole access road, which is reduced to one lane hugging the cliff face; the other has been washed down into the steep valley far below.

It's the first time I've been back in a couple of years, since Georgina's wedding. Today Heaven is empty, and the Frog and Fern is closed. The local wovits are on the warpath here too, and Chimanimani Village is desolate. I wander over to the Msasa café. I find the owner, John Barlow, a young white man who is a master carpenter, in the back carving an African drum from a log of blue mahogany. His newly renovated café is empty, and we sit by the fire sipping fresh local coffee and discussing evacuation routes. It is the hot topic around many Zimbabwean dinner tables this week.

Most white Zimbabweans, and many middle-class black people, have what they call gap bags packed and ready, in case the election results trigger a spasm of violence. *Gap bags* because that's all you have when you "take the gap," that is, flee from the country through a pass—a gap—in the mountains, the reverse of the trek

WHEN A CROCODILE EATS THE SUN • 91

made by the pioneers in their covered wagons. Georgina and her friends have a complicated plan that involves various rendezvous along the route from Harare, with prearranged fuel sources, then crossing the Zambezi into Zambia. They have organized food supplies and visas and vehicle carnets. Some have acted preemptively, going "on vacation" for the next couple of weeks, deaf to the entreaties of the MDC to stay and vote.

The evacuation plans now seem prudent, given the white-hot racial rhetoric pouring out of the state media, and Hitler Hunzvi reinforcing Mugabe's mantra of malice by saying that if ZANU-PF loses the election he and his men will go back to war. Add to that conveniently color-coded culprits, and it's beginning to look distinctly scary for white communities, especially isolated ones like this.

The whites here in Chimanimani have already evacuated once, last month, when several truckloads of vets became incensed at a rumor that Hunzvi's private clinic in Harare (where opposition members claim to have been held and tortured) had been torched — it was just another in a spate of rumors — and decided to take out their ire on the local whites. There aren't very many of them left, about twenty families. Warned first by their domestic workers and black colleagues, and then by the local police chief (who was demoted and transferred for his trouble), the whites formed a convoy and drove up to Skyline Junction and out of the valley to lie low until tempers cooled.

Evacuating now from Chimanimani is particularly tricky, with its back to the soaring mountains, and one of its two access roads washed away by Cyclone Eline. If the other one is controlled by war vets, how to get out?

John Barlow was loath to leave last time, but now even he's taking evacuation seriously. "You know, if it comes down to it, the only way out may be to grab the kids and do a *Sound of Music* — climb up over the mountains and into Mozambique."

The very idea of going to Mozambique for sanctuary strikes me as absurd: it is officially one of the poorest countries in the world after being ravaged by thirty years of civil war. But that's what we've come to.

The war vets here in Chimani have been conducting a sporadic reign of terror. They have stripped and beaten black schoolteachers in front of their pupils, threatened the black managers at some of the sawmills, forced locals to attend ZANU-PF rallies. But now their venom is directed overwhelmingly at one man, a white man—Roy Bennett, the local MDC candidate. Charleswood, his seven-thousand-acre farm, is arguably the prettiest in the country, tucked up against the national park. It is latticed with irrigation canals, which feed neat rows of coffee bushes. The local Ndau people call Bennett *Pachedu*, which means "One of Us."

A pitch-perfect Shona speaker, who often walks around without shoes, Bennett arrived in the area about a decade ago. He did what very few farmers bother to do; he went first to pay his respects to the local chiefs, to get their approval of his presence on Charleswood—a matter way outside their modern jurisdiction, and just good neighborliness on his part. He divvied up his need for seasonal labor among the chieftaincies, and only then did he get on with farming. But he continued to be a good neighbor. When Cyclone Eline struck, for instance, and his workers were cut off from their homes in the tribal areas, he got tired of waiting for the government roads department to come. So he took all his farm equipment and his own workers and fixed the roads himself. And so he was approached by a delegation of local ZANU-PF councilors and *kraal* (village) heads to stand as their candidate for Parliament.

Every election, they said, the same thing happens. The party chooses a candidate for us from somewhere else, someone we don't even know. He comes here for a few weeks before the election, he wears a smart suit and makes a lot of promises, and then, once he is elected, he never really comes back, and we are left to cope on our own. We would like you to be our candidate this time, because you live here and we know you.

At first Bennett said he was a farmer not a politician, but they pressed him and pressed him, and eventually he agreed. So they went to Harare and told the ZANU-PF officials there that they had chosen Roy Bennett, a white farmer, as their candidate for the next parliamentary election. The officials just laughed and said, "Don't be stupid. We will decide who your candidate is, and it certainly won't be a white man." And the local councillors came back disconsolate. But then they heard about this new party, the MDC, so they went to Roy again with an idea. How about if they all joined this new party, and he stood as their candidate? The MDC was delighted, and this is how a white man came to run in a rural constituency where over 99.9 percent of the electorate is black.

Bennett is expecting me, and his workers direct me to his farm office. He is burly, uncomfortable behind a desk, a tanned outdoorsman who was once a champion polo-cross player. He is just finishing going through election correspondence in a file fat with constituents' letters. I ask to see them, and he turns the file around, while he answers the phone. Some address him as Father Chimanimani, others thank him for helping to repair bridges after the cyclone. There is a poignant tone of optimism to them, though many are afraid to sign their real names. One reads: "I tell you that I am one of the people who was beaten by those thieves. They beat my flesh but not my mind or brains. . . . We are not going to be intimidated by ZANU-PF anymore. . . . Let's change things. This is our time. Say hi to your wife and family."

Another writes of distributing Bennett's campaign pamphlets, inserting them under doors at night, and it ends with a postscript: "We would have liked to talk to you live, but with the situation as it is I guess it's too risky."

Bennett's rival, the ZANU-PF candidate chosen by the central committee in Harare, is Munacho Mutezo. He wears well-cut suits and Italian loafers and has postgraduate degrees from universities in England and Scotland. His family originally came from this area, so he is the right tribe, but he lives far away from here, in Harare.

And so the battle lines are drawn. The homeboy is a barefoot white farmer without a college degree who lives just down the road,

and the interloper is from the capital, a black man with a postgraduate, First World education and expensive shoes.

Judging by his reception from the locals, Bennett is probably a
shoo-in — if he can just stay alive until the polls open. He has had a
steady stream of death threats. His farm is guarded by dozens of
youths armed with knobkerries and iron bars, and he has supporters in the village and the black township who warn him of approaching danger.

Bennett tells me that he has only just moved back onto his farm
after war vets invaded it. He was away at the time, he says, and they
seized his wife, Heather, who was three months pregnant. They put
a panga to her throat and made her dance around the house and
chant ZANU-PF slogans until she collapsed from fear and exhaustion before they let her go. As a result she miscarried. They beat up
the farmworkers and occupied the farmhouse, ransacking it and
daubing the walls with their own shit. They emptied the urn of
Bennett's father's ashes and cut the paws off the lion-skin rug to use
for *muti* — traditional medicine.

"These white farmers who appease — I've got no time for them,"
says Bennett. "Appeasement has never worked, just look at history.
What's so heartening about these elections is that there's a good
percentage of Zimbabwean whites who've said, 'Damn it, let's get
involved,' and we've suffered together with the blacks and feared
together with them. We've made a stand and shown that we're prepared to sacrifice ourselves for this country. And isn't that what a
patriot is, after all? It's the first time in my life I've felt really Zimbabwean."

We eat supper in the Mawenje Lodge, which Bennett built as
accommodation for the Chimanimani National Park above us, and
where some of Georgina's wedding party had stayed. He moved in
here with Heather when their own house was trashed.

As we sit talking under the tall open thatch eaves by the fire, the
two-way radio crackles to life. "It's my security bloke," he says.
"They've spotted a truck of war vets coming this way."

Bennett's hunting rifles—even though they are correctly licensed—have been confiscated by the police, but one of his mechanics peels down a horse blanket on the sofa to reveal a shotgun and a belt of cartridges.

Bennett's MDC guards, our guys, as he calls them, are gathering at strategic points to repulse the attack. Having seen what they did last time, he is going to make a stand, however unequal the fight. "I'm sick of running now," he declares. "If they're gonna come, they must just come and let's get this over with."

We take up positions by the windows and arm ourselves with knobkerries and pangas, and we wait there, listening. The Haroni River burbles below the lodge, and the wind rustles the bamboo grove, and the baboons bark up in the mountains, and the nightjars call, and we wait to be attacked. "So this is democracy Zimbabwe style?" I say to Bennett, and he just laughs and shakes his head and keeps on looking out the window, scanning the bush. We stay like that, alert, waiting for a gunshot, a gasoline bomb, a hail of stones. How it will start we do not know exactly. I feel strangely calm about an impending attack. It seems somehow predestined, as though I have been drawn back across the globe to meet this fate at home.

And while we wait, the moon rises over the Chimanimani Mountains, glittering the quartz of their jagged granite peaks. I have climbed the range so many times, first as an infant strapped onto the back of my nanny, Violet, and then as a boy, scrambling up on my own into this enchanted kingdom in the air. Later I learned that the winding passes we climbed were ancient slave routes along which captured tribesmen, yoked together by logs at their necks like oxen, were prodded by Arab traders on an enforced trek to the slave brigs that awaited them on the coast of Mozambique. In the Zimbabwe independence war, they became guerrilla infiltration routes, and now their latest bit part in the unfolding history is as *Sound of Music* escape routes.

I am dozing, my forehead on the windowsill, when finally, in the early hours of the morning, Bennett's guards radio in to say that the party militia have turned back. I fall asleep in my bed to the gurgling of the river and the call of the nightjars. I wake up once to the sound of murmuring outside the window and look out to see the young opposition activists huddled around a fire there, blankets draped over their shoulders, hands clasped around enamel mugs of steaming coffee. These are brave men, many are kids still, who are taking on the full wrath of the state, and they are in just as much danger as Bennett.

The next morning I accompany Bennett to the police station, where he has been summoned for a meeting. The wovits' leader, a tall black man who will not look at Bennett directly, tells him that they intend to reoccupy his farm, by force if necessary, but they are prepared to do it peacefully, "cooperatively."

"That's what you said last time," spits Bennett, raising his voice and reeling off a litany of the crimes they committed when they first visited Charleswood. The room is thick with tension, and several of the vets look as though they will quite probably shoot him in a heartbeat, given a pretext. The police officer is doing his best to calm them down, but Roy's not interested in compromise now— he's had a gutful of these guys. I try to work out how many of us are armed. Neither Roy nor I are, but I can see that some of the wovits have pistols. The police officer follows my eyes and nods. He gets up from behind his desk and walks over to the bureau, and on the way back he whispers to me, "You must get Roy out of here." So I remind Bennett that he is running late to address his rally at Ingorima communal lands this afternoon. He looks at the clock and scoots his chair back and thankfully we are out of there.

From the Land Rover, Bennett calls his election agent and friend, James Mukwaya, who says that he has had to cancel the rally. Gangs from ZANU-PF have been there overnight, moving from house to house, warning people that if they attend they will be killed. But Bennett is not downhearted. "They're all on our side anyway," he says, "so why risk their lives with public rallies? We know how they'll vote when the time comes."

* * *

ON MY WAY out of the village, early the next morning, I drive once around the old square and there, faded now and chipped, is the little sign to the elementary school I'd attended up on top of the hill overlooking the village. On impulse, I follow the sign and drive up past banks shouting with bright blue morning glories. I get out and survey the long low buildings.

"Good morning, may I be of assistance?" A tall, tidily dressed black lady introduces herself as Iris, a teacher. When she hears that I once studied here, she offers to show me around. Most of the children are away for a long weekend, she says, but one of them has not been reclaimed by his parents. His name is Honest, and he is a tiny boy in a khaki uniform with a green jersey and serious, dog-dark eyes. He is obviously dejected at having being left behind but determined not to show it. I know exactly how he feels, having been in the same position all those years ago, when my mother was frequently delayed by medical emergencies.

"I am pleased to meet you, sir," Honest says, and he stands very straight, with his chin out, like a little soldier.

On Iris's instructions, he takes me to the spartan classrooms, their ceiling panels hanging down to reveal the metal ribs of the roof struts, and past the empty swimming pool to the threadbare playing fields with their crooked goalposts. He shows me the shower block with its missing tiles and ruined porcelain toilets, and finally he takes me to the boarders' dormitory. I point out the bed where I slept when I was six, the first bed to the right of the main door, the bed traditionally reserved for the youngest boy. It is the very same narrow iron bed with sagging diamond wire mesh under the mattress that I once used to wet.

"It is my bed also," says Honest. "I am the youngest, so this is where I sleep, the same as you."

Iris comes to say good-bye, and Honest strides away over the gravel driveway. When he reaches the red-cement veranda, he turns and holds his hand up in solemn salutation like an Indian chief in a Western.

"Some months," Iris says quietly as she looks over at Honest, frozen in his gesture of farewell, "there is no budget left for the boarders' food, so we have to ask the day students to bring extra food with them, to share."

As I drive slowly away, I feel the distinct sensation that I am on the stern of a ship pulling away from a dock and that soon I will be separated from Iris and Honest by a vast ocean.

The sun is just breaking through the granite ramparts of the mountain, dissolving the mist, as I drive up and out of Chimani-mani to Skyline Junction. But there is no skyline today, just fat gray clouds sitting heavily on the hill, and rain. Work gangs in olive green plastic ponchos dig in the downpour, trying to keep the road open. As I drop down the other side into the Biriwiri Valley, the rain stops, and the clouds lift and the baobab trees begin. I come up behind an old, slow-moving Land Rover pickup. The back is filled with young black men singing exuberantly. They wave me the open-palmed sign of the MDC and throw some fliers up into the air. For a brief moment one sticks to my windshield, and I see the grinning face of Roy Bennett and the headline "*Chinja Maitiro*—Change Your Ways—Vote MDC," and then it blows off into the bush.

eight

June 2000

THE ELECTIONS ARE CHAOTIC. In the cities, long lines form, with some people waiting for days to vote. There is a polling station at Oriel Boys School, right across the road from my parents', and they wait for the throng to thin out, but it never does, so they take folding chairs and join the line. It's a hugely partisan crowd, overwhelmingly in favor of the opposition. There is a carnival atmosphere—a feeling that the old guard is about to be swept away, that we are on the brink of momentous change.

Every few minutes, my parents get up and move their blue-striped camping chairs a few yards on as the line snakes slowly in long switchbacks through the school grounds. The sun blazes down, and everyone shares water and refreshments. Eventually Dad becomes exhausted, stooped with back pain, sodden with sweat.

"You go home," says Mum. "One vote won't make the difference here."

But he refuses, and eventually he casts his vote, and they walk slowly back over the road. He can barely catch his breath, but he is triumphant.

And Stalin Mau Mau does not become the member for Harare East. Stalin Mau Mau comes away with less than 20 percent of the votes cast, trounced by Tendai Biti. In fact, the ruling party gets almost no urban seats at all, and none in the entire southern province of Matabeleland, and few in Manicaland, where Roy Bennett romps home to become member of parliament for Chimanimani.

I leave a few days later for New York, as the last results come in, from constituencies deep in the bush. The MDC has just failed to tip over into outright victory—they are four seats short, fifty-seven to ZANU-PF's sixty-two. And according to the constitution, the president gets to appoint another twenty seats.

My father insists on driving me to the airport, and on our way we are overtaken by the police motorcycle outriders of the presidential convoy. A policeman jabs his finger toward the side, and Dad veers off the road, as we are required to do by law when the president approaches. More squad cars stream by, lights flashing, sirens wailing—the locals call the presidential convoy Bob and the Wailers, after Bob Marley's band, which played at independence celebrations here. Now truck upon truck of soldiers from the presidential guard roar by, bristling with machine guns and AK-47s with which some of them take beads at cars and people as they pass. I count ten trucks of soldiers before Mugabe's black armored Mercedes finally reaches us.

"I saw the inside of his car once when I worked for the Ministry of Transport," says my father as we wait for the convoy to pass. "It was specially modified in Italy. It has a bomb-resistant floor, bulletproof windows, no outside door handles, an intercom for passengers to speak to those outside. The glass is also one way."

I imagine what it must be like for the president looking out of his smoked-glass windows at the city around him, knowing that not a single constituency voted for him in the entire metropolitan area—knowing that he is driving through enemy territory. Knowing that the only way he has been able to stay in power at all is through massive electoral fraud. In the coming months, court challenges show the extent and detail of the cheating, especially in the rural areas, where his men used intimidation and bribes and vote rigging. In some constituencies, the vote tally exceeded the entire population.

A FEW MONTHS later, after secret negotiations, Georgina finally leaves her job at ZBC and joins Capital Radio, a new independent station, Zimbabwe's first, which will be critical of the government, moving into what the political commentators are calling "democratic space." They import a transmitter from South Africa and set it up in a rented room on the top floor of the Monomotapa Hotel. They scramble up onto the rooftop to erect the antenna, and then they realize they have no idea what frequency to broadcast on, so Georgina phones Dad, and he looks it up in his radio manual and tells them that 100 FM is free, so they begin broadcasting on 100 FM that night.

And while Georgina broadcasts her show, and Xanthe rolls around on the carpet at her feet, she looks out the window toward Pocket's Hill and sees the towering antenna of ZBC, whose monopoly they have finally broken. Sunset streaks the sky with ocher, and across it sails a hot-air balloon. It is one of those moments of pure happiness, she tells me. One of those moments that you must commit to memory and savor in the dark days ahead. For those days will come soon enough.

The morning after her epiphany, Georgina and her colleagues are tipped off that they're about to be raided, that the president is signing a special decree to close down Capital Radio. As a precaution, they set up to transmit prerecorded programs and leave the hotel. One of the technicians, Brendan, goes back up to check on the studio, and as he enters the elevator, a posse of armed policemen crowd in behind him. When they get out on the same floor, Brendan pretends to be going to another room and watches as the policemen kick down the door of Capital Radio.

It has been on the air just six days.

*   *   *

THE PRESIDENT'S RHETORIC gets steadily more incendiary. At his party's congress, he says the whites have "declared war" on the people of Zimbabwe.

"We must continue to strike fear into the heart of the white man, our real enemy," he tells his audience of party faithful, and they cheer him wildly and chant, *"Hondo! Hondo!"* — "War! War!"

And Hitler Hunzvi takes the stage to warn, "Whosoever is killed, it's tough luck."

I phone my parents from New York and say it might be time for them to think of leaving. But my father is still unimpressed with the president's blood-curdling threats. Ordinary people don't hate us, he says. They couldn't be nicer.

And anyway, he says, he's no *soutpiel*. It's an Afrikaans word meaning "salt penis," a term for us Anglo-Africans who, they say, have one foot in Africa and the other in Europe, causing our genitals to dangle in the ocean where they pickle in the brine of cultural confusion. *Soutpiels* are not "real Africans." We are the first to cut and run.

But people of all races are starting to leave — even Thomas Mapfumo, troubadour of the liberation war, who virtually invented *chimurenga* music, a blend of electric guitars over *mbiras,* the traditional metal-pronged thumb pianos.

When I was a teenager, and my father worked at Mhangura Mine, I used to sneak down to the beer hall in the black township to hear Mapfumo play with his band, then called the Hallelujah Chicken Run Band (because some of them had day jobs in the mine chicken coops). I was an avid guitarist, and I could barely contain my excitement when, on occasion, he would let me jam with them. Later they called him the Lion of Zimbabwe, and he played at the independence celebrations in 1980 with Bob Marley and the Wailers.

But Mapfumo becomes disillusioned. His new songs attack corruption and nepotism. So the government bans them and threatens to arrest him and Mapfumo leaves for Oregon. There is only "disaster" now in Zimbabwe, he says. "The government has done nothing good for the people."

And then the war vets come to town. Hitler Hunzvi, now a member of Parliament, announces that the party is establishing "mobilization bases" in the cities, as part of "an aggressive plan." The plan is put into practice by one of Hunzvi's lieutenants, Joseph Chinotimba, a huge bull of a man, with an attempted-murder charge hanging over him. His first task is to bring down the last of the independent judges who have been trying to curb the government's excesses and are hearing the MDC cases that challenge the election results. Chinotimba leads a column of war vets to the supreme court building in central Harare, where he threatens to kill Chief Justice Gubbay unless he steps down. And when the government says it cannot, will not, protect Chief Justice Gubbay, he reluctantly resigns, and the vets stand on the steps of the supreme court and they hoot and cheer and whistle. Mugabe appoints one of his own cabinet ministers to replace him.

The pace of violence picks up too. Gloria Olds, the seventy-year-old mother of Martin Olds, is herself gunned down by wovits, her body riddled with eighteen bullets. Again, just as they did after her son's murder, the police wave the departing gunmen through their roadblock. At her funeral, the priest says that Gloria Olds's blood is on Mugabe's hands. A week later the priest is expelled from the country.

From the rural areas come reports of opposition witch hunts. Some of these incidents rise to a new level of the grotesque — clearly designed *pour encourager les autres.* When Mugabe's youth militia catches Robson Chirima, a young opposition supporter, they gouge out his eyes before killing him.

Chinotimba declares himself the new leader of the Zimbabwe Congress of Trade Unions and organizes the wovits and party militias to do to factories and businesses what they have done on the farms. They invade in force, punching and kicking managers and owners, spitting on them and pelting them with rocks, and forcing

workers to do the same. They set up kangaroo courts for labor dis-
putes and use them to extort money, taking half of anything handed
over by the frightened managers. The Avenues Hospital and Meikles Hotel are both targeted. So are nongovernmental organizations, including the Red Cross, where the son of the director is
abducted from the Harare International School by war veterans
and assaulted.

When wovits invade Lobels Bakery, the country's main bread
maker, they are assisted by the police, who arrest a white manager,
Ian Mel, after finding MDC e-mails on his computer. The vets
gather the bakery workers together and tell them that if they don't
support ZANU-PF, they will be "beaten to death." They also tell
them that all whites are to be driven from Zimbabwe.

MY ANXIETY GROWS as I watch all of this from afar, and I call
my parents every few days from New York, just to check. But they
assure me they're fine. And that I really shouldn't worry. But of
course I do. I discuss it with Georgina, who is thinking of leaving
the country herself.

"Maybe they're falling victim to the boiled-frog syndrome?"
she suggests.

I have never heard of this.

"Well, apparently, in experiments, if you put a frog in a shallow
saucepan of water and heat up the water very slowly, the frog will
never quite notice how hot it's getting. It won't actually jump out.
Until it's too late. Until it's boiled alive."

"Perhaps it's time we told them to jump," I say.

"Oh, I'm constantly pestering them to leave. But you know what
they're like. They won't even consider it."

This is their home, and they're damned if they will allow
Mugabe to drive them out, to win. They still believe that change is
coming soon and that they have an obligation to stay to help usher
it in. Besides, they feel responsible for so many people — colleagues,
friends, employees — people they will not abandon, a way of life
they will not surrender.

To find out for myself just how hot the saucepan is getting, I look for another assignment to get me to Zimbabwe. I find one for *Men's Journal,* a feature on Victoria Falls, "adventure capital of the world."

At least it will take me home.

n i n e

May 2001

T HE LAST TIME I was at Victoria Falls, ultralights and hang
gliders, small planes and helicopters, hot-air balloons and
bungee jumpers, gorge swingers and rappelers and cable sliders
were jostling for the air space above the falls and the canyons that
slice through the black basalt below them. Launches, rafts, jet boats,
riverboards, kayaks, and canoes tussled for Zambezi River space. It
had become the biggest commercially run river in the world.

I have pitched the place to *Men's Journal* as having all the raucous feel of a frontier souk simultaneously servicing different fan-
tasies — from the top-dollar Edwardian silver-service safaristas in
their designer khakis, reliving the glory days of the African Raj in a
town that still bears the name most redolent of the British Empire,
to Generation X jungle junkies in neoprene, Velcro, and *kikoyis*,
striped cotton sarongs; a world heritage site that has been transformed into a Babylon of adrenaline that conservation purists see
as merchants running riot in the temple of Nature.

I check in at the Kingdom, a new hotel that echoes the style of

Great Zimbabwe—the soaring drystone palace built in the southwest of the country by Shona-speaking Rozwi people in the fourteenth century. Here it is rendered in rococo riff by a camp designer from Cape Town. Its thatched towers are crowned with fiberglass elephant tusks. Its rooms open onto a decorative lake, fringed with reeds and slung with rope suspension bridges and signs warning, "This lake is a natural water habitat and could contain small crocodiles. Children playing around the lake need parental guidance."

But as soon as I venture into the usually riotous town, it's clear that my "adventure capital of the world" story is going to require some fundamental retooling. The place is ominously quiet.

I go over to see Rita, one of Georgina's bridesmaids, who works here organizing safaris through the Zambezi Valley. She tells me that because Vic Falls is an opposition stronghold, war vets have recently been bused in to teach the locals a lesson. On Monday, militants from the ruling party marched through the city center singing liberation songs, scaring the tourists and beating up opposition supporters.

"They're still around," she warns, "frightening all the tourists away."

As I walk back, a crowd of people sprint around the corner past me, yelping and squealing. I flatten myself against the wall, expecting a column of party thugs to come marauding down the dusty street brandishing weapons. Instead, a massive red-bottomed baboon lopes into sight, clutching a bag of groceries it has stolen. It scrambles up onto a roof and examines its haul, looking up occasionally as the locals throw stones.

Things are quiet too down in the Backpackers Bazaar. Usually there would be a line out the door of people waiting to book for rafting, jumping, viewing, paddling, flying, sliding, swinging, but today the agents are idle. On the table in the waiting area, among the sports magazines and the fliers, is a huge jar with a label that reads: "AIDS Kills So Don't Be Silly, Put A Condom On Your Willy." Inside is a single foil wrapper. Years too late, Zimbabwe has launched an AIDS education campaign.

"They take them by the handful," says one of the agents without looking up from her magazine.

I have arranged to meet Rita later at the Croc and Paddle pub, known variously by the locals as the Crotch and Straddle, the Crap and Piddle, the Crook and Fiddle, and the Clit and Nipple. From there, we embark on what they call here a "booze cruise" on one of the boats that chug leisurely up the Zambezi River above the falls. The trip is always laced with the frisson of what would happen should the engines cough and die. Will you get sucked down the biggest drain in the world and spat out a thousand feet below in the so-called boiling pot, the deep pool carved out of the black basalt bedrock by the staggering force of the water?

Up here, though, the great Zambezi is lazily benign, palm-fringed and gentle. We glug our gin and tonics and palm our roasted nuts and gnaw our buffalo wings while the setting sun struts its stuff. A hippopotamus's snout and eyes break water alongside the boat, and the small contingent of elderly French tourists applaud wildly—not necessarily a good way to welcome a proximate hippo. As any Africa hand will tell you, the hippopotamus, though a bona fide vegetarian, kills more people here than any other mammal.

Of all the theories for the hippo's antisocial behavior, my favorite is the one offered by the San, the Bushmen with whom I have recently spent so much time for *National Geographic*. They believe that the hippo was the last animal to be created and was made of parts left over from the construction of other beasts. When the hippo saw its reflection in the water, it was so ashamed of its ugliness that it begged the creator—Kaggan—to allow it to live underwater, out of sight. But Kaggan refused, worried that the hippo would eat up all the fish with its huge mouth. The hippo promised that it wouldn't eat any living thing from the water, and Kaggan relented. A deal was struck that the hippo must return each night to the land to eat and to shit so that the other animals could examine its dung to ensure that there were no fish bones in it. The regular humiliation of public fecal inspection could well account for the hippo's irascibility.

Much of the tourism scared away from Zimbabwe is migrating across the border to Zambia, where new hotels are rapidly being constructed. The two sides are joined by the Victoria Falls Bridge, which was supposed to be the crowning jewel of Cecil Rhodes's Cape to Cairo railway, but the line never got farther than the Congo frontier before the onset of imperial fatigue syndrome.

From the middle of the bridge you get a stunning view of the main falls, and usually there are dozens of tourists milling around there waiting to bungee jump, and a boom box whose bass riff can be heard even above the roar of the falls. But this morning there is only one jumper, a middle-aged German in a denim suit who insists his name is "OK." He emits a Teutonic yodel and dives with arms outstretched into the circular rainbow below, and the bridge is empty of tourists again.

At dawn the next day, I go for a walk along the footpath that follows the lip of the falls. As I approach the gate, the curio sellers and the money changers, frenzied by lack of customers, descend on me like mosquitoes on warm flesh. "The tourists, they have all flown away," they complain when they realize I am local. "It is bloody Mugabe's fault. Give us a gun, and we will shoot him!"

As I wait to pay my entrance fee, a large black man patiently hoes the edges of the path. He wears a torn T-shirt with a logo that announces "I have AIDS—Please hug me—I cannot make you sick."

I walk along the riverbank until I reach the Devil's Cataract, where the flow of the falls is greatest, a huge frothy torrent churning over the edge of the fault line. The normally taciturn Scottish explorer David Livingstone raved in his journal in 1855: "On sights as beautiful as this Angels in their flight must have gazed." He carved his initials into a tree trunk here, the only place, he later admitted, that he had ever surrendered to such vanity.

Prince Charles, whose visit here I once covered for the London *Sunday Times,* was not so poetic. When first presented with this wonder of the natural world, which Livingstone named after his great-great-grandmother, Prince Charles peered at the spume, then turned to his host, the Zambian minister of tourism, and asked, "So how many people commit suicide by throwing themselves over here?" But Africa later wrought its revenge on the House of Windsor. At a formal dinner in the recently postapartheid South Africa, Prince Philip, presented with a menu choice of duck or beef, apparently asked his waiter, "What's the duck like?" The waiter is said to have pondered a moment and then replied: "It's like a chicken, only it swims."

Dr. Livingstone is my only companion here today, sculpted in a twice-life-size bronze, greened by the constant spray. He gazes sternly down at his "wondrous sight," with a Foreign Legion–style peaked cap and kepi on his head to protect the back of his neck from the African sun. His boots are planted apart, and puttees are bound tightly around his ankles. One hand clutches a Bible, and the other grips a walking stick. A pair of binoculars hangs from his shoulder. A bronze plaque bolted to the massive granite plinth on which he stands is inscribed with three words: "Liberator. Explorer. Missionary."

When he finally succumbed to malarial fever nearly 130 years ago, dying on his knees in prayer, Livingstone's two faithful bearers, Sussi and Chuma, carved his heart out and buried it under a banyan tree, as he had requested. Then they dried and cured the rest of his corpse and lugged it fifteen hundred miles across the African interior to the east coast port of Bagamoyo (a trip that took them nearly a year) where it was loaded onto a ship and taken to be entombed at Westminster Abbey.

Today, Livingstone—his efforts to end the African slave trade notwithstanding—has many detractors. Revisionist historians say he failed as a missionary, actually converting only one African, who later lapsed. They say too that he was a failure as an explorer, misidentifying the Congo as the Nile and wrongly believing the Zambezi to be a commercially navigable river. The epithet "liberator," in particular, galls President Mugabe, who views Livingstone as a pious hypocrite who cast a cloak of moral respectability over early colonialism. He has threatened to have the statue uprooted.

The fact that Victoria Falls still retains the name that Living-stone bestowed on it is hardly due to nostalgia on Mugabe's part—he has changed virtually every other colonial name in Zim-babwe. It's due rather to a lack of African unity: Zimbabwe and Zambia can't agree on a new one. The inhabitants on the Zambian side, the maKololo, call them *Mosi oa Tunya*—"The Smoke That Thunders." The Ndebele, on this side, call them *aManzi Thun-gayo*—"The Water Which Rises Like Smoke." But tourism consul-tants warned that neither exactly trips off a midwestern tongue, and that in Victoria Falls they have a universally recognized brand name.

I'm still trying to breathe some air into my flagging Adventure Capital story, so I meet Rita for supper at the Boma. We are almost alone there. A sultry black waitress named Temptation talks us through the menu: smoked crocodile, tiger fish mousse, roast mopani worms, ostrich terrine, impala stew, warthog steak. While we eat, a woman offers to braid my hair with extensions, and a man in a loincloth declares that he is PingePinge, a witch doctor, and would like to tell my fortune. The beating of drums interrupts his pitch as an Ndebele troupe launches into a vigorous tribal dance, rustling the thatch and the leaves on the overhanging mopani trees.

I wander back despondently to the casino at the Kingdom. The sunken pit of slot machines, roulette, and blackjack tables is sur-rounded by a rotunda of fast-food outlets, shops, and bars. Beneath a giant TV screen and a spinning disco ball, suspended dugout ca-noes and an inflated raft, a handful of people—young overlanders who have been trucked down east Africa, Birmingham secretaries and bookkeepers from Melbourne, Canadian physical therapists and German students—already giddy on cheap dope are now get-ting smashed on tequila shots, cane spirit, and Zambezi lager. A tall Nordic girl in flared jeans, spaghetti-strapped tank top and a flaxen bob nudges an anxious black boy onto the dance floor.

Down in the gambling pit, I take up a position at the green baize of the blackjack table, flanked by two giggling Chinese businessmen mainlining Fantas. My funds hemorrhage steadily until I'm down more than $8,000. But these are only Zimbabwe dollars, so my losses are less than US$200.

I try to recoup them at the one-armed bandits. The most highly rewarded icon in the spinning windows is the serpent-headed Zambezi River god, NyamiNyami, highly revered by the local baTonga people. You know when he has swum by you, legend goes, because the water is stained red with blood.

BACK IN HARARE, 2 St. Aubins Walk looks unchanged. I give an intricate series of honks at the gate: short, long, long, short—a gap, then—long, long, short. It is the Morse code for my initials, something my father has requested each visitor do so he can identify us, as a security precaution. My mother comes limping out.

"Where's Mavis?" I ask while she fiddles with the padlock on the gate.

"We finally persuaded her to retire," says Mum. "She was getting so frail that we were doing all the heavy work anyway. She's part of a housing cooperative—Dad used to drive her to their meetings every Sunday—and she's renting a nice little co-op house with her nieces. She's got a good pension annuity, and I've arranged for her to be supplied with hypertension drugs. She left a card for you and a little good-bye gift."

As I lug my bag to the front door, I see that my father's Peugeot isn't in its usual parking place.

"Is Dad out?" I ask.

"No."

Then I see him sitting in his chair, but he doesn't rise. As I get closer, he lifts his glass of faux cane-spirit-based scotch and toasts me. "Welcome home, son."

He takes a sip and only then, as he rests his head back against his antimacassar and into the pool of light cast by his reading lamp, do I see him clearly.

I drop my bag to the floor. "Christ, Dad, what the hell *happened* to you?"

"Oh, it's not as bad as it looks," he says, smiling his lopsided smile. His left eye is swollen shut, and a scab covers that cheek. There are deep cuts in the bridge of his nose and forehead, and his broken glasses are taped together at the bridge and the earpieces, one lens cracked. There is an angry gash along his left forearm.

"He was hijacked," says Mum, handing me a drink.

"Where?"

"Right here, at our front gate."

"It wasn't very late," says Dad, "just after dark. I drove up to the gate and I got out to unlock it, and then suddenly there were all these armed men, about eight of them. They'd blocked my car in with some big vehicle — a Toyota Land Cruiser, I think — I never saw the license plate. You know, it all happened so quickly. Of course, I realized what was happening — there's been a spate of them recently — so I was just about to say, 'Take whatever you want,' when . . . Well the next thing I knew I'd been hit from behind and I was on the ground. Someone wearing a big boot kicked me in the chest, my glasses were knocked off and stomped on, and I couldn't really see what was going on. They took my wallet, ripped off my watch, and stole the car. End of story. The whole thing was over in a few minutes, and there were no witnesses."

"Why didn't you tell me?" I say.

"Because it would only have worried you unnecessarily," says my mother. "There's nothing you could have done. No point in fussing."

"The car was insured," says Dad, inhaling on his cigarette. He starts to cough and winces, holding his bruised ribs. "But with inflation being what it is, the payout won't cover a replacement."

Later, my mother tells me that Dad suspects the men who carjacked him were off-duty soldiers. They were armed, she emphasizes, and seemed to have a military bearing. They knew what they were doing, had obviously done it a lot. And they weren't nervous at all. They were almost casual about the whole thing. He reported it to the police, but nothing has come of it.

Later, as we eat, I look at Dad unobserved. He seems smaller, hunched over, as though he has lost some essential core of self-confidence. And I feel a rage building up inside me, a fury at all the people I have seen being humiliated and beaten, at the powerlessness of them all, at my own impotence.

"Why didn't *you* tell me?" I ask Georgina later.

"They made me promise not to," she says.

She and I set about persuading my parents to hire a security guard for the nights. They are unwilling at first, even though we offer to pay, but in the end they reluctantly accept, and we make all the arrangements. I go up to the back of the garden to tell Isaac, the gardener, the new security procedures. I find him on his knees planting reeds into the swimming pool, their roots encased in hessian sacks of earth. It is the final stage of its conversion into a fish farm. I ask about his daughter, Cheesely. I no longer notice her name—it was given to her, he once told me, because her mother had a craving for cheese when she was pregnant. Isaac's wife commutes back and forth from their small farm in their tribal area of Mount Darwin, but Cheesely mostly lives here, and Dad pays for her to attend an upscale school around the corner. Every morning, Cheesely puts on her gray and green pinafore and trots off to the school where she is educated with the children of cabinet ministers and Reserve Bank governors and senior civil servants—most of whom she regularly outperforms, even though she never speaks English at home.

"It is winter coming," Isaac is saying. "And they should have a different uniform for winter, a warmer one. And she needs sports whites too. And tennis shoes. I did tell Mr. Godwin . . ." He trails off.

"I will make sure it is done," I tell him, and only then do we discuss the security changes.

The next day a man in an olive uniform with an orange lanyard and a nightstick reports for duty and takes up his position on a garden chair at the gate. I feel slightly more secure in leaving. The four Dalmatians are roaming the front garden, and Isaac still lives up at the back.

"Oh, do stop fussing," says my mother. "We'll be fine."

I look skeptical so she puts the knuckle of her index finger on her nose and waggles the fingertip. We call this a "box elephant"; the finger is supposed to be a trunk, and it is our family sign. Years ago, in Chimanimani, Jain was opening one of many barbed-wire farm gates one windy night, not long after our neighbor had been murdered in the first guerrilla attack of what was to become the civil war. Everyone was feeling jumpy, and my mother kept a loaded pistol in the glove compartment. As Jain struggled to get the gate pole out of the wire loop, a huge shape suddenly loomed across the headlights toward her.

"It's an elephant!" she screamed, and bolted back to the car.

Mum scooped up the gun. Ahead the shape took form: it was a large cardboard box, sailing on a gust of wind, its side tabs flapping like elephant ears. Ever since then, a box elephant has meant for us, "take courage, things aren't necessarily as bad as they look." Although, depending on the context, it can also mean, "I know all your embarrassing secrets," or, "The person you are being rude about is approaching from behind you."

Despite my mother's breezy assurances, Dad seems distracted. He is even more difficult to talk to than usual and has a distant, preoccupied expression. He doesn't want to talk about the hijack anymore, or their security; he gets irritated when I try to raise the issue again.

"Is he OK?" I ask my mother.

"Given what he's gone through, I think he's bearing up rather well," she says. "You know your father. He would never admit it, but I think it was pretty traumatic. He told me he thought he was going to be killed. That one hijacker pointed a pistol at him and sort of smiled like he was going to shoot Dad, even though he was offering no resistance and was already lying on the ground; like he was going to shoot him just for fun, just because he could."

ON MY LAST DAY, I hear hammering in the living room, and later, when I go in there, I see a new picture hanging on the wall. It is a

framed photograph I recognize as the one I had found stored behind the circuit tester in Dad's "light" workshop when he was in the
hospital, the one of a middle-aged couple and between them, a
young girl. I look at it more closely this time. The man wears a
three-piece suit, a white handkerchief peeping from his top pocket,
and a dark necktie with little stars speckled across it. The woman
has an aquiline nose as she looks across in profile at the girl. They
are both wearing summer dresses with busy floral prints, and the
girl has a daisy-chain headband holding down exuberantly glossy
dark hair. She is trying to suppress a smile.

"Who are these people?" I ask my mother when Dad is out of
the room.

"These people," she says, taking a deep breath, "these people are
Dad's parents and his younger sister — your grandparents and your
aunt."

It is the first time my father has ever displayed any photos of his
family. I look at it again, and now I see the family resemblance. The
man, Dad's father, has his same important ears. His strong sloping
brow is absolutely Dad's. The woman, his mother, shares her nose
with him. The girl — the girl looks oddly familiar. I adjust my focus
to catch my own reflection in the glass over the photo, and then
back to her again. Of course, the girl looks like me.

When was this picture taken? Why isn't my father in it? Why
has it suddenly appeared now, after half a century?

I ask my mother all these things; they come out in a rush.

"Listen," she says in a hushed voice so as not to be overheard by
my father. "I'm afraid we haven't been entirely honest with you.
Dad's family wasn't from England. They were from Poland. He's
from Poland. They were Jews."

"Jews?"

"Yes, Polish Jews. Like him. He's a Jew. He changed his
name."

For a moment I still can't quite grasp what she's saying. My father, as I know him — George Godwin, this Anglo-African in a safari suit and desert boots, with his clipped British accent — is an

invention? All these years, he has been living a lie? His name—my name—is not our own?

But even as I struggle to absorb this, aspects of his character begin to fall into place. His truculence, his intense privacy, the minefield he has laid around all things personal. He has been sitting on this huge secret all this time.

"What's his real name?" I ask my mother.

"Goldfarb," she murmurs.

"Goldfarb?"

"Yes," she sighs, and spells it out. "G-o-l-d-f-a-r-b. Kazimierz Jerzy Goldfarb."

"Why did he keep all this a secret? Why did *you* keep it a secret?"

"I gave him my word," she says, and then she is cut short by my father's arrival. We stop talking as he walks through the room, and I find myself looking at him differently—shorn now of his cover, his assumed identity. He seems to look different, more . . . more Middle European. His handlebar mustache no longer looks like a Victorian English accessory, but a Slavic one. Stalin as rendered by Peter Ustinov. I find myself examining him for stereotypical Jewish features.

"I'm going to ask him about it," I say to my mother as soon as Dad leaves the room. "He did display the photo. He must be ready to talk."

She looks immensely weary.

"Please, Peter," she says, and she reaches out and holds both my hands in hers. "Can you wait a while? Just a little while longer? He's really not up to it yet. He's been badly shaken by the attack. Much more than he's letting on to you. Let's do it next time you're back, when he's feeling stronger. Please?"

ten

August 2001

I REALLY DON'T KNOW what to do with my father's Jewish secret. Initially I think that perhaps I should just let it lie. After all,
if it was so important for him to keep his Jewish identity hidden,
then he can continue to do so.

And then I begin to wonder what this means for my own identity. I'm already muddled enough trying to work out where I fit
in—between Africa, England, and now America, where I've been
living for four years. Everyone in my own home—Joanna, our son,
Thomas, me—speaks with a different accent; it's a Babel of dia-
lects. What am I supposed to do now? Garnish myself with a dash
of ethnic condiment, instant Jewry? Cast off eight years of Jesuit
education and convert? I vaguely recall that Judaism is passed down
through the female line, so I probably can't achieve genuine Jew-
hood anyway. I think of that Jonathan Miller (himself a Jew) quip,
"I'm not really a Jew, just Jew-ish." Perhaps I can be a drive-through
Jew, a semi-Semite, deploying my postponed part-Jewishness only
when it suits me.

Back in Manhattan, I tell Joanna.

"How do you feel about it?" she asks.

"I don't know," I say. "I really don't know."

She begins to reel off recent late-onset public "Jewish revelations": Madeleine Albright, John Kerry, Christopher Hitchens. And she points out that to be Jewish in New York City is pretty commonplace. It has the largest population of Jews of any city in the world outside Tel Aviv.

"Anyway, everyone's a mishmash here," she says. "I'm not really English either, if you go back a bit. I'm a Viking, a Dane. Lots of us in Yorkshire are."

Later I pull on my black jogging suit and sneakers and pound off down Riverside Park to try to clear my head. I cut right off the boulevard and down along the bank of the Hudson River, running faster and farther than usual, until my chest is tight and my arches ache and a stitch throbs in my side. It's a good pain, a penitent pain, as my Jesuit athletics coach at school once said, like the Roman centurion's spear in Christ's side. Run on through the pain to your salvation. But today it feels more like the Zulu stabbing spear, the *ixlwa*, plunging in and out of my flesh. My Anglo-African-Ashkenazi-American flesh. Finally I turn and head for home. When I'm nearly there I remember that I've promised to pick up food, so I cut east onto Broadway to Barzini's, a deli.

As I walk back, north up Broadway, weighed down with shopping bags, I become aware of a fluttering figure on the sidewalk ahead, canvasing passersby. Closer up, I see he is dressed all in black, like me. He wears an ill-fitting black suit, black shoes, black hat, and he has some kind of tatty string knotted around his waist. His face, though, is white — an etiolated unhealthy white, as though he never goes outdoors — and a ginger fuzz of baby beard inhabits his cheeks and chin. His broad-brimmed black hat is set back on his head, framing his pale face in a dark halo.

His manner is insistent; even as I try to walk around him, he steps into my path and blocks me with his clipboard.

"Are you a Jew?" he asks, without preamble.

I think I have misheard him, transposed my internal dialogue onto the world outside.

"What?"

"Are you a *Jew?*" He looks at me intently with black eyes.

"No," I say. "No, I'm not," and I shoulder my way past him.

Georgina and I talk on the phone about Dad's Jewish secret. Mum has told her too.

"It's like that changeling syndrome," she says, "when adopted people first hear that they're adopted, it suddenly all falls into place."

There is a long pause on the line, and when she speaks again it is in a reverie. "Dad only ever took me to see two movies when I was kid," she says. "You know what they were? *Raid on Entebbe,* and its remake, I think it was called *Operation Thunderbolt.* Strange, huh?"

"I suppose it makes sense that he took you to see a movie about the Israeli commandos going to great lengths to rescue Jews held hostage in Africa."

"I suppose so," she says. "I suppose lots of things start to make sense. Have you heard the proverb 'When the bird alights too long upon the tree it will have stones cast upon it'?"

"No."

"It's a Yiddish saying I found. It explains why we're always moving around."

"Maybe we do have the nomad gene," I say. "I wonder why he kept it a secret all these years?"

"You should ask him," she says.

SINCE CAPITAL RADIO was raided and closed down, Georgina has been feeling increasingly under threat. She is only mildly cheered by the timely death of Hitler Hunzvi, of AIDS. In June, there is a total eclipse of the sun, and she drives north down into the Zambezi Valley to view it. As the moon blots out the sun and skies grow dark, the animals of the bush are confused. Birds begin to roost, bees return to their hives. Frogs come hopping out at midday, owls hoot, hippos make for the shore, and hyenas stir. It's an event so rare that panic spreads among the remote villagers. The Shona call an eclipse *koura kwezuva* — "the rotting of the sun" — and they say it's caused by angered ancestors. Some of Prince Biyela's people, the Zulus, and the Vendas too, believe that a solar eclipse occurs when a crocodile eats the sun. This celestial crocodile, they say, briefly consumes our life-giving star as a warning that he is much displeased with the behavior of man below. It is the very worst of omens.

Georgina is deeply affected by it. Mugabe's clan totem is *garwe*, she reminds me, a crocodile. And she has a premonition of terrible days ahead. Not long after, she writes to tell me that she is planning to leave Zimbabwe for London with Xanthe and Jeremy. She is helping to start a new radio station there, Radio Africa, a successor to short-lived Capital Radio, which will broadcast into Zimbabwe via satellite.

THE ATTACK ON my father increases my own sense of unease, especially now that Georgina will be leaving. Her presence has enabled my absence. She promises that she won't go without setting up all sorts of support systems. Mum and Dad seem unperturbed by the idea of her departure. She says they have been encouraging her to go, knowing that it is in her best interest. But I feel like our family is starting to disintegrate, spreading out across three continents — a minidiaspora of Godwins.

I feel too that the gap between my new life in New York and the situation at home in Africa is stretching into a gulf, as Zimbabwe spirals downward into a violent dictatorship. My head bulges with the effort to contain both worlds. When I am back in New York, Africa immediately seems fantastical — a wildly plumaged bird, as exotic as it is unlikely.

Most of us struggle in life to maintain the illusion of control, but in Africa that illusion is almost impossible to maintain. I always have the sense there that there is no equilibrium, that everything perpetually teeters on the brink of some dramatic change, that society constantly stands poised for some spasm, some tsunami in which you can do nothing but hope to bob up to the surface and not be sucked out into a dark and hungry sea. The origin of my permanent sense of unease, my general foreboding, is probably the fact that I have lived through just such change, such a sudden and violent upending of value systems.

In my part of Africa, death is never far away. With most Zimbabweans dying in their early thirties now, mortality has a seat at every table. The urgent, tugging winds themselves seem to whisper the message memento mori, you too shall die. In Africa, you do not view death from the auditorium of life, as a spectator, but from the edge of the stage, waiting only for your cue. You feel perishable, temporary, transient. You feel mortal.

Maybe that is why you seem to live more vividly in Africa. The drama of life there is amplified by its constant proximity to death. That's what infuses it with tension. It is the essence of its tragedy too. People love harder there. Love is the way that life forgets that it is terminal. Love is life's alibi in the face of death.

For me, the illusion of control is much easier to maintain in England or in America. In this temperate world, I feel more secure, as if change will only happen incrementally, in manageable, finely calibrated, bite-size portions. There is a sense of continuity threaded through it all: the anchor of history, the tangible presence of antiquity, of buildings, of institutions. You live in the expectation of reaching old age.

At least you used to.

But on Tuesday, September 11, 2001, those two states of mind converge. Suddenly it feels as though I am back in Africa, where things can be taken away from you at random, in a single violent stroke, as quick as the whip of a snake's head. Where tumult is raised with an abruptness that is as breathtaking as the violence itself.

By Thursday evening, the wind changes. It brings with it the acrid fumes of destruction, which sting our eyes and catch in our chests. Late at night, a dramatic electrical storm strikes, and with the first great roll of thunder, lights go on all over the city as nervous residents check that it is indeed only the weather. The lashing rain turns the smoldering disaster site into a quagmire.

On Friday, I take my son to a candlelight vigil at the 1913 Firemen's Memorial on 100th Street and Riverside Drive, just a block away from our rented apartment. It is a marble sarcophagus fronted by a bronze frieze of a horse-drawn fire engine at full tilt, flanked by two statues, representing "duty" and "sacrifice," erected "by the people of a grateful city" in 1912, "to the men of the fire department of the city of New York who died at the call of duty—soldiers in a war that never ends." Now the monument has been transformed into a shrine to the hundreds of firefighters who perished in this disaster, men who struggled up those stairs as everyone else struggled down. On the wall, someone has taped a stanza from canto twenty-three of Dante's "Inferno," from *The Divine Comedy:*

> *A painted people there below we found*
> *Who went about with footsteps very slow*
> *Weeping and in their looks subdued and weary.*

The memorial plaza is laden with flowers—roses and lilies, daisies and sunflowers—and ringed with cards, posters, and flickering votive candles. A teacher from the nearby Booker T. Washington Middle School methodically lays out the cards that her class has prepared. "To all those who risked their lives to save our families, you make all the difference in the world, love from Zoey." Zoey has drawn a heart and colored it in with stars and stripes, and rent the heart in two.

Hundreds of our neighbors have gathered silently, overflowing down the slope toward Riverside Park. I hoist my son onto my shoulders.

"Look at all the candles," he exclaims, and begins singing "Happy Birthday" in a clear, piping voice. The woman next to us breaks down in racking sobs. Above us, golden in the final rays of the setting sun, an F-16 fighter jet banks steeply over the southern tip of Manhattan, turns and prowls back up the Hudson.

The week after the attacks, I begin working occasional shifts at St. Paul's Chapel, which once numbered George Washington among its parishioners. It is right across the street from the downed towers and yet has escaped unscathed; not a pane in its windows has been broken. The main force of the blast was borne by a massive syca-more tree, which now lies uprooted in its small cemetery. The vicar there, Reverend Lyndon Harris, recently served as the chaplain at my son's school, St. Hilda's and St. Hugh's, on West 114th Street, and has called in dire need of volunteers. Mostly we unpack provisions being trucked in from the Midwest, and then we don surgical masks and trundle coffee and bottled water and sandwiches into Ground Zero to feed the volunteers and construction workers toiling there.

In those early weeks after the attacks, Armageddon really does seem to stare down at us. Anthrax mailings and rumors of dirty bombs abound; terrorist cells are poised to visit new calamities upon us. Wrenched from its muddling mundanity, life here too, as in Africa, is suddenly rendered exquisitely perishable and precious.

In October, when city hall reopens after the disaster, Joanna and I join a long line at the heightened security checkpoint to do something we have previously neglected: marry. We joke that it is a trade-off: she will get my forthcoming green card, and in return I will be covered by her health insurance. But in this changed world, an institution that we had both thought unnecessary suddenly seems relevant. In a small, neon-lit room with a view of the Brooklyn Bridge, a pleasant Hispanic matron intones a heavily accented Esperanto of vows. She is completely unfazed by the fact that Joanna is eight months pregnant with our second child. We conclude festivities with a brisk brunch at Bubby's, an upscale diner in TriBeCa, and then Joanna goes back up to Midtown, to her job at *New York* magazine, and I go on shift at Ground Zero.

* * *

AT THE END of one shift I escape the blackened cinders of the ruins and stroll across to Battery Park and down the Hudson, and I find myself looking up at the Museum of Jewish Heritage. So I go in and sit in their empty cafeteria and order kosher vegetable rissoles and knishes and drink coffee with nondairy creamer and look out over a gray Hudson to the old Ellis Island immigrant station and the Statue of Liberty. I have hardly been thinking about my father's secret past; it has been crowded out by 9/11. But now I make my way into the museum itself. I skip the floors of Jewish folklore and religious rites, and go right to the Holocaust floor. And there unfolds in front of me an instant history of what happened to the Polish Jews. A chart on the wall lays out the timetable of their torment, the closing of the vise. In the early hours of September 1, 1939, German panzers thundered into Poland. Four weeks later, Warsaw was theirs. On October 26, the new Nazi overlords passed a decree that all Jewish men between fourteen and sixty were to do forced labor; three months later this was extended to women. On November 23, all Jews were made to wear yellow Star of David armbands. Warsaw's Jews, four hundred thousand of them, were then forced into the ghetto, and within a year it was sealed.

Before the death camps were set up, I learn, German mobile killing units, the *einsatzgruppen,* did much of the Jew killing. The firing squads made victims dig their own graves before they were shot. In one grainy thirty-second loop of footage that shows continuously on a TV monitor, Jewish prisoners are unloaded from a truck in front of a large group of spectators, some of whom are smoking and chatting. The Jews, confused and unresisting, are herded into a large shallow pit and gunned down by a firing squad. A pet dog, frightened by the gunfire, runs through the frame and is comforted by its owner. I watch it again and again, the same grainy loop — genocide's *Groundhog Day.* The Jews are unloaded from a truck. The audience smokes and chats. The rifles fire. The Jews fall dead in a heap. The little dog bolts. Its owner gathers it into his arms and comforts it.

I have heard about Auschwitz and Belsen, but here, I learn the names of the rest of the Polish camps: Chełmno, Bełżec, Sobibór, Majdanek, and Treblinka.

On the museum wall dedicated to these death factories are some magnified quotes from the diaries of inmates. One is written from Treblinka:

> We secretly placed in the walls of the graves whole skeletons and we wrote on scraps of paper what the Germans were doing at Treblinka. We put the scraps of paper into bottles which we placed next to the skeletons. Our intention was that if one day someone looked for traces of the Nazis' crimes, they could indeed be found.

The writer's name is Goldfarb, Abraham Goldfarb.

GOLDFARB'S SECRET MESSAGE in a bottle feels like a personal rebuke. Even as he faced death, he reached out to speak to future generations. I phone my mother and ask her whether we might now discuss my father's family history.

"In fact, he's been working on a letter to you," she says.

Soon, a letter does arrive from my father. Only it's not a letter as such. It's a family tree, meticulously plotted in his draftsman's hand on sheets of graph paper taped together. They fold out like an expanding concertina—an intricate origami of our origin. It goes back five generations, and many of the names have footnote numbers by them, fourteen footnotes in all. I notice that he has referred to himself cryptically, by the initials of his assumed name, *GG*—George Godwin—and has deliberately omitted his birth date. Footnote number eight is marked next to his name. But the footnotes themselves are not enclosed.

They arrive a few weeks later, mailed only after I have confirmed receipt of the family tree, so that it cannot be deciphered on its own, if intercepted. Footnote eight, after my father, *GG*, reads simply, "You can work that out yourself." Even now, in his moment of candor, he cannot bring himself to use his original name. It goes against all that he has struggled to hide for half a century, his self-imposed witness protection program. On the same line as his, he has used his sister's real name, her only name, *Halina Goldfarb*. The twelve-year-old girl in the daisy chain headband, suppressing a grin.

Next to her name he has written: "Born 1926. d. H. X."

His footnotes explain the code.

> *d = died*
> *H = Holocaust*
> *X = extinction of branch of family*

I count the symbols. Of the twenty-four family members in Poland at the time, sixteen were killed in the Holocaust, including his mother and sister.

The footnotes are accompanied by some terse instructions. It seems that my father does not really want to discuss his former self with me. What he wants is for me to initiate a Red Cross tracing inquiry for his sister, Halina, and his mother, Janina.

I write to the American Red Cross, and I get a reply from their Holocaust and War Victims Tracing Center. It says that hundreds of thousands of names of victims imprisoned by the Third Reich have recently come to light in newly acquired documents, which has greatly expanded their ability to trace missing relatives. Enclosed are two Tracing Inquiry forms. I fill them out, such as I can from the bare bones my father has sent me.

> *Name:* Halina Jadwiga Goldfarb
> *Occupation:* schoolgirl
> *Address:* No. 5 Kredytowa Street, Warsaw
> *Nationality:* Polish
> *Religion:* Jewish

Under "*Last Contact With Sought Person,*" I write: "Disappeared from a Warsaw Street in 1942/43."

That's all my father has written.

I go back and review the form and realize I have missed the first line. At the very top it says: "*Sought person is my . . .*" and I write: "Aunt."

And then I turn to the next form and write: "Grandmother."

Only then does it really sink in. This is not just my father's history; this is my family too; these *are* my people. Just as Abraham Goldfarb had intended, this Holocaust is reaching forward in time to snag me with its icy claw, to confound me with its counsel of despair. But still I want to resist this inherited burden. My father's antique associations have nothing to do with my life. These are not my fights. That was there, then. This is here, now.

I used to think that we white Africans were hard to sympathize with because we were that least defensible of constituencies, the unwronged. Now I am having thrust upon me the poisoned chalice of historic victimhood. But notwithstanding Abraham Goldfarb's hidden bottle, the hemlock of the Holocaust is not something I wish to drink.

I know that Jews call the Holocaust the Shoah, which in Hebrew means "catastrophe." I dimly recall reading Anne Frank's diary as a child. I once read Primo Levi's account of Auschwitz; I saw *Schindler's List*. I studied the Nuremberg trials in history. But it really wasn't something I had dwelled on in any detail.

Holocaust. *Holo caustum*. From eight years of schoolboy Latin I knew it meant "whole burned." Burned whole. Even the phoenix of Zionism that rose from those ashes—the muscular sabras trying to reestablish a home in an unforgiving land surrounded by hostile Arabs—resonated too closely with my white African narrative. The parallels with South Africa in particular seemed uncanny. Israelis were building barriers to separate themselves from those who threatened them, just as white Africans had tried to do. Both had created odd-shaped, artificial homelands, isolated dust bowls for those they had displaced, and said to Palestinians or to blacks: live there and rule yourselves, you are no longer a subject people.

The Red Cross writes back to acknowledge my tracing requests, saying that it will take at least a year for them to be processed. And a few days later, our second son, Hugo, is born. We give him George as a second name. George, after my father. George, which is English for Jerzy. I phone my parents to give them news of their new grandchild. My father comes on the line, and we talk of the baby for a while, and then I tell him that I've sent off his tracing inquiry to the Red Cross. It is the first time we have ever referred directly to his real past.

There is a pause on the line, and then he says gruffly, "Thanks."

"Do you think you could tell me more . . . more about, it all?"

"Well, Pete," he says, his voice now flat and guarded. "I'll try. What do you want to know?"

I struggle to keep the exasperation out of my voice.

"What do I want to know? Who you are, Dad? I want to know who you are."

And so, as an old man now, my father tries to reintroduce himself to his own son, finally acknowledging his real identity, hidden from the world for half a century. Eventually, I receive an e-mail from him. It is headed "My Life History: Part One — Childhood." My mother says he has been working on it for months, sitting at the computer for hours at a time, staring at the screen between little bursts of two-fingered typing, while she pads in and out with trays of coffee and sandwiches.

"It is so hard, Pete, after all this time," he says. "I find it quite amazing how little I remember."

It is as if my father has made so few forays into the hidden landscape of his past that the neural pathways leading to these memories are choked with foliage, just as a footpath in Africa disappears soon after the people stop walking there. His e-mails read like reports from an archaeological dig: little random shards of a reconstructed life, the barest facts, shorn of their emotional context.

He is finally trying to discard a mask, and yet it seems that when he peels it off he cannot easily access what's underneath. The mask, the superimposed visage that he has shown the world, this concocted exterior, has become his only reality. It is more than just a mask; it is a suit of armor that hasn't been shed for so long it has fused onto the milky body within, the body it was fabricated to protect.

He has thought and thought about it, sitting in front of that computer screen in his room in Africa, looking out onto the gaudy tropical garden and bright African birds, but not seeing any of it, trying instead to see into the heart of a Polish boy in Warsaw a lifetime ago. Trying to reimagine who he once had been. And, in time, a few iconic moments emerge from the penumbra like tiny points of light in a wide dome of darkness, beams of a far-off search party coming to rescue him from a cliff face of autobiographical amnesia.

KAZIMIERZ JERZY GOLDFARB is born in 1924 in apartment fourteen at 5 Kredytowa Street next to the Hunt Club in central Warsaw. He weighs only three-and-a-half pounds — about half a normal baby's weight — and is initially kept in cotton wool in a cigar box on the study desk. Everyone calls him Kazio.

My father has even found two photographs of the address, one as it was in 1939 and one now. He has translated the caption from Polish: "A wonderful building on the corner of Kredytowa Street and Dabrowski Place was lowered after the war, and the majority of interesting architectural details were removed."

There are shops underneath, he remembers. On one side, a barbershop, run by Mr. Majewski. Every day, when his father, Maurycy, finishes his breakfast, Mr. Majewski comes up with his little leather case and shaves him with a straight razor at the dining table.

Maurycy is a shipping agent, and his father before him had been a wine taster. Kazio remembers being beaten by his father only once, when he left a hairbrush—bristles up—on his chair, and Maurycy sat on it.

His mother, Janina, makes cherry schnapps. Her maiden name is Parnas, and though she no longer practices, she is one of the first women in Poland to qualify as a lawyer. Her father is an optician who has a shop called Iris in which he also sells electrical gadgets; the whole ceiling is hung with glowing chandeliers.

Around the corner on Jasna (Bright) Street is a nightclub, with a black doorman—the only black person Kazio ever sees in Poland. And, nearby, an open-air café run by Philips, the radio manufacturers, with colored bulbs hanging from the trees, and loudspeakers playing music in the summer. He remembers going to sleep, serenaded by Chopin's polonaises and mazurkas, waltzes and nocturnes.

There is a live-in cook, a washerwoman who comes twice a week, and a succession of maids, country girls. He has a steel bed, which, he is assured, is the same model used in army officer training schools. There is a desk, rather like a school desk, with a top hinged in front. All his furniture is painted in royal blue with the edges in red.

On top of the cupboard stands an 8mm film projector and an 8mm cine camera. Photography is his passion. He is allowed to use his mother's folding camera, covered in tooled gray leather, and then he graduates to a black enamel Kodak Bantam Special with a chrome finish and an F2 lens.

He plays with his sister in Saski (Saxon) Gardens, near their grandmother's flat. When they are still small, he sits on a little seat fixed to his sister's carriage, facing the nanny. Later on he plays in the park with his friends, Jurek Bregman and Wacek Binental.

Their favorite game at home is Operations. He is always the surgeon. Anne, his cousin, is his assistant, and his sister is the patient's mother. Her job is to cry. The patient is one of her dolls.

He remembers a fancy-dress party. He is dressed as a lancer. He wears long slate blue breeches with red stripes down the sides, a tunic with crimson piping and white buttons, a lancer's czapka and a real saber. The outfit is based on a carefully studied picture of a Polish officer in a book of French military uniforms during the Napoleonic Wars—Poles served in the French army. His sister is dressed as Marie Antoinette in a long white dress. She has long curls and a little white bonnet.

When Maurycy's business is in trouble, during the Great Depression, he withdraws all the savings out of Kazio's savings account and empties his piggy bank. But the economy recovers, and their wealth is soon restored.

He remembers his nursery school teacher, Miss Bronia Dekler, a large elderly spinster who teaches him to write, and the day that he is finally allowed to graduate from pencil to pen. He remembers going to the collegium by streetcar, and being the teacher's pet; being given as a present a book by Jan Korczak, about the boy-King Matt, hunting in a forest. He remembers his school uniform, a double-breasted navy blue suit and a soft square cap. And on his sleeve a badge, in the form of a shield, with the number of the school, 89, in blue for the lower years, red for the upper.

He remembers taking his camera to school, taking photographs in the classroom, and producing an album of photographs with a double page for each subject and captions in cardboard lettering, which he shows the teachers on the last day of term.

His two best friends at school are Jasio (Jan) Matecki and Genio (Eugene) Moszkowski. Jasio's father is a doctor, specializing in psychoanalysis, who has corresponded with Sigmund Freud. Genio's father is a lawyer. The three of them found a make-believe aircraft manufacturing company, called MGM after their surnames, and they take long walks in the evenings and discuss world affairs.

During their summer vacations, they go into the forest to try smoking, and as soon as they light up, a forest ranger appears and scolds them for causing a fire hazard.

His first vacation, he thinks, is to Copoty, better known by its German name Zopot, which is part of the Gdańsk (Danzig) free city. Wacek Binental is there too. He remembers subsequent summer vacations in rented gingerbread villas, fifteen miles from Warsaw by a narrow-gauge railway, in a spa called Konstancin, or, next door to it, Skolimov. A small river flows through the spas, with a few sandy beaches. The one near Konstancin is next to a wooden railway bridge, from which you can dive into the river. He loves to kayak there. His favorite is No. 4, a single-seater painted red and white. And later they go to Orlowo, between the new Polish port of Gdynia and Gdańsk. And on his return, his parents take their vacation, alone. Two weeks on the French Riviera, every year.

When he is twelve they go on a cruise to the Norwegian fjords on a brand-new Polish passenger ship, the fourteen thousand–ton *Piłsudski,* which has just been built in Italy. He sits at the bar drinking fresh orange juice. They go as far north as Tromsø, where he refuses to go to bed until the sun sets, well after midnight.

The summers of 1937 and 1938 he remembers spending in the Swiss Alps, at La Clarière, "École pour Jeunes Garçons" (which the young John Kerry was later to attend), learning French and climbing in the mountains. And during the summer of 1937 his parents also take him with them to Paris to the World's Fair. He remembers riding in a Citroën taxi specially modified to run on a battery. One of his father's business contacts invites them to dinner at a cordon bleu restaurant and brings along his son, my father's age, who wears a dinner jacket. Kazio is humiliated because he has on a brown suit with plus fours.

He remembers winter vacations in Otwock or Srodborow, and in Zakopane, at the foot of the Tatra Mountains, part of the Carpathian range, where he learns to ski.

THE GOLDFARB FAMILY is nonobservant. Kazio cannot speak Yiddish, has never been inside a synagogue, considers himself a Jewish Pole not a Polish Jew. And yet he is aware of the steady drumbeat of anti-Semitism. Aware how carefully his father avoids ostentation, for fear of exciting envy, eschewing a car even when they can clearly afford one. He recalls a law being passed that requires the owners to put their full names on their shopfronts, so Jewish merchants can be identified and boycotted. He remembers an elderly German woman in Berlin who, discovering he is Jewish, begins harassing him, saying Jews should not be allowed in Germany. His host, a family friend, turns on the woman. "Don't you know the Führer wants to promote tourism?" she says.

Although most "educated" people in Poland can speak French and German, and the elderly also speak Russian, compulsory during the Russian occupation, English is an almost completely unknown tongue in the 1930s. But Maurycy, a great admirer of Churchill, says it will be the language of the future. So Kazio begins attending evening classes at the language college, when he is thirteen. He is the youngest student. Mrs. McAvoy, a middle-aged English lady, is the teacher, and everyone assumes her husband to be a member of the British Secret Service.

Lessons begin with the singing of current English popular numbers, and he remembers belting out the "Lambeth Walk," where the chorus "Oi!" has to be shouted loudly. They use Eckersley's *Essential English* textbook, and read "The Selfish Giant," by Oscar Wilde, and practice conversation, and within ten months he thinks that he can make himself understood in English.

After a lot of discussion with his parents, he writes to the *Daily Mail* in London asking them to recommend places where he might study English for the summer. The Goldfarbs choose Greenhayes, in St. Leonard's-on-Sea, East Sussex, where Mr. V. S. Ward, MA (Cantab), and his wife run a residential English-for-foreigners course. Kazio sets off for England in late June 1939.

Later, he will wonder whether the whole thing was a ploy to get him out of the country, in expectation of what was to happen three months later, but he has no inkling of it at the time. He sails on an old twelve-berth steamer called the SS *Baltrover,* sharing a cabin with three men on their way to America. None of them can speak any English, and they ask him to arrange for warm water to shave. But when he asks the steward for "varim vater," his Polish accent is so thick that the steward cannot understand him.

The *Baltrover* docks just below Tower Bridge. He has been sent written instructions to take a taxi to Charing X, and a train from there to St. Leonard's.

"Sharing Ex, Sharing Ex," he says to the driver, who has no idea what he is talking about until Kazio shows him the note.

"Oh, Charing *Cross*," the driver says. "Why didn't you say so?"

And Kazio realizes that perhaps his English is not so good after all.

There are few other guests at Greenhayes, the residential-hotel-cum-language school. They include a Dutch girl, related to the owners, and a middle-aged Frenchman, M. Askenazi, who spends all his summer vacations there. Vincent Ward, a retired school-teacher, spends a couple hours a day with Kazio, improving his English, and slowly my father's Polish accent fades.

By the middle of August 1939, it begins to look as if a war is coming to Europe. Hitler has already occupied Czechoslovakia and clearly has designs on Poland. Kazio wants to move up his return to Warsaw, but Vincent Ward says that is not necessary. Later, he suspects that his father has contacted Ward and told him not to let Kazio leave. The Germans invade Poland on September 1 (the Soviets invade from the east, part of the secret pact with Hitler to partition the country), and on the following Sunday, September 3, Chamberlain, the British prime minister, hitherto bent on appeasement, finally declares war on Germany. That morning the first air-raid warning sounds in St. Leonard's.

AFTER THAT, HE remembers, everything changes. All the other guests at the Wards' leave except for M. Askenazi, who stays on a while, making blackout screens on wooden frames for all the windows. Vincent Ward becomes an air-raid warden, going around the area shouting at people who expose any lights. Peggy, their grown-up daughter, comes home from Canada to be with her parents when they are bombed. All cars are fitted with covers for their headlights, and driving after dark becomes dangerous. Everyone is issued a gas mask, to be carried in a cardboard box that hangs from a piece of string from one's shoulder, and an identity card. My father still remembers his number: EIBL 134-3.

Kazio is stranded. He knows no one but the Wards. He has left Poland expecting to be gone for only seven weeks. Now the summer is over, and the new school year has begun. Vincent Ward enrolls him at King's College, a private school down the road. It is named not after the monarch, but after Lieutenant Colonel Wally King, the headmaster and owner, whose military rank is in fact in the cadet corps. There are only four teachers for two hundred boys, mostly sons of local shop owners and tradesmen. Wally doesn't really know what to do with this stranded Pole from a different educational system, but Kazio stays there until the following summer. He receives very occasional letters from his parents, smuggled out via Sweden, not saying much, but reassuring him that they are well, they are alive.

In Britain men are drafted and children are evacuated from major towns into the countryside, complete with their schools and teachers.

In April 1940, Hitler launches his Blitzkrieg, starting with Denmark and Norway. Weeks later the German army attacks the Low Countries and then pushes south into France. And by the end of May, the remains of the British Expeditionary Force are chased to the channel ports, mainly Dunkirk, and are being evacuated back to England. In England, the panic starts in earnest; an invasion is expected daily. Something has to be done and done quickly. Local Defense Volunteers, later called the Home Guard, and consisting mostly of elderly men armed only with sticks and pikes, begin to patrol, looking for Germans. And the next thing that comes to somebody's hare brain, my father says, is to get rid of all the foreigners living in possible German landing areas. There is no time to see if they are likely enemy sympathizers, and Kazio, like everybody else without a British passport, is ordered out of St. Leonard's. He has one small suitcase of clothes and a few books, his camera, a bicycle, and ten pounds. He is still a boy. He is in a foreign country. And now he is on his own.

twelve

1940

I N JUNE 1940," WRITES my father, "I became an adult. It was
a somewhat traumatic change from a schoolboy, especially because it was quite unexpected."

With his experience in amateur cinematography, he finds a job
as a rewind boy at a cinema in Bulford, on Salisbury Plain, called
the Garrison Theater. The pay is thirty shillings per week, which is
not enough to live on (three pounds was considered a living wage).
However, with air raids expected at any moment, the cinema also
employs its staff as fire watchers, and so he volunteers, for which he
is paid an extra eighteen shillings per week, plus one Coke per
shift.

He finds a room with a retired sergeant major and sells his prize
camera to help pay the rent. The cinema manager is Mr. Piper, and
his daughter, Cecilia, plies the aisles with a tray hanging from her
neck, full of sweets and Cokes for sale. The chief projectionist is
Norman Taylor, who says "fucking" every four words. The projec-
tors have arc lamps, whose carbons Kazio has to adjust as they burn

out every minute or so. He also does all the rewinding. There is a second cinema in Bulford called the Beacon, which shows the same films an hour after the Garrison, so he has to shuttle the films back and forth between them.

The situation is quite comical, he says. He has not been allowed to live at St. Leonard's because he is considered a security risk — as a foreigner, he might cooperate with German invaders. But there seems to be no objection to his living on the edge of the Salisbury Plain, which is full of military establishments. One of them is Boscombe Down, a huge Royal Air Force (RAF) airfield, where you can easily see experimental aircraft being tested.

Kazio saves up his pay and eventually acquires a brown double-breasted suit and a blue belted overcoat, which he wears with the collar up at the back just like the film stars. Later, with another lad, the grocer's son, he buys an old Ariel 600cc motorbike for six pounds, putting a beer-bottle label in the license-plate holder. He joins the Church of England and is prepared for confirmation by an army padre, who seems to spend most of his time drinking in the officers' mess, and confirmed by the bishop of Salisbury. "There is no shame in being a Jew," the bishop says. "Jesus Christ was a Jew."

Jewish or not, at heart he is still very much a Polish patriot, so when General Sikorski forms a Polish government-in-exile in London in June 1940, Kazio writes volunteering to join their army and does so as soon as he can, even though he is not quite seventeen.

From time to time I try to interrupt my father's chronicles of Kazio. "But what did it feel like, Dad," I ask, "to be stranded like that; to be cut off from your family in a strange place?" But he can tell me little of his emotional state.

THE POLISH FORCES in Britain that started forming in 1940 are a very mixed bunch, my father remembers. There are fewer than twenty thousand men, most of them members of the defeated army who have somehow managed to get out of Poland. Many, if not most of them, are officers and noncommissioned officers (NCOs). Others are Poles who were living outside Poland when the Germans invaded. In Kazio's unit, there are miners from the coal pits of northern France, a Jewish tailor from the East End of London who can hardly speak Polish, a student from San Francisco, and a steward from a transatlantic liner. It is quite difficult to transform this bunch into a fighting unit. The RAF takes on any trained pilots and when their numbers become sufficient forms them into Polish squadrons.

Soon Kazio is stationed at the Firth of Tay, in Scotland, where the Poles are guarding the coast against possible invasion. Initially he is part of a rifle battalion dedicated to Mary Queen of Scots. On the front of their forage caps they wear the Polish eagle, but on the side is pinned a little Royal Stuart tartan flash and the Scottish lion. He is placed in the machine gun platoon, which uses World War I vintage Vickers .303 machine guns. Their firing range is on the edge of a moor, firing over the sea. There is a lookout, who waves a red cease-fire flag if a ship approaches. As the lookout is out of direct sight of the troops, another man is posted in between to alert the gunners that the red flag is aloft. Kazio has that duty once when a British submarine sails past on the surface. Unfortunately, he is color-blind and doesn't see the red flag waving against the background of green grass. The captain of the sub gets a bit upset when his vessel is fired on by several machine guns at once. He dives the sub and later lodges an official complaint. Kazio is reprimanded.

Soon his unit converts from machine guns to three-inch mortars and is issued with armored carriers, but Kazio is sent to St. Andrews on a matriculation course to qualify for officer training. It is held in a small hotel, facing the sea, and not far from the Royal and Ancient Golf Club.

One Sunday afternoon, taking a break from homework, he strolls across the road to the sea wall and leans on it and looks over the water and wonders about Poland and his family there. Then he notices another young man next to him, in the uniform of a Polish paratrooper, also looking out to sea. It is Wacek Binental, his childhood friend, whom he has not seen since before the war. Each has assumed the other dead. They embrace, my father says, "and I rather think we were both crying. Fortunately no one saw us." Wacek is on a weekend pass from parachute training near Manchester. Later, he breaks his back jumping from a plane and spends much of the war in the hospital recuperating. After the war he emigrates to Australia.

By the time Kazio joins the First Polish Armored Division in 1943, after his matriculation, the whole Allied force is preparing for the invasion of Europe. The soldiers are gradually shifting southward, and his battalion is now in Yorkshire. In his four-man carrier is a young soldier nicknamed Cania, Polish for "bird," because he is small and agile and fast. The two of them become firm friends.

They make their way farther south to an embarkation area near Southampton. His unit sails for Normandy in a U.S. Navy motor torpedo boat and disembarks onto Juno Beach from a "Mulberry harbor" at the end of July, seven weeks after the first D-day landings. One of the ships scuttled to provide the breakwater there, remembers my father, is the only Polish cruiser, the *Dragon*, a gift from the Royal Navy—recently holed by a German torpedo.

Polish morale is high. As they set out inland into Normandy, they hear the first reports of the Warsaw uprising. Kazio's unit is attached to the First Canadian Army, which is to form the left wing of the forces advancing into France, parallel to the coast. They camp near Bayeux, and together with the Canadians, move on through the ruined city of Caen, which has only just been liberated.

OUTSIDE CAEN, THEY pause just short of a big concentration of artillery, says my father, row upon row of guns of all calibers, firing at the German positions until their barrels glow red. The Americans are meant to join in this bombardment from the air, with their B-17 Flying Fortresses. But something goes wrong. The system relies on a master bomber, and when the master bomber drops early, the rest follow suit. Kazio and Cania watch in tears, appalled, as the Flying Fortresses drop their bombs on the Canadian and Polish gun crews, who are unable to communicate directly with the air force to stop the "friendly fire."

British army spotter planes, little unarmed Austers, fly in and out of the American formation, with no direct radio contact, their pilots desperately waving their arms and firing signal rockets, trying to stop the bombing. It seems a very long time before the bombs cease. The casualties are especially high because the gunners are about to move forward and are not dug in.

This is the first of three times that Kazio is to be bombed in the war, he says, twice by Allies and only once by Germans.

The Poles advance toward the town of Falaise, trying to complete the Allied encirclement of a huge German force—fourteen divisions, about one hundred thousand men. They manage to dislodge German infantry dug into positions on top of two thickly wooded hills that straddle "the Falaise gap," the last escape route for the Germans. The Poles nickname the feature *Maczuga*, "the Mace," because of its shape on their contour maps.

Almost immediately Kazio and his comrades come under ferocious and sustained counterattack by German forces desperate to break through Allied lines, and also by two elite SS armored divisions returning from outside to help. Largely surrounded and running out of ammunition, their Sherman tanks outgunned by the German's latest Panther and Tiger tanks, the Poles are mistakenly bombed again by their own allies.

The fighting, much of it at very close quarters, blurs in Kazio's memory. Once, he recalls, he finds himself alone, caught in open ground, armed only with his rifle, as a Panther bears down on him. He crawls under the wreck of a Sherman tank abandoned in a ditch, and watches, terrified, as the Panther's barrel rotates slowly toward him. It lowers until it is trained on him, pauses for a long moment, then the German tank abruptly accelerates away.

He remembers too being slumped, exhausted, on the edge of a road, in a rare gap in the fighting, with his corporal, a man in his early twenties, the son of a well-known Polish actress. There is a deafening roar, and when Kazio's ears clear, he realizes that the corporal, still sitting beside him, is dead. Kazio starts removing the dead man's personal items to return them to his family. He unbuckles his watch and reaches into his breast pocket where he discovers a small diary with a bullet lodged in it. But there is no visible wound. He still can't understand how the corporal died.

The Poles hold their ground for four long days until, finally, they are relieved by the Canadians. By then, according to their battle report, nearly six hundred Poles are dead or missing, another one hundred fifty wounded. They have killed more than two thousand Germans and captured another five thousand. General Stanislaw Maczek, the officer commanding the First Division, later wrote, "Of all the battlefields in Normandy, none has presented such a picture of hell, destruction, and death."

A memorial is later built there. It reads:

Between the 18th, 19th, 20th and 22nd of August 1944, this vast panorama of the Oren countryside stretching away to the horizon, with its gaily colored pattern of crops and fields dotted with apple trees hemmed by hedgerows, was the scene of a battle of unprecedented importance, which was to determine the outcome of the Second World War. At this historic spot, the First Polish Armored Division closed the last escape road out of the "Falaise Gap" (Chambois—Montormel) to the German VIIth Army, thus playing a decisive role in its destruction and hastening the liberation of France.

Over the next few days the German retreat turns into a rout, as soldiers flee down what becomes known as *Todesgang*, "Death Road." Allied fighter planes relentlessly attack the withdrawing troops. Kazio recalls that road, strewn with the wreckage of charred vehicles and choked with carnage; corpses lined thick along the roadside—human and horse—both distended by gas, their innards busting out.

The Poles advance north at a punishing pace, covering three hundred miles in nine days to liberate Abbeville. They cross into Belgium, and on September 6 they help to liberate the ancient city of Ghent. There, at last, they are allowed a few days' rest.

* * *

WHAT IS HAPPENING back in Poland, Kazio knows only vaguely. His elation at news of the Warsaw Uprising has turned to disbelief as he begins to hear reports that the Russians approaching the city from the east have stopped their advance on the banks of the Vistula, their guns silent, allowing the Nazis to crush the uprising and raze the city.

Since the outbreak of the war, Kazio has received three letters from his father. They are carefully written to include virtually no personal details, in case they are intercepted. In the final two letters, his father asks him for any news of his mother and sister. Kazio's letters to his father ask the same question. Their letters have crossed. In his last letter, Maurycy has enclosed a copy of a snapshot of himself as a keepsake. Kazio peers at it with a magnifying glass and thinks he can make out the letters *ECUA* across it. He assumes his father has acquired an Ecuadorian passport to enable him to get out of Poland, and Kazio carries the passport photo around with him in his tunic pocket as a talisman. When he discovers that there is an Ecuadorian consul in Ghent, he goes to see him, hoping he can find out his family's whereabouts. But the man is only an honorary consul and can do nothing, and anyway, Kazio's unit moves out of Ghent the next day.

They make their way to the Dutch town of Breda, which they liberate without a single civilian casualty. But some stubborn German troops take up defensive positions on an island in the middle of the river Maas and refuse to budge. So the Poles dig trenches facing the island and trade mortar and rocket fire daily with the German holdouts.

Kazio turns twenty-one years old in that dugout by the river Maas, celebrating with a large, round Gouda cheese shared with Cania and other friends from his unit. Later, when he falls ill from a cheese overdose, he is ordered to the hospital. He finds it full of Dutchmen all slowly going blind from bingeing on German rocket fuel.

Just as his unit is about to advance north into Germany itself, Kazio is selected to attend Officer Training School. So he says good-bye to Cania and the others and sails from Ostend for Britain. On the ship, he gets drunk with a Polish sailor whom he last saw four years before, when they both volunteered at the Polish Army head-quarters in London.

KAZIO IS STILL IN the officers' training course at the Crieff Hydro Hotel in Perthshire, when the Germans surrender and VE Day is declared in May. But Poles like Kazio remain in limbo.

Back home, the Soviets have already selected and eliminated the flower of the Polish intelligentsia, in a calculated act of cultural genocide. Almost twenty-two thousand people were killed — many of them executed in an abattoir in the Russian city of Smolensk and buried in the forests of Katyń. (The dead include an admiral, 2 generals, 103 colonels and half-colonels, 258 majors, 654 captains, 17 naval captains, 3,420 NCOs, 7 chaplains, 200 pilots, 3 landowners, a prince, 43 civil servants, 20 professors, 300 doctors, more than 100 writers and journalists, and hundreds of engineers, teachers, and lawyers.)

When the Polish government-in-exile demands an international inquiry, Stalin uses this as a pretext to break off relations with it, and imposes a puppet communist regime on Warsaw. He then persuades the British to withdraw their diplomatic recognition from the Polish government-in-exile in London. The "Free Poles" have now become an official embarrassment, marooned by the tide of history. They have helped to defeat one occupier, Hitler, only to find him replaced by another, Stalin.

In the summer of 1946, the huge victory parade takes place down the Mall in London. Two million onlookers cheer wildly as King George VI takes the salute from Allied soldiers of dozens of nations. In the skies overhead there is a massive flyby. But though they are the fourth biggest Allied army, no Polish forces march that day. The new Warsaw regime, at Stalin's insistence, ignores the British invitation and stays away. And the Free Poles have not been invited. Anyway they have nothing to celebrate. While everyone else is jubilant, many of them watch the victory parade in tears.

"The new Polish government said we were traitors, just a bunch of fascist thugs, and I realized I would never be able to go home to Poland," says my father. "And Cania, who had stayed behind with our unit in Germany after I'd been sent back for officer training, realized the same thing. He couldn't bear it. He walked out of his tent one evening and shot himself."

MAURYCY WRITES AGAIN at the end of the war to say that he has still heard nothing from Halina and Janina. Both father and son know by now in their hearts that there is little hope of finding them alive. "All he told me," says Dad, "is what I told you. That they were picked up by a Nazi patrol and never seen again." Maurycy was hidden by his barber, Mr. Majewski (who, despite his middle syllable, was a Gentile). He spent two years in hiding, finally emerging from the ruins toward the end of the war.

"I knew then that everything I had known in Poland was gone, destroyed. And that I would never go back," says my father.

KAZIO ENROLLS at Medway Polytechnic to complete his preuniversity matriculation, and he starts calling himself George, the better to fit in. And there, in the common room one day, when they both reach for *Punch* magazine at the same time, he meets an ex-Wren who has also just been demobilized. Civilian clothes are rationed and hard to find, so she still wears her navy-issue bell-bottoms. Her name is Mary Helen Godwin Rose.

Helen has straight Titian red hair, hazel eyes, creamy skin. She comes from four generations of Anglican churchmen. Her father, the Reverend C.P.G. Rose, was an author (of *The Christian Case for Birth Control* published, precociously, in 1924, and *Antecedents of Christianity* published in 1925) and a naval chaplain who served on the dreadnought HMS *Colossus,* in the Battle of Jutland during World War I, and proposed to her mother high up in the crow's nest of HMS *Invincible.* Helen is their second daughter, ten years younger than Honor, and she grows up in a succession of naval bases in the south of England. Her mother, known as Baha, is a charming and strong-minded woman, an enthusiastic espouser of causes, a vegetarian and a suffragette, a despiser of corsets and of cosmetics, who throws out the family's refined china and makes them eat from rough pottery bowls. She holds militantly progressive views on everything from birth control to macrobiotic diets, and it is generally acknowledged that her eccentricities cost her husband the chaplain-generalship of the fleet. So denied, he resigns his commission and accepts a living from Lord Darnley of Cobham Hall in Kent, one of the many civilians who had traveled great distances to hear him preach.

Cobham is the site of the half-timbered Leather Bottle Inn, which Dickens used as a setting in *The Pickwick Papers,* and the home in retirement of Sir Herbert Baker, the imperial architect who had designed so many public buildings for Cecil Rhodes, founder of Rhodesia. The Reverend Christopher Rose and his family live in the ten-bedroom vicarage, where he names each room after a ship he served on. His liberal views soon provoke the ire of his superior, the bishop of Rochester. When he refuses to take down a notice on his church door welcoming visiting nonconformists to worship and receive communion there, the bishop takes him before the ecclesiastical court for breaking his oath of canonical obedience.

But before he can be disciplined, Christopher Rose goes swimming in the Thames one morning after having nicked his chin shaving. He develops septicemia — it is just before Alexander Fleming discovers penicillin in a garret in St. Mary's, Paddington — and dies a few days later at the age of fifty-one. Helen is not quite twelve. Her mother survives on the charity of others and by running a guesthouse in Cobham. Helen is sent to St. Margaret's boarding school, on a bursary for the orphaned daughters of Anglican clergymen. Honor clashes often and violently with Baha, from which Helen learns the tactical advantages of passive resistance and evasion.

In the school summer holidays of 1940, at home in Cobham, Helen remembers, she lies on the daisy-filled lawn watching the dogfights of the Battle of Britain far above in the clear skies over the rolling chalk ridges of the North Downs. Soon an antiaircraft battery is placed in their orchard and, night after night, the guns pound, filling the sky with fire and smoke. The gunners are aiming at German bombers lured by decoy city lights constructed in fields west of Cobham. In a single night the local batteries bring down fourteen bombers within three miles of their house.

Helen returns to St. Margaret's, Bushey, on the northern periphery of London, in early autumn, just in time for the beginning of the Blitz. At night when the air-raid sirens wail, the girls troop down into underground bomb shelters where they sleep so tightly squashed together that they must turn over in unison. They get exam points for every night they spend down there. Above them, London is pulverized. Over a million houses are destroyed, 43,000 people killed, another 139,000 injured by the time the bombing lets up that summer of 1941.

As soon as she turns eighteen, Helen follows her dead father into the Royal Navy and becomes a Wren. She is stationed at Folkestone and spends many of her nights on the end of the dark, bomb-mangled, wind-whipped pier, where she uses an Aldis lamp to signal by Morse code to ships at sea. She remembers the Christmas eve after D-day, listening to the soldiers singing carols as their ship set sail from the adjacent harbor, and knowing that many would not return. And while she listened to the haunting sound of "Silent Night" floating over the water, military policemen dashed up and down the pier, chasing deserters who were desperate to avoid embarkation.

At the end of the war, she decides she wants to become a doctor, a frustrated ambition of her dead father and still very much a pioneering profession for women. She enrolls at Medway Polytechnic to complete her premed courses. When she realizes that she's behind in physics, George Goldfarb offers to help, and they become friends. Soon, she introduces him to her mother, who at first sees him as a charity case, a displaced Jew whose life has been devastated by the Holocaust, a deserving cause for her energetic altruism.

Helen is accepted by St. Bartholomew's Hospital, the oldest

hospital in Britain, founded in 1123 by Henry I's court jester, Ra-here. It is the first year women have ever been allowed to train as doctors there. Many of the hospital's ancient buildings are still bomb damaged, and the women's segregated common room is an old air-raid shelter. In the chemistry lab she is teamed with an Egyptian student who deeply disapproves of women being trained as doctors and is appalled that he is having to work in such proximity to one. But eventually he is sharing the strong Turkish coffee he brews up in a beaker over their Bunsen burner.

George goes on to study engineering at the University of London, and they continue to see each other. When he first asks her to marry him, she just laughs, knowing that it is socially impossible, that Baha—despite her progressive views in some areas—will never stand for it. He waits a bit and then asks again. And again. And on his fourth attempt, in early 1948, she narrows her eyes and looks up at him and says, "You know what? Damn them all. I *will* marry you."

Together they go to the Old Curiosity Shop next to the post office in Cobham. It has bay windows with mullion panes and sells Victorian bric-a-brac, postcards, and Dickens memorabilia, mostly to literary pilgrims who have come to see the Leather Bottle Inn. In a dusty velvet tray at the back of the shop, they find a Victorian ring, gold with a topaz set in the middle, flanked by a pearl on either side. Helen tries it on and it fits. It costs a modest £4 10s (about US$18), a large sum to them then, but George buys it.

He places it on the finger of his new fiancée, and after admiring it, she takes it off and wears it secretly, on a long chain around her neck. One day when Helen is carrying Christen, Honor's daughter, the little girl reaches in and fishes out the ring in front of Baha. She asks why Helen is hiding it, and Helen confesses that it's an engagement ring.

Baha is incensed. To George's father in Poland, she writes furious diatribes accusing his son of being a gold digger and an opportunist, a Jewish cuckoo in the nest of her Christian charity.

* * *

ONLY THREE OF MAURYCY'S letters survive, all written in 1948 and saved by Helen's elder sister, Honor; the rest of his weekly letters are to his son, and George destroys them when he erases his old identity. For reasons of self-preservation, Maurycy Goldfarb has changed his own name, even before his son. His letterheads now bear the name Stefan Golaszewski, a name he has taken from a Warsaw tombstone. The letters beg Helen's family to look kindly on George. Letters written in a formal, stilted English, full of courtly foible and florid phrasing, heartbreaking in their earnestness. A man who has lost his wife and young daughter to the Holocaust, a man who has lived hidden underground for two years, kept apart from his only son, a man writing to a hostile stranger in another land, saying: We are not the wandering itinerant Jews you think we are, we are not a family to be ashamed of and to be disdained, we are something, we are cultured and cosmopolitan and proud. Do not denigrate my son; he is worthy of your daughter. The letters of Maurycy Goldfarb, a man writing in a foreign language, under a dead man's name, to a stranger, appealing for respect.

To Honor and John, her husband, who are supporting Kazio and Helen in the teeth of Baha's venomous onslaught, he writes:

> I thank you very cordially for your kind letter of the 16th inst. It gave me gladness and comfort all the more if I compare it with the letter received from Mrs. Rose which struck me like a thunderstorm from the clear sky so that I could not find the right words to reply. . . .
>
> I know it from my Kazio that they fell in love with one another, and is there anything more beautiful than such strong love in the juvenile age? I must admit that I appreciate my son's calm and composure towards Mrs. Rose all the more because he had a very caressed childhood. It proves only how much he loves Helen. . . .
>
> My son wrote to me lately that he wants to defer his wedding till my arrival at London. Their wedding will be the only happy day in my life since 1939!

And again, two months later, he presses his son's case, a son he has not seen now for nearly ten years:

> We had in our family a great many intelligent people, but Kazio was the most distinguished of all. I may assure you that as soon as my Kazio has finished his studies he will be able to keep his own family, and Mrs. Rose will surely be proud of her son-in-law.

And though life in war-shattered Warsaw is grim, he manages to send a little gift to my mother.

> My much beloved Helen,
> Some days ago I have sent you 3 pairs of nylon stockings and shall be very please to hear from you as soon as possible that you have received them in good order, and that they have pleased you well. I got your 3 photographs and find them very nice and lovely. Your common photo with Kazio reminds me of Kazio in 1939 when he was hurrying from school home. He looks like in 1939! I may stress that you will be happy with Kazio all your life. When I shall be with you, you will be convinced that my words become true!
> My projected trip to England must be again delayed but I hope to get a passport in the course of the next weeks and then I shall come over to you.
> Many kisses my beloved daughter from affectionate yours,
> Stefan Golaszewski

The stockings never arrive. And of course, as he already suspects, he never does get a passport. He is never able to leave. And George and Helen go ahead with their wedding, at St. Mary Abbots on Kensington High Street, without him. And without Baha, who boycotts it. George has relatives in Norfolk, Virginia, who own a clothes factory there and have been sending him care packages, but when they hear that he is to marry a Gentile, they cut him off.

(Years later, when I am living in Notting Hill Gate, I walk down Kensington Church Street to St. Mary's to look for their register entry. But of course I scan down the columns looking under the wrong name, Godwin, and never find them.)

The young couple work hard to complete their degrees. Surviving solely on ex-service student grants, they have little money for diversions. As they come to the end of their courses, Stefan, né Maurycy, writes to his son telling him that he has decided to marry again. His second wife is a childhood friend. She has a son the same age as George, a son who—coincidentally—is also called Kazio, George's old name. The two boys knew each other growing up, but were not friends. George is numb at the remarriage. In some ways he feels that his father is being disloyal to the dead Goldfarb women. And that he is being replaced by a namesake.

When, a few years later, he receives a cable from Poland that Stefan Golaszewski has died, George is unable to weep, my mother says. He tears up the telegram and refuses to discuss it with her.

George has already applied to be naturalized, though there is a five-year backlog of applicants, Poles and Czechs and Hungarians, whose countries are now behind Stalin's Iron Curtain. But before Princess Elizabeth could marry Prince Philip of Greece and Denmark, in late 1947, he too needed to be naturalized. And rather than let the prince be seen to line jump, the Home Office clears the logjam, and my father finally becomes a British citizen in early 1949.

Once he is naturalized, my father changes his surname too. First my mother has to change hers. She drops "Godwin," her third Christian name, an old family name. And my father adopts it as *his* surname, and so it now becomes my mother's married name. When he emigrates to Africa, he is George Godwin. A new man. A man fleeing racial persecution and war, mayhem and genocide. And with him, a woman who will keep his secret, even from their own children.

THE AFRICA IN WHICH my parents arrive after the war is a hopeful place, at least if you are white. It is still entirely white ruled. The better part of a decade is yet to pass before Harold Macmillan, as British prime minister, will make his famous 1960 "Wind of Change" speech, which signals Britain's flagging imperial energy and its intention to shed its African colonies.

At first George is sent out by his employer, Gwynn's Pumps of Lincoln (whose machines drain the Fens of East Anglia), to install a new water supply system for Blantyre, the capital of Nyasaland — a country named after the lake that forms its core. David Livingstone had so named it after pointing at the lake and asking the local Yao people what it was called. "Nyasa," they said. So he named it Lake Nyasa. In chiYao, *nyasa* means "lake." Lake Lake. So good they named it twice.

It is here in Nyasaland (now Malawi) that George poses for the earliest photos I have so far seen of him. In one he's on the veranda of Riley's Hotel, a liveried black waiter at his side in the act of serving him a frosty beer on a tray. In another he stands against the majestic backdrop of Mount Mulanje, wearing small aviator shades. His legs are planted apart, his fists are on his hips, and he is grinning at the newness of it all, grinning at this place that seems to have no history, a greenfield site for Europeans of energy and aptitude. You can almost see him deciding that he wants to stay.

For him, Africa is clearly the antidote to Europe's great burden of history, the blood feuds and the destruction, the prejudices and the pogroms and the Holocaust. It is a place where he can wipe his memory of past hurt and start again. It is the final phase of establishing his new identity. Once he arrives he breaks off all contact with the past.

"I arrived in Africa, in Nyasaland, for the first time in October," he tells me. "And the hotel I stayed in, Riley's, was on the corner of two streets with views up both, lined with jacarandas in full bloom. Pete, I thought it was one of the most beautiful sights I'd ever seen." His heart was lifted by the sheer exuberance of it, the extravagance of the blossom. Though he didn't know it then, he was responding to something not indigenous to Africa at all — jacarandas were imported from South America. One exotic was luring another.

He finds a job in Nyasaland's near neighbor, Rhodesia, and one for Helen too, with the Ministry of Health. And he writes persuading her that this is the new start they need. This is their destiny. So, as soon as she finishes her first-year medical internship, she boards an airliner on the Zambezi service of Central African Airways. Her plane hops from London to Nice to Malta and then down colonial Africa, stopping at Khartoum, Entebbe, and Victoria Falls, until finally she reaches Salisbury, the Rhodesian capital.

My father's parents and his sister, shortly after the war began.

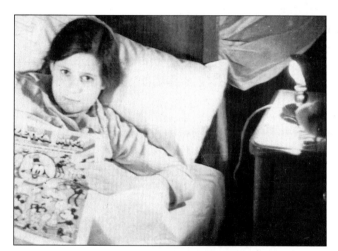

My father's sister,
Halina, with her
comic at bedtime
on the eve of war.

A Good Man in Africa: my father, the engineer, who could fix anything, Nyasaland, 1954.

My parent's wedding, London, 1948.

Dad and a waiter at Riley's Hotel, Malawi.

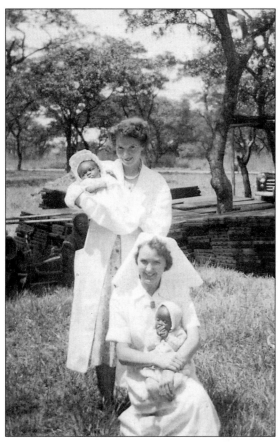

My mother *(standing)* and my godmother, Margaret, with their tiny patients, Harare Hospital, Mbare township, 1955.

My parents at a party in Rhodesia in the mid-1950s.

My father and me on the veranda of our house in Silverstream.

Mum and me at the Silverstream estate.

Me and Nomore, our cook's son.

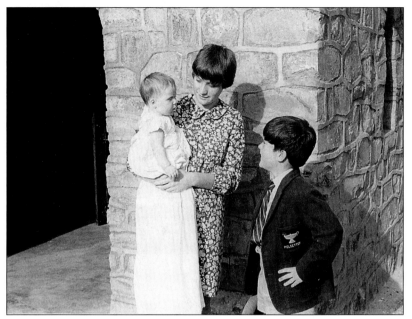

Jain holding Georgina outside St. George's-in-the-Mountains, Chimanimani, where she had just been christened, and me.

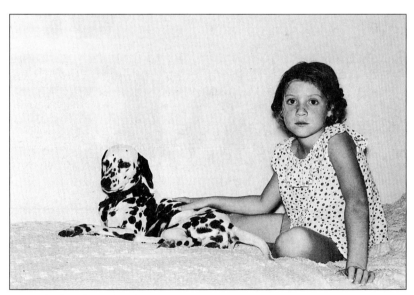

Jain at bedtime, with Judy the Dalmatian, at Mhangura.

Margaret and me, with her dogs, Nyanga.

Me, covering the Ugandan
War for the *Sunday Times*
(London).

My parents and Georgina, at her wedding, Bridal Veil Falls.

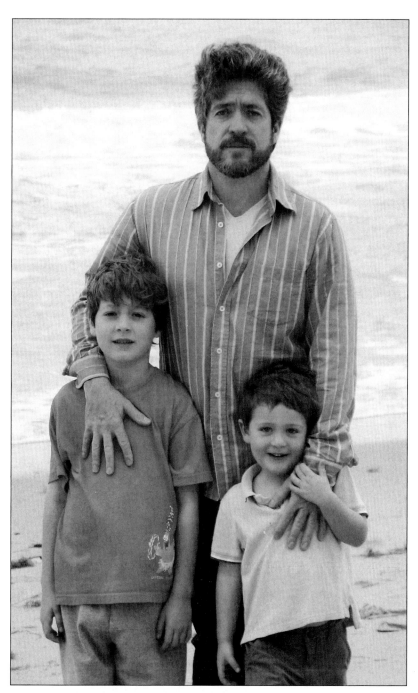

Me and the boys, Thomas and Hugo.

"A bicycle made for two."
My parents in a borrowed
wheelchair, visiting
Margaret in Harare.

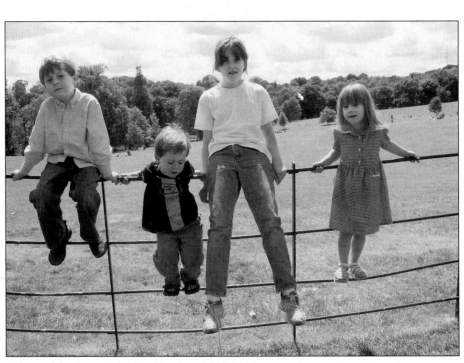

The next generation: Thomas, Hugo, Holly, and Xanthe, in London.

thirteen

February 2002

I⟶ IS SOMETIMES SAID that the worst thing to happen to Africa was the arrival of the white man. And the second worst was his departure. Colonialism lasted just long enough to destroy much of Africa's indigenous cultures and traditions, but not long enough to leave behind a durable replacement.

There is a paradox at the heart of Africa: it is mankind's crucible, the motherland, the place where early hominids evolved and, presumably therefore, the environment originally most hospitable to man, yet Africa is now the economic laggard, the Cinderella continent, a byword for poverty, disease, and underdevelopment; the Third World's Third World. In 1963, Zimbabwe had the same gross domestic product as South Korea. Now South Korea's economy is a hundred and twenty times the size of Zimbabwe's. Africa accounts for more than 11 percent of the world's population and less than 2 percent of its trade.

Zimbabwe is undisputed leader of the comparative economic decline. It has the world's fastest shrinking economy. Today the average Zimbabwean has a standard of living that is half what it was at independence in 1980.

The paradox has long bewildered me, and I get a chance, in 2002, to examine it when asked by the British TV station, Channel 4, to make a documentary. They want me and Aminatta Forna, a writer (and former colleague at the BBC) whose Sierra Leonean father was executed by the local dictator when she was a child, to answer the question, Do Africa's problems reside principally in the continent's underlying environment, or with imposed colonial distortions, or with the travesty of Africa's postcolonial leadership? We are not proposing solutions here; we are just conducting a biopsy of the blame.

The historic lack of big cities is certainly one clue. The city is the petri dish of civilization, a marketplace for produce and ideas, a site where man can specialize. But sub-Saharan Africa had few cities of any size at the time it was "discovered" by Europeans, as Jonathan Swift noted in a satirical ditty:

> So geographers, in Afric maps,
>   With savage pictures fill their gaps,
> And o'er unhabitable downs
>   Place elephants for want of towns.

You need a food surplus to establish real cities, and Africa's uniquely hostile environment conspired against this, the anthropologist Jared Diamond explains to me. The continent was dealt a hand perversely plagued with pestilence, which kept Africans largely isolated from each other and from the rest of the world until relatively recently.

"It seems that for our sins," one sixteenth-century Portuguese explorer of Africa despaired, "or some inscrutable judgment of God, in all entrances He has placed a striking angel with a deadly sword of flaming fevers." Today, we find, the limits of Islamic conversion in Africa tally roughly with the range of the dreaded tsetse fly, which wiped out the horse-borne northerners in the west and limited Arab traders to the coast in the east.

Diamond also explains that Africa has no indigenous beasts of burden. For a wild animal to be domesticated, it has to possess a series of attributes, including a follow-the-leader social structure, a nice disposition, and a tendency not to panic. "Rhinoceroses, boy would they be fantastic meat production animals," he says. "But there are two things against rhinos: they have a nasty disposition, and they have a territorial social structure, so you cannot herd them. If that had not been the case, then the Zulus would have ridden into Europe on rhinos and just plunged through the ranks of European cavalry with their wretched little horses—but it never happened."

So African agriculture remains at only a subsistence level for millennia because without draft animals nearly all tilling must be done by hand. As the old African axiom goes, "It's a wise man who cultivates just as much land as his wife can conveniently hoe." Unsurprising then, that by 1500, sub-Saharan Africa had a population density of only 4.9 per square mile—when Japan had 120.2 and Europe, 35.4, and where cities flourished.

The notable African exception is the highlands of Ethiopia, which remain free of malaria and sleeping sickness. And it's no coincidence that this rugged region is where the ancient stone city of Aksum rises, where an indigenous form of writing is invented, and where a strong centralized government evolves. No coincidence either that but for a tiny window of five years when Mussolini tried vainly to subjugate it, it's the one African country that largely resisted European colonization. (Liberia, on the west coast, was settled and effectively colonized by freed slaves from the Americas.)

When the first Europeans arrive in Africa, they bring their territorial imperative with them. And once the dust settles from the "Scramble for Africa," the continent finds itself sliced up into bizarre and arbitrary shapes. Kilimanjaro, for instance, is said to have been given by Queen Victoria as a birthday present to her cousin, the Kaiser, because she has two snowcapped African peaks, and he has none. Many of these new states lump together ancient antagonists, cut across cultural and economic hinterlands. Europeans take Africa by the scruff of its neck and shake the bejesus into it, knocking it clear off its cultural fulcrum by doing good things and bad on so many fronts: religion, trade, infrastructure, health. Societies that are built on the mathematical fundamentals of women giving birth to twelve babies in order to bring two or three to maturity suddenly find themselves with five, seven, nine children and all the attendant cultural chaos. Europeans entice them to want stuff—soap, clothes, bicycles, radios, stoves; turn them into impoverished consumers; co-opt their chiefs, tax them, and compel them to leave home to labor for wages.

WE CRISSCROSS THE CONTINENT, puzzling over this blame game, from South Africa to Sierra Leone to Ethiopia. There, sitting in Emperor Haile Selassie's lovingly preserved imperial railway coach, I ask the country's leading historian, Chifera Aberkelly, what the advantages are of never really having been ruled by the white man. Certainly Ethiopia has been as plagued with dictatorship, war, and famine as anywhere else in Africa.

"This is a very tricky question," he says. Dodging the bullet of colonialism means that Ethiopia has never benefited from sustained colonial investment in public works, in infrastructure, however lopsided that might be. The water-supply networks that my father came out to build in colonial Nyasaland were never built in Ethiopia. But on the other hand, says Aberkelly, "we were able to maintain our identity, our national language, our national traditions and institutions, and this kind of independence had a big impact on the national psyche of the people, on our pride."

THERE IS ONE CONTEMPORARY Zimbabwean writer who has wrestled more than most with the bear of African identity. His name is Dambudzo Marechera, and I met him once in Harare: slight, bespectacled, and cursed with a most terrible affliction for one so enamored of words—a maddening stutter.

Later, when I try to write about him, I find that there are many different versions of his life. Just like my father's, Marechera's biographical facts changed like the *njuzu*, the mythical manfish that populates his writing and is constantly altering its form. As a boy, Marechera scavenged the local rubbish dump for old books and magazines tossed away by the white community. His father, a mortuary assistant, was run down and killed by a car when Dambudzo was in his second year of a scholarship at St. Augustine's, an Anglican mission school in the eastern Highlands. His mother turned to prostitution to make ends meet. Marechera was expelled from the University of Rhodesia for taking part in student protests in the dog days of the white regime. But he went on to Oxford.

Like a great river, education seemed to swirl him downstream, farther and farther from his roots, marooning him on a cultural sandbar far from the banks of belonging. He felt within himself a number of different identities, and it was the conflict between these that he mined to such good effect. Even as he castigated himself as "a keen accomplice in my own mental colonization" for his enthusiasm for Western education, he remained unapologetic about his catholic thirst for literature. He wanted to escape the ghetto of "African" writing to claim a broader, universal canvas.

Marechera's refusal to trade on blackness as his defining trait, but rather to remain a free literary spirit, annoyed many of his fellow African writers and soon the badge of heretic—one he wore with pride—had been applied to him by the orthodoxy of black nationalism. "No, I don't hate being black," he wrote crossly. "I'm just tired of saying it's beautiful."

He had shunned those who wanted him to become a literary champion of the African cause, accusing them of "trying to reduce me to some kind of Bantustan writer with all the fucking Boers applauding. . . ."

When he was decried in some quarters for choosing to write in English, the tongue of the "colonial oppressor," which was seen by some as an act of subjugation in itself, he wrote, "I prefer to go along with Caliban's theory: 'You learned me your language, now I can insult you in it.'"

And he pointed out that Shona (his native tongue) in its written form was covered with the white man's fingerprints—it was, after all, missionaries who standardized it and rendered it onto the page, largely to facilitate their Christian proselytizing, which often functioned as the Trojan horse leading to full-blown indigenous cultural servitude.

In the light of recent events in Zimbabwe, his views on the corruption of the elite — the so-called *chefs* — and their betrayal of the *povo* — "the people" — who delivered them to power were more than prescient. "Ring studded black fingers / Around the pink gin of change," he wrote of the new leaders. But his criticism of the new black elite in Zimbabwe came unfashionably early. In the days when almost all Zimbabweans had been dyed in the vat of optimism, Marechera was already the canard at the party, blowing raspberries at the heroes — sometimes literally. When Robert Mugabe visited London in 1978, at the height of the war for Zimbabwean independence, Marechera was the lone heckler in an audience full of sympathizers.

He felt strongly that there was something of the emperor's new clothes in the specter of new African leadership, that African postcolonial identity provided a protective fog of black culture to obscure a multitude of sins against the people. In his poem "Oracle of the Povo" he talks of those "Who yesterday a country won / And today poverty tasted." And he mocked the patronizing white liberal cheerleaders of the African cause for falling for a sentimentalized view of the "African image." He wished to break out entirely from the sterile binary bout between colonizer and subject, oppressor and victim, exotic and indigenous — the lazy, generalized shorthand of evil and good that seemed so natural to impose on Africa in the first flush of independence. In fact, he questioned the whole foundation of Africa's newly independent states, based as they are on these flawed colonial territories, "nations" invented by whites. Was independence nothing more, he asked, than a rebranding of essentially the same product?

I'd like to speak to Marechera for this documentary, but I can't. He died of AIDS-induced pneumonia at the age of thirty-five, a homeless pauper on a Harare park bench. A prophet without honor in his own land.

THE IDEA IS THAT I will complete the filming by going on to Zimbabwe for the forthcoming presidential elections (which are held separately from parliamentary elections), to take its democratic pulse. Prospects for a free and fair election there are, once more, but dim indeed. The general in charge of the defense forces, Vitalis Zvinavashe, goes on TV to say that his soldiers will not permit the victory of any candidate who has *not* served as a guerrilla in the war for independence, which would preclude Mugabe's main opponent, Morgan Tsvangirai. The warning is tantamount to a preemptive coup. Then Tsvangirai himself is charged with high treason for allegedly fomenting plans to assassinate Mugabe. The evidence comes from a grainy videotape secretly recorded by an Israeli con man, the voices on it largely inaudible.

BY THIS TIME, Mugabe has made it illegal to hold dual nationality and banned long-term residents who give up their Zimbabwean passports from voting. Mugabe's move affects mostly whites, and many are torn. Some suspect that he may push through laws forbidding nonnationals to own property or businesses. But there is also a fear that by giving up rights to a second nationality they will forfeit foreign refuge in the face of a complete meltdown in Zimbabwe. My parents decide to spread the risk. One will keep a British passport and the other will forfeit it and remain Zimbabwean. Because Dad is British, not by birth, but by naturalization, he will keep his British passport. A legal appeal has been launched against disenfranchisement of registered voters, like Dad, as being unconstitutional, so he hopes he will keep his right to vote. Mum, a Briton by birth, will give up her British passport. Hoping that the Queen will understand that circumstances require it, she sends her British passport off to the Zimbabwean Ministry of Home Affairs as stipulated by the new law. But because it actually belongs to Her Majesty's government, the ministry, under diplomatic protocol, has to forward the passport to the British High Commission, which in turn — much to Mugabe's chagrin — sends it back to my mother. Several months after surrendering her British passport, she finds it back in our mailbox.

So Mugabe tries again. This time, he orders all those with even a notional birthright to a second nationality to bring him proof of repudiation of that right. My mother signs a form that states that she turns her back on the Queen and on any possibility of a British nationality, that she is irrevocably African. She lines up at the British High Commission to sign the documents, and the British charge her — at the higher black market rate — for the privilege.

For some, however, the process of preserving their Zimbabwean citizenship is positively Kafkaesque. Robin Watson, my honorary godfather, and one of my father's best friends, was born in India when it was still a British colony. When he goes to the British High Commission to sign a form saying he renounces all claims to be British, they say they cannot cosign it as he was born in India. "You need the Indians to sign," they tell him. But when he goes to the Indian High Commission, they turn him away, saying it is a British matter, nothing to do with them.

"I can't get anyone to accept my surrender." He laughs, shuttling between embassies.

I GET AS FAR AS South Africa before Mugabe bans all foreign press from covering his election. We consider trying to sneak into Zimbabwe to film clandestinely, but Channel 4 forbids it — their production insurance will not cover the loss if I am arrested and unable to complete the series. Instead, we watch the elections from South Africa and then we go up to neighboring Mozambique and make our way northwest to the border with Zimbabwe. Here in Manica Province, a group of white Zimbabwean farmers have resettled at the invitation of the Mozambican government. It's a bizarre situation; some of them are starting again within sight of their farms on the hills across the border.

John Coetzee (not his real name) is living with his wife and son and daughter-in-law in a canvas tent just as their forefathers, the Voortrekkers, did more than a hundred years ago when they came up to Zimbabwe in ox wagons from South Africa. They have been in Mozambique for less than a year but already the virgin bush around them is cleared and plowed and bursting with rows of sunflowers, eight feet tall.

In fact, the bush is not quite virgin. A Portuguese farmer worked this land until FRELIMO guerrillas in their war for independence drove him off forty years ago. You can still see the ruins of his brick house. After guerrillas took it over, it was strafed and bombed by Rhodesian forces. And now it is farmland again, husbanded by Coetzee, a white Zimbabwean. When the Coetzees began to dig ditches for stream-fed irrigation, they discovered that the earth along their chosen canals was soft and giving. They were actually digging into the old irrigation furrows of the Portuguese farmer, following the unseen architecture of his contours, happening on the archaeological remains of a previous era. All else may have been turned upside down in the meantime, but the laws of gravity never change.

Every day at a preappointed time, Coetzee gets on the two-way radio to talk to the few remaining employees on his farm across the border in Zimbabwe, which has been invaded by war vets. He has been bringing farm equipment over the border. His men back on the old farm break down tractors and pumps and mills into their component parts, and the local tribespeople load them onto donkeys and mules to carry them along the old slave trails over the Chimanimani Mountains.

Here, in this poor region of Mozambique, the Coetzees have been welcomed by the local chief and already employ several dozen of his tribespeople. Other white Zimbabwean farmers have been similarly welcomed in Zambia and Nigeria.

"The white people that came to Africa did a lot of things wrong," admits Coetzee. "But history has proved that the white farmer, the Zimbabwean farmer, is a producer. There's no way that anybody can tell me that the white farmer in Africa hasn't benefited Africa."

On the second day of my visit, a local government official drives up in his air-conditioned Pajero SUV to check on the new white farmers. The official wears a well-cut dark suit and a dazzling white shirt with a starched collar. He eases down the electric windows a crack, not wanting to step out into the hot fuggy air. He has trouble talking to the local people Coetzee employs, for he speaks only Portuguese and a little Sena, while the locals speak only the chiNdau dialect of Shona. Coetzee has to interpret. It is all beginning to remind me of Roy Bennett just across the Chimanimani: local whites forming alliances with local blacks to the fury of the ruling clique in the city.

How long will it be before there is an official Mozambican backlash against Coetzee and his ilk? How long before they become victims of their own agricultural success? The local villagers here may be materially better off because of his presence, but how long before the politics of envy kick in once again?

On our last night with the Coetzees, Max, John's son, adjusts the tall antenna, and we listen to news of Zimbabwe's presidential election coming in over the shortwave radio. It is tuned to Radio Africa. Instead of broadcasting from the nineteenth floor of the Monomotapa Hotel overlooking Harare Park, it now broadcasts by satellite from an office park just north of London.

My sister's voice sounds metallic and distant here in the hills of western Mozambique as she tells us that Robert Mugabe has been reelected president. She tells us, too, that all Western observers have concluded that the polls have been massively rigged, that many people were not allowed to vote, that ballot boxes were stuffed with hundreds of thousands of bogus ballots, that voters were intimidated, that by any definition of the word Zimbabwe is no longer a democracy. Thanks to Mugabe's latest citizenship changes, my father — although he again waits in line for hours to vote — is turned away at the ballot box.

John Coetzee switches off the radio and slumps back down on his camp chair outside his tent in the middle of the Mozambique bush, and he just shakes his head. "Fucking Africa," he says, and takes another slug of his Dos Equis cerveza.

fourteen

September 2002

Bᴀᴄᴋ ɪɴ Nᴇᴡ Yᴏʀᴋ, Joanna and I have decided to buy an apartment because we are hemorrhaging rent. I sell my flat in Notting Hill and we start to look at property in Manhattan. We first look downtown, as post-9/11 bottom-feeders, but the market has frozen. Everyone is waiting. So we look in the Upper West Side, where we rent now.

One day we are shown into a ruinously dilapidated apartment on Riverside Drive, overlooking Joan of Arc Island, a small grassy tussock dominated by a statue of the French martyr on horseback, brandishing her sword at the Hudson River and the New Jersey shore beyond. The owner is an eccentric rabbi who first moved in as a student at Columbia University forty-five years ago and hasn't touched it since. He doesn't seem to notice the great chunks of plaster missing from the peeling walls, or the huge water-leak stains on the ceilings, or the grimy black wooden floors. The living room is headquarters of his radical green Jewish environmental group, and along one wall rests a thicket of vintage Israeli protest placards all proclaiming: BIBI — STOP THE TRANS NEGEV HIGHWAY. The master bedroom is a jewelry workshop where we find Rikki, an Ethiopian Jewish refugee, a Falasha, in a leopard-print leotard and safety goggles, armed with a soldering gun, bent over a trestle table making exquisite pendants and earrings of silver and nickel and amber. The rabbi is unable to shoulder his way into the dining room at all; the door opens only a chink to reveal floor-to-ceiling stacks of banana boxes, overflowing with musty documents. In another bedroom, Joanna gives a squawk of alarm as the door of the walk-in closet springs open and out steps a small, elderly man impeccably dressed in a white linen suit and spats. He doffs his panama hat and introduces himself as Mr. Goradevski. He is a recently arrived Polish Jew, he explains. A duo of Polish Jewish girls also lives here, accessing their bedroom from the fire escape, through the window.

"I'm a Jew too," I find myself saying to the rabbi, trying to boost our chances as prospective buyers. It is the first time I have said it in public.

"Observant?" he asks, looking me up and down.

"No," I confess. "I only recently found out."

In the end, he sells it to us anyway. And we mortgage ourselves to the hilt to buy this Jewish halfway house.

"It has a great karma," declares Joanna as we survey the wreck we have purchased. Thomas, now four, takes one look at it and bursts into tears. "It's broken," he wails. "And dirty. I want to go home."

As we begin the arduous task of making the apartment livable, I teach part-time at Princeton, where I have been appointed for a semester as a visiting professor of journalism. Though my green card hasn't come through yet, I now have a temporary work permit. With two little boys, a new, ruined apartment, and a temporary job, it is starting to feel like I am finally nesting. But I still miss Africa and follow events there compulsively. And when *National Geographic* magazine suddenly shows an interest in the Zimbabwe land conflict, I head back to Africa again as soon as I can.

* * *

TRAVELING WITHOUT a TV crew this time, and without an impending election, I risk crossing into Zimbabwe, although of course I can't tell the immigration officers that I plan to write a story—that would require a special visa that I would never get. For "purpose of stay," I write "tourism."

On the drive from the airport I notice new graffiti, "Exodus 20:17," scrawled on various walls along the way. At a red traffic light a group of ragged, feral children swarm around the car with cupped palms. One small boy comes up to my closed window. When I don't open it, he wipes his hand across his runny nose and writes on the glass in yellow snot: "help me."

I sit with my parents under the jasmine pergola drinking tea, looking out at the swimming pool. It has now completed its transformation into a fishpond and is alive with water lilies, cream and mauve. Papyrus reeds pierce its surface, rising to large green mop-like flower heads, and the shafts of bulrushes too, with brown tips like Zulu spears. A great clump of orange crane flowers grows on what used to be the love seat. Around the edges grow yellow daylilies, white alyssum, and orange nasturtiums.

"Where's the security guard?" I ask as darkness falls and he fails to appear.

"We dropped the service after a few months," says Dad.

"It didn't make sense," says Mum. "Having a guard just signals to *tsotsis* [criminals] that you have something worth stealing. And the guards themselves are often in cahoots with the robbers, providing them with inside information about household precautions and routines."

"Anyway," says Dad, "our guard seemed to sleep most of the time."

I don't bother to argue and change the subject.

"What's Exodus 20:17?" I ask. "I keep seeing it written on walls."

"Oh, Peter. I'm *ashamed* of you," says my mother, in mock rebuke. "A chaplain's grandson, and you don't know that? Exodus 20 is where God lays out the Ten Commandments for Moses. Verse 17,

I think, is number ten: 'Thou shalt not covet thy neighbor's house, nor his wife, nor his manservant, nor his maidservant, nor his ox, nor his ass, nor anything that is thy neighbor's.' "

"It must have been daubed by evicted farmers, come into town," says my father.

THE NEXT AFTERNOON I head out to Woodleigh Farm, east of Harare, to visit the Drapers, an elderly couple who have just been attacked by those trying to evict them. Still sprightly at eighty, Dubble Draper meets me at the ivy-layered arch leading to her low-slung, utilitarian farmhouse, with an offer of tea.

"But not cake. I'm too depressed to bake," she says, limping over the red-cement floor of the kitchen.

She has a bandage on one leg; bruises and gashes cover her thin, tanned arms.

In the living room, leaning against the mantelpiece, is her chain-smoking daughter, Lee, whose face is puffy and bruised, one eye swollen shut. Lee gingerly eases up the back of her blouse to show a large mulberry bruise in the shape of a boot tread. Her hair is matted with blood from a deep cut on her crown. Yesterday, at about this time, just after the sun dipped behind the jacaranda tree in their garden, Dubble heard a commotion and came in to see "this child of mine with eight monsters on her, her face already a pool of blood." One of the attackers stood over Lee with an ax held aloft, ready to swing. Dubble hurled herself at him.

When Bob, Dubble's infirm husband, staggered onto the scene with his flashlight, muttering, "Who are these? Who are these?" they turned on him too, but the ringleader cried, "Leave him, he's half dead already," and snatched his flashlight, then disappeared down the corridor into the gathering darkness. As he left, he lashed out with a bottle at the photos that line the wall, a gallery of Dubble's triumphs as one of the country's premier horse trainers.

"Pack your things and leave, white bitch! Take your pictures and get out! This is all ours now!" he screamed, and then was gone.

Dusty outlines on the wall mark the missing frames, but some survive. Here is Dubble as a glamorous young matron in a slim-cut white cotton dress she made herself, court shoes, a fox fur cape, black velvet headband, black lace veil, and pearls strung around her slender neck. She holds the reins of the sleek mare that has just triumphed at the Mashonaland Turf Club. "Mrs. A M Draper (trainer) leads in Snow Princess, 1959," reads the caption.

In the middle of the lawn, there is a large patch of burned grass from the wovits' huge bonfire. All night they pranced with a high-kneed march and beat a metal pipe on a large empty drum and chanted, "Kill the Drapers! Kill the Drapers!" The family huddled inside, behind closed curtains, while their security guard, a diminutive man called Decent, told the crowd that he would set his dog on them if they tried to come inside. For hours they taunted and abused him, calling him a white man's lackey. But Decent remained there, standing at attention, with his Labrador sitting beside him, refusing to let them in.

Dubble tells me that, for weeks now, the cottage at the bottom of the lawn has been occupied by "the pastor," who claims he is the new owner of Woodleigh Farm, and indeed of their house, which they should vacate immediately. He has begun plowing up their horse paddocks, which are on nonarable land, and he has cut down their avenue of fifty-year-old fir trees and sold them for firewood. The "pastor" is in fact a librarian at the *Herald,* the government newspaper. He commutes out to his new farm from Harare every weekend, and during the week he leaves his nephew, Liberty, there to watch over his interests. He has brought farming activity almost to a standstill, turning the Drapers' head groom—whom they adopted as a nine-year-old orphan thirty-two years ago—against them. The pastor has persuaded the grooms to go on strike for millions of dollars of "retrenchment money," compensation he says they will be paid by the Drapers when they leave.

This is not how Bob Draper expected to end his life. At eighteen he ran away from school to join the Royal Navy and fight the Nazis. His destroyer was sunk in the eastern Mediterranean and he floated for days in the oily sea.

"For years after," interjects Dubble, "he used to get these terrible boils that would eventually burst and oil would come out."

Bob was captured in German-occupied Greece and thrown into a POW camp, escaped, found his way to the British headquarters in Alexandria, where he was dispatched to the Far East. When the war ended, he returned to Rhodesia and Woodleigh Farm.

He is a talented rider himself, captaining the Rhodesian polo team for several years. "We even had a practice ground right here on the farm," he says, with nostalgic reverie.

"Great life, great life," says Dubble.

"Yes, lots of good fun," agrees Bob, and you can see that the memory of those days is more real to him now than yesterday's beating in his own house by frenzied squatters intent on taking over the farm.

"Are you bitter?" I ask him.

"What?"

"*Bitter?*" I repeat. Bob is pretty deaf now.

He blinks at the word. Then an anguished look spreads across his deeply scored face. "Yes," he says slowly, trying it out. "I suppose I am. There's cause for bitterness, let's face it. I was born here. I served my country through World War II, worked here all my life, paid my taxes, and you wonder what it was all for. Bitter? Yes, I do believe I am."

"I never dreamed it would get to this stage," says Dubble. "I mean this is just plain, unadulterated anarchy. It's the mob running the country. There is no help from anywhere."

Dubble is too traumatized for me to contradict her, but of course it's not really anarchy at all, though many are calling it that. Anarchy? Just look at the word's origin, from Greek *anarkhos: an,* "without," *arkhos,* "chief or ruler." Without ruler? Not in Zimbabwe, we aren't. Our problem is the opposite. We have an oppressive, overbearing ruler. We have a dictator.

I can think of other words that far better describe what we are enduring. *Fascism,* for one. *Anarchy* here is nothing more than a fig leaf to hide the heavy hand of the state. In fact it is all pretty well organized. The original wovits I met more than two years ago on the first occupied farms are fast disappearing, turfed off by the real players, the elite: the ministers and the generals and the judges and the ambassadors. Other farms, like Woodleigh, are being divided into smaller plots for lesser-ranking functionaries.

AT HOME FINALLY, I tell my parents about the Drapers, and they nod sagely and exchange glances.

"Uh, we had a little labor trouble of our own," says my father.

"Mavis," says Mum.

"But I thought she'd retired," I say.

"Yes," says Dad, "but she came back."

And slowly the full story comes out. Mavis turned up one day with goons from Joseph Chinotimba's pseudounion, who accuse my father of having underpaid Mavis, of not having given her a proper pension, of owing her a "retrenchment package" even though she retired and was not laid off.

"What's this all about, Mavis?" my father asks.

She sits in the back of the goons' car, her eyes downcast, frowning.

"Why don't you tell them these allegations are untrue? We have always paid you well and looked after you."

But Mavis says nothing.

So my father goes to his filing cabinets and returns with his double-entry ledgers and contracts and receipts for her wages and interest-free loans and pension records and private health insurance, going back more than twenty-five years: all is meticulously recorded there. But the two large men will not even look at his proffered evidence. Instead, they demand he go with them to the police station. So over my mother's objections, he puts on his outside shoes and his jacket and accompanies them to Highlands Police Station.

They sit there in the charge office for hours, the four of them, Dad and the union enforcers and Mavis, waiting their turn. And eventually they are ushered in to see a junior policeman. The union men speak to him first, and then Dad.

"It is not our jurisdiction," says the young officer quickly, clearly nervous to contradict Chinotimba's men, and he suggests the matter is one for the Ministry of Labor.

So the next day, Dad humps a large briefcase with all his receipts and contracts and files to the ministry. He sits in the ministry waiting room for most of the day, eats the ham sandwich Mum has made him for lunch, and, finally, in the late afternoon, he is ushered in front of an official, a black middle-aged lady. He explains the visit by Chintotimba's men.

"These people, these people . . ." she says, and shakes her head and sighs.

He spreads out his records on her desk, including the thirteenth-month salary checks he has paid Mavis each year as a bonus. She looks at them all carefully and deems everything to be in order.

"You have been generous," she says, and she writes at the end of the pay book that it has been examined and approved by her, and stamps it with the ministry stamp.

Dad thinks this is an end to it all. When Mavis and the thugs return, the same two men and a woman too, Mum ushers them into the courtyard and offers them tea, which they refuse. Dad shows them the pay books with the labor ministry's approval stamps on them, but they dismiss them without even looking.

"We decide, not the ministry," says their leader. "We are the ultimate authority."

"You should be ashamed, trying to cheat your faithful servant," says the woman.

"Have we not always treated you well?" Mum asks Mavis. She draws breath to answer, but looks up at Chinotimba's men and says nothing.

"What about the clothes you are wearing?" asks my mother.

Mavis looks down at her navy blue tailored jacket. "Yes," she says, suddenly brightening. "The madam gave me this jacket. But it is not an old one of hers. She made this jacket for me from new cloth." And she mimes how my mother had measured her, and cut the cloth from a paper pattern, and pinned the material. "She sewed it on her sewing machine and made the buttonholes and bought the buttons." Mavis stands up and smooths the jacket and twirls slowly so the union leaders can examine it. "It is a beautiful jacket," she says. And they all nod.

When Dad gets up to go to the study in search of yet another document, the two men follow him.

"You have been wasting our time," says the less big of the two men, though he still looms above my father. "And now we have run out of patience."

"It is time for you to just pay us," says the bigger man, his voice rising.

"Yes, pay your maid," corrects the less big one. "It is too dangerous to make us angry."

"We know where you live," says the bigger one, unnecessarily. He starts jabbing Dad in the V of his farmer's tan. "We will come and get you. Do you understand?"

And finally, Dad does understand. He understands that this is extortion. My father, who has never given a bribe in his life, for whom bribery is anathema, who believes that the bribe giver is just as morally corrupt as the bribe taker, realizes that he now has no option but to pay them. So he goes to the bank and comes back with a dozen bricks of Zimbabwe dollars. But even then, he insists on giving it to Mavis—and getting a receipt. She lowers the car window, scribbles her initials on Dad's invoice book, and he hands her the money, which she quickly gives to the bigger man. He counts out the bricks, takes half of them, and hands the other half back to her. And suddenly, all jovial at his hoard, he comes over and tries to shake Dad's hand, as though they have just finished a legitimate business transaction. My father just shakes his head in disgust. "You are nothing but a thief," Dad says, and the man looks at him like thunder.

By now, Mum has come out of the house. She raps on Mavis's window, and Mavis lowers it again.

"How *could* you, Mavis?" Mum says. "How could you do this to us after all we've done for you? How could you bring these people here and steal from us?"

Mavis finally breaks down and begins to weep. "It was my nieces," she says, finally meeting my mother's eyes. "They made me to do this. They are too greedy."

My mother just walks away.

And the goons drive Mavis back to her house, where she stops taking the hypertension drugs that Mum has stockpiled for her and dies a few months later.

ALTHOUGH HER BACK PAIN — sciatica that ebbs and flows — is quite severe now, and she sometimes finds it difficult to walk, my mother says she doesn't want anyone else inside the house. "We'll just cope on our own," she insists, and she retreats to her bed to listen to Georgina on the radio, even before it is dark outside.

Dad and I are sitting alone in the living room. The picture of his parents and his sister still hangs on the wall where he nailed it on my last visit. I walk over to look at it up close. He watches me but says nothing.

"I wish you'd told me before," I say finally.

He gives a long sigh. "What real difference would it have made, Pete?" he asks. "It's all so long ago."

"I don't know," I reply truthfully. "I suppose it might have made us closer, as a family."

My father shrugs.

"Well, I just wish I'd known," I say. "You know I was *in* Poland once, when I was East European correspondent for the *Sunday Times*."

"Oh," he says.

"And I probably walked right past your old home on Kredytowa Street."

"What did you think of Warsaw?" he asks.

"Well, those were the dark days before the Iron Curtain was lifted, and Solidarity was being harshly repressed. I don't know. It all seemed so foreign to me, and it was midwinter, freezing cold, and there was nowhere to eat, and I was being followed around by the secret police."

"Just as well I moved, then," he says, and laughs harshly.

"One image stands out from my time there," I continue. "It was a demonstration one evening in Old Town. It's been restored, you know."

"No," he says. "I didn't."

"The protesters were met by a solid phalanx of black-helmeted riot police, the ZOMO. And as the two sides fronted up to one another, I thought it was about to get, you know, really violent. Then the protesters reached into their pockets and began throwing handfuls of pennies, zloty coins, at the officers, and chanting, 'Ju-das! Ju-das! Ju-das!' and the coins tinkled as they fell onto the cobbles, and the police just stood there looking ashamed."

My father lights a cigarette and says nothing.

"And shortly after that, I was banned from going back to Poland, because the government didn't like a piece I'd written."

"Oh," says Dad.

"Why did you conceal the Jewish stuff anyway, Dad?" I ask.

He looks at me as though I am being deliberately obtuse.

"Why?" he says. "For my children. For you. So that you could be safe. So that what happened to them," he nods toward the photo of his mother and his sister, "would never happen to you. Because it will never really go away, this thing. It goes underground for a generation or two, but always reemerges."

I wonder if he's right, if this hatred of Jews is one of those atavistic urges we will always return to. That it is aimed as much against assimilated Jews as it is against those who keep themselves distinct. That the fear and suspicion may be even greater against those who seek to assimilate, to pass. The fraud, the impostor, the enemy in disguise, an infiltrator who appears in many forms, like Marechera's *njuzu, the manfish.*

In fact there is a small Jewish community in Zimbabwe. The Shona call them *maJuta,* and they are mostly descendents of Jews who fled the Baltics to escape Russian pogroms in the early 1900s. They had originally set off for South Africa but found the "quota" for Jews there already full, so ended up as accidental immigrants to Rhodesia. From a peak of around three thousand, there are now only a few hundred left.

But they are not quite the only Jews. Some of the Lemba, a small tribe who straddle the South Africa–Zimbabwe border, have long claimed to be a "lost tribe of Israel," a claim treated until recently with some doubt, as they are classically Bantu in appearance. But when the men volunteered for Y chromosome DNA tests, they proved not only that they *are* of Jewish descent, arriving on the African coast about a thousand years ago, probably by ocean-going dhows from Yemen, but that they hail from the rabbinical Cohanim line.

Dad looks at his watch and switches on the ZTV news. It's preceded by an advertisement extolling the current "fast-track" land reform campaign. The ad begins with a jingle: "*Chave Chimurenga*—'Now it's war.'" Then a well-dressed black man opens his refrigerator and, seeing that it's empty but for a couple of wilted lettuce heads, he leaps into a yellow Mercedes and drives to a supermarket, only to be met by more empty shelves. He drives on into the countryside in his search for sustenance, stopping briefly at a farm gate adorned with a sign reading: WELCOME TO THE LITTLE ENGLAND HOMESTEAD — MR. BIG WHITE. Frightened off by cutaways of lion and leopard—for farms that have been turned into wildlife conservancies are also being seized—he finally arrives at a resettlement farm where he joins other well-dressed settlers in spirited hoeing of the soil followed by some boisterous dancing, albeit still on an empty stomach.

Dad switches it off. "Fine lot of good it's done us anyway. Being a white here is starting to feel a bit like being a Jew in Poland in 1939—an endangered minority—the target of ethnic cleansing."

THAT NIGHT, I sleep in the converted garage, with the dogs groaning contentedly in their creaking wicker baskets outside. And on the bedside table still sits the Greek mythology book I had been paging through when I was last lying here, listening to the war vets banging on the sides of their trucks as they went to invade the farms. I pick it up again and examine the picture of the Chimera on the cover. Since I saw it last I have looked up the word to discover that *chimera* has another meaning. In biology, it is any organism that contains tissues from at least two genetically distinct parents. So I suppose I am a chimera of sorts too. Half Jew, half Gentile. A hybrid, a crossbreed. A mongrel.

THE NEXT MORNING, I get back to work on my *National Geographic* piece. Mugabe's farm-seizure program is now in its final stages. By the latest count, 97 percent of six thousand white-owned farms have been served with eviction notices. But the one I'm visiting today—Zanado—is not one of them. The Selbys show me a high court order pinned to the wall of the farm office. It proclaims that the Selbys are still its legal owners. But in reality, Zanado Farm is already occupied. Major Kanouruka has taken over the front half and Mrs. Molly Mapfumo, a senior government official, has taken the back. After a four-month legal tug-of-war in which the Selbys have been chased off and then returned by court order no fewer than nine times, they are losing heart. Mick Selby, who farmed here with his parents, Jeremy and Janet, had his house broken into and occupied two months ago by the major and his men, a cadre of young toughs from the major's home area down in the Zambezi Valley. They are graduates of the ruling party's Border Gezi militia-training camp and have their own riff on the history of land ownership in Zimbabwe. When the first white pioneers approached Chief Lobengula to ask for a land grant, he was seated on a revolving chair, they tell me. Beguiled by his first taste of sugar, a sly gift from the whites, he raised his hand meaning only to indicate a small portion of land for the whites to farm, but the chair spun a full circle, suggesting he would give it all away. Thus was the paramount chief outmaneuvered by a sweet tooth and an item of well-lubricated office furniture.

"Zimbabwe for Zimbabweans," chant the major's young toughs.

"I was born here, I'm Zimbabwean too," Mick points out, in Shona, but they aren't listening.

Each Saturday morning at 9:00, Major Kanouruka drives down from Harare, thirty miles away, in his company car, an olive green Peugeot sedan with military plates. He sits on his veranda, fires up the barbecue, and chugs his way through a bottle of Glenfiddich. From time to time, if he catches sight of Mick, he calls out in a not entirely believable way: "Hey, Mickey, come over and have a shot with me."

Today, I have come to see the Selbys supervise a squadron of combine harvesters churning through their winter-wheat crop. That they have been allowed to plant the wheat at all is due only to a desperate deal they have made with the major to prepare, plow, plant, fertilize, and harvest a similar field of wheat for him. For this, the major has promised to pay them back, once he sells the crop. But they have little hope of recouping the debt. The major has already seized their bakery, which supplied fifteen thousand people in the neighboring Chiweshe tribal reserve with bread, and their butchery. He has expropriated their flour and sold their loaves and their meat.

After the winter wheat is reaped, there will be almost no more agricultural activity on Zanado Farm. The fifty acres of citrus trees are wilting and will soon die. The irrigation piping on which they depend has been dug up and sold by the major's boys. The greenhouses are nothing now but torn skeins of plastic that flap in the stiff breeze against their exposed wooden ribs. The main homestead is already looking derelict. The swimming pool is dark with rotting leaves. The clay tennis court has sprouted a quiff of elephant grass. Goats nibble at the lawn, and the flower beds are rapidly returning to bush.

Mick Selby and his mother, Janet, survey the ravages of neglect with mournful disbelief. Their two dogs lurk in the trees, thin and tick infested, reduced to cowering curs by the continuous taunting of their new overlords. The previous week, Mick had to shoot their two horses. And before the sun sets this evening, he must take the dogs to the vet to be put down.

Janet Selby, armed with pruning shears and spade, walks purposefully to the rose garden. Her mission today, she tells me, is to retrieve the rosebushes given to her by her mother-in-law as an anniversary gift, twenty-five of them, one for every year of her marriage. She manages to unearth two, which Panga, the family cook, places in their pickup truck. But as she kneels to dig up the third, Kumbirai, one of the major's enforcers, strides over to her, an open quart bottle of Lion beer sloshing in his pocket. "Put those down now!" he screams.

Janet Selby rises from her knees and, in a somewhat tremulous but determined voice, reminds him that this rose retrieval has been negotiated with the major. With his mouth only several inches from her face, Kumbirai issues another spit-flecked command. "You shaddap!"

Mick strides over, his fist already clenched to thump Kumbirai, but I restrain him. If he hits this youth we will probably die here this morning. All the while, Marumbu, a tall and somewhat drunken youth, dances around us, throwing kung fu punches and kicks into the air.

"Sabotage! Sabotage!" he shouts to no one in particular.

Panga looks down at the lush kikuyu grass beneath his laceless shoes. "God sees everything," he says in a quiet voice. "They will be made to suffer, these ones, for what they do." But his tone is one of defiance, not prediction.

FIFTY MILES AWAY, in Marondera, Roy and Louise McIlwaine take a similar sanctuary in the idea of some kind of divine accounting.

Today is the day that Roy and Louise must leave their farm, Larkhill. Today is D-day, the expiry of the notice period on their "Order to Vacate." Most of their household stuff is already gone—pictures, photo albums, rugs, books—and the place has a desolate air. The farm equipment is still there, though. That *has* to stay. This is how the latest iteration of the land reform formula works: the government confiscates the farm without compensation. It then insists that the farmer pay large "retrenchment packages" to the labor force. To guarantee this payment, the labor force is encouraged to set up a barricade to ensure the farmer doesn't try to "smuggle" out any of his assets.

The entire Larkhill Farm, including the farmhouse and well and fields, has already been divided into hundred-hectare plots and allocated to black settlers. They have responded to advertisements in the *Herald* and on ZTV offering free land under the "A2 resettlement model." For months, you could see the applicants in their jackets and ties lining up around the block outside the Ministry of Land in Harare. The only lines that are longer are those for bread, cooking oil, cornmeal, fuel, and South African visas. Many of the prospective settlers are already visiting their plots, even before the McIlwaines have gone. Most of them are civil servants and office workers from town. Few of them intend to live here or farm full-time.

Roy opens a dusty manila file to show me the history of Larkhill Farm. It has been in McIlwaine hands since Major Mac, a retired British artillery major, who had played for England in eight rugby internationals, saw a stand at Earls Court Olympia with a big banner declaring, COME TO ROMANTIC RHODESIA. In 1927 Major Mac came out and toured the country with his wife and four kids in an old Model T Ford. He wanted to start a dairy farm and supply butter and cheese to the capital, so he bought Larkhill because it was close to the railway line.

Major Mac told his wife, "Shin up that tree, dear, and see what the view's like."

"Marvelous," she replied, so he traced the outline of their house with the heel of his boot. There they constructed a pole-and-mud hut and a long-drop privy and set about making a farm. But when a depression struck in 1930, Mac, along with many pioneering white farmers, went bust. It was only years later, after he came back from World War II, from fighting in the western Sahara and in Italy, that he finally got out from under his original debt.

Yesterday afternoon, seventy-five years after Major Mac bought this land, Louise hears the singing start up outside. She has been expecting it. It is *jambanja* time. *Jambanja*. In Shona it means "to turn everything upside down, to cause violent confusion." That is what they call it now when they drive a farmer off the land. Louise goes out to see the crowd that has gathered there. They are led by strangers, agitators who have come to orchestrate the McIlwaines' eviction. But some are their own workers, scared, greedy for the huge retrenchment payouts they've been promised, or just worried about their future. The farm is their only home. They have seen other white farmers leaving and so they have changed sides. Changed masters. Among them are the three orphaned black youths that the McIlwaines adopted after picking one up as a tiny hitchhiker fifteen years ago.

"The way they've divided up the farm makes no sense at all," says Roy. "The guy who's been given this house and the surrounding land, Mr. Munyawarara, he has no water source on his plot at all. His sister works at the Zimbabwean Embassy in Rome, and the plot is in her name. He comes to visit occasionally on Sundays in his SUV. One Sunday he came to me and said, 'Do you mind, Roy, if we take some pictures of our house?' And he posed there, smiling, on our front doorstep, while his friends photographed him.

"Another settler, a senior civil servant who works in town, has already moved her stuff into my mother's cottage. She arrived one day with an entourage, and I said to them, 'The Lord forbids that I should give you the inheritance of my fathers,' and they laughed and laughed.

"Mr. Sekeremai, who is related to a government minister, he has another of the hundred-hectare plots. He came to me and asked if I would plow one hectare for him. So I did it, and when I'd finished I asked him, 'What about the other ninety-nine?' And he said, 'No, I only have a small family, one hectare is enough to feed them.' That's the real tragedy. Most of these people won't actually farm much of the land at all."

As he knows it's his last season, Roy has virtually stopped farming the land, planting nothing but one small plot of corn, so that his labor force will at least have some food when he's evicted.

"I call it the 'well-watered garden,' " he says, "after the biblical garden. But the pump switches for the irrigation were stolen. I replaced them and they were stolen again, so it's not so well watered anymore."

Among the cornstalks Roy has hammered in wooden stakes that bear placards of biblical quotes. As far as my eye can see, this little placarded plot of corn is now the only crop growing. This well-watered garden, no longer watered at all, is the only agricultural activity. In this whole district, less than 5 percent of farms are still operating.

"I keep thinking of the scriptural readings of the desolation of Judah," he says.

"What will you do now?" I ask.

"I don't know. It's difficult to start again at fifty-two, with no capital. If I leave, I think I will lose my self-worth entirely. Everything I have is in this place. I'm not sure where we'll go."

"What about going to South Africa?" I ask.

"Hmm. I'm not so sure about that," says Roy. "My aunt was murdered in South Africa. It was a ritual murder, you know, a *muti* killing. I heard that they cut off her hair and cut out her eyes and her heart to use in traditional spells. But I think the police caught the guy who did it."

BACK AT THE HOUSE, another evicted farmer, Bux Howson, has arrived with his pickup to help them cart away the last of their personal belongings. We finish loading the boxes as darkness falls around us. Bux latches the tailgate, leans back on the pickup, and looks out across the gloaming.

"You know, we're Africans, but we will always be the scapegoats, the aliens," he says. "My philosophy now is that you have no security in Africa. We've tried to kid ourselves that it was going to be different here. We plowed everything back into our farms. It was all reinvested. And now look. We've lost everything."

fifteen

September 2002

E VEN FROM THE AIR, when we go up in a little Cessna to get some aerial shots, it is obvious that everything has been *jambanja*'d, turned upside down. At this time of year, you should see freshly tilled soil planted for the new season. But as we circle over the highlands of Mashonaland, in central Zimbabwe, there are few fields planted. Many of the peasants who have been allocated small plots on seized farms still wait in vain for the seeds and the fertilizer and the squads of tractors that the government has promised them. Irrigation has been destroyed, wells ruined, electricity cut off for nonpayment of bills. Some have reverted to medieval agricultural methods on what were, just the year before, highly sophisticated, productive farms. Unsurprisingly, yields have plummeted. Cereal production is already down 57 percent from last year, and corn 67 percent. And as the hunger spreads, Mugabe's men are using it to their political advantage, controlling the supply of grain through the monopoly of the grain marketing board and trying to prevent aid agencies from delivering food relief to areas associated with the opposition.

Some of the main casualties of *jambanja* are the two million black farmworkers and their families who lived and worked on the commercial farms.

Bigson Gumbeze is the displaced farmworkers' project manager at the Farm Community Trust. From his high-ceilinged office within an old colonial house in central Harare, he follows the growing humanitarian disaster on the farms as the workers are thrown off with their old employers. On a whiteboard in his office he updates the tally: last month there were eighty thousand displaced farmworkers. You see them along the roads, sleeping in the open, little knots of people like remnants of a defeated army, with nowhere to go.

Today, Gumbeze and I drive east out of Harare with a delivery of clothes donated by a local factory. At the massive balancing granite boulders of Epworth, as featured on the country's beleaguered currency, eroded by 200 percent hyperinflation, the paved road narrows and then runs out altogether as we come to Rock Haven Refugee Camp, an expanse of olive tents where several hundred farmworkers have lived for the past nine months. They sit, mostly barefoot and ragged, under a grove of musasa trees as Gumbeze and his assistants dole out their bounty. The clothes, it turns out, consist of just three oufits, and soon we are surrounded by refugees in a surreal uniform — the women all in matching housedresses, yellow floral swirls on orange; the men in identical khaki chinos with cuffs and sharp creases, and dark green golf shirts; the kids all in the same jaunty Hawaiian shirts. And they assemble in rows and begin to sing a thank-you song, their words floating up in effortless four-piece harmony.

Many of these workers are from one farm — Chipesa, owned by Ian Kay, who paid the price for openly campaigning for the MDC in the recent general election.

James Sani, twenty-six, tells me what happened: "One day, the war vets and party youth arrived on our farm and said it belonged

to them now," he says. "They put a gun to Ian Kay, but he managed
to escape. The vets beat us with iron bars and axes, and they looted
our property and burned down our houses and chased us away."

"They called us *mwengi*, which means 'enemy,' because, they
said, we supported the opposition party," says Armando Serima.
"We hid in the bush for two months eating roots and leaves and
begging food from other farmworkers at night, until our employer,
Mr. Kay, came and found us hiding there in the mountains just
when we were about to die of hunger, and he brought us here."

"So we have nothing," says Sani. "There are no jobs, and now
this drought . . . I was born at the farm, grew up at the farm, went
to school on the farm, worked for the last eight years on the farm,
my father died on the farm. All we know is farming. That's what we
want to do again."

"We did try to lease another farm for them to set up agricultural projects," says Gumbeze. "I took twenty-one of the workers
from here to prepare the land there. The day after we arrived, at
1:30 a.m., when we were all fast asleep after digging in the fields all
day, the riot police surrounded the building and arrested us all.
They bundled us into trucks and took us to prison. Then they kept
moving us about from prison to prison so that our lawyer couldn't
find us. They charged seventeen of the workers with undergoing
military training, and they charged me with coordinating an un-
lawful public gathering. The charges are ridiculous."

THE NEXT DAY, I visit my sister's grave, something I try to do
every year. Neither of my parents feels up to the trip, but my mother
calls Isaac to help her cut a selection of flowers. She calls and calls,
but he doesn't come, and she gets irritated. Then we see him cycling
up to the gate. He is wearing long trousers with the hems rolled up
and Wellington boots. And over a pressed white shirt he wears
Dad's hand-me-down herringbone-tweed jacket. In its top pocket
he has carefully placed a handkerchief, its corner showing, just as
Dad does. He has pinned a miniature rosebud to his lapel. And
around his neck is one of Dad's old paisley cravats. Mum remem-

bers Dad has given him time off to attend the PTA meeting at Cheesely's upscale school, Lewisam.

"How was the PTA?" I ask him after he has changed back into his gardening clothes, and Mum is pointing out flowers for him to clip for Jain. I wonder how he has fared, Isaac, the gardener, among the black diplomats and the bankers and the government ministers.

"They did not elect me to any committees," he says glumly, "though I volunteered."

Mum points to tall blue and yellow crane flowers, and sprigs of yesterday-today-and-tomorrow, forget-me-nots, strelitzia, soft ivory kapok blossoms from the tree that Mum transplanted from Jain's garden after she died, green mop heads of papyrus from the pool and blue plumbago.

"I want her to see how the garden's doing," Mum says as she helps Isaac tie the selection together into a huge, unruly posy. At the center of their floral architecture are two long spiny stalks of aloe, "to ward off Kipling's hyenas," says Mum, and a clutch of white arum lilies, "as symbols of purity."

Isaac puts the flowers into a bucket of water and jams it in the foot well of the passenger seat of the car, and I drive it out along the Bulawayo Road to Warren Hills Cemetery. Since I was last here, the adjacent township, Warren Park, has swollen and is now garlanded with improvised shacks, which press hard up against the cemetery boundary. I park the car and carry the flowers up the hillside to the garden of remembrance, where all cremated remains are entombed in rows inside long, low, curving stone walls, under a canopy of wild musasa trees.

As I approach, I see that something else has changed since my last visit. The fence that used to separate the township from the cemetery has been dismantled, and there is a new network of footpaths where the residents have taken shortcuts through the graves. Closer still, peering over my flowers, I see that they are also using it as an open-air lavatory. There are little clumps of soiled toilet paper scattered around and a fetid smell. And in among the graves at the top, people have started to cultivate little patches of corn. Then I notice that the brass plaques that were bolted onto each mini-tomb, inscribed with the names and details of the dead, are missing. Every single one. The wall is just a long line of blank niches. I have no idea which is Jain's. Some of the tombs themselves have been broken open and the urns removed.

I stride down to the cemetery office, but there is no one there. Finally, I find a gaunt man leaning against the crematorium wall, smoking and coughing.

"I am not the in-charge," he says, when he sees I want to complain about the state of the place.

"But how did this happen?" I ask.

He shrugs and exhales his smoke and coughs a bit more. "We have a guard only in the day. When it is dark, those people come from the township and they steal the fence, and sometimes they take gravestones too, to build their houses; and others, they steal the plaques from the tombs. They melt them down to make brass handles for coffins for the people who die of this AIDS."

"Well, where can I put my flowers?" I say miserably. "We picked all these flowers and now I can't even tell which one is my sister's grave."

He nips the stub of his cigarette between long dirty nails, and sucks one last lungful of smoke, burning it right down to the filter, and he throws it down on the stone path.

"Let's we go," he says, and I follow him as he coughs his way down to the office. He wanders off into the back. I hear drawers opening and closing and more coughing, and then he returns with a big ledger. "When did she die?" he asks.

"April twenty-second, nineteen seventy-eight."

He flips through the book and then turns it around to me so I can see the names for 1978, and I move my finger down the column until I find Jain's name. Next to it is written "U.160."

"I can show you where that one is," he says, and he coughs back up the hill, and down one of the walls, and as we go, he counts the blank tombs and then stops. "This is the one," he says, pointing and coughing violently. "This is your sister." And then he leaves me alone.

At least her tomb has not been ripped open. The plaque is gone, of course, but the rough cement plug still seems intact, which should mean that the urn with her ashes is still inside. I move the flowers away from my face and, losing their sweet masking scent, am assailed again by the overpowering smell of human shit. I see now that there is a fresh mound of wet turds right in front of me, right in front of Jain. In the time we have been down at the office, someone has crapped here. I kneel down to prop my mother's unwieldy flower bunch against Jain's blank headstone. But when I stand back up, the flowers slowly topple over. I dive to save them, but I am too late, and they fall across the stinking mound. I pick them up to see there is a wide streak of mustard shit all across the white arum lilies. Symbols of purity, my mother had called them.

"Fuck this!" I shout, and I hurl the flowers away, up in a wide parabola. It lands near two women who are bent over, hoeing their cemetery corn, their babies strapped to their backs. They stop their hoeing, look up for a moment, and murmur to each other, and one laughs. And then they go back to their digging. I wonder which one of them crapped here.

Back in the office, I bang repeatedly on the bell that sits on the wooden counter. Eventually I hear the coughing getting closer, and the gaunt man shuffles in.

"I want to move my sister. I want to take away her remains. How do I do it?"

"Ah, it's too difficult," he says, shaking his head. "You need special documents. You need permission to disinter, permission to uplift ashes. And you need to relinquish ownership of the burial plot."

His voice is no longer flat and bored, and he has stopped coughing. "It is too, too *difficult*," he repeats.

He is looking at me expectantly and I realize that he's probably fishing for a bribe. That he is going to hold my sister's ashes hostage in their crap-strewn resting place unless I pay him to spring her. I find the idea of rewarding this man repugnant. And I know it would appall my father.

So I turn on my heel and walk away from that terrible place.

I TRY TO CALM MYSELF as I drive fast, back into town, late for a meeting with Meryl Harrison. By the time I get to the Italian bakery in Avondale, across the road from the Phreckle and Phart, she is waiting for me on the veranda. She is a tall, imposing woman in her late fifties, wearing the uniform of the Zimbabwe National Society for the Prevention of Cruelty to Animals—a royal blue shirt with ZNSPCA shoulder flashes, and dark trousers. As chief inspector of the ZNSPCA, she's had a ringside seat at Zimbabwe's farm invasions.

Two years ago, while watching BBC World Service TV, she saw a Great Dane called Black Jack lying unconscious on a homestead lawn while Mugabe supporters danced in a circle around him to the beat of a tom-tom, darting in from time to time to bash the dog's head with knobkerries and rocks and to hack at his neck with pangas. Meryl realized that the ZNSPCA had to act. (Incredibly, Black Jack is still alive; blind, deaf, and a little lame, but alive.)

ZNSPCA inspectors have the right to arrest those who perpetrate cruelty to animals. But Meryl is well aware that the country's legal system is in ruins, so she goes directly to Hitler Hunzvi, the man masterminding the land takeover for Mugabe, the man who is supervising the torture of scores of suspected opposition supporters in his medical offices in Budidiro, on the edge of Harare.

"I am the biggest terrorist in Zimbabwe," he boasts to her and laughs.

"All I want," she says, "is to do my job, to prevent the abuse of animals. I'm not interested in politics."

Eventually he agrees.

"But only on strict conditions," he insists. "Only black inspectors, in uniform, traveling in official vehicles, may go onto the farms; there must be no publicity; and they mustn't take anything except for pets and domestic animals that are being mistreated. Disobey, and you will be banned from visiting any more farms."

The first rule Harrison has to brush aside immediately when she finds that the only way to get the militant farm invaders to take the ZNSPCA seriously is for her to attend herself. The last rule has proved very difficult to keep—she often has to refuse the tearful entreaties of farmers' wives to retrieve wedding photos, passports, legal documents.

She's been at just about every farm where there's been a major confrontation.

"We are doing this in a war situation," she says. "At least when the British RSPCA operated in Bosnia, they went in *after* the fighting. I have to go in while the conflict is still in full throat. We often have situations where the farmers are warning us that farms are no-go areas and that we'll be attacked by the war vets if we venture there," she says. "But still we go."

Harrison slides a pile of snapshots across the table to me. They are gory fare. Here's one of a field of dead racehorses, killed when their field of grazing is set afire by war vets; this one is of a young heifer with half its face ripped off by wovits' packs of dogs. Here is a Staffordshire bull terrier, axed in the ribs. An emaciated two-month-old foal lies on the ground with a huge gash around her neck from a wire snare. A great pink pile of pigs that have starved to death after wovits refused entry to trucks sent to remove them.

From her bag she takes out a large blue diary. On the cover, below a smiley face sticker, she has taped a quote from Mahatma Gandhi: "The greatness of a nation and its moral progress can be judged by the way its animals are treated." Inside, the book is filled with her dense back-sloping handwriting. She starts to flip through it, picking out entries at random. Danbury Park Farm: a white couple, the Bayleys, Edith, seventy-nine, and Thomas, eighty-nine, are barricaded in their house, surrounded by wovits. The Red Cross is allowed in to take the old couple food, and then their son asks Harrison if she can help to get their dogs out, because every time his parents try to let them out onto the lawn to pee, the vets throw rocks at them. The "base commander" is named Never, and he marches around with a wooden replica AK-47 under his arm. He has tied a serrated carving knife on the end as a bayonet. Eventually, Never allows Harrison in, and she taps on the window. Old Mrs. Bayley, who has palsy from advanced Parkinson's, peeks through the curtains and begins to unlock multiple padlocks.

"We've been here for thirty-three days," she says in a trembling voice as she passes out the first of her dogs, four Jack Russells and a fox terrier.

The police will give Harrison an escort, as a ZNSPCA officer, to rescue the animals, but they still refuse to provide an escort to the old couple themselves to leave. That is "a political matter," they say, beyond their powers. A few days later, however, old man Bayley falls from his walker, breaking his leg, and the police do allow an ambulance in to take him (with his wife) to the hospital. He dies days later.

After the old couple has left Danbury Park, their son Tommy asks Harrison to go back with him to rescue the remaining animals. They manage to get one cat out, but though they call and call and lay down a trail of food, they cannot find the last one. Just as they are about to give up, Harrison hears a tiny meow coming from under the bathtub. Tommy gets down on the floor and reaches his hand in through a hole and feels the cat lick his fingers, but it won't come any farther. And Tommy just lays his head on his arm and begins to sob. Great racking sobs. It is his last day on the farm His father is dead. The cat is too frightened to come out from under the bathtub.

Harrison decides that she will bloody well get this cat back for him, if it's the last rescue she ever does. So she goes to Never, the base commander, and bargains with him—as it is now his house—to be allowed to knock out the base of the bathtub. She offers to treat his dog and to give him blankets and some food. Never finally comes to attention with his wooden rifle, the one with the carving knife tied to the end of the barrel, and he says: "Permission granted." So Harrison and her inspector, Addmore Chinembe, find a hammer and a crowbar and start to knock down the bath wall. Finally the cat flies out, and they manage to cage it.

The next day Harrison returns, gives Never the blankets she has promised him and treats his dog, a Rhodesian ridgeback called Rambo that needs deworming and vaccinations for rabies and distemper.

Never says to her, "You are the only white person I trust," because she has kept her end of the bargain, and so she is allowed to follow the *Treasure Island*–style map that Tommy Bayley has drawn for her, entitled "Danbury Park tortoises." In red, he has marked every tortoise hole and enclosure on the property. In the end she finds all twelve of them, including the seventy-five-year-old.

But it doesn't end there for the Bayleys. After the trauma of losing their farm, and the death of his father, Tommy and his wife, Trish, and their two-year-old daughter decide to drive down to South Africa to escape for a short vacation. On the way down, just north of Bulawayo, a cow has wandered onto the highway, and they round a bend and slam into it. The toddler is only slightly injured. Tommy is badly hurt and spends months recovering in the hospital. Trish is killed instantly.

THE NEXT PICTURE is of Terry Ford, one of the country's premier horse breeders. He lies dead, a blanket over his body, shot by war vets. And curled into the crook of his arm is his Jack Russell terrier, Squeak, who is refusing to leave his dead master, snarling at anyone who tries to remove him. After Ford's funeral, Harrison gets a call to rescue four dogs belonging to Mwambo, the man who, eyewitnesses say, killed Terry Ford. Mwambo has been arrested and has left his own dogs unattended at the Ford farmhouse, which he has taken over. Harrison takes the dogs to the ZNSPCA, vaccinates them, deworms them, and treats them for bilharzia. Then she returns them to Mwambo's relatives. When Mwambo himself is released by a government that declines to prosecute him, he moves back into the house of the man he has murdered and is reunited with his own dogs.

"It's the nature of our job," shrugs Harrison. "It's the animal not the owner that we must focus on."

Another picture shows two of Ford's thoroughbred racehorses with deep cuts and abrasions on their chests. Mwambo has harnessed them and tried to make them pull a plow.

AT HOME I tell my mother that I'm considering getting a few friends together, arming ourselves with sledgehammers and chisels, sneaking into the unguarded cemetery at night, and smashing into Jain's tomb to liberate her ashes. But my mother counsels caution and instead steers me to Keith Martin, an undertaker friend of hers. Until recently, he was managing director of Mashfords, the country's oldest funeral home, with branches all over. But at lunch at the Brontë Hotel, he tells me how he was fired. A black businessman named Philip Chiyangwa, a former vegetable vendor and police officer (and a relative of Mugabe) who became rich riding the crest of the indigenous business advancement campaign, buys Mashfords outright in cash three years ago. Chiyangwa lives in a luxury villa he has built in Borrowdale, which features eighteen bedrooms, each with a bath; "computerized closets" for his three hundred suits; a helipad; and a ten-car garage. Initially, he tells the sixty Mashfords staff members, four of them white, "You are the value of the company to me, I want you all to stay on." But, disappointed at profit margins, Chiyangwa soon tries to dismiss Martin. He sends him disciplinary letters, one for not coming to work by car but instead "Walking to work, like a beggar, through the dust. We are shocked and surprised and it is going to stop." One for taking a bottle of wine, which is part of the rite, to a Greek Orthodox funeral. Finally, the senior staff are snatched from their offices by security guards, who haul them off to Harare Central Police Station while their houses are searched.

Now Martin is back at the university, training to be a doctor, while also working in the deceased-estate department of a law firm in Harare. Having been in the death business for so long, he knows where many of the bodies are buried.

He has seen the corpses of several cabinet ministers who were supposed to have died in "car accidents," whose bodies were "pulverized until they were almost unrecognizable." He also once had a unique view of Robert Mugabe after the death of his first wife, Sally.

"Sally Mugabe died in January 1992, and his mother, Bona, a few months later. These were the only two people whose opinions Mugabe cared about, and he lost them in quick succession. I embalmed Sally and put her, as ordered, in an open casket, where she remained at Mashfords for nine days until the state funeral. And Mugabe came on each of those nine days to visit Sally and to sob over her casket.

"Of course, it's true that he already had two kids with his mistress, Grace, by then. She was a secretary working in the protocol department of the president's office."

Martin isn't surprised by my experience at Warren Hills, and he promises to look into it. The whole way of death is collapsing, he says, just like the way of life. Many bodies are now just left on the street by black families who cannot afford a funeral. The Social Welfare Department piles hundreds of the bodies of the "indigent dead" into common graves. In the smaller towns like Kadoma and Rusape, Zvishavane and Masvingo, for hygiene reasons, they burn the bodies on open pyres, "like huge barbecues," he says.

I ask Martin about possible retirement homes for my parents. Athol Evans is the best, he says, because they have the most access to foreign currency. Some of the others are terribly short of funds. The junior staff in one home are so hungry that they sometimes steal the residents' food. In another, he says, when a son leaves some pocket money with his mother, her nurse's aide demands it as soon as he has left. She refuses, so the aide beats her head against the basin, shouting, "You fucking British bitch," until the old woman hands it over. One old woman has her wedding ring torn off her finger, skinning it. The thief is also one of her caregivers, but because the victim has Alzheimer's she can't make the identification.

"Jesus," I say, "that's a grim picture. I don't know what to do with my parents. What I need right now is someone to help them inside the house, part-time, because they clearly can't cope alone. But they're very gun-shy after what happened with Mavis."

"I have just the guy," he says. "Adston. He was this old lady's cook. Comes from Mount Darwin. His wife died in childbirth. His two young daughters are looked after there by an aunt, I think. He did everything for the old lady, lifted her from bed, got money for her from the ATM, and cooked for her the only thing she would ever eat: butternut and pumpkin puree. When she died, he got on his bicycle and rode into town to tell her attorney that she was lying dead in her bed."

Adston, it turns out, can live on in her house, which is near ours, caretaking it for at least six months while her estate goes through probate, and work part-time for my parents to supplement his salary.

"You thinking of leaving yourself?" I ask Martin as we get up from lunch.

"Nah, we've been here forever. My great-grandmother gave birth on Salisbury Kopje during the 1896 Mashona Rebellion. She cut the umbilical cord herself with a pair of pinking shears, while her husband was out securing the defensive camp. In 1921, she went back home on vacation to County Wicklow, in Ireland, only to have her house there burned down by Sinn Féin, as planned by her servants. We never went back after that."

WHEN I EXPLAIN the Adston arrangement to my parents later, they seem relieved. I have only a few days left before I have to get back to classes at Princeton, a world away, and it has been such a rushed visit that I have had no time to talk to them properly. I've hardly been in Harare, just hopping from farm to farm, *jambanja* to *jambanja*. But now my father asks me to do something for him before I leave. He wants me to go, as a family representative, to the memorial of Garfield Todd.

Originally a churchman from New Zealand, Todd was the prime minister of Rhodesia from 1953 to 1958. He introduced universal primary education for blacks, doubled the number of schools, and tried (unsuccessfully) to legalize sex across the racial divide and move the country toward one-man-one-vote, moves considered far too radical by most whites. They voted him out of office and later chose Ian Smith, who led them into seven years of civil war. Todd established a school at Dadaya, where he lived, and one of the teachers he employed was the young Robert Mugabe. During the independence war, Todd secretly helped the guerrillas.

In recent times, Todd had been critical of Mugabe and, because he is foreign-born, like my parents, he was stripped of his citizenship and his right to vote. He had gone from prime minister to pariah under white rule, and from hero to heretic in the time of Mugabe. His daughter, Judith, a friend of mine, supported the Zimbabwe African People's Union (ZAPU), one of the two nationalist groups that fought for independence. It turned out to be the one that came second, in a continent where the winner takes all and there are no second places. ZAPU was humiliated, crushed, and dismantled. Now Judith is a fiery critic of Mugabe, the more effective, and the more reviled by him, because of her impeccable *chimurenga* credentials.

On the day of the memorial, I arrive early, so I wait across the road in the Monomotapa Hotel, downstairs in the Safari Bar. The last time I was here, the place was bustling with the Harare International Festival of the Arts. Now I am the only customer, eating a sandwich at an empty bar, trying to read the paper, but reflecting really on the ironies of Todd's life, on the weird circularity of his roller-coaster ride.

"Hi there?"

The voice that breaks into my Todd reverie is startlingly close. It belongs to a young black woman now sitting on the next stool. The stools are fixed to the ground so close together that the silver-sequined leg of her skintight jeans touches my knee, and her prominent cleavage looms over my chicken sandwich.

"Ah, hello." I nod curtly and turn back to my paper.

"I'm a little thirsty," she says. The bartender has materialized from his stocktaking and is hovering to take her order. But she is not speaking to him; she is addressing me. Though I'm pretty sure she must be a hooker, I'm somewhat nonplussed at how to get out of buying her a drink without being rude. So I nod to the bartender and he immediately mixes her a piña colada, without asking her what she wants to drink.

I retreat behind my paper again, swinging away from the insistent pressure of her leg.

"Ahhh," she moans loudly, smacking her lips after the first sip.

I ask for my bill and hide again behind my newspaper.

Tap, tap, tap. She is tapping on my newspaper with her swizzle stick. I lower the paper, obviously annoyed now. But she doesn't seem to notice. "Are you on business?" she wants to know.

I slide some cash over the counter to the bartender for the drinks and the sandwich, and her eyes follow the money like an egret hunting fish.

"Actually, no, I'm local," I say curtly, getting up to leave. "I live here."

"*Tsssk.*" She makes the Shona sound of disgust. "You people," she says.

I shrug and start to walk away.

"You are a *racist,*" she says, her voice rising and attracting the attention of a newly arriving cohort of Chinese visitors. "You don't want to go with a black woman because you are *racist.*"

I flee through the revolving glass doors out onto the street where I am mobbed by a throng of desperate curio sellers and money changers and kids selling toy cars made of scavenged wire and tins, and a begging cripple who sits on a little wooden cart, propelling himself along the road with his heel-hard hands. I hurry to the church for the memorial, trailed by my needy retinue and by the hooker's accusations of racism.

Inside, the pews are full; Todd has lived a life of public service, of charitable deeds. Pius Wakatama, father of Ellah, Georgina's best friend, is one of the eulogizers. He tells the story of how, after he lost office, Todd went back to his farm near Zvishavane and founded a school that took the children of poor black families and gave them a thorough education, turning them from peasants into teachers, lawyers, accountants, university professors, cabinet ministers. But the path of the righteous man is not always a straight one. In 1990, a student dispute over food at Dadaya escalates and they burn down their classrooms, their chemistry labs, their library, and the principal's house. And Robert Mugabe, whom Todd had treated so kindly, strips him of his right to vote.

LATER I DRIVE OUT to visit Meryl Harrison at the ZNSPCA headquarters, to say good-bye. Her position is becoming increasingly perilous. The wovits have lost patience with her interference. Her life is in danger. At one rescue, she tells me, a policeman who was supposed to be guarding her directed her to go around the back of the house where she found herself surrounded by Mugabe's militiamen. One started swinging a golf iron menacingly at her; another loaded a slingshot with a rock and held it at her temple. "If you ever come back here, we'll kill you," he said.

She is also getting death threats by phone. They call and say, "We are coming to cut your throat next."

And there are written threats too. She brings out a folded piece of lined paper on which is handwritten in ballpoint pen:

Mrs. Harrison,
    Be warned that the days of serving the interest of the white at the expense of blacks are over. We know you are 100 percent a racist who does not deserve to live in a liberated Zimbabwe. You are only interested in the plight of dogs and cats left by white farmers.
    You love dogs and cats, at the same time you hate blacks. Your days in Zimbabwe are numbered. Take this seriously. You

are given 24 hours to leave Harare where you are operating from.

Thank you for your racial attitude.

Vying for your head, you are under spotlight.

What annoys her most is the accusation that she cares only for the animals of whites. "We've rescued animals of black owners too," she says. "Opposition supporters who have had to flee, and I've treated war vets' goats and donkeys as well. It's immaterial to me who the animals' owners are. And when people say to me, 'Why do you worry about the animals and not the people?' my retort is this: 'There are over seven hundred welfare organizations for people in Zimbabwe, and only one for animals.' " But now, more and more of the animals she rescues have to be put down later.

"Every riding school in Harare is groaning with horses," she says. "We've run out of room. With euthanizing we can promise them a good death, because here in Zimbabwe, we can't promise any animal a good life right now."

She suddenly bows her head across the desk, and I see the stoicism drain out of her at the bloody madness of it all. Risking your life to save animals you then have to kill.

"Sometimes," she says quietly, "I sit on the end of my bed and think, *I can't face one more farm*. It's so depressing walking around empty farms — people's whole lives on the floor, trashed, smashed."

ON THE LAST DAY before I leave Africa, I go out to a farming community nestled against the Mvurwi Range, north of the capital. Here at Tsatsi, the farmers have decided to mark their own extinction with a farewell party — to themselves.

When we arrive, we find four generations of white farmers gathered under a large thatched gazebo on a lakeshore. They have literally come to toast their own demise. Lion and Castle and Zambezi lager flows freely, and the atmosphere is thick with the unaccustomed emotion of a tough, taciturn people.

Rod Bowen, a tall ex-cop, taps his glass to speak. Until recently, he was employed by the local farmers' association to help whenever one of them was invaded. In the end, though, he could do little.

"This is a farewell to those displaced persons of this parish who have had to move out so fast they had no time for individual fare-wells," says Bowen. "This is a party for all the wrong reasons. Six months ago we were more or less in one piece, and just look at what's happened now. This is our home—we built it. But now the Tsatsi farmers' community has been totally dismembered. This is mad-ness. This is utterly unbelievable. And the same thing is happening all over the country to other farmers' associations.

"For the past two years this community has had a two-pronged approach—some of us have appealed all the way to the very top, right up to the president himself, to try to save our farms. Others would not talk to a government that was acting outside the law, would not sup with the devil. Neither approach got anywhere. Today, four farmers of sixty remain. The situation is being orches-trated to destroy order here, to destroy the fabric of society, to rid this country of its commercial farming community."

He bids the assembly raise their glasses to absent friends and then, as the sun dips behind the green hills of Africa, a young farmer walks slowly out along the jetty over the golden lake, tartan bag-pipes under his arm, and pipes them out. Pipes them away into their diaspora, to Britain, to Australia, to Canada, to America, and points beyond.

IT'S A RELIEF to get back to New York. The boys mob me, but Jo-anna seems uneasy. When I finally get them into bed, she tells me that the FBI has been looking for me. Two special agents from the counterterrorism task force want to talk to me urgently. She hands me their cards, embossed with gold shields. At first, I assume that it has to do with security clearance for my green card. But when the two special agents arrive the next morning, it quickly becomes ap-parent that they have something else on their minds—my contact with Dr. Stephen Hatfill, a bioterrorism expert who has become their main "person of interest" in the anthrax attacks. They have searched his apartment in Maryland and drained a nearby lake looking for anthrax-handling equipment.

My interest in Hatfill was originally piqued when I read that he studied medicine in Zimbabwe and subsequently practiced in South Africa. I have been talking with him for months now, trying to negotiate an interview—so far he has not talked publicly at all. After hours of questioning by the FBI special agents, during which it becomes apparent that they know the content of my e-mails, phone calls, and letters, we finally close in on the nub of their suspicions: an incorrect date on one communication from Hatfill, which makes it look as though I had preknowledge of the anthrax attacks; and the fact that I was teaching at Princeton at the time that one of the anthrax letters was mailed—from a Princeton mailbox.

Even then, the FBI remains interested in me, and I get the distinct impression they want me to get close to Hatfill, to see what I can learn. And I worry that if I refuse, my green card will never come through.

I tell my parents none of this. Instead, I keep up my regular calls in which they always assure me that all is well, when everything I read describes Zimbabwe collapsing in a quickening downward spiral.

Two months after the Tsatsi farmers' farewell, there is yet another full eclipse of the sun there. Two total eclipses within less than two years. This is very rare—no one can recall such a thing, even in the stories handed down through the generations. People are saying that the celestial crocodile must be truly furious to be back so soon, threatening us again with perpetual darkness. The approach of the second eclipse has a chilling effect.

Even my mother, now finally retired, becomes uneasy. Despite her medical training, she remains at heart a superstitious woman. She drops her bright assurances, and for the first time she admits that her back pain is now unbearable. It has been tracked to her hip, which is collapsing with avascular necrosis and needs to be replaced.

Although there are a couple of surgeons still performing the procedure there, she says, artificial hip joints are difficult to get in Zimbabwe. So I start looking into how I can buy one for her in America. It proves tricky. The socket and cups come in a confusing array of materials: titanium, ceramic, cobalt-chrome alloys, zirconium, polyethylene. I am leaning toward the metal ones, which seem more durable, and are more expensive. But then I read that some of them exude trace metals into the blood, and worse, that the leading manufacturer has withdrawn one of its hips because of a glitch in its construction. Surgeons around the country have had to saw it out of nearly eighteen thousand people and replace it. A class action is pending. It hasn't been a stroll for the ceramic kind either. One model has been recalled after it began disintegrating. Without any notice, apparently, it is prone to give way with a loud *pop*.

I worry about how I will get the artificial hip to my mother. If I try to import it officially, I will almost certainly get bogged down in Zimbabwe's baksheesh bureaucracy. Or it may simply go missing en route. If I take it in my carry-on luggage, it will probably get nixed by security. It looks like an offensive weapon of some sort; a high-tech knobkerrie, a hockey stick with a metal hemisphere bonded onto the blade. Finally, to my relief, Mum reports that her surgeon has secured one himself. She is all set.

sixteen

May 2003

I BUCKLE MYSELF into the seat of the South African Airways flight from JFK, and the screen lights up with the physical reality of my separation from Africa. Distance to destination: 7,969 miles. And then I still have to connect from Johannesburg up to Harare. After several hours, I give up trying to contort myself into sleep and switch on the seat-back TV screen to the progress map. The blinking red plane is flying directly into the armpit of West Africa, the infamously fever-ridden Bight of Benin, which I always used to think deserved to be called the *Blight* of Benin. English sailors evidently agreed — they used to sing:

> *Beware, beware the Bight of Benin*
> *Twenty come out of a hundred go in.*

Our flight path takes us down a continent of catastrophe. Many of the conflicts thirty thousand feet below I have covered in my time as a foreign correspondent. It unfolds like a geography of doom. Sierra Leone, where the hacking off of limbs was standard practice; Liberia, where peacekeeping Bangladeshis in blue helmets were struggling to separate teenage gunmen wearing women's clothing; Ivory Coast, divided between bitter ethnic rivals; Congo, where civil war still raged in a nation that has ceased to be and probably never was; Sudan, where a civil war still rages and triggers frequent spasms of famine; Somalia, which has no government at all now, a country that deserves the description anarchic.

And of course, everywhere, AIDS.

Africa seldom makes it into the American media; even the venerable *New York Times* mostly smuggles in its Africa coverage as soft features on slow news days, or six-line bulletins in the news-in-brief section. Yet every single day, newspaper headlines can legitimately announce: "Another Five Thousand Africans Die of AIDS." Nearly two Twin Towers' worth of humans *every day*, dying quiet deaths, unobserved and unclamored.

THE PLANE DESCENDS over Zimbabwe to a wintry dawn. Plumes of mist trail with the prevailing breeze from rivers and dams below, ghostly ribbons garlanding a bleak khaki landscape. The fields of Mashonaland stand reproachfully uncultivated. Large-scale farming here is all but at an end.

The new airport is still paint fumed and contractor fresh. It has royal blue wall-to-wall carpets and large expanses of plate glass. It feels expensive. It is. The airport is one of the biggest examples of the corruption now rampant here. A country that has not been particularly dishonest in the past is now a den of deceit. Leo Mugabe, the president's nephew, brokered this particular contract. His proposal for the new airport was awarded over five competing bids (as stipulated by law), even though it was the most expensive one, it came in after the bid deadline, and it didn't meet the requirements. None of these are obstacles to Leo, the First Nephew.

You can bet Rustic Realist has something to say on the matter. The selling point of the new airport plan, my father explains, was its patriotic control tower, which was to have been a stylized replica of the acropolis at Great Zimbabwe. It was only after the bid was awarded that anyone bothered to run it by the international civil aviation regulators, only to discover that such an edifice ran foul of safety rules, and if built no mainstream airlines would land there. So it was hurriedly modified and now resembles a vast white artichoke. It stands in the sunshine, glittering in all its pompous redundancy, completed just in time for the total collapse of tourism.

Most airlines have now canceled their flights to Harare, and Air Zimbabwe, the national airline, is increasingly unreliable. Behind the new terminal stands one of its Boeing 737s, mysteriously damaged — one of only five planes in its fleet. The airline is struggling to retain technicians and find spare parts to keep the fleet airborne. The fact that the president commandeers a plane whenever he needs it to attend an international function or to take his new wife, Grace, on a shopping trip also makes Air Zimbabwe's schedule extremely tentative. Three journalists who have pointed this out in print have been arrested and charged under the law that makes it a crime, punishable by two years in jail, to bring the president into "ridicule or disrepute."

THOUGH IT IS RUSH HOUR in Harare, there is little traffic. At every fuel station along the way, long lines of driverless cars have formed, waiting for the next delivery. There has been no fuel here for weeks.

My promised vehicle, borrowed from Murelle, a friend of Georgina's, has been in an accident, so she offers me a substitute: a tiny, ancient, pimento red pickup that has the word *CHAMP* emblazoned on its sides in sloped letters, as if they have been thrown backward by the immense speed of the vehicle. It has no immense speed; I can coax its little engine up to about sixty miles per hour. Champ's interior is so small that my knees are up near my chin, and my head brushes the roof. Every bump and pothole threatens to break my neck.

I have convinced myself that about the only compensation for the pimento Champ (which my father immediately christens the Noddy car) is that it is unlikely to be carjacked. But Robin Watson soon disabuses me. The Nissan Champ, old as it is, and tiny, has a reputation for great reliability and convenience, while offering enviably low fuel consumption. It stands high on the hijack desirability list, and I am constantly fending off suitors who want to purchase it.

At home, I find that Mum has retreated to her bed permanently, such is her pain. Dad has rigged up a metal gantry over her bed, and from it hangs a "monkey chain" with a handle that dangles over her head. Whenever she wants to sit, she hauls herself up on this contraption. She has hung other useful things from it too, a short-wave radio and an electric bell she buzzes if she needs something. Adston comes in for just a few hours a day to vacuum and do laundry, so it's been Dad responding to her buzzing, Dad doing all the fetching and carrying and cooking and after-hours gate opening and fuel queuing and shopping, even though he gets very easily exhausted.

Although he has been responding well to new drugs, and is, my mother says, much better than he has been, my father has shrunk, and he now walks permanently stooped at an acute angle, the result of his own back problems, which cannot be operated on because his heart is not strong enough to withstand major surgery. His legs, I notice, are dappled with a livid trellis of veins.

Adston knocks gently at the outside door to say that he is going now.

"Hello, Aston." I have only met him once before, just for a few minutes, when I initially interviewed him.

"Hello, sir." He is tall and strong. He looks down, a little embarrassed. "Adston," he says. "My name is Adston, not Aston."

"I'm so sorry," I say. "I heard my parents calling you Aston."

"Yes," he agrees. "That is what they call me. I think they didn't hear properly at first. And afterward . . . I never corrected them. But my name is Adston."

"I will tell them to use your real name. I'm sorry for our mistake."

"It is no problem." He hesitates. "Actually, Adston is not my real name either. It was the name given to me by the old lady I worked for before. My birth name, my African name, is Gomo."

"Gomo? 'Hill'?"

"Yes, because my mother walked up a hill, and then grew tired and went into labor and I was born."

"Why didn't he tell us?" says Dad when I explain the misunderstanding. My mother is mortified.

I offer to make them lunch, but I find that the refrigerator is nearly empty, just like the one in the *Chave Chimurenga* commercial on ZTV. It contains half a lemon, hard and dry with age, and little portions of leftovers and scraps: two hard-boiled eggs on a saucer, a few shavings of stiff ham — Dad buys only six thin slices at a time now — and bread crusts and cheese rind saved for the dogs. My mother has also stored a small bag of cornmeal in there, which I toss out as it is mildewed and inedible.

I look around in the pantry for something to eat and find a couple of avocados that are almost ripe and a tin of pilchards, but no bread or rice. Mum's friend Linnea is visiting and she suggests I mix the two. So I mash up the avocados and mix them with the pilchards. The result is an unappetizing olive green mush in which I can identify the tiny spines of the fish among the hard nodules of underripe avocado. I add a little salt and pepper and a squeeze from the elderly half lemon.

Then I taste it.

Immediately my eyes tear up, my lips burn, my nose leaks. I grab the can and inspect it. Underneath the word *pilchards* is written, in faded red script, *chakalaka*. Next to it is a tiny picture of a red chili pepper with little comic-book lines of heat radiating from it.

"It's a bit spicy," I warn Mum and Linnea before they dig in, but they gamely proceed. And though they are soon damp eyed and gulping at their water glasses, I am amazed to see they seem to quite like it.

Later that afternoon, though, Mum buzzes me to her bedroom.

"I'm feeling a bit queasy," she complains, and she hoists herself up on her overhead monkey chain. "I think you're going to have to help me to the loo. But there's no water at present."

"So what's the toilet protocol?" I ask as I maneuver her out of bed.

"Well, every time you need to go to the loo, you have to go out to the swimming pool and fill a bucket with water and pour it into the cistern."

When I go out to the garden, there is a white egret standing on the step of the swimming pool peering intently into the green water to see if the fish there are big enough to bother with yet. It flaps away when I appear, and I get busy clearing a patch of the scum and weeds from the surface and filling my plastic bucket.

"It's the pilchards *chakalaka*," declares my mother. "They're the culprit. I'm going to be struck down by a major tummy upset just as I set off for surgery, and I'll be shamed in front of all the hospital staff, and they all know me. How humiliating!"

I scoop the considerable remnants of the pilchards *chakalaka* into the trash and scrub the fridge clean. Then, as evening draws in, I am looking around for something for their supper when the house is suddenly plunged into darkness.

"Oh, I meant to tell you," my mother calls from her bedroom. "There's a brownout too." Electricity is intermittent because the state-owned national power utility rations it around the different parts of town. It is another reason why my parents stopped buying perishables in larger amounts; the refrigerator keeps cutting out.

AROUND US, the country seems to be reaching a breaking point. The opposition has declared the following week to be a week of strikes and protests culminating in a march on the State House. They are calling it "the Final Push" and have been running full-page ads in the independent press announcing the action.

"Any thought of the dictator giving up power quietly is sheer delusion," declares one. "The real African drama . . . begins to un-fold in a few days' time, sadly, in our streets." Other ads appeal to "our brothers and sisters in the armed forces. . . . Be part of the solution and not part of the problem."

As I drive along, I notice freshly stenciled signs on walls and curbs—one huge word: zvakwana! In Shona it means, "It's Enough!"

The government is calling the Final Push "a British-sponsored plan to subvert a democratically elected government," which is "tantamount to a coup" and will be put down ruthlessly. ZTV, the mouthpiece of Mugabe's ruling party, announces that "Security agents have been put on high alert" and all police leave canceled. A ZANU-PF spokesman appears to relish the coming confrontation: "The time has come for a showdown with the MDC," he says. "Their activities can no longer be tolerated." Businesses that heed the opposition call to close their doors for the week are also threatened. "They close the shop on Monday," promises a senior minister, "they close the shop *for good.*"

A confrontation is imminent. It is not a good week to be undergoing major surgery.

THE DAY BEFORE my mother goes into the hospital, I try to stock up with essentials before the protest begins. The first thing I need is cash. ATMs have long since run out in the panic so my father has written me a personal check for the princely sum of Z$100,000, which, at the local black-market rate of Z$2,000 to US$1 (which even government ministries, not to mention the British High Commission, openly use—hell, it's even printed daily in the paper), is actually worth US$50.

The check can be cashed only at the bank branch where my parents have their account—in Sam Levy's Village, an open-air shopping center on the northern edge of the city. I join a long line of customers also trying to get emergency cash before the protest shuts everything down. When I finally reach the bank teller, she says they have long since run out of Z$500 notes, the largest Zimbabwean bills, worth about twenty-five U.S. cents. She gives me the money in

Z$100 bills, each worth five cents, counting out ten thousand of these bills in bricks of notes, each bound with an elastic band. I stuff them into my briefcase, and there are still more, so someone in the line gives me a plastic shopping bag and I stuff that too. It isn't quite the wheelbarrows of the Weimar Republic, but it's getting there.

As I'm leaving, I hear the teller apologize to the line that she has run out of money, and she puts up her closed sign. The line starts to mutiny, and the bank manager comes over from the back to see what the trouble is.

"We have no cash left in the entire bank," the manager confirms. "Or indeed in any of our other branches. We have no money left at all. This man," he says, as I pack the last of my money bricks, "has got the last of our cash." Everyone looks crossly at me, and I slink out of the bank.

Later, Dad explains to me that with hyperinflation, prices have been doubling every four months, but the Reserve Bank hasn't put any more banknotes into circulation.

"Why not?" I ask.

"Why not?" He chuckles. "Because the banknotes are printed overseas, and the Reserve Bank doesn't have the foreign currency to pay for them."

Next, I need to get fuel, if we are to be visiting Mum in the hospital for several weeks. But everywhere there are cars waiting in lines outside fuel stations. Some lines are a mile or more long and have been there for weeks. They have become campsites, surrounded by rubbish—wads of toilet paper and thin plastic bags blowing in the wind, all the detritus of delay. Fuel prices went up 300 percent several weeks ago, but there is still no fuel to be had. We have enough for about six round-trips to the hospital.

John Worsley-Worswick, an old school friend of mine who now works for Justice for Agriculture (JAG), a new farmers' group struggling to resist the land seizures, says some farmers—who are allowed to buy in bulk for their businesses—may have fuel to spare, especially as most have stopped active farming, so on the way home

I call in at the JAG office to source the fuel. The little house is being used as a logistics center for the strike, and it is bustling with activity. In the yard, Caro, a British colonel's wife who fell in love with Africa and remained behind when the colonel was reassigned home, is assembling tear gas solvent kits for protesters — bottled water and breathing masks. A team of young black MDC members, many of them still in their teens, are loading the kits into the back of her cherry red pickup truck, throwing them one to the next in a chain from the veranda, while the sound system belts out Oliver Mtukudzi's "Wasakara" ("You Are Worn Out"). Roy Bennett comes careening in with his own team of MDC youths, who load up with tear gas kits and dash out again.

Inside, Worsley-Worswick sits behind his wooden desk in the open-plan room squinting through his cigarette smoke, phone clenched between shoulder and ear, flicking through papers and barking out instructions to farmers calling in for advice.

Everyone is buzzing with anticipation. This is it: the Final Push, the big one, the one that will finally get the momentum going to eject Mugabe, the Emperor of Borrowdale Road. Their enthusiasm is infectious — maybe this time something really *will* happen?

I drive home as darkness settles over the city. It is winter in Africa, when the warm breath of day dies quickly on the lips of dusk. The city is as quiet as a cave. A city waiting to be liberated. Large parts of it are without electricity, and along the entire length of Enterprise Road not a streetlight shines. Many of them stand at drunken angles, downed in old accidents and never repaired, like snapped stalks of elephant grass.

THE NEXT DAY, I help my mother prepare for her hospital stay. Under her close supervision I pack her various sets of color-coordinated nighties and bed jackets into separate Bon Marché shopping bags and carefully decant white glops of moisturizing cream into a small jar, assemble hair clips, brush, plastic shower cap, and toothpaste and pack them all carefully into her black toiletry bag.

Because she can no longer reach back to do her hair, which is still long enough for her to sit on, she asks me to weave it into a single thick braid. I can follow her age by her hair, as by the rings of a tree trunk — closest to her scalp it is quite white, then it gradually reddens farther along, and the last few inches are still Titian red. She asks me to write her name in the books she is taking to the hospital. I feel as though the roles are reversed from the days when I was going off to boarding school and she was sewing name tags onto my uniform. She gives me the key to the gun cabinet and shows me where the loaded .38 revolver is and the extra ammo. She shows me again how to lock the newly installed "rape gate" across the corridor at night to seal off the bedrooms in an inner sanctum, inviolable — they hope — even if the rest of the house is being ransacked.

"Do make a bit of a fuss over Dad," she says. "He's feeling exhausted and neglected, having had to look after me when he's got a bad heart. And try to make him eat regularly."

I get down on my knees to pull her new elasticized terry cloth slippers onto her cold, dry feet, and tie the furry sash of her homemade fleece robe, decorated with gamboling reindeer. She thrusts her shoulders back and takes a last look around the room that has become her prison these last three months.

"Right," she says decisively. "I'm ready to go now."

THE SUN IS already low in the sky and drained of heat. The journey to St. Anne's Hospital in Avondale is a quick one. It is Africa Day, a public holiday for those few with jobs, and the deserted city is preparing itself for trouble.

We decant Mum into an old wheelchair at the ambulance bay. From an alcove above us, a large plaster Virgin Mary trades glances with the mandatory unsmiling photograph of President Robert Gabriel Mugabe, complete with his little toothbrush mustache — the man who would grimly turn his country into an African Albania rather than relinquish power.

We follow the orderly pushing Mum along the polished red-cement corridors and settle her into her room, with its high white ceiling and a long veranda overlooking the crisp, winter-dry lawn.

After my mother is admitted, I drive Dad home. He doesn't like being out after dark since his hijacking. And his smaller, older replacement car has been stolen too, this time from within the yard, at night. The dogs failed to bark, and shortly afterward one of them died. The usual method of pacifying dogs is to infuse slabs of meat with horse tranquilizer and toss them over the fence. The intruders used industrial bolt cutters to cut the heavy-duty padlock off the barbed-wire-topped iron gate. Neither Mum nor Dad woke up. The first Dad knew of it was when he went to fetch the newspaper early in the morning and found that the car was gone—again.

Now he has taken a number of extra precautions to prevent Mum's small, elderly Mazda from being stolen. He has welded a metal plate to the gate so that the padlock is not exposed and cannot be pried or cut off as easily. He has purchased a massive new padlock that doesn't have a cuttable U and fits so tightly it's almost impossible to get a blade or screwdriver in. Only Dad has the keys to this master lock. Neither Gomo nor Isaac is allowed a key. They might be threatened to hand it over, he says.

In addition Dad has devised a number of antitheft rituals. The car is, of course, wired with an electronic alarm and engine kill. He has also fitted a crook lock on the steering wheel and another lock over the stick shift, making it impossible to change gear, as well as one that locks the accelerator to the clutch. He parks the car right beneath his bedroom window, as close as possible to the wall. He manages this by hanging a tennis ball from the eaves: when the ball touches the windshield, the bumper is an inch from the wall. After Dad switches off the engine, he turns the radio to full volume, so that even if someone breaks open the gate; neutralizes the car alarm; pries off the gear lock, the accelerator lock, and the crook lock on the steering wheel; bypasses the engine kill and hot-wires the ignition—the radio will immediately burst into life at full blast and, he hopes, wake him up.

I think he has been seriously considering roping himself to it somehow, through the bedroom window, but so far wiser counsel has prevailed.

I RETURN LATER that night to the hospital to deliver Mum her watch and her shortwave radio so she can listen to Georgina broadcasting on Radio Africa from London. I find her in the middle of a supper of chicken, sautéed potato, and red jelly. She is wolfing it down—the best meal she's had in months, she says, certainly an improvement on pilchards *chakalaka*. I tease her that when the orderly arrives to remove her tray prematurely, she bares her teeth at him, like a lioness protecting its kill.

While she finishes her supper, we listen to the radio together. Everyone believes that the revolution is nigh. In response to the threatened street demonstrations, the government is going to deploy its new riot-control vehicles, freshly imported from Israel. They come equipped with water cannons that, apparently, can target demonstrators with high-pressure bursts of military-strength mustard-gas solution, which causes a painful stinging, or indelible dye, which stains both the clothes and skin of those sprayed so they can be identified later.

While we listen to the radio, I page through the billing paperwork for Mum's surgery, and I see that she is to have the cheap plastic version of a hip joint, instead of the more expensive one with a ceramic ball and titanium setting, which I have been looking at in the United States.

"If only I'd known you were getting a plastic one," I tell her, "I would have brought the good one."

"But this is the one they are experienced at putting in here," she says. "If you'd got the fancy one, they probably would have made some mistake putting it in."

I continue to look penitent.

"Heavens," she says, impatiently. "It's not as though I'm going to be training as an Olympic hurdler. I just want to be able to shuffle around the house. And it won't have to last for that long. The plastic one will do fine."

Our last conversation the night before her surgery is in no way maudlin or even portentous. She may be seventy-eight, but this is a routine procedure, she says, and she clearly doesn't expect to die. She is looking forward to being out of pain, to being mobile again. But, by now we both know there is no such thing as a "routine procedure" in Zimbabwe, especially on the eve of an attempted revolution.

THAT EVENING, my father follows his normal ritual: a fake scotch and soda and a prolonged coughing fit. He sits in his armchair trying to listen to Radio Africa, trying to get news of the Final Push. But the signal is terrible, smothered by waves of static interference and violent atmospheric raspberries caused by distant thunderstorms. From time to time, the manic sawing of high-pitched violins encroaches from Radio Taiwan, which has the neighboring frequency.

Dad sits with his eyes squinched shut in concentration behind his bifocals, trying to hear his daughter in a studio in North London, five thousand miles away from home. Occasionally he descends into another bout of what my mother would describe as a "productive cough," swats the radio irritably, and mutters, "It's hopeless, hopeless."

But he never switches off the radio.

THE GENERAL STRIKE begins the next morning, but hospitals and emergency services have a dispensation, and at 11:00 a.m., as planned, my mother goes under the knife. Her surgeon is Mr. Bowers (in the English tradition, Zimbabwean surgeons are still referred to as Mr. or Mrs., not Dr., a custom dating back to the days when their trade was plied by barbers), whom I have met several times, and who looks disconcertingly young—barely in his mid-thirties.

Dad seems oblivious, puttering around the house while Mum is on the operating table. I keep imagining the scalpel slicing open her thigh, Mr. Bowers prying out the old joint of her hip, tossing it into the garbage bin of medical waste, and attaching the plastic ball joint in its place.

By midafternoon, we have heard nothing. I begin to wonder what I am going to do if she dies. How Dad will cope without her. Where he will live. Where we will bury Mum. By 4:00 p.m., I can stand it no longer and call St. Anne's. I am transferred from extension to extension, but nobody seems to know where she is. Finally, we get in the car and drive over through the deserted streets.

Her room is empty, but her belongings are still there. I start to get a bad feeling. Several nurses we ask don't know where she is. One suggests we try the critical care unit, and there we finally find her, flanked by unconscious black men with heavily bandaged heads. She is giddy still from her anesthetic, speaking in an excited, slurred whisper. As she can't talk properly, and Dad can't hear properly—a result of prolonged exposure to gunfire during the war—I find myself interpreting for two people who've been married for fifty-five years. Dad holds her hand while she tells us how things have gone.

She says that when the anesthetist (a black man) injected the anesthetic, "Instead of asking me to count backward, he grinned at me said, 'I hear you are the mother of *infamous* children?' " And she replied, "If you mean that my son was declared an enemy of the state, and my daughter is on the current list of people banned from entering Zimbabwe, then yes, I am." And then she lost consciousness.

A male albino nurse comes over and adjusts the IV in my mother's arm. Mum says she feels fine and can now wiggle her toes and flex her leg muscles. It is the first time she has been pain-free for more than six months. She is elated and high on the drugs.

Nurses and aides whom she has treated in the staff clinic at the Parirenyatwa keep appearing at her bedside to pay homage. They come shyly up to her and curtsy.

"Dr. Godwin, it is me, Patience."

"Doctor, remember me? I am Charity."

"Doctor, you looked after me—my name is Ruth."

And my mother says, "Yes, yes, of course I remember you, and how are you feeling now?" She can't possibly remember them all—she has spent the last twenty-five years seeing up to eighty patients a day.

THAT EVENING I go to supper at Barker's Lodge. Once the smartest boutique hotel in the city, it consists of a series of stone buildings with steep cathedral eaves and pristine thatched roofs, the work of Zimbabwe's legendary thatchers. But with the general collapse of tourism, Barker's is closed. It has stood empty for some months, and now the Worsley-Worswicks are living here, since they've been kicked off their farm. A fire is roaring in the huge mock-medieval fireplace, the stone floor is scattered with impala skins and the walls are hung with dusty wildlife prints. The electricity is out, so we sit around a table made of old teak railroad ties, and eat by candlelight.

Around the table are MDC supporters, elected councillors, and members of other civic groups. All of them are white. The MDC has warned whites that it has heard the police and army will specifically target us, so we should stay in the background and provide logistical and planning support. There is also the propaganda value to the government of large numbers of whites at the barricades, which would help it to portray the MDC as a puppet to white interests.

Everyone is worried that the protest hasn't been properly organized. The "stay-away," as strikes are called here, is already almost total—the MDC, with its trade union roots, is good at those. But getting people out in large numbers to march into town is a different matter entirely. A people who once rose against white rule and joined guerrilla movements in the thousands has now been cowed by a twenty-three-year dictatorship.

There are all sorts of rumors flying around: the government has infiltrated the MDC, the army has orders to shoot to kill. On the other hand, the MDC claims to have been assured by two army units, the Commandos and the Paras, that they will not fire on civilians. The actual routes of the marches have been kept secret, but there are only a handful of main roads leading into the city center from the townships, with relatively few choke points.

"Maybe we shouldn't have called it the Final Push," I suggest. "It sounds awfully, well, final. What if it doesn't work?"

"What would you rather have it called?" says Dale, an MDC councillor. "The Initial Push?"

"Or how about One of Several Pushes?" offers John.

IN THE CRITICAL CARE UNIT the next morning, my mother is in a querulous state—tearful and angry and indignant. She has woken up to find herself paralyzed from the waist down. After having been able to use her legs the day before, she assumes that there has been some awful nerve damage. Then she discovers that during the night, without any complaint of pain on her part, the nurses have taken it upon themselves to turn the epidural way up. This is contrary to all the principles of pain management, she declares, which is to keep medication to a minimum. She strongly suspects the staff has knocked out the patients so they can enjoy a hassle-free shift. When she complains to the white physician on his morning rounds, he eyes the nurses over at the ward station. "I see," he says, nodding gravely. But my mother doubts he will do anything.

Later that day, after her legs regain some feeling, she is returned to her own room, relieved to be back within the warm realm of a head nurse she knows. I take her a bunch of tall yellow and blue crane flowers, and she seems calmer, rousing herself to berate me for trimming the flowers with her good nail scissors.

But things soon deteriorate as the national strike takes effect. Most of the nurses get stranded in the townships where they live, as there is no public transportation. Food supplies are erratic. Milk runs out, then bread. Strawberry-flavored jelly begins to feature heavily on the menu.

On our next visit, Mum looks pale and shaken. Late that afternoon she was taken out to the end of the veranda to enjoy the last rays of the winter sun, but no one came to collect her—with the staff shortages she was forgotten. She shouted weakly for help, but no one heard her. Hours later, in the gathering gloom, a nurse finally stumbled upon her, in tears, trembling with cold.

"It's all right, madam, it's all right," she soothed, and helped her back inside.

But it doesn't stop there. In the middle of the night, when she needs to use the bedpan, she presses her buzzer again and again, but no one comes. Eventually, she can hold on no longer and wets the bed.

The entire hospital is hanging by a thread, with just a few senior nurses keeping it going.

That afternoon I decide I will ignore the visiting hours and camp out there to make sure that she is taken care of. By now she looks terribly pale and subdued, crying at the slightest problem. I fuss around, fetching her books and water and adjusting her bed. She asks me to pick up the comb she has dropped on the floor, so I feel around under her bed for it. The cement down there is wet and sticky to my touch. My fingertips are coated with a viscous red substance. At first I think it might be floor polish, but then I realize it is blood.

"Jesus!" I peel back her blankets to look at the dressing on her wound. It is bright red. When the surgeon arrives, he says she lost two pints of blood during the operation and more from the wound. Her red cell count is now dangerously low: six and falling.

"She needs a blood transfusion," he says.

"Not bloody likely," says Mum, and rolls her eyes.

He leaves us alone for a moment, my cue to persuade her. But no one knows better than her how high the country's AIDS rate is. "Let's just say that the screening of blood stocks is less than perfect," she says.

As I draw breath to begin bullying her into compliance, she hands me a copy of the *Daily News*. "There's an ad in there from the National Blood Service," she says.

I open it and page through until I find the half-page advertisement announcing that it has essentially collapsed. It has no fuel, no foreign currency for plasma, no "refreshments," which are used to entice indigent blood donors.

The head nurse comes in, and I try to recruit her to my cause.

"If you were in my position, would you have a blood transfusion?" asks Mum.

The nurse looks around to make sure the doctor has gone. "Nuh uh," she says, and she shakes her head vigorously.

In the mayhem of that week, as St. Anne's teeters on the brink of collapse, the person my mother fixates on as her potential savior is her physical therapist, a young woman called Sue Francis. She has just the right blend of strictness and sympathy.

When Mum falls off the commode and thinks she's dislocated her new hip, I buzz Sue and she arrives within minutes, out of breath. After she has calmed down my mother, I walk her outside, out of earshot, and tell her how much my mother has come to rely on her. Sue looks stricken, and she takes a deep breath.

"I'm so sorry, but tomorrow's my last day at work," she says. "I'm emigrating to the U.K."

Her eight-year-old son has managed to get a cricket scholarship at a private school in North Yorkshire, and her husband—a game warden who has lost his job since the collapse of tourism—is going to be a groundsman there. Sue will work as a physical therapist at the local hospital.

How strange is that? A whole family getting a lifeboat out of here on the back of an eight-year-old kid's talent with a cricket bat and ball.

Sue suggests that I move my mother to Dandara, a small nursing home annexed to a gated retirement community next to the Borrowdale Race Course, just up the road from the State House. "They're still short staffed," she says. "But they're smaller, and they seem to have planned better for this strike."

So we load Mum into an ambulance and take her to the new hospital. For most of the way, the city is still deserted, but outside the university an air force helicopter clatters overhead, a green armored personnel carrier full of riot police roars by, and we hear the *puh, puh* of distant gunfire coming from the campus.

DANDARA CLINIC is small and clean and modern and almost empty. My mother has a private room with her own bathroom and a bedside window that looks out onto some rosebushes. She is immediately calmed by her move, and her spirits improve. Without a blood transfusion, her recovery will take much longer, but now that she realizes she is out of danger, she becomes appalled at how her illness has drained my father. "I think I may have killed him," she says, aghast.

Once I have settled her in, I go and collect Dad for a visit. He sits by her bed and they hold hands, and I leave them alone together, while I take a look around. In the next room there is an elderly emaciated white woman, who lies on her back, staring at the ceiling, waiting to die. On the other side is middle-aged woman with a hacking cough who sits on her bed, smoking, with the door open, surveying the comings and goings.

As I drive Dad back from Dandara, I see that the fuel gauge is dipping into the red reserve zone. I have failed to get any fuel at JAG, and there is still none available at any fuel station, so I have no option but to try to acquire some on the black market. There are several problems to overcome — quite apart from breaking the protest strike. Black-market fuel has to be bought in U.S. dollars, possession of which is now a criminal offense. It's also a crime to carry fuel around in a jerrican (to discourage hoarding, the government says). But I am due to depart within the week, and I want to leave Dad with enough fuel to visit Mum while she recuperates.

One of the places to meet "private" fuel suppliers, apparently, is the Italian bakery in Avondale Shopping Center. I have been wondering how I will identify the black-marketeers, but once there, it's immediately obvious. A young white man at one of the veranda tables is doing deals on his cell phone in a booming voice.

"I've got plenty of both, gas *and* diesel. I know it's four times the official price. If you can find any at the pumps, good luck to you!

OK, then, you've got the address? That's right, just past the white wall, the sign says *Kuala*. I'll be there. Ciao."

I'm just getting ready to make my approach when an elegantly dressed black woman sits down at his table. She discusses golf with him for a few minutes—they are evidently occasional golfing partners—and then she does a fuel deal with him too.

Now is definitely my chance, before his phone rings again. I get up and walk over, but just as he looks up at me, a young white man at the next table who has also been listening in, leans across to the black-marketeer.

"You know, you make me *sick!*" he says vehemently. "You're a bloodsucker. You should be ashamed of yourself. Haven't you, haven't you got any . . . any *decency?*"

The crowd goes quiet, and I retrace my steps to my table, pretending I have just been checking on my car.

"Hey, man, I'm just trying to help," shrugs the dealer.

"Bullshit," says the young man, pushing back his chair and standing up now. "You're exploiting all of us."

He looks around for moral support, but no one backs him up. The dealer stands up too. He is taller than his critic.

"Listen, china, you get out of my fucking face, OK? I'm not hassling you, I'm just going about my business, so why don't you go about yours."

The critic turns as if to leave, but he is just winding up to throw a punch. The dealer deflects it with his forearm, and then they are grappling, tumbling to the floor, upsetting a table and spilling cappuccinos, until they are pulled apart.

The critic seems suddenly deflated. "I *was* going about my own business," he says. "But we got thrown off our farm and lost everything. And here *you* are growing rich on it all. Guys like you make me wanna *puke*, man." He picks up his keys and stalks off into the parking lot.

I wait for a few minutes, working up the nerve, and then I make my approach.

"Jeez," says the dealer. "What a fuckin' idiot. Dunno what *his* case was."

I know what his case was, and I feel grubby and ashamed to be making this deal, but I must.

So the next day I drive over and pay my U.S. dollars and fill the tank of my car and drive back to my parents' house, and Isaac siphons the tank into the fifty-five-gallon drum hidden in the back of the garage, and I repeat the journey several times until the drum is full to the brim, and the needle on the fuel gauge in the car is hard over to right, as far as it can go.

THE FOLLOWING MORNING, the protests are to start in earnest. The city is in lockdown. On my drive to the hospital, there are soldiers and policeman at almost every corner, and plainclothes officers from the CIO or C-10 as it's now nicknamed by the young activists, and roving squads of party youth militia jogging importantly down the middle of the road, and helicopters clattering overhead. It seems that every member of the security forces is out in the city today, and I am pulled over several times by sullen and suspicious policemen. There are policemen outside Dandara too. When I finally get inside, I notice that the rooms are all occupied, with murmurings behind closed doors.

"What's going on?" I ask my mother.

She tells me to close the door.

"They've been admitting women who've been beaten up by the police," she whispers hoarsely. "Women who were trying to join the protests."

I venture out of her room and a nurse emerges from the room opposite—inside I can hear a woman groaning with pain.

"What's happening?" I ask the nurse, who has also been looking after my mother.

"Ah, it's too terrible," she says. "They have all been beaten, with rifle butts and sticks and *sjamboks* [heavy whips]. They have broken arms and broken legs and lacerations, and some have head wounds, and one has a gunshot wound. But if they are found here they will be arrested," she says. "And probably us too."

In Zimbabwe it seems that injury has become proof of guilt.

Later, a delivery truck pulls up to the laundry bay. There is a flurry of nurses, and instead of laundry, several more injured people come in. Their clothes bear the overwhelming aroma of tear gas. Not ordinary civilian tear gas, but the potent, military-strength stuff. Soon, all our faces are streaming with tears.

A blue-overalled gardener pressed into emergency indoor duty squeaks into my mother's room in his Wellington boots, holding out a rattling tray in work-horned hands. His face is a study in fierce concentration—he too is in tears but he ignores them. He lays the tray down gently and, drawing himself up to his full height, gestures grandly at the cup and the teapot and the milk jug. "Your afternoon tea, madam," he announces.

Then he wipes his tears away with the back of his sleeve and withdraws, walking squeakily backward out of the room.

"Thank you. Thank you so much," my mother calls after him, and she is crying too. Whether it's from the tear gas or not, I no longer know.

WHEN I GO TO SEE if there's anything I can do for the injured women, they ask to use my cell phone to call their families. Most of the women are from Women of Zimbabwe Arise! (WOZA), and they had been trying to march into the city center when they were attacked. They are middle-aged black ladies—the pillars of society, normally to be found at the Women's Institute or organizing church teas. Yet here they are, their arms in casts, patches over their eyes, and bandages around their heads. And still they are spirited and indignant. This, it seems to me, is true courage. These women had a pretty good idea of what would happen to them and *still* they marched.

AFTER VISITING HOURS, my father and I have an appointment at Christchurch, nearby. Keith Martin, the former funeral director who knows everything about death in this country, has suggested this as a suitable place to rebury Jain, and now I want to get Dad's approval before I leave. Father Bertram, the white-bearded parish priest, shows us around the sheltered internal courtyard that serves as a small garden of remembrance for cremated remains. It is well tended and invisible from the road. We are trailed by the church gardener, Rodgers, who adjusts the sprinklers—the church has its own well, which makes its garden a lush oasis of magnolia and agapantha, pride of India and frangipani, in a desert of crisp khaki.

"What do you think, Dad?" I ask gently.

"Very nice," he says. "Yes, very nice."

"Actually," explains Father Bertram, pointing out the vacant spots among the rows of gravestones set into the lawn, "I've got some extra plots available, for the rest of the family, if you like? These had all been booked and paid for in advance, but so many people have left the country . . ."

I'm appalled—it seems wrong to be offering to sell Dad his own grave, as if we are giving up on his health improving. I start to decline, but Dad interrupts. "Oh, we might as well, Pete," he says, trying to sound lighthearted.

So we agree to reserve the extra graves, one for each of us—because in the end, I suppose, you want to be buried where you belong.

THAT NIGHT over dinner at the house of Richard and Penny Beattie, local architects, I hear the first reports about the progress of the Final Push, from two MDC members of Parliament, Tendai Biti, their justice affairs spokesman, and Paul Themba-Nyathi, their foreign affairs shadow minister. Themba-Nyathi I have known for years. During the independence war, I fought—on the opposite side—in his home area of Gwanda, in southern Matabeleland. After independence, I worked with him as a lawyer, defending his ZAPU colleagues who were charged with treason by Mugabe. Now he seems depressed at the conduct of the protests. The "secret" marches, which were supposed to be taking routes from various townships into the city center, were not secret at all, and were broken up almost immediately. I mention that some supporters are disappointed that the opposition leader Morgan Tsvangirai has not led the marches himself, but Biti points out that to do so Tsvangirai would break his treason-trial bail conditions and be imprisoned immediately.

A guest admires Biti's Nigerian garb—a white brocade dashiki tunic and trousers, and a kente kofi hat. The hat is obviously terribly itchy, and every few minutes he removes it and scratches his head vigorously.

"No, no, it's not Nigerian," he says crossly, "it's *Ghanaian*. Why does everyone think it's Nigerian?"

The Nigerians are unpopular here because their president, Olusun Obasanjo, has just hosted Mugabe, and they appeared together on the local TV news last night, holding hands on a brown sofa.

Tendai Biti is also angry that the marchers today have been so easily cowed. A single CIO officer driving by in an old unmarked VW Golf turned an entire column of protesters back.

"All he had to do was to pull his pistol out of his waistband and fire it into the air once, just once, and they all ran away," he says in disgust.

Others, though, have been dealt with more savagely. Beattie's kitchen has been turned into a major supply and logistics center for the protest, with MDC members cooking vats of food to take to all those hundreds who have been arrested. Joel Mugariri is organizing things. He is an accountant who ran—and lost—as an MDC candidate in Rushinga, down in the Zambezi Valley. After the elections, his house was burned down, so he rebuilt it, and they burned it down again, and, because he's brave and stubborn, he rebuilt it a second time, and this time they came openly during daylight and torched it.

"Staying in Rushinga has become very dangerous," he says unnecessarily. "They can come and kill you at any time."

Joel was forced to move into a Harare township where he set up a house that serves as a refuge for other opposition supporters from his tribal home, people who have lost everything, including their homes, for daring to oppose the government in what they misunderstood to be free elections.

"None of us can go home or we will be murdered," Joel says. But apparently he hasn't run far enough away. "At noon on Monday they came to my house, the riot police together with soldiers and youth militia, and they just began beating whoever they found there, my wife, my sisters, even small kids, beaten on the head with batons."

He pauses to stir a huge aluminum pot.

"I was taken away with four of my guys, and they drove around picking up other activists until there were thirty-three of us in the back of the truck. And then we were taken to Makoni Police Station, where there is also an army base. There we were made to lie flat on the ground, and they beat us with different kinds of whips. They did the beatings in teams of six, taking turns so they wouldn't get tired.

"After that, they dumped all thirty-three of us in a police cell designed to hold eight. There was no flushing toilet, no beds or blankets, no food, no water to drink, and yet we were kept there for more than forty-eight hours.

"We weren't charged or registered as prisoners, so no one knew where we were. Eventually one of our activists tracked us down and had the courage to bring food to us, and he came back with a lawyer.

"When we were finally released, they kept all our belongings, our money, cell phones, our IDs and driver's licenses. One of our guys who went back to try to reclaim his things—they threw him in the cell, and he's still there."

The young man preparing food next to him is Henry Chimbiri, a photographer, who's been trying to record the police abuses and been arrested nearly forty times for his efforts. He has downloaded some of his photos onto Richard's laptop, and he scrolls rapidly through them, giving me a guided tour of the brutality.

"This one is Conrad, he has a broken arm, seven stitches to the head. He was sleeping in his own bed when they burst in and began beating him."

He clicks on the next thumbnail.

"This here is Tobias. He was shot in the leg and had his neck fractured."

Click.

"This is an MDC councillor's house. They smashed the TV with a rifle butt and tried to demolish the walls with a pick ax."

Click.

"And this is all that's left of a small factory, a cooperative making fiberglass bathtubs and basins. The soldiers burned it down."

Click.

"This is a woman who was forced to sit on the electric ring of her stove. Look how badly her thighs are burned—look, you can actually see the spiral mark of the red-hot element."

Click.

"And this is a one-day-old baby, born at home during the protests because there was no transport to get her mother to the hospital. The baby was teargassed. Her mother—who has nothing to do with politics at all—was pointed out by an informer and beaten until her arm was broken. I think they did it just for fun."

Pearson Mungofa, an MDC member of parliament from Highfield, is also in the Beatties' crowded kitchen. He was accused of organizing mass action and arrested too. "We were marching peacefully," he says. "And all of a sudden two trucks of soldiers drove up and began firing at us without warning. Not in the air, but among us, with live bullets. Some of us fell down . . ." He lowers his voice. "I don't know what happened to them, those ones who fell down. I ran away," he admits. "Later the police arrested me."

"How was your evening?" asks my father when I return.

"It was fine," I say. "Fine."

He asks me whom I met, and I gloss over it all. I can't bring myself to tell him what is happening around us. His life is difficult enough as it is.

And the next day, unbelievable as it seems, I leave. I have commitments elsewhere: assignments, appointments, inflexible tickets, children, deadlines. My mother is much improved, though she is staying on in Dandara for a few more days because of its convenience, mostly, until she is fully mobile again. And Dad has enough fuel now. There is a support system of sorts with Linnea and the Watsons, and Gomo is coming for a few hours each day to help with the cleaning and clothes washing. And I'll be back soon, I promise.

My mother is enjoying a supper of sweet-and-sour pork when I say good-bye to her at Dandara. Dad sits by her bed, holding her hand, and they are murmuring to each other like new lovers. He looks up and sees me looking at them.

"I'd miss the old girl if she died," he says, and grins.

Mum gives him a box elephant. And me one too.

AND THEN, suddenly, I'm gone. It's like the end of a macabre fairground ride. From my expense account seat, I listen to the comforting tones of the British Airways captain wafting through the air-conditioned cabin. I look out my window to see three helicopters lift off from the air force base. They hover briefly over the runway, their snouts tipped down like malevolent dragonflies, then they swoop off low over the tin roofs of Harare township to deal with the morning's opposition marches, ready to rain tear gas on Joel and his friends, ready to direct the police and the army, the militia and the party youth, to beat the protesters and arrest them, to put them in jail and leave them on cold cement floors without blankets or food or water or access to lawyers.

And as we soar away into a crisp, cloudless sky, I feel the profound guilt of those who can escape. I am soaring away from my fragile, breathless father with his tentative hold on life. I'm soaring away from my mother, who still lies in her hospital bed surrounded by wounded demonstrators—the trembling black women with broken limbs and puffy eyes and backs striated with the angry whip marks of the dictatorship. Away from John Worsley-Worswick, squinting through his cigarette smoke, phone clenched between ear and shoulder, trying to encourage evicted farmers. From Caro, the British colonel's wife, now ferrying around anti–tear gas solvent kits and bottled water, her toenails painted a riot of different colors, her posh Home Counties diction already absorbing the shortened vowels of our southern African dialect. From Roy Bennett, gray-haired now with his tribulations, but still bloody well *there*. The marchers for democracy are being shot at and teargassed, and I am flying away from it all. A nation is bleeding while I sit here cosseted with my baked trout and crispy bacon, my flute of Laurent-Perrier brut champagne, my choice of movies and my hot face towel.

I am abandoning my post. Like my father before me, I am rejecting my own identity. I am committing cultural treason.

WHEN I GET BACK to New York I am listless and distracted. In my head, I'm still in Africa. I sit online at my computer, following the increasing pace of repression in Zimbabwe and listening to African music, cranked up fat and sweet. Mostly I listen to Oliver Mtukudzi, who I last heard live at the Harare International Festival of the Arts. And I listen to his fellow Zimbabwean, Thomas Mapfumo. The intricate cyclical melodies of his *mbiras* are almost narcotic in their trance-inducing effect—quintessentially African, though they are being played and recorded now in Oregon.

No one knows exactly how many of us have fled, because few of us emigrate officially. But the numbers are high—between one and two million, mostly black, energetic, educated, experienced people, the leadership cadre of a country—the Katyń cadre. And the irony is that from our exile, we, whom Mugabe has chased away, inadvertently contribute to his survival. The money we send home to our relatives, our hard currency remittances (often multiplied by the black-market exchange rate), supports millions of people in Zimbabwe and helps to defer the country's continuously imminent collapse.

Thomas and Hugo, my sons, dance around me, trying to get my attention, puzzled at my detachment. I know I must snap out of this. That I cannot live the life of an exile, a perpetual sojourner, feeling my past more emphatically than my present, carrying this sadness within me, this spiritual fracture, unspoken mostly, but always there, an insistent ache. I must become a real immigrant, positive, engaged, hopeful.

At night I lie awake, listening to the roar of air conditioners all around me, until finally, in the glow of first light, I fall into a shallow, dream-tossed sleep. And I dream a version of a dream that Joanna once had when she was pregnant with Thomas: I am trying to sing "The Star-Spangled Banner" in front of a huge Superbowl stadium crowd before the game begins, but when I reach for the high notes I start coughing up blood.

JOANNA DECIDES we all need a break, that we will take the kids on vacation to Jamaica. But I am wrestling with "resident alien" restrictions. My green card still hasn't come through, and I worry that it's my Hatfill anthrax "connection" that's holding up my security clearance. Every time I leave the country I need an "advance parole" to travel (they use the terminology of the penitentiary for us foreign supplicants) or my application for permanent residence will be considered "abandoned." Though I have applied in plenty of time for the parole renewal, this time it is late in coming.

Then I receive a letter from the Immigration and Naturalization Service informing me that my application for advance parole to travel has been denied and must be resubmitted, with all the contingent delays. I have sent them a passport-style head shot, which is not sufficient: they insist on a three-quarter view that must include one ear (and only one), for reasons of closer identification. They enclose a sample photo of a model, smiling coquettishly, her ear peeking out from behind a curtain of glossy black hair. I stomp around our apartment threatening to do something van Goghian. Staple an ear to the picture and return it, a bloodstained three-dimensional ID. My error only seems to underline the tentativeness of my presence here.

There is ominous news from home on the health front too. My mother tells me that Dad has "a tiny touch of gangrene" on the tip of one toe, but that it should "resolve itself." I start to plan a return trip. A friend at *Forbes* commissions me to write a piece on luxury safaris in South Africa, and I quickly book my flight over Joanna's objections.

"But you've only just gotten back," she complains. Increasingly she sees Africa as a capricious mistress, something she must compete with, something dangerous and diverting.

seventeen

November 2003

O N T H E W A Y to Zimbabwe I stop over in London. I find Georgina exhausted and demoralized. Every day she catches the Thameslink train across London to the Radio Africa studio in an office park on the city's northern edge. (We jokingly refer to it as "an undisclosed location" because there are fears that, even in London, they are not beyond the reach of Mugabe's goons, so none of the staff is permitted to reveal its address.) Here she spends hours on the phone with people in Zimbabwe, and broadcasts morale-raising programs back to them. She works straight through the weekends, and in the evenings she attends political functions, lobbies members of Parliament, gives evidence to the foreign-affairs select committees, and does TV and radio interviews. But she is starting to lose faith in the prospect of change. Like so many members of the opposition, she has set out on a sprint that has turned into a marathon, with no finish line in sight.

And now her marriage has collapsed. Jeremy, who has been unable to find a job, has been going through a crisis of his own. After protracted agonizing about it, he has decided that he is, after all, gay, and has moved out. Like so many young gay men from the infamously homophobic Zimbabwe, where the consequences of coming out can be so extreme, it has taken him all this time to come to terms with his own sexuality.

Auxillia, Xanthe's Zimbabwean nanny, who came over with them from Harare and lives with them in North London, has also announced that she too is decamping. Since they arrived she has had her teeth fixed, smoothed out her Shona accent, and—largely through Georgina's efforts—obtained a residence permit. Now she wants to go to Birmingham to join a friend who is a real estate agent of sorts, selling property in Harare to Zimbabwean exiles for pounds sterling.

I sleep that night under an Angelina Ballerina duvet, in Xanthe's small, pink-walled room, surrounded by her Barbie dolls and the tiny plastic cups and saucers from their tea service. A fairy costume with white-sequined wings hangs on the back of her closet door.

In the morning Georgina makes coffee and we sit at the dining table. The room is furnished with Shona soapstone sculptures and oils of the African countryside. As I check my ticket to Harare, she bursts into tears. "It's not bloody fair! I want to get on the plane with you and go home too," she sobs. "And I can't. I work all God's hours and for what? I've no idea who listens to us, or whether we make *any* difference at all. We just broadcast into a vacuum. Nothing changes over there, and I'm stuck here. And now my whole damn life is collapsing around me. My marriage is over, even Auxillia's deserting me. I so miss my life in Africa. I just want it back."

She is crying hard now, taking in big gulps of air. I put my arm around her shoulders and try to comfort her, but it only seems to make it worse.

"Your sacrifice *is* worth it," I say. "People *do* notice. They *do* listen. It helps them feel that they're not alone to hear your broadcasts."

But she doesn't really hear me.

"Xanthe will never know Africa the way we did," she weeps, and lowers her head into her hands. She is crying still when I leave for the airport.

AS THE PILOT TELLS the passengers to prepare for our descent into Harare, I begin patrolling the aisle to scrounge used flight socks from fellow passengers. My mother has asked me if I can collect them, as she finds stretchy airline socks to be ideal for holding Dad's foot dressings in place, much better than bandages.

Several passengers hand theirs over wordlessly, but then a frequent-flying banker bridles. "Why do you want them?" he asks brusquely.

"They're for the sick in Zimbabwe," I say.

I have not told a lie.

At Harare, I line up to pay for my visitor's visa, now US$55, hard currency that the government is gasping for. Then I join another line to clear immigration. This is always where it starts to get nerve-racking for me. Although I have been on the "banned" list for years, I have managed to get in and out under the protection of Dumiso Dabengwa, the cabinet minister I once helped defend from a high-treason charge. But all that has changed now. Dabengwa has lost his seat to the MDC. And my sister is broadcasting daily under our surname on Radio Africa, a station that so infuriates Mugabe that he has ordered the CIO to jam it. And now entering the country as a journalist without a special visa has become its own crime with a minimum two-year jail term.

The immigration officer wears a threadbare white shirt and a sad, patient face as he sits behind a counter in his booth. When I finally reach him, I proffer my passport with an affected world weariness. While he examines it, I focus on the top of his lowered head. His bald spot gleams like a burnished conker. I stand on tiptoes to examine his workstation.

"Still no computers," I say, trying to conceal my relief. No computers means no searchable database.

"No," he sighs, head still down. "We are so behind here now." He glances up at me and down again at my passport.

Then he makes a little *hmpf* noise, half through his nose, half in his throat, a noise that, frankly, does not sound good.

"G-o-d-win," he says, drawing out the first syllable. I concentrate on his gleaming conker, trying to beam thoughts into it. "I know who you are," he says.

He pauses, as if inviting me to guess who he thinks I am, but I remain silent.

"You," he announces quietly, looking up briefly, "are a *troublemaker*. And so is that sister of yours, Georgina, broadcasting on that rebel radio station."

As he speaks, I think, at least I can tell her someone *is* aware of her programs. Then I am overcome by a hernia of panic. Great polyps of fear threaten to burst through the wall of my resolve. I am terrified that they will dump me in Chikurubi Prison, as an example. That they will dust off all the old spying allegations, put me in front of a pliant judge, and lock me up for years in a filthy, crowded, shit-fumed cell, where my teeth will fall out as I succumb to malnutrition or tuberculosis or cholera, and I will never see my kids again.

Getting caught like this suddenly feels so inevitable. I have become too complacent, too impatient to bother with the circuitous route through Victoria Falls that I used to take — attaching myself to tour groups and following the raised umbrella of their guides through the Falls Airport — and now I have to pay the price. I do not argue with the immigration officer. I just smile weakly and shrug, trying to stay calm, waiting to see what happens next. His head is still bowed, his eyes cast down. And, oddly, I hear the thumps of what sounds like stamping, coming from his desk.

"Tell her I liked last night's program," he murmurs, handing over my passport and grinning broadly. "Welcome back to Zimbabwe. Welcome home."

I feel dizzy with the reprieve.

"Next," he says.

*　*　*

I COLLECT MY BAGGAGE in something of a daze, and the customs officer waves me through the green channel. On the other side, the Watsons are waiting to meet me. They are accompanied by Ephraim, their cook of forty years, in his police reserve special officer's uniform—bronze serge safari suit and cap, his shoes shined to mirrors. He sits up front so as to face down any militia roadblocks. Robin drives, and a great glowing shoulder of moon rising low in the east over Mukuvisi Woodlands follows our progress.

Robin's daughter, Fiona, with whom I grew up in Chimanimani, is telling me about their recent burglary. She and Robin, and her mother, Sydney, had rushed to the local shops on rumors of salt—another commodity in short supply. They returned, triumphantly clutching a very small bag of salt, to find their house ransacked. Alasdair, Fiona's younger brother, and Ephraim are missing—kidnapped, they assume. The Watsons are distraught, but after a frantic half hour Alasdair and Ephraim arrive, cut and bleeding, in a car with two policemen, driven by Mrs. Muguti, a black surgeon's wife, who is a member of their local Catholic congregation. They tell them that robbers barged in, armed with pistols and knives, and one held a knife at Ephraim's throat. Alasdair was out on the veranda so Ephraim, with the blade still at his jugular, shouted, "Run, Alasdair, run!" Alasdair sprinted out, dived through the three-foot-thick hedge and onto the road where Ephraim joined him (once the robbers took off), and there Mrs. Muguti spots them fleeing along Montgomery Road and offers them a lift.

The next Sunday, after the service at Rhodesville church, says Fiona, Sydney shakes hands with the professor's wife, and as she draws her hand away she realizes that Mrs. Muguti has pressed a wad of notes into her palm. "Buy yourself some cheese," she murmurs, " . . . as a treat."

Tonight we take a route past their house, where we stop briefly at the gate for Robin to give a cryptic sequence of honks in Morse code. Standing inside, silhouetted in the window, Sydney acknowledges us with a double-handed wave; now she will rush to the phone to warn Mum of our impending arrival, and Mum will set off for the gate, as Isaac, the gardener, will have knocked off for the night.

It is five months since her hip operation, but she is still on crutches.

"I don't really need them," she quickly insists. "I only lean on them when I'm tired. But they're a good defensive weapon." She lifts a crutch and makes sharp jabbing motions with it, nearly toppling over in her enthusiasm. Then she begins the painstaking and elaborate ritual of unchaining and unlocking the gate. Special Officer Ephraim stands a benign guard over her, gazing sternly out at the horizon.

My FATHER is noticeably more stooped and frail, though his head remains imposing and Rushmorish, his hair leonine and full. When the Watsons have gone, I lay out my bounty on the living room carpet. Dad's eyes glitter as he surveys the hoard, and he absently squirts a Nicorette inhaler into his mouth.

"It has been four weeks since his last cigarette," says Mum proudly.

This must be about the tenth time he's tried to quit. His doctor has told him that giving up may boost the oxygen in his blood by up to 5 percent, which will improve the circulation in his feet.

My main haul consists of various medications he needs that are impossible to get here. They include an experimental transdermal foot cream called Healthibetic that I discovered online in an issue of *Diabetes Care*. According to a pilot test—on only eleven people, it's true—it increased blood flow to the feet by an average of 10 percent. I contacted the doctor running the test and bought several jars of the stuff, enough for about six months.

"I hope it's more rigorously administered than the last 'wonder drug' I cadged," I say to Mum out of Dad's earshot.

The rest of the loot includes single-malt scotch, a pair of nail clippers, a dozen books, and printer cartridges that my father has specifically requested. There are four of them sealed in their crinkly silver foil cocoons, and Dad fondles them, as valuable to him as Fabergé eggs.

"I won't need any more," he says. "These should be sufficient to see me through." He is measuring out the remains of his life in printer cartridges.

I offer him a bag full of diabetic chocolate that Georgina has sent, and he seizes it with relish.

"When I was a child," he says, "I had a ritual with my mother. Every evening, after dinner, I would approach her as she sat reading, and in silence she would break six squares of chocolate from the bar—never more, never less—and hand them to me." He pauses to wince as his foot touches the table and shoots a bolt of pain through him. "Even to this day," he goes on, "I eat chocolate in units of six squares. It's somehow imprinted on me."

I PHONE NEW YORK to tell my family that I've arrived safely.

Joanna tells me that Thomas came through to our bedroom this morning asking, "Where's Daddy?"

"In Africa," she replies.

"Oh," he says, as though Africa was on the next block, and he trots through to the kitchen for breakfast.

Hugo, she says, is barreling around the apartment singing the first line of a song I have taught him in Shona, the old Zimbabwean national anthem: "*Ishe Komberera* Africa"—"God Bless Africa." He puts manic emphasis on the first syllable of the continent: *Ishe Komberera Aaaaa-frica.*

I CARRY MY BAGS into the guest room, which now doubles as a study. Over by the computer, where my father has sat for hours typing out e-mails to me about himself, there are piles of medical and engineering papers, which he recycles by printing on their backs. New paper now costs Z$100 a sheet.

Mum has cleared some space in the closet, and I hang my New York clothes next to a row of her white doctor's coats.

My parents turn in early, but with the time difference, sleep eludes me. I lie on the single bed staring at the widening structural cracks that fracture the walls, the white ceiling panels discolored by repeated leaks, and I listen to the rats scurrying frenetically back and forth up there. I cannot go out onto the veranda, as I'd have to unlock the rape gate, which would wake my light-sleeping mother. So I get up and stand at the window and look out through the curli-cued burglar bars, out across the swollen profusion of our garden, to the massive bowers of bougainvillea that mark the boundary of Fort Godwin. My parents have had Isaac plant sisal bushes along the inside border of the hedge and now their savagely serrated blades form an interlocking barrier. Still, through it all, I can make out the flickering of the fires of the street hawkers camped out along Hind-head Avenue. During the day, they sit at their pathetic rickety wooden stands and sell groundnuts in tiny bags, single mangos, ba-nanas, tomatoes, and cigarettes, and they roast corn on small fires and sell half a cob at a time. Sometimes, they don't even make enough for the bus fare home to the townships, so they sleep right there, under our bougainvillea hedge, like tonight. I can hear them murmuring to each other, gently scolding their children. I can hear their liquid coughing and spitting, and their babies mewling. They must be lying fifteen yards away from my bed, and the harsh smoke from their fires seeps though the hedge and in through my open windows and catches in my throat.

My parents are wary of them. They feel watched all the time. The hawkers know everything about their routine—when the dogs are fed, when Isaac is out. My parents worry that the hawkers will provide intelligence to attackers.

FOR BREAKFAST Mum makes my father a fried egg on a slice of "cake bread," a dish worthy of Marie Antoinette. There is a price control on ordinary bread made from flour, a control that pegs it at such a low price that the bakers take a loss on every loaf they sell. Long lines form for the few loaves produced. The bakers have gotten around the price control by introducing "fancy loaves" with a smid-gen of sugar and the very occasional raisin in them, which are not controlled by the price-fixing statute, and are very expensive—way beyond the reach of most people. Mum worries that Dad is losing too much weight. After his lavish breakfast, he has nothing for lunch, and then another two thin slices of bread with either a single sliver of ham or cheese on them for dinner, washed down by cane-spirit whiskey. Mum herself has given up bread completely, she confides. The cake bread is simply too expensive for both of them to eat.

"I eat cabbage instead," she says. "And minced pork. It's the cheapest meat at the moment, it's going for four thousand dollars for five hundred grams."

Beef has suddenly quadrupled in price because the national herd, 1.4 million strong three years ago, has been decimated.

"People are saying that a chicken breast goes farther," she muses. "A small tin of tuna will last for four meals, if you mix it with cabbage. And we don't drink real coffee anymore, we drink chicory."

"If you've taken the decision to live, you have to spend a lot on food, and that's that," says Dad, munching his way through his second slice of cake bread.

As he eats, I notice that his arms are lined with plum-colored contusions. "What are they from?" I ask.

"Your mother," he replies, in a false falsetto, "she beats me up when I don't behave."

Mum snorts on her chicory. "It's his anticoagulant drugs," she says. "They make him bruise very easily."

In front of him, she has lined up the drugs he needs to take after breakfast: salbutamol, to assist his breathing; glibenclamide, to control his type 2 diabetes; aspirin, to thin his blood and prevent a stroke; digoxin, to strengthen his heart muscle and moderate its beat; indomethacin, to ease the inflammation and pain of his lumbar disc lesion; furosemide, to help his kidneys work more effectively; Slow-K, to counteract the potassium loss caused by furosemide; becotide, a corticosteroid to alleviate the congestion in his lungs; and doxypol, a light morphine-based painkiller.

After he's swallowed the last of them, he stands up to leave the table. The legs of his shorts flap around his much-reduced thighs, and his feet are encased in dark blue terry cloth slippers that bear the slogan "*GOLF*," a game my father says he has never played, nor indeed shown any interest in. As he boasts that he has not purchased a single new item of clothing since he retired three years ago, I challenge him on the slippers.

"Real shoes are too painful for him," says Mum. "These are the only things that don't put pressure on his toes." He eases his feet up onto a wicker stool, and up close I see that the slippers do not bear the word *GOLF* at all, but *GOIF*.

"Yes, they misinterpreted the *L*," he laughs.

And the little club underneath it, on closer inspection, looks suspiciously like a croquet mallet. Obviously the people at the Chinese factory churning out *GOIF* slippers have even less sporting knowledge than my father.

After reading the paper, he retreats to his bedroom, groaning in pain. I can hear the murmur of Mum ministering to him. Eventually she emerges.

"Is he OK?" I ask, though it is quite clear that he is not.

"He's in acute pain," she says briskly, "a stabbing pain that shoots up his legs. He's complaining that it's unbearable. So I told him that women put up with acute pain in labor, knowing that it's only going to last so long, and that he should just shut up and breathe through his mouth and it'll ease soon."

Mum has arranged for me to see Dad's doctor, Mr. Bowers, the man who replaced her hip, so that I can help decide what we should do. I sit in his waiting room in a suburban house at the bottom of Tongogara Avenue looking at Bowers's world-class qualifications on the wall: MBChB (Zim), LRCP (Edinburgh), LRCS (Edinburgh), LRCPS (Glasgow), FRCS (England). He is one of the last orthopedic surgeons in the country. On the wall are his latest financial rules for patients: "Due to current harsh economic conditions, consultation and operation fees are being reviewed continuously," it warns. "Please check with the office closer to your consultation or operation to confirm the current fees."

"Gangrene almost never resolves," Bowers tells me. When he

worked on a vascular ward in Glasgow, they were forbidden to cut off toes. "You would simply cut one off, and then another, and then the foot, and finally what you should have done in the first place, take the leg off below the knee and fit a prosthesis." But he agrees that Dad may not be strong enough for that operation, the amputation of both his legs. His only chance of surviving is to *want* to have it done and to have the will to live afterward.

"The pain your father feels at present, ischemic pain, is the pain of a muscle being deprived of oxygen. It is," says Bowers, "the very worst, most intense kind of pain there is."

DESPITE HIS LEVEL OF PAIN, Dad continues to do the shopping. It's a duty he has long claimed and clearly enjoys. And some weeks it is all that prevents him from tipping over into complete misanthropy. Today, he takes me with him. First stop is Vasilly's, the bakery, which apparently invented the Marie Antoinette "cake bread" exception. Dad loads his little basket with a small selection of loaves, which he will later freeze, and, as a special treat, he says, because I am here, two croissants. The assistant wraps them individually and rings up the total on the till. It comes to Z$12,000.

"What!" says Dad. "How can it *possibly* be that much?"

The black shop assistant manages to look sympathetic and embarrassed at the same time. "It's the inflation," she says, and looks down at the till, waiting for Dad to make a decision.

Dad slowly counts out all the notes in his wallet but they fall short of the total required. I haven't yet changed any money so I am unable to make up the difference. Vasilly's, like most shops here, stopped taking checks ages ago—they are not worth their face value by the time they clear. He points to one of the loaves, and she removes it and subtracts it from the total. But the total is still too much, so he hands back the rolls one at a time until finally all that's left are the two "special treat" croissants.

But then, inexplicably, the cashier wraps up the whole order, including the items he cannot pay for, and presents them to Dad.

He is confused, as am I. The cashier nods her head toward the line that has formed behind us, to a tall, well-dressed black woman. "She is paying the extra for you," says the cashier.

I am not sure whether to offer to pay her back, or if that will offend her, and clearly neither is Dad.

"Thank you so much . . . for helping us," I say as we leave.

"You are welcome." She smiles. Dad just looks at the floor.

"Many's the time," my mother says, when I tell her about it later, "that we have done that for a black person struggling to pay."

DAD IS INDIGNANT rather than humiliated. People like him who rely on pensions that are not adjusted to inflation have to live on less and less with every passing month. Some have simply run out of money. A few have committed suicide at the shame of it.

Dad's British pension—for the years he worked in England before he emigrated—is £36 a month, about US$60. Mum's pension for working as a government doctor here for the past twenty-five years amounts to Z$15,000 a month—just US$5 at black-market rates.

Next stop is across the road at Bon Marché, where Dad wants to return empty bottles to collect the refund. As we wait, the only white people in line, a steady stream of customers push bulging carts out of the supermarket. Our line sullenly watches these diplomats and black-marketeers, expatriots, and corrupt government officials packing their Pajeros and Range Rovers and Mercs with mountains of groceries.

On our return, Isaac shlumps over in his Wellington boots to help us unpack, but the haul is so meager his help is unnecessary.

"You know he's leaving in December," Mum says, "going back to his tribal area in Mount Darwin to try farming full-time."

"Why now?" I ask.

"Well, the government has increased the producer prices for corn, trying to offset the collapse in production on the former white-owned farms, so he thinks he can turn a profit," she says. "Anyway, he's gone a bit peculiar."

"How?"

"Recently we were gardening together perfectly amicably, when he turned to me and said, 'I want a tea break.' Quite forcefully," my mother adds.

So she says, "Very well, off you go, have a break."

And he says, "No, every day."

"But you have one every day," she says.

"No," he says. "I want one at a set time."

"OK—how about ten to ten thirty?" she says.

"Right," he says triumphantly. "You owe me a lot of money for all the years that I have worked without a tea break. You must add up those half hours and pay me for them."

"Well, you must talk to my husband about that," my mother says.

And so he does. Dad shows him a copy of the domestic workers' statute. "Each employee has the right to a forty-five-minute lunch break and two fifteen-minute breaks during the working day," he reads.

"At present," says Dad, "you take two hours at lunch and another hour over the course of the day."

Isaac nods, for he knows this to be true.

"In that case," says Dad, "you should pay *me* back for one and a quarter hours a day."

Isaac drops the demand. My father hasn't needed to mention that he pays Cheesely's school fees and pays for her uniform, and has given Isaac my old motorbike, with a market value of Z.$5 million. There is a premium on motorbikes in these fuel-challenged times.

Shortly after the pay dispute, says Mum, she is on her dusk patrol of the garden—a very slow patrol—when Isaac's wife, who is a Mapostori, starts praying "aggressively" at her. I hoot with laughter when Mum tells me this and she looks offended.

"Well, she was. As I approached, she was on her knees facing the setting sun. I was careful not to walk in front of her, but she turned toward me, and she raised her voice until she was shouting. Frankly,

I felt as though she was trying to put a curse on me. It gave me quite a turn. And it wasn't the first time."

"What was she saying?"

"I don't know," says Mum glumly. "It was in Shona."

Things finally come to a head one afternoon when they hear a terrible ruckus outside the gate—men shouting and a woman screaming. The gate bursts open, and Isaac appears, shoving his wife in ahead of him, pursued by three men.

"We're under attack!" shouts Mum. Dad emerges from the house with the .45 revolver in his hand and sits on one of the chairs he has placed strategically five paces apart along the drive—his "resting chairs"—with the gun on his lap. Two of the men—one of the hawkers on our corner, and an off-duty security guard—run away when they see the gun. But the third man, who has a clubfoot, remains, and he and Isaac begin to brawl, and as they trade blows, the clubfooted man drops the little plastic shopping bag he is holding. Inside is a small bottle of cooking oil, precious because it is so scarce now. It shatters, and at this, the fight drains out of him, and he begins to weep. Isaac runs off to his house, and Mum tries to soothe the man with the clubfoot. She sits him down on one of Dad's resting chairs and gives him a glass of water and a wet washcloth for his face, and he explains the root of the dispute.

Isaac, he says, has done a painting job for him—with our paint, of course—and the man gave Isaac a bicycle tire as security. "But now I have paid in full," he says, "and Isaac is still refusing to return my tire. He has stolen it."

This is what this vile president has done to us—made scavengers of us all and stripped these grown men of their dignity as they fight over a worn bike tire. Reduced us all to desperadoes and thieves, made us small and bleak and old and tired. Made us lose our love of life itself. Split our families and left my parents impoverished, alone, afraid.

THE NEXT DAY Mum summons me into my father's bedroom to observe the daily ritual of the Changing of the Dressing. She wishes me to see this so I will be better informed of his condition, so I can help with the decisions that lie ahead. She gets down on her knees, "like Mary Magdalene," she jokes, and Dad makes the sign of the cross, bestowing a blessing to the top of her head. She gingerly pulls away the gauze that covers his feet, right one first. As it comes away, Dad does not look down. The foot is swollen and puffy, and the toes and the pad underneath are blackened and oozing. I had no idea it was this bad. It is an appalling sight, and the smell is rancid. I feel a retch rising from my chest into my throat. I am going to throw up at my father's feet.

"This is the good one," I hear my mother saying for my benefit, "and I must say, it looks a little better this morning."

I battle to swallow my own vomit.

"Hmmm, distinct improvement," she continues. She gently massages the new diabetic cream into it, while Dad winces and squinches his eyes shut in pain. Then she moves to the suppurating ulcerous ruin of his left foot.

I rise to flee, but she fixes me with a steely gaze that says, don't-you-bloody-dare-wimp-out-on-me. So I sit back down and make small talk to Dad, as though this is no big deal, really, rotting alive from your feet up.

Finally the phone rings in the hall, and I gratefully leap up to answer it. Mum follows me out a few minutes later. She has been trying to suggest bringing forward his next doctor's appointment. But Dad will have none of it; he wants to avoid amputation, any amputation, even of individual toes.

"He's suicidally depressed, you know," she sighs. "I'm worried he'll go for a gun and shoot himself."

We decide that if he's going to kill himself, he'll most likely do it while I am here, so as not to leave Mum to deal with the aftermath on her own. So together we remove all the guns — the .38 pistol and the .45, the .410 shotgun and the .303 rifle — from the safe and hide them right at the top of the cupboard in the study, where I'm staying.

"Maybe we should move his extra medical supplies," she suggests, "in case he decides to OD." So we gather up the pill bottles from the medicine cabinet, and I take them away and conceal them in my room, under my New York clothes.

Later we discuss his pain threshold.

"He's on the maximum doses of pain relievers already," says Mum. "That's why he keeps falling asleep."

"What else can we do?" I ask.

"It could be time to move him on to morphine." She pauses. "I wonder how soon he'll get addicted?"

DAD RALLIES later that evening and settles into his old armchair, munching his cake bread supper. Though I have offered to pay for it, my parents refuse to get satellite TV, refuse to retreat into the expatriate compound of the mind. They prefer to wrestle with the country that is all around them, to remain engaged. Their only concession is the BBC World Service radio news, which they've listened to for fifty years, and Georgina's Radio Africa.

Next to Dad's chair is the Tempest Super Sixty stereo. "Super Sixty" because when he bought it in 1970, sixty watts was something to boast about. It is finished in wood veneer and is the size of an oven. Each speaker is as big as a tea chest, and they emit a background hiss when music is played through them. But it is an old Sony shortwave radio of mine, linked to an outside antenna Dad has strung up along the avenue of cypress trees, that provides their only window on the world now.

The BBC World Service for Africa is trailing a story that a new guerrilla group called the Zimbabwe Freedom Movement is launching an insurgency to overthrow Mugabe. The leader of the new group goes by the nom de guerre Charles Black Mamba. Their rather unlikely spokesman is Peter Tatchell, the gay rights activist from Outrage! who ambushed Mugabe outside Harrods. He says he's been in contact with Black Mamba for eighteen months and that Mamba and his men are all serving members of the Zimbabwean army.

"What do you reckon?" says Dad.

I am skeptical and so is he. After seven years of guerrilla war, followed by the Matabeleland massacres after independence, few here have the appetite for more armed conflict, even as the opposition falters and the dictatorship tightens.

KEITH MARTIN has now managed to secure Jain's ashes, and we are clear to rebury her at Christchurch in Borrowdale. It will be a small ceremony, just us and the Watsons. And then I wonder whether we should invite Aunt Margaret.

Margaret Gray is not my real aunt, she's my godmother. She was a nurse back in England, where she had looked after George Bernard Shaw. Then, responding to the "Sunshine Girl" campaign, she was recruited to work in Rhodesia after World War II, and went on to become a senior nurse at the hospital in Mbare township. On Sundays she and her husband, Derek, a retired policeman, used to fetch me from boarding school and take me back for the day, to their small farm at Christon Bank near Mazowe. I haven't seen them in years.

"I'm so ashamed," says Mum. "We've quite lost touch with them."

Last she heard, they had sold their house and moved into managed care.

With Keith's help, I call around to the various nursing homes and finally track her down to the B. S. Leon Home for the Elderly. It's OK, he says, it's one of the good ones.

"Remember," says Mum, as I leave for B. S. Leon, "Margaret Gray saved your life — twice."

This is the first I've heard of it.

"I had a pregnancy that went wrong, before you were born. The placental tissue grew uncontrollably into the wall of my womb to form an invasive hydatidiform mole, and the gynecologist was all set to do a hysterectomy, which was then standard treatment, but Margaret talked me out of letting him do it, and I went to another doctor who spent hours dissecting it out instead. And later, when you were conceived, they said my womb would tear, and I should have an abortion, but Margaret persuaded me to keep you. That's why I made her your godmother."

There is no obvious reception area at B. S. Leon, and I find myself in a large room where dozens of chairs have been arranged in a semicircle around a TV set. About fifteen very elderly white men and women and several black aides are watching a pop video through the snowstorm of static. It is "I Could Be the One" by Donna Lewis and the volume is turned up, way up. The nursing aides are bopping to it while the old folks just sit and stare at the snowy screen in silence.

One of the aides directs me to Margaret's ward, and I walk to the end of a long linoleum-covered corridor that smells of cabbage and disinfectant. I find her, short and grizzled, in a pink housecoat, sitting at a Formica table with her back to the window, reading *This England* magazine, issue of Spring '93. It is open at an article entitled "The Spirit of England," illustrated with a portrait of Winston Churchill and quotations from him on the eve of World War II, warning his people that "Appeasement is feeding the crocodile, hoping it will eat you last," and imploring, "Nothing can save England if she will not save herself." In her hand is a green plastic flyswatter. Two other elderly ladies sit hunched over on the ends of their beds, observing me silently.

Margaret looks up and sees me. She frowns for a moment and then her face brightens.

"Peter. Well, I never!" she chirps in the Shropshire accent that fifty years in Africa have failed to dent. "It's been years."

She flicks deftly at a fly and kills it. I congratulate her.

"I killed twenty-one in a single day once," she says, and gives her little signature hoot of laughter.

I sit down on her narrow iron bed and fill her in on family news, and then I ask, "How's Derek?"

"Derek." She blinks. "Derek?"

"Yes," I say, nodding at the framed wedding photo on her side table. Margaret with soft blonde hair and Ming blue eyes, in a feathery flounce of taffeta; Derek in British South Africa police dress uniform—diagonal leather Sam Browne belt, jodhpurs, puttees, silver sword snug in its scabbard.

"Derek's dead."

"Oh, God. I'm so sorry."

"It was a few months back I think. I never went to the funeral," she says. "I don't really go out anymore, I get . . . tired. I don't even know where he's buried, you know."

I go over and hug her awkwardly, and she starts to cry. "I miss him terribly," she says into my shoulder.

I SIT ON THE SOFA that night, letting the ZTV news wash over me. Canaan Banana has died in a London clinic. An undertaker condemns the local hospital's practice of dumping bodies in mass graves after relatives fail to claim them because they cannot afford funerals. A poet, Bernard Sibanda, is interviewed. "How is it? To be a poet?" he is asked. "Ah, you have to be *tough* to be a poet," he says, and he assumes a boxer's stance. President Obasanjo of Nigeria arrives tomorrow to try to broker a deal to keep Zimbabwe from being expelled from the commonwealth. "He comes to Zimbabwe after a display of white arrogance by Australian Prime Minister John Howard." The Chinese Embassy has donated eight electric sewing machines to a secondary school in Goromonzi. Prior to this, more than a hundred students have shared each machine.

Later, Dad listens to Georgina again. She is interviewing a protest leader who has just been arrested and locked into the back of a police Land Rover. He has hidden his cell phone in his sock and is now calling in his version of events. "I must stop now," he whispers. "They see me." There is a squawk and the line goes dead. "We apologize for technical difficulties with that interview," says Georgina, and goes on to the next item: Roy Bennett's farmworkers have been attacked, shot at by a combined force of army, police, and party youth militia. There are casualties, but no one knows how many yet. This attack is despite a high court order excluding the security forces from the farm.

I think of that evening two years ago when we waited for just such an attack. And I know the young men who are in the firing line this time are the same ones as back then — those boys drinking raw farm coffee from chipped enamel mugs, waiting for an ambush or dawn, whichever came first.

KEITH MARTIN has given me the "authority to disinter" document for Jain's ashes, and I ask Dad where to put it.

"Put it in the Jain file, in the top drawer of the filing cabinet in the study," he says.

Way at the back of the cabinet, jammed in behind a screed of engineering standards files, I find a set of hanging files labeled "Jain." I heave them out and lay them in a pile on the desk. Together they form a complete record of my sister's life — twenty-seven years of it. Her first school reports, theater programs, team photos, applications for teachers training college, letters from ex-pupils, grateful parents. It takes me several hours to work my way through the counterfoil of her existence, until there is only one file remaining. It is a dusty, plum-toned folder. I know what it must be, and I don't want to open it. I sit for a long time looking out the study window at the swimming pool fishpond. Dragonflies hover over the murky water, mating, and masked weavers fly back and forth collecting pink-headed pampas grass for their nests. And the kapok tree that Mum transplanted from Jain's garden after she died is blossoming with small, soft, ivory flowers.

Finally, I flip open the folder. Inside is all the documentation of Jain's death — first the clipped obituaries and condolence notices from the newspaper, browned now, with age. Then the inquest report, the Warned-and-Cautioned Statement for the possible culpable homicide charges against several soldiers, the sudden-death docket, witness statements from other soldiers detailing the disputed sequence of events, the injuries sustained by Jain, Neville, and Mark, who'd died where and how. As a former policeman, I have written reports like these, but this is different. This is the one that has torn my own family apart, that has created two worlds for us: before and after.

I'm terrified that I am going to encounter photographs of Jain's battered corpse—an image I cannot bear to hold within me. Georgina and I have heard that Jain was decapitated. As I turn each page, I look first through half-closed eyes, to censor whatever is next. Finally I reach the autopsy report. Under "Cause of Death," it concludes simply, "extensive head injuries." And it confirms one small mercy—that she was killed instantly. Thankfully there are no photos of her body.

There are other photos, though, which Dad has stored at the back of this folder, early ones of Jain as a toddler on the lawn in Cobham, ones I have not seen. For me, these pictures are almost unbearable. I cannot look at them without also seeing the police forensic photos of her crushed vehicle, the black type of her death report. And yet here she is, holding the hands of the parents who will soon take her out to Africa and ultimately to her death. And here she is again wearing a little white dress with short puffed sleeves, her grass-stained knees peeking out below the hem, dimpled fists clutching the handle of her doll's carriage, practicing to be the mother she will never become. She is smiling shyly up at Dad's camera. A dying man's photo of his dead daughter on a lawn in Kent.

But in that telescoping of lives, in that wrangling of memories with the rough rope of hindsight, madness lies. I close the folder, replace it, and slide the drawer shut.

RETURNING TO THE STUDY DESK, I see a pile of letters waiting to be filed. One is a copy of Mum's letter to Joan Simpson, the wife of my old headmaster at Chimanimani School. When her husband died, Joan finally left Zimbabwe and her younger daughter, Liz, to go to live in Scotland with her middle daughter, Elaine, a doctor. Now Elaine has died of breast cancer. I begin to read.

My dear Joan,

Liz rang me with the news last night. How cruel and senseless it all seems to be. I ache so much for you and know only too well how you are feeling. The only consolation is that you had a wonderful daughter who fulfilled her potential and gave so much of herself to everything she did. "More geese than swans now live."

How do you see your future? I am sure it pleased Elaine very much that she had arranged a safe and secure place for you to live. Life really is very uncertain here and I no longer go out anywhere. You-know-who is obviously quite mentally unstable. Anyone who was a polling official for the MDC is being hunted down ruthlessly and very severely beaten if not killed and their property destroyed, and the white farmers increasingly savaged. The town whites must obviously be the next targets. We have got gap bags packed and what an upheaval that was with essential documents missing and turning up in the oddest places and just a handful of clothes suddenly becoming so heavy. And one doesn't know what to pack for: walking to Beira; a transit camp in Messina; freezing in U.K. or arriving in a heat wave. You have already done all that in a composed and orderly fashion, and I do so admire you for all the traumas you must have gone through and yet hidden from the rest of us.

If we do have to go it would probably be to remote wildest north Wales where my sister has this cottage that is cut off by snow every winter and threatened by floods every spring and a car is essential to get to the nearest village. My sister is permanently in a nursing home with a speech defect, which sounds like Mrs. Thatcher's, and other problems resulting from a series of small strokes. Her husband died last year.

Your Liz is the only person I know who, while remaining well aware of all the problems and choices confronting her and her family because of the situation here, yet continues calm and serene and a pleasure to talk to. You raised her well. Everyone else is bewailing fate and starting to panic.

I wish this letter could get to you more quickly as I want to beg you not to make the same mistakes I made when Jain was killed, but you are probably much more sensible anyway. I went all aloof and introverted, as I couldn't talk to anyone about it because I would cry, and I spurned offers of help and companionship and as a result it has taken me all these years to get back to normal. Do keep in very close touch.

Much love from us both,

Helen

That night, the night before we are to rebury Jain, I ask my mother about the letter she has written to Joan Simpson.

"Losing a sister was bad enough," I say. "I can't imagine what it would be like to lose one of my children. I think it would kill me."

"Fifteen wild Decembers," she murmurs.

"What's that?"

"Don't you know the poem? It's by Emily Brontë. It's called "Remembrance" and was inspired, as I recall, by the deaths of her mother and two elder sisters when Emily was a little girl, more than fifteen years before."

She goes to the bookcase in the living room and brings back a battered hardback with hand-tooled leather cover and a broken spine and pages unthreading from their binding. She lays it carefully on the dining table next to the silver donkey cruet holder and begins to read aloud.

> "Cold in the earth—and the deep snow piled above thee,
> Far, far removed, cold in the dreary grave!
> Have I forgot, my only love, to love thee,
> Severed at last by Time's all-severing wave? . . .
>
> "Cold in the earth—and fifteen wild Decembers,
> From those brown hills, have melted into spring;
> Faithful, indeed, is the spirit that remembers
> After such years of change and suffering!

"Brontë ends with a warning," says Mum, and goes to the last verses.

> "Then did I check the tears of useless passion—
> Weaned my young soul from yearning after thine;
> Sternly denied its burning wish to hasten
> Down to that tomb already more than mine.
>
> "And, even yet, I dare not let it languish,
> Dare not indulge in memory's rapturous pain;
> Once drinking deep of that divinest anguish,
> How could I seek the empty world again?"

"That's the danger of grieving," she says. "The dead can become more real to you than the living."

THAT NIGHT, Dad listens to Georgina on Radio Africa and breaks into his last bottle of soda water. The radio tells of Zimbabwe's collapsing hospital system, a matter close to my mother's heart. Both nurses and doctors are on strike—their salaries have lagged badly behind hyperinflation. No new patients are being admitted. Three "airport personnel" and one army doctor are trying to assist all new inpatients at the entire giant Parirenyatwa Hospital.

Dad keeps interjecting over the broadcast, as though he's having a conversation with Georgina. The air traffic controllers are also on strike. So are university students, post office workers, garbage men. "But it's difficult to tell the difference these days," says Dad. "Everything is such a shambles anyway."

A court order has been successfully sought by Morgan Tsvangirai to imprison the registrar general of elections for contempt of court for refusing to bring all ballots to Harare for safekeeping, as specified in the Electoral Act. "But we all know it will never be acted on," pipes Rustic Realist.

I sit on the sofa half listening and half reading back issues of the newspapers that Dad has saved for me. One carries a Reuters report headlined "Rent-a-Corpse," which starts, "Two Zimbabwean mortuary workers have been arrested on charges they rented out corpses to motorists to enable them to take advantage of special fuel preferences given to hearses."

In the *Zimbabwe Independent,* an opposition weekly paper, I read the "Hijack Update" headed "Mayhem Continues." The Update is sponsored by Track-it, makers of a car-tracking device, whose logo is a man pointing a pistol at a driver's head.

Another paper carries a story about the burning down of the synagogue in Bulawayo a few weeks ago on the eve of Yom Kippur, under mysterious circumstances. A government commentator, under the pen name "Busybody," is alleging that the city's tiny Jewish community—now down to only 159, nearly all more than seventy years old — were hoarding contraband there: foreign currency, and even black-market fuel, which, "Busybody" claims, boosted the fire. "Busybody" knows this, apparently, because of "the amount of emotion, dejection, and desperation on the faces of the victims that fateful Saturday."

THE NEXT DAY, the day we are to rebury my sister, my father calls me into his room. He sits hunched on his bed.

"Sit, Pete," he says, gesturing to a hard plastic chair. "Let me tell you where I am." He sighs and gathers his thoughts. "I'm going downhill fast. My memory's shot. I tire easily. I can hardly walk. I could go at any time. We have almost no real income left, Pete. I'm so sorry, son. The thing you will have to decide is what to do with Mum when I'm gone — which could literally be at any moment. I'm finished, Pete. Finished."

I sit there wondering how to respond. "Don't worry about Mum. I'll make sure she's OK," I say.

Mum shuffles through the door, as if on cue. "What are you two moping about?" she inquires brightly.

We both remain silent. She doesn't press it.

AS WE ARE getting ready to leave for the cemetery, I realize that we have no flowers.

"We can buy them from the flower hawkers at Chisipite Shopping Center," I suggest.

"No! They're probably *blood flowers*," Mum hisses, meaning the looted produce of ejected farmers whose in-the-field crops have been taken over by ruling party fat cats.

I carry the wooden box containing Jain's ashes out to the car and place it gently on the backseat. I wonder about strapping it in with a seat belt. Then, as I wait for my parents to make their slow way out, I notice that Isaac had been pruning the tall bougainvillea hedge. Cerise branches lay thick on the drive, destined for the compost heap. So I gather up a great armful of the thorny clippings and put them in the backseat next to the wooden box.

We drive in silence across town, me at the wheel with Mum up front, and Dad in the back with Jain, in her box, nestled in her thorny crown of bougainvillea. I try to think of the last time all four of us were on a drive together, sometime before Georgina was born. Fate seems to have conspired to keep our family apart from each other, especially at death. Dad was stranded in England while his mother and sister were killed. His father died in Poland, unable to get out to the West, and Dad was not able to be at his graveside. And after my mother's father died—when she was eleven—she was kept from the funeral by her mother, had barely known he'd been ill. At Jain's first funeral, I was the absentee—my parents not wanting me to come back to Zimbabwe-Rhodesia (as it then was) and risk being called up again into the army. And at this second one, it is Georgina who is persona non grata. Why is it that we can never seem to mourn together, to have unity in our grief?

And I realize that for three generations, men in our family—my grandfather, my father, and I—had fought in battle. Yet it was our women—my grandmother, my aunt, and my sister—who got killed in war.

AT THE CHURCH, Father Bertram greets us, and the Watsons, in a white cassock with a busily purple-patterned surplice. I hand him the wooden box of ashes, and he puts them on a little table next to a square hole, freshly dug in the courtyard lawn by Rodgers the church gardener. Fiona, the Watsons' daughter, takes the bougainvillea branches and skillfully arranges them into several sprays, which she ties together with hair bands and places at the graveside.

Father Bertram begins the obligatory reading from John, of Lazarus being raised from the dead. Then he turns to me and asks whether I should like to place Jain's remains in the grave. It is a shallow hole, no deeper than my elbows, with a small ledge around the rim on which to rest the tombstone. The earth is rich, red, and loamy. I kiss the box and set it down. Above and behind I can hear my mother quietly weeping, and Sydney and Fiona too.

Dad has said that he does not wish to say anything at this inter-
ment, but that I should. I have written down some thoughts, but
they seem trite now. What can I say about Jain that her own parents
and godparents don't already know?

I start to speak but my voice sounds far off.

What I want to say is that even though she has now been
gone for almost as long as she lived, I still miss her. That even now
when something funny happens I sometimes find myself wanting
to recount it to her, just for the reward of her laugh. That her pre-
mature death has rendered her forever young in our memories,
overtaken in years by the younger siblings she once protected and
nurtured.

What I want to say this afternoon is that it was Jain's death that
sealed for me the utter futility of war. That when our civil war was
over in 1980, I remember half expecting that the dead would be restored to us, like some weary column of POWs returning after an
armistice. And that it was only then, a full two years after her death,
that I finally realized she was really dead. That there is no literal
Lazarus. There is only a void where once there was a life.

And the only solace I can find in all of it is that Jain has been
spared the intervening tragedy in which we are all now embroiled,
the needless moral and physical debasement of this place we used to
call home. She has been spared the scattering of so many of its sons
and daughters in a far-flung diaspora from which each passing day
makes a return less likely.

Robin reads from a piece of liturgy from the Russian Orthodox
panikhida, selected by Anastasia Heath, my mother's cousin in England (who changed her name from Rosalind when she converted
to Russian Orthodoxy many years ago).

"With the saints give rest, O Christ, to the soul of thy servant,
where there is neither sickness, nor sorrow, nor sighing, but life
everlasting."

But in this place, this here and this now, there is still sorrow and
sighing and sickness.

A dog in a neighboring garden barks urgently, but we ignore it, and Father Bertram starts reading from Psalm 121. It begins: "I lift up mine eyes to the hills. From whence does my help come?"

From whence indeed, I find myself thinking bitterly.

Dad can stand no longer, and he shuffles slowly over to a wrought-iron bench in the corner of the cemetery and eases himself down onto it.

Next to the hole, Rodgers stands with the new headstone. It is made from natural unpolished granite, chiseled with an exact copy of the inscription on the original brass plate, which now probably serves as someone else's coffin handles.

> *Jain Godwin*
> *daughter of Helen & George*
> *sister of Peter & Georgina*
> *killed near Shamva*
> *aged 27*
> *on 22nd April 1978*
> *together with her*
> *fiancé Neville Williams*

At a sign from Bertram, Rodgers kneels down to place the stone over the casket. But the hole he has cut in the lawn is slightly too small. He struggles for a while to force it in.

"She always was an awkward fit," I say, and Sydney laughs through her tears.

Then I kneel down to help Rodgers while he grabs his shovel and cuts an extra sliver of turf away, and finally the slab slips in.

Father Bertram gives a final blessing, and the breeze picks up, and we can hear rain showers approaching fast from the south. We don't bother to move inside, enjoying the fat, cool drops splattering on our warm faces. The shower passes in a few minutes.

We drive home in silence, in convoy with the Watsons, for a little wake. On the veranda under the jasmine pergola, we drink tea and eat scones freshly baked by Fiona and then we graduate to pizza, which I collect from Chisipite Shopping Center. Take-out pizza is the biggest extravagance my parents can think of. Dad suggests I break out the good whiskey, the single-malt scotch I have brought with me. I pour shots for everyone, and we sit in the gloaming and toast my sister. The streetlights flicker on, and we all give a ragged cheer. The light nearest us is immediately surrounded by a hazy halo of flying ants. On the hillside across the valley, the rest of Chisipite lights up too.

Then the lights sputter and die, and darkness is restored to our corner of Africa.

eighteen

November 2003

Before leaving on the *Forbes* side trip to South Africa that is both the pretext and the paymaster for my visit to Zimbabwe, I drop off my car—rented from a dispossessed farmer's wife—at the JAG offices, with a full tank. I have managed to find the only place in the city with fuel, a party-owned station on Manica Road. The JAG offices are bustling with farmers. Kerry Kay, whose former employees I had met at Rock Haven Refugee Camp, is there, like a whirlwind, trying to record what is happening to evicted farmworkers. And so is Marcus Hale, whose farm has just been *jambanja*'d by no less than the Very Reverend Nolbert Kunonga, Anglican bishop of Harare. (Kunonga has also thrown off fifty farmworkers and their families.) This is the bishop's earthly reward for preaching in favor of the president, which has caused a mutiny among Anglican rank and file. (Pius Ncube, the Catholic archbishop of Bulawayo, by contrast, is a major thorn in Mugabe's side.)

"We sent a letter of complaint to the archbishop of Canterbury," says Hale, "and he wrote back to say that he was 'very annoyed,' but Bishop Kunonga continues to squat on our farm nonetheless."

For my *Forbes* assignment, I am to sample luxury hotels in Cape Town and then three high-end safaris. Mudiwa Mundawarara, an old school friend from St. George's, is on the same flight so he gives me a lift to the airport in his pickup truck. His sister, Mandisa, broadcasts alongside my sister for Radio Africa in London (as does Ellah's husband, Richard). Mudiwa's father was a doctor, a colleague of my mum's. He was Shona, while Mudiwa's mother is Xhosa, and his wife, Julia, who teaches English literature to twelfth graders at our old school, is Ugandan. They are a true pan-African family, the kind of people who give me hope that this place *could* work. As an American-qualified pharmacist, who was CEO of a large pharmaceutical company in Zimbabwe, Mudiwa can emigrate tomorrow, but has so far chosen not to join the swelling diaspora.

As we drive slowly through the city, he talks enviously of the velvet revolution presently unfolding in ex-Soviet Georgia. "Why can't that happen here?" he wonders. "It's so humiliating, all of us just waiting for the old man to go, while the country dies around us."

"Behold the great image of authority . . ." I say.

". . . a dog's obeyed in office," he completes, from *King Lear*, required reading at St. George's.

"We're like a goat being slowly devoured by a python," I say as we drive through the moribund city to the airport. We bleat a bit, twist a little, and occasionally kick feebly, but on the whole we're afflicted by some lethal lassitude that allows us to accept that we will slowly rot in the belly of the beast.

Later generations will shake their heads in incredulous contempt and ask: But why? Why didn't you do something? Why didn't you rise up? How could all of you, so many millions of you, stay in the thrall of this one old man? Look at him, he looks almost fragile, effete even — *this* little man was your ogre? *This* was the man who had his heel on your throats for so long? And they will despise us. I wonder what happened to Tatchell's Black Mamba guerrillas?

At the airport, the customs officer wants to know if I have local currency, which it is illegal to export.

"No way," I say. "With this hyperinflation, I have none left over at all," and we all laugh.

"I have no more questions," he declaims in mock stentorian tones. "And no answers either." And he chortles some more.

Airside, Paul Themba-Nyathi, dressed in a Cuban shirt and a baseball cap, ambles over to greet me. It is his penance now to circle the globe, in perpetual motion, drumming indefatigably for The Cause. Nyathi is on his way to appear before an open session of the South African Parliamentary Select Committee on Foreign Affairs, which I promise to attend.

I HAVE ALWAYS wanted to love Cape Town, and I still do. In many ways it is the perfect place for me, a compromise city between Africa and the First World. I used to come here often over the five years I was stationed in Johannesburg, and in 1997, following my father's heart attack, I tried to live here, but after six months, I gagged on its isolation from the rest of the continent.

Somehow, Cape Town doesn't feel like part of Africa. The real Africa, Black Africa, stops five hundred miles to the east at the Great Fish River. Jared Diamond explained that to me when we were making our Africa film. The Great Fish River is where the climate changes from a tropical one, with dry winters and wet summers, into a Mediterranean one, with wet winters and dry summers. And the crops that the Bantu people grew up in the tropical north — millet and sorghum — didn't work down here; they didn't germinate at the right time. Because of that, the Great Fish River is where the Bantu's southern migration fizzled out. That is why the western Cape doesn't really feel African. It isn't. That's why the Dutch were able to establish a beachhead so easily here in 1652; there were no regiments of Xhosa to drive them back into the sea at spearpoint. There were just the retreating remnants of Bushmen and their pastoral cousins, the Khoi.

It sometimes feels to me as though Cape Town might also serve as the white man's last redoubt, where our vanguards will hold back the onslaught—the *swart gevaar,* the "black peril," as P. W. Botha used to call it—while our women and children board lifeboats out to the tall ships waiting in False Bay, ships that will sail over the horizon taking us back to England and Holland and France and Germany, or on to ex-colonies where we have conveniently decimated the indigenous inhabitants, to North America and the Antipodes.

I check in at my hotel, the Twelve Apostles, nestled under the west side of Table Mountain past Camps Bay, and then dash to Parliament for Themba-Nyathi's show-and-tell. I arrive late, and he is already being grilled by parliamentarians who ask obvious and repetitive questions. He answers patiently, explaining over and over how bad the situation has become in Zimbabwe, and why South Africa must take a strong line against Mugabe. Themba-Nyathi seems so much more intelligent and sophisticated than most of his interrogators and yet he is the humble mendicant here, pleading for help. But it is obvious that these people will never help us. He knows it, and so do I.

Afterward, a reception for Themba-Nyathi at the Institute for Democracy in South Africa is almost empty. No one is interested; no one here cares that our democracy has been trampled. The fact that many black South Africans, in particular, continue to salute Mugabe when his policies have destroyed a once-promising nation depresses Themba-Nyathi. They don't seem to care that the vast number of Mugabe's victims are his own people, black people. Maybe, I say to him, South African blacks, with only a decade's distance from white rule themselves, are still partial to Mugabe's race-baiting stagecraft, "the righting of historic wrongs" plume of dry ice that he has pumped over his real machinations.

I remember this conversation later, when Mugabe arrives at the celebrations in Pretoria to mark the tenth anniversary of the end of apartheid, and he is greeted with what looks like a standing ovation (although I am assured that some of the crowd booed). It gives me a shiver of negative epiphany—a zemblanity, a fear that we will never really surmount race here. And when *New African* magazine surveys its readers to find the top African leaders of all time, they rate Mugabe third (behind Nelson Mandela and Kwame Nkrumah, first president of Ghana), and that fear only deepens.

How many generations will it take before the taste of colonialism has been washed from our mouths? And I have to live my own life in the meantime. I can't bear the guilt, the feeling of responsibility. I can't lug the sins of my forebears on my back wherever I go. I will be just like my father. I will dispel from my head all the arcane details of this place, the language, the history, the memory. I will turn my back on the land that made me. Like Poland was to him, Africa is for me: a place in which I can never truly belong, a dangerous place that will, if I allow it to, reach into my life and hurt my family. A white in Africa is like a Jew everywhere—on sufferance, watching warily, waiting for the next great tidal swell of hostility.

After another drink at the desultory reception, Themba-Nyathi reminds me that not all Africans are cheering Mugabe as he stands on our throats. Many of the continent's moral standard-bearers are not fooled at all. Dambudzo Marechera wasn't. Wole Soyinka, the Nobel Prize–winning Nigerian writer, compares the Zimbabwean land program with Stalin's land collectivization in Soviet Russia, designed to get rid of the kulaks, the prerevolutionary commercial farmers whom he saw as a political threat. And Archbishop Desmond Tutu, another Nobel laureate, calls Mugabe the "very caricature of an African tyrant."

THERE IS ONE PLACE I have told my father I will visit in Cape Town before I head back to Zimbabwe: the Holocaust Center, to learn more about how his family met their end.

"He's always distressed about what happened to his mother and sister before they were killed," says Mum. "He's still haunted by what they must have gone through in their last days, their last hours."

In my briefcase I have the reply I have just received from the Red Cross tracing service. I sit on the terrace at the Twelve Apostles with the South Atlantic Ocean lapping below me, across the bay from Robben Island where Nelson Mandela was incarcerated for eighteen years, and reread it.

> We deeply regret we could not provide you with the information you sought. Though the Third Reich documented the names of many of their victims . . . many records were deliberately destroyed in occupied areas as the Allies advanced; others were accidentally destroyed during the course of the war. Finally, Nazi authorities did not always record the fate of individuals, including those sent to ghettos or concentration camps.

It is from the children of Sophie, my father's aunt, that I have found out a little more about the fate of his mother and sister. Sophie is his mother's younger sister. Her husband was killed in Auschwitz. But Sophie, a chemist, survived, shielded by her colleagues at a Warsaw hospital, sleeping every night on a doctor's examination table, and giving up her infant son, Alexander, to be looked after by Catholic nuns. At the end of the war, she retrieves him and escapes to France, where she settles near Bordeaux, remarries, and has another child, Jeannette. Since going to Africa, my father has cut off all contact with Sophie, and she, just like Dad, keeps her Jewishness secret until shortly before her own death in 1989. Only then does she start to tell her children some of what she can remember.

It seems that by late 1942 or early 1943, the Goldfarbs, who have managed to remain outside the Jewish ghetto, finally get hold of foreign passports. They are preparing to leave Warsaw, when mother and daughter, Janina and Halina, are arrested. Either an informer "denounces" them as Jews to a German patrol or they are caught up in a street cordon-and-search, nobody knows. And then they are put on a death camp train. Sophie has drawn a family tree of her own, which Jeannette later sends me. Under both Halina and Janina it says *"morte à Treblinka."*

THE CAPE TOWN HOLOCAUST CENTER is near Parliament, on the lower slopes of Table Mountain, just below the handsome pink-and-white confection of the Mount Nelson Hotel. It features a

1:400 scale replica of Treblinka made by Peter Laponder, a Dutch model maker, based on maps and eyewitness testimony from Yankel Wernik, a prisoner who worked there as a carpenter for more than a year and finally escaped. Treblinka was a new species of camp. It was not a *Konzentrationslager*—a "concentration camp"— like Dachau and Buchenwald, ghastly places to be sure, where many people died. Treblinka was a *Vernichtungslager,* an "extermination center" designed with a single purpose: the annihilation of the Jews of Europe.

There were six extermination camps built in Poland: Chełmno, Auschwitz II, Majdanek, Sobibór, Bełżec, and Treblinka. The last four, all in the east of the country, were part of Operation Reinhard, named after Reinhard Heydrich, the man who had planned the genocide, the "Final Solution" for Europe's eleven million Jews. And of these four, Treblinka was the most lethal. It opened in July 1942 and was an industrial-scale killing factory where the average stay for new arrivals was about an hour. I know that no one can truly imagine the reality of what it must have been like for those taken there. But I look at this replica of the camp and I feel that I must try.

The train from Warsaw is made up of fifty to sixty freight cars, packed eighty people to a car for the four-hour journey. The small vents are wrapped with barbed wire, and the smell of chlorine is overwhelming. Many vomit or faint. The train crosses the Bug River and stops at Treblinka Village Station, where it is uncoupled and the locomotive pushes twenty railway cars at a time down a specially built spur line to the camp itself.

The doors open and everyone is ordered out onto a ramp. On the walls are signs for a ticket office, a restaurant, a telephone kiosk, and train schedules, posters of vacation destinations, and a clock. All are fake. The hands of the clock are always at three o'clock. The windows don't open, they are painted on the walls. The German SS officers, who designed and oversee Treblinka, are trying to postpone the passengers' understanding of their fate, for once the full horror becomes plain, they will panic and try to escape, or to commit suicide, and killing them will take longer. So the SS officers tell them that this is just a transit camp from which they will shortly be transported to the east, to work in factories.

But sometimes the deadly charade is impossible to maintain, especially when the pace of the arrivals accelerates to twelve thousand Jews a day. Then many deportees die of exhaustion or suffocation in the cattle cars. And those who have realized what awaits them have to be forced to disembark. In his testimony, Abraham Goldfarb, our namesake, records the mayhem of his own arrival.

> When we reached Treblinka and the Germans opened the freight-car doors, the scene was ghastly. The cars were full of corpses. The bodies had been partially consumed by chlorine. The stench from the cars caused those still alive to choke. The Germans ordered everyone to disembark from the cars; those who could were half dead. SS and Ukrainians waiting nearby beat us and shot at us.

On the scale model, with a red cross on a white flag in front of it, is the infirmary. If you feel unwell on arrival, you are escorted here, joining the elderly and the handicapped. Though the "doctors" wear white aprons and red crosses on their sleeves, this is not an infirmary. Patients are told to sit on a long wooden bench facing a ditch. Guards come behind them and shoot them in the back of the head, and they topple over into the ditch. When it is heaped with bodies, the guards pour on gasoline and set the bodies on fire.

The rest are divided, males from females and children, and sent to separate disrobing sheds where they are told to undress and hand over all their valuables, wedding rings and other jewelry, cash; all must be surrendered, and they are given receipts to prolong the illusion of a future.

The barbers arrive in the women's disrobing shed to shave their heads. Hair falls to the floor where it is collected in big bags to be used to make insulation felt for U-boats and the boots of German soldiers. I think of Halina's glossy dark hair — that exuberant mane in her family portrait, disciplined by a headband in front and a long plait down her back. Does Janina know yet that their deaths are imminent? Does she still try to reassure her daughter that all will be well soon?

Now the naked women and girls are told they are going to shower, and they are herded into a long tunnel that the SS guards have nicknamed the *Himmelfahrtstrasse*—the "road to heaven." The women and girls are made to run up an incline to raise their heart rates. An attendant yells at them to hurry before the water gets cold. The guards have even allowed some women to bring towels and soap, to prolong the illusion. The entrance they arrive at is decorated to look like a mikvah, a ritual Jewish bathhouse, with a large Star of David on the gable, and an Aron Kodesh curtain. It bears a Hebrew inscription: "This Is the Gateway to God, Righteous Men Will Pass Through." Naked and bald, the women and girls climb five wide steps, between potted plants, to reach the showers. The Nazis call this Jew Town.

As they arrive, most of the women know now, beyond all doubt, what lies in store. They are terrified in those final minutes, panicked by the imminence of their own deaths, and many lose control of their bowels.

The men are usually killed first, and as soon as their bodies are dragged out of the gas chambers, the guards force the women in—arms raised above their heads so more of them will fit. The ten gas chambers, five on each side of a central corridor, can accommodate over two thousand people.

"Ivan, water!" shouts a guard. This is the signal for the gassing to begin. It is done with exhaust fumes from the engines of captured Soviet tanks, and it can take up to twenty-five minutes for the carbon monoxide to do its job, turning the women yellow as it kills them. The gas chambers have low ceilings, only six feet high. The less air in there, the quicker the women will die. But sometimes the engine malfunctions, and asphyxiation can take longer. There is a little peephole next to the doors for the guards to check if those inside are dead yet. When they finally die, they do not fall. They remain standing, packed up against one another.

The *Sonderkommando,* Jewish prison workers, open the doors to remove the bodies, many of which are bloodied and disfigured, their faces scratched and ears bitten off, in the terminal frenzy to escape. The prisoners shine flashlights into the mouths of the corpses and wherever they see the gleam of a gold filling, they must take the corpse to waiting "dentists" who wrench out those teeth with pliers. They sort the pulled teeth into cairns, according to the amounts of gold they contain.

As the bodies are dragged out, the fresh air starts to revive some of them, especially children. The guards shoot or club them with rifles, or simply jump on their necks to snap them, and their bodies are taken with the rest, and thrown onto giant grids made of railway tracks on concrete pillars, under which fires are lit. A thousand bodies can be burned at a time, sending up a billowing black tower of smoke with a stench that can be smelled ten miles away. The bodies take five hours to incinerate. Then the ashes are sifted again for valuables, and shoveled into huge pits.

For wealthy Jews from Warsaw, like my family, the whole experience could be even worse, writes Yankel Wiernik:

> The Warsaw people were treated with exceptional brutality, the women even more harshly than the men. Women with children were separated from the others, led up to the fires, and, after the murderers had had their fill of watching the terror-stricken women and children, they killed them right by the pyre and threw them into the flames. This happened quite frequently. The women fainted from fear, and the brutes dragged them to the fire half dead. Panic-stricken, the children clung to their mothers. The women begged for mercy, with eyes closed so as to shut out the grisly scene, but their tormentors only leered at them and kept their victims in agonizing suspense for minutes on end. While one batch of women and children were being killed, others were left standing around, waiting their turn. Time and time again children were snatched from their mothers' arms and tossed into the flames alive, while their tormentors laughed, urging the mothers to be brave and jump into the fire after their children and mocking the women for being cowards.

In the summer of 1943, after fifteen months, Treblinka is being wound down. Yankel Wiernik helps to lead a *Sonderkommando* breakout on August 2, and the last gassing is carried out on August 21. German courts later calculate that the death toll was at least nine hundred thousand people. Some of the Treblinka guards put the figure at above one million. One third of those killed are children like Halina. Among them are all 192 children from the Warsaw Ghetto orphanage, led by their founder, the author Henryk Goldschmit, who—under his Gentile pseudonym, Janusz Korczak—wrote the King Matt books my father was given as a child. Goldschmit is offered a way out of the transports but refuses. Instead, he marches at the head of his column of kids to the railway station. One of the children holds the banner of the boy-King Matt. On the reverse side is the Zionist flag, now the flag of Israel.

By the time Vasily Grossman, a Jew himself, from the Ukraine, arrives at Treblinka as a correspondent with the advancing Red Army in the summer of 1944, there is little to see. It has been demolished and planted over with lupines. He walks across the unsteady earth of the leveled camp and finds a sack of human hair that has been left behind. "Some yellow hair, wavy, fine and light, glowing like brass, is trampled into the earth, and blond curls next to it, and then heavy black plaits on the light colored sand, and then more and more."

At the sight of it his heart breaks.

> The last, lunatic hope that everything was only a dream is ruined. And lupine pods are tinkling, tinkling, little seeds are falling, as if a ringing of countless little bells is coming from under the ground. And one feels as if one's heart could stop right now, seized with such sorrow, such grief, that a human being cannot possibly stand it.

ONLY A HANDFUL of perpetrators are brought to trial for the genocide at Treblinka. Among them is Kurt Franz, its last commandant. When police search his apartment in Düsseldorf in 1959, they find a photo album from his Treblinka days. Inside are the only photographic records of Treblinka, souvenir snapshots taken by SS officers—pictures of themselves jogging, riding, sunbathing. Pictures of the little zoo they made the prisoners build for them, in which they kept foxes, rabbits, doves. Pictures of themselves posing jauntily on the iron-clawed bucket of the giant crane excavator they used to dig the mass graves.

On the cover of the album Franz has written a title, *Schöne Zeiten*—"Pleasant Times."

MY SAFARIS SWEEP BY in a flash. At MalaMala we are charged by a bull elephant. The late sun reflecting on the moisture at his temporal gland shows he is in musth, and mad with lust, and we have inadvertently separated him from the breeding cows of his desire. I try to see if his ears are flapping out for a mock charge. They are folded back. This one's no box elephant; it's for real. The ranger has his .375 bolt-action rifle clipped across the dash but no time to reach it, chamber a round, turn, and fire as the dully gleaming arcs of tusk bear down on us. I shrink back in my seat, awaiting impact. Then the vehicle is lurching forward, engine gunning us over the bush and out of danger. The whole thing has lasted less than fifteen seconds. Fifteen life-affirming seconds. Even the taciturn Shangaan tracker is impressed. "That was close," he admits.

At Singita Lebombo on the eastern edge of Kruger National Park, we drive up onto the Lebombo Mountain Range in the late afternoon for sundowners. These are the mountains that in 1986 claimed the life of Samora Machel, Mozambique's first black president, the one who told Mugabe that you might as well keep your whites, they can be useful. The Russian pilots of his presidential plane en route back from South African peace talks to the Mozambique capital, Maputo, descended prematurely and hit the ridge—lured, some still suspect, by a South African decoy radar beacon.

The border with Mozambique here is marked by a huge fence—five strong cables webbed with diamond wire stretched taut between ten-foot lengths of railroad track anchored in concrete. Parallel to the fence on this side, I notice little clumps in the ground, regularly spaced every few feet. I ask the ranger what they are. In the old days, he says, the South African army planted a double row of sisal bushes along much of the 250-mile border between Kruger National Park and the badlands of Mozambique to prevent insurgents and refugees from crossing over, just as my parents have done along their bougainvillea hedge. But the architects of this strategy didn't realize that elephants like nothing more than a baby sisal plant to snack on. The little clumps are all that survive.

MY LAST STOP is on the very northern tip of the Kruger, in Makuleke, where I camp on the banks of the Luvuvhu River under a giant sycamore fig tree that also serves as a baboon roost. Across the river are the ruins of Thulamela, a drystone citadel, an offshoot from Great Zimbabwe, built by one of the Shona-speaking peoples. The local Venda say it was ruled over by a mystical *khosi*—the sacred leader, who never left his high-walled enclosure and was called "the crocodile that does not leave its pool."

The valley is scattered with huge baobabs, some over a thousand years old, and with acacias and appleleafs, corkwoods, silver cluster leaves, and mountain aloes. The trees are filled with turtledoves and Cape parrots and gray hornbills. Mosque swallows dart across the sky catching flying ants, and golden-tailed woodpeckers tap at baobabs to encourage bugs to come out and be eaten.

Thulamela is set among red-tinted sandstone mountains, the eastern edge of the Soutpansberg Range. To the north I can see across to a ridge on the other side of the Limpopo that is Zimbabwe.

Early in the morning I drive down to Crooks' Corner on the river's edge, where Mozambique, South Africa, and Zimbabwe meet up in a three-way border. It was once a hideout for fugitives like the famous ivory poacher Bvekenya Barnard, who could hop across the frontier when being pursued by the law. White traders would come here to barter provisions and hard liquor with the Makuleke tribesmen in return for ivory. The concrete foundation of their old trading post is still visible, marked now with a faded white *H* from its use as a heliport by the South African army in its war against African National Congress guerrillas. In the flesh of a nearby baobab is the graffiti of one army unit, "Alpha Coy—1979."

I scramble down the riverbank, and there before me is the wide, sandy Limpopo riverbed, several miles across. It is mostly dry today, as it has been for nearly two years of drought. In an isolated pool at the confluence of the Luvuvhu, a pod of hippo are squeezed shoulder to shoulder, sixteen of them, just nostrils and eyes and ears and humps of back. There are crocodiles here too, and one is slowly approaching an Egyptian goose, which has moulted and so is temporarily unable to fly. The crocodile glides up behind the goose and takes a snap at it; feathers fill the air, but the honking goose manages to paddle away, and the chase continues around the pool.

During the night the wind rises, flapping the sides of my tent and unsettling the baboons above; it is raining to the west, upstream. In the distance, lions roar in expectation of the rain. It will wash away their territorial urine markings, so they must bellow to warn off rivals. The next morning, when I return to the Limpopo, it is just beginning to flow; muddy fingers of water are creeping along the sand, joining up and filling the dips and overflowing into new streams. The hippo snort and whinny and heft themselves up out of the confines of their pool.

There are huge elephant herds here too that migrate back and forth across the Limpopo. But these days, when they return from the Zimbabwe side, the elephants are often agitated and skittish. Poaching has surged there as the people grow hungry and the law breaks down. Most of the privately owned game conservancies have been *jambanja*'d, along with the farms, their wildlife largely eradicated, their trees hacked down for firewood. The taupe eland that used to graze so securely on Pork Pie Mountain in Chimanimani Game Sanctuary are gone, some of them shot and roasted on the orders of the ruling party to feed supporters at a political rally. Emboldened wovits have marched into Victoria Falls National Park and tried to demolish the statue of David Livingstone. Thwarted by the monument's size, they contented themselves with prying off its big bronze plaque—the one that reads: "Liberator. Explorer. Missionary."—and flinging it down the rushing torrents of Devil's Cataract.

On the Zimbabwe side of Crooks' Corner, the wovits are deliberately herding elephants toward the old border minefields, which are still littered with live, unstable mines. They follow the bloody footprints of the injured animals and harvest the ivory.

Today, the old elephant trails are being used by desperate Zimbabweans searching for food and refuge in South Africa. They cut across the wildlife reserve to avoid the authorities who will arrest them and send them back. Up against the electrified fence along the Zimbabwe border, we find logs jammed by the refugees to form makeshift ladders. Once across the border some of the Johannesburg-bound refugees follow the corridor under the power lines, where the bush is cleared. But lions, lazy predators who sleep twenty out of every twenty-four hours, have taken to waiting along the route and picking off Zimbabwean refugees. Once lions become man-eaters, the rangers must shoot them. When we drive around the bush, we come across odd shoes and remnants of clothing, miles from anywhere: all that remains of some fleeing Zimbabweans.

Just last week, the locals tell me, they came across a Zimbabwean man trying to coax his ninety-year-old mother through the game park. He had returned home to Zimbabwe to find her starving and was trying to bring her back with him to Johannesburg. So enfeebled was the old woman that she had managed to move only a few hundred yards in several hours. The trackers tell of other, terrible sights too. Young girls who have been raped when they stopped to ask for help. One girl was barely fifteen years old, her clothes torn off her, weeping copiously, so traumatized she could scarcely talk. She had been serially raped and had turned back, walking north through the wildlife reserve, desperately trying to go back to the home she fled. They tried to help her, but she just kept weeping and walking, through the bush. The rangers say too that some of the guards at the border fence see it as their "rent" to rape women who cross over, and so do groups of black-market traders who happen upon them.

THE NEXT DAY, I am back in Zimbabwe. I collapse into bed early, exhausted from all the predawn starts required on safari. But I am awoken in the middle of the night from a deep sleep. All is confusion — shouting, flashing, crackling, the smell of smoke, our dogs barking in the garden. I hear Mum calling out. I pull the curtains aside and see that our bougainvillea hedge is on fire. Flames, already tall, are dancing up toward the fir trees. Spark showers are bursting up into an indigo sky. The weaverbird nests that hang on the ends of the bougainvillea branches are burning too, the little yellow birds swooping above them and calling in alarm.

"It's the damned hawkers," says Mum. "Their fire has got into our hedge."

I pull on some clothes, unlock the rape gate and the door to the veranda, and go out into the garden. I fumble in the dark to find the hose and connect it to a garden tap. But there is no water. I get a bucket, fill it from the pool, and throw it onto the flames. It makes no difference, but I keep doing it, running back and forth with buckets of water, the dogs following me, barking. Mum and Dad appear on the veranda in their bathrobes. Dad has the .38. "Just in case it's a setup," says Mum. "It could be deliberate."

Dad calls the fire brigade from his cell phone, as our landline has been cut, perhaps by the flames burning the overhead wires. Or perhaps, Mum worries, by would-be robbers in cahoots with the hawkers. The fire burns for an hour or so, and just as it is dying down, a fire engine finally arrives. The firemen slowly unroll their hoses and douse the embers of the hedge.

It is nearly dawn, and Mum brings out a tray of milkless tea — milk is unavailable again. We sit on the patio, watching the sunrise through the smoke. The bougainvillea bowers have more or less vanished, and the sisal has been reduced to blackened hulks like the innards of airplane wreckage. The fence that winds its way through the middle of the hedge is charred and sagging and broken in several places. And as the day lightens, we see that we are completely exposed, looking directly into the hawkers' camp and the busy throng of curious passersby beyond. The hawkers sit there at their little stalls, staring in at us, murmuring to themselves, unapologetic for burning down our barrier. Several of their kids stand by the ruined fence, coughing their liquid coughs, watching us drink our milkless tea.

My parents have spent the last fifteen years tending this barrier against the huddled masses outside, reinforcing it until they have judged it impregnable, and it has been incinerated in an hour.

"We could replace it with a wall," I suggest.

"No," says Mum. "Too expensive. And anyway, if you have ostentatious security it makes it look like you have something worth stealing. It only encourages robbers. That was the whole beauty of the hedge."

As we sit there, the mournful wail of the air-raid siren marks the first class of the day across the road at Oriel Boys School.

"Always reminds me of being in London during the Blitz," says Mum. "Feels like it now too," she says, surveying the smoldering cinders of Fort Godwin's bougainvillea battlements.

The breeze is picking up again, swaying the fir trees on the other boundary. Crows, with their awful cawing, used to gather in the hundreds on these trees.

"No crows," I say.

"What?" says Dad.

"Where are the *crows*," I say, louder, pointing up at the firs, and the hawkers all look up at the firs too. "What happened to that great flock of crows that used to congregate around the school?"

"Not the *flock*," says Dad, ever the stickler for his adopted tongue, "the *murder*. They disappeared recently. I have a theory: since the food shortages, the Oriel schoolboys have been eating up all their packed lunches. They no longer strew bread crusts and bits of fruit and the like on the playing fields and courtyards. Everyone's hungry now. Nothing is wasted. So no scraps for crows."

At the siren, Isaac appears.

"Well, well, not a moment too soon," says Mum under her breath as he approaches.

"Ah! Ah! It is too bad," he says, surveying the scorched earth.

Mum tasks him to dig holes along the fence line. I start mending the wire breaks while he transplants yesterday-today-and-tomorrow shrubs to obstruct the hawkers' sight line. But to little effect. We remain totally exposed; anyone can peer straight into our inner sanctum, the little patio where my parents habitually sit on their white garden furniture under the jasmine pergola and drink their weak tea and read their plastic-covered library books.

Dad retires to his room in pain. Later that evening he calls me in. "Shut the door, Pete," he says.

Once again, he is sitting hunched over on his bed. His arms are wreathed in bruises from the anticoagulants, which have also made his eyes bloodshot. "This fire is the last bloody straw," he says. "This whole place is going to hell. I'm in so much pain now, Pete. I've taken all my meds at once, and I'm still in pain. I think this is the beginning of the next stage: permanent pain. I'm not fit to go on. My bloody memory's gone. I forget to pay bills. We'll soon be cut off from services. We spend over five hundred million Zimbabwe dollars a month on medications. Our savings are gone. If it goes on like this, I'm going to end it myself. I want you to cremate my body, Pete. Put it in a hole in the garden for all I care. Nothing fancy. But be sure to cremate me. I don't want to be buried whole, with worms eating my flesh. And you must look after Mum. You're the only one now who can arrange it all."

I sense he is not to be mollified, that his rage needs to flow freely. So I just stay quiet and, after a while, he continues. "I mean, Derek died, and I didn't even know about it. No one did. Well, that's what can happen to me. I can die, and no one will know. No one needs to know."

Outside, Isaac calls the dogs to their supper bowls. A bus chugs noisily down Hindhead Avenue, its sound amplified by the loss of the bougainvillea baffling. When he speaks again, my father's voice has changed; it is softer, less angry. "What did you manage to find out about my mother and my sister?" he says. "How was it for them? At the end?"

Of course, I have been expecting this conversation, rehearsing different ways of telling him what I've found out. I can't possibly tell him the real details of how people died at Treblinka.

"From all the research I've done, the books I've read, it would have been quick, Dad. They wouldn't have suffered much."

He closes his eyes and nods. "Well, that's something, at least," he says. "I'm glad of that." And he reaches across and pats my arm. "Thanks, Pete, for doing that."

I can see, though, that he is just pretending to believe me. He knows that they probably did suffer terribly. But he wants me to believe that I have successfully reassured him. I am lying, and so is he. We are lying to each other.

ON SATURDAY MORNING, I go through to the study and squeeze the one-eyed wooden frog clip that sits on the desk, to make it re-gurgitate its diet of letters and lists and utility bills. Dad has asked me to check them — a huge concession from someone as organized as he. It soon becomes apparent that our phone is not out of order; it has been cut off because the check he sent to pay the bill has been returned. The figures he has written do not jibe with the words.

Among the bills is a newspaper advertisement he has clipped.

It's another "Hijack Update." But the sponsorship has changed. Now it is: "A community service brought to you by TV Sales and Hire." Under that is the headline "Watch Out—You Could Be Next! If you are the victim of a hijacking or are sure you are being followed, these are the numbers to call. Cut them out and if you have a cell phone, program one or two of these numbers into the phone. These numbers will go directly to the vehicle theft squad and they will respond." These instructions are followed by news of recent hijackings, in particular a spate of SUVs being driven into neighboring Zambia. "Hijacking causes many problems within the victim's family, sparked off by their terror and fear of reprisal. Mrs. C lost her twin cab in Marondera last week. The thieves were lying in ambush for her and were armed with AK-47s."

WE HAVE SATURDAY LUNCH with Georgina's in-laws, Shaina and Gerald, in their garden. Their tame crow sits in the munhondo tree above. "It's called Jekel," says Shaina. "It had a mate called Hekel who was in the habit of eating from our Rhodesian ridgeback's bowl until last week, when the ridgeback bit Hekel's head off." Their cockerel leaps up on the back of the guinea fowl and tries to mate with it; their peacock trumpets loudly until fed tidbits from the table.

Mum is telling them about the fire, and Shaina offers to give her some shrub cuttings to help fill the gaps in our hedge. Gerald hollers for Naison, the gardener. As he approaches, Shaina's tiny Yorkshire terrier yaps and nips at the back of his blue-overalled legs, but Naison ignores it.

"It's a very good watchdog, you know," says Shaina. "I use it to alert the bigger dogs. It never gives a false alarm. Last night it was growling and growling, and then suddenly there were four gunshots right by our bedroom window. They keep trying to steal the neighbor's swimming pool pump, and he was shooting at them. He has a very high-powered rifle, you know. You could hear the bullets zinging through the trees."

Naison is assembling a variety of plants, placing them carefully in Bon Marché bags for Mum.

"He's a lovely old chap," says Shaina of her gardener. "He's the only one of them I really trust. Shame, he lost his girlfriend and his daughter to AIDS. And now his real wife has died too. And the bastards, her family, they said that he'd never finished paying *lobola* to them for her so they wouldn't let him bury her body. It lay there in the reserve, getting all stinky, for about a week, until he sold three cows and paid off the bride price. These people, honestly. Imagine holding a corpse hostage. Now he's dying of AIDS too, poor old bugger. Every time I see him he's got a new blister on his lip or something and I think, *Oh, oh,* and I rush off to give him extra treats to eat. You know that's my instinct, to nourish the sick. I used to work at the hospice, you know. There was a picture in the *Herald* yesterday of a little black boy who died of meningitis. It said his last words were, 'Look, Dad, I'm flying.' That's what that famous author Kubla something says, isn't it? That when you die, your soul flies out of your body. When I worked at the hospice, the dying always used to say they were flying."

"When we drive down to South Africa we prefer to go through Botswana," Gerald is saying to Dad. "It's much more *civilized*. I hate the Beitbridge border crossing. You line up inside for hours while outside they steal the headlights from your car."

Shaina is telling Mum about the contentious divorce of her daughter, Jacaranda, whose ex-husband accused her of withholding some of his belongings, paintings, and other valuables, hiding them here at Summerfield Close. When marshals of the court arrived with policemen to raid the house, they mistakenly arrested the other daughter, Topaz, who had just arrived from Los Angeles.

"Topaz went to Chikurubi Prison for the night, you know, with her baby, Sable, not even two years old. They were crowded into a cell with thirty-one others. There was menstrual yuck all over the floor, but the other prisoners, all of them black women, they were so kind to her, they all moved to the side and put their blankets together so she could have a bed. And the black lady warden took the baby and mixed some powdered milk and gave her a bottle."

Now Shaina turns to me to ask about the recent breakup of her son's marriage to my sister. Jeremy has written to Shaina, trying to tell her he has finally accepted that he is gay.

"You know I wrote back to Jeremy saying we'll always love you whatever you are, but I'm hurt that you never felt you could tell me. And he wrote back saying he'd assumed I'd always known." She pauses for a sip of her iced water. "So do *you* think he's really gay?"

"I'm not sure," I say, not wanting to get involved.

"Well, I wish you'd ask him, man to man. I think it's just a state of mind. That you can come out of it. Anyway, there's been nothing like this in our family. Only one of Gerald's distant relatives who's a bit effeminate."

"But he has kids," objects Gerald mildly.

"Yes," concedes Shaina, playfully, "but he only *really* came alive when he was playing the dame in the pantomime."

MY PARENTS ARE EXHAUSTED after their outing. Mum is fast asleep before 6:00 p.m. Her glasses are still on, and one hand clutches the corner of her Sony radio, which hangs by its black nylon strap from her monkey-chain stand. Unheard by her on Radio Africa is *A Different Point of View,* in which an American accent is calling for "days of prayer to get rid of Mugabe and his whole regime."

Prayer. Is that all we have left?

I remove Mum's glasses and gently pry her fingers from the radio, and she snuggles under the duvet. "Night, night," she murmurs, without really waking up.

In bed I lie listening to the hawkers quarreling. The walls dance with the shadows caused by their fires, fires that now burn along the edge of our garden and seem to surround us.

ON SUNDAY, for a break, I go out by myself. American aid-worker friends have invited me to a barbecue—what we call a *braaivleis*—at their house high on Hogerty Hill, in Borrowdale. It is raining as I drive there, a tropical downpour that overwhelms the little wipers of my small blue Korean rental car with a blanket of water, but in this blighted country even the rain is bad news. The small winter-wheat crop is largely unharvested, its new black farmers unfamiliar with the ritual of advance booking combine harvesters. Rain will rot it in the fields.

Later, up on Hogerty Hill, the clouds clear to reveal a wide view across the valley toward a broken farm, and on the other side of the hill, red scars where the earth is being excavated to construct mansions for the new elite. One of the barbecue guests, a rhino expert, plays the bagpipes, while his wife accompanies him on the accordion, a hauntingly melancholy medley of Gaelic laments and Slavic ballads.

Out on the porch, an elephant expert from the States, Loki Osborn, is telling me about his dissertation on elephants' abhorrence of pepper, something I can understand after my chili *chakalaka* experience. This matters because it provides a nonlethal way for tribespeople to keep elephants from eating their crops. If you spray an elephant with pepper, he says, it will stay away from that place for years. He's been working with a small group of villagers in the isolated Dande tribal area down in the Zambezi Valley. As they have only one spring and walk miles each day for water, Loki says he wanted to help them by drilling a well. They welcome the idea, though doubt he can pull it off. When his drilling crew finally hits water, the villagers start feuding furiously about the altered walk-to-water hierarchy, and Osborn is eventually forced to fill the well back in. Now the tribeswomen once again spend hours each day trudging to fetch water, and calm has returned.

It's always instructive to observe the life cycle of the First World aid worker. A wary enthusiasm blooms into an almost messianic sense of what might be possible. Then, as they bump up against the local cultural limits of acceptable change, comes the inevitable disappointment, which can harden into cynicism and even racism, until they are no better than the resident whites they have initially disparaged. Even those like Osborn, who have learned the language and done thorough research, often have their faith eroded by the vagaries of Africa, which can start to look horribly like irrationality to the northern eye.

Witchcraft still grips Dande, says Osborn. "They have cleansing ceremonies where they dance around, get possessed. They accuse the old women, their own grandmothers, the *ambuyas,* of being witches. And the amazing thing is that the *ambuyas* play along with the accusations: 'Do you promise to stop eating babies?' 'Yes, we won't do it anymore.' The people slice the *ambuyas*' foreheads with razors and rub dirt into them. Then they all become possessed with the spirits of baboons and leap around making baboon calls."

The next day, he says, everything is as normal—except that the old ladies have cuts on their foreheads.

The jealousy in traditional societies can be extreme if someone garners any sort of advantage. This is the downside of their egalitarianism. When big shots who have made money in the city return to their home areas to build grand houses, these rural mansions are often vandalized and stoned. Of course, anyone who has better crops or cattle is at risk of being accused of witchcraft. And such allegations often come from family members. Osborn shakes his head at it all.

His adventure in elephant pepper has finally become victim to the cult of *jambanja* too. It happens when he tries to turn his research trust into a company so that he can encourage the tribespeople to grow pepper commercially. He explains to his own staff—his drivers, translators, and research assistants, with whom he's been working intimately for five years—that they will all still be employed under exactly the same conditions, but that as a *bonsela,* a "bonus," he will give them a month's salary for each year of their employ when he switches their contracts. But still they bring in the war vets and demand "retrenchment packages" of about twice their annual salaries (of which the war vets will take half).

Now Osborn is packing up and leaving. No new well for Dande. No pepper cash crops. No jobs for his own staff. Nothing. He has moved his projects to other African countries, ones where things are a little less deranged.

WHEN I RETURN at 10:00, our house is ablaze with lights. Usually my parents are in bed by 8:30 p.m. and though I have my own keys, they are both still up, waiting to lock down Fort Godwin. We congregate in Mum's room. She hauls herself up on her monkey chain and demands a debriefing. Dad arrives, very slowly, wearing only his sleeping shorts, airline socks over his bandages, and his *GOIF* slippers. I tell them about all the new mansions springing up in Borrowdale Brook, and they request a tour of it soon.

After I've put my parents back to bed, I test the phone line. It has been reconnected since I paid the bill. It takes almost an hour to get an international line, and when I get through it is crackling with static.

"Have a quick word with the boys first," says Joanna, and Thomas comes on the line.

"Have you seen baby rhinos?" he asks, and before I can reply. "And elephants?"

"Yes," I say. I have seen both on safari.

"Will you bring me back a Power Ranger costume?"

"No," I say. "They don't have Power Rangers in Africa."

I take a breath to offer alternatives, but in the pause, he darts away like a silver minnow in the surf. "Bye, then," he says, and hangs up.

I'm too tired to try again. I flop into bed. The rats scurry back and forth across the ceiling, their claws scrabbling for traction, and in my half-asleep state it feels as though they are scrabbling within my skull. Finally I sleep, and in my restless dreams, the Hindhead hawkers are barking and whooping like the Dande *ambuyas,* the grandmothers forced by their own children to imitate baboons. They are scampering up and down the foot of our garden. Their eyes reflect the flames of their fires. They are whooping and barking and waiting.

MARGARET'S ROOM at the B. S. Leon Home for the Elderly is down the end of a long corridor, way too far for my father to walk, so I ask the staff if there is a wheelchair I might borrow.

"They all have people sitting in them," the caregiver says. Then another remembers where there is a spare one and she skips off and returns with an extraordinary contraption, a massive antique iron wheelchair that looks like a Victorian bath chair. Its brake is tied with wire, and its footplate is missing, but it's a set of wheels.

"It used to belong to an old lady. But she died," an aide says to me. "Ah, but that one was very fat!" She giggles.

My parents look at it doubtfully.

"Come on, Dad, it's better than walking," I say, and I help him up into the chair. He scoots over to one side, and there is so much room left that I suggest that Mum get in too, which she does, and they both fit quite comfortably into this great old boat of a wheelchair. They look rather regal, the two of them, enthroned, and I trundle them down the linoleum corridor much to the mirth of the nurses and the residents.

Margaret is at her Formica table again, against the window. She looks blankly at my parents for a second and then gives a hoot of delight.

"Good 'eavens! Helen and George! I 'aven't seen you in years."

Mum gives her a little bag of chocolates, and Margaret immediately tears open a Crunchie bar and tucks into it, chewing in a circular motion, like a ruminant, all the while eyeing the ward warily for potential poachers.

I listen to them reminisce. They tally up how long they've known each other — forty-seven years. Dad reminds Margaret that she has been awarded an OBE (Order of the British Empire) for services to health care.

"Oh, that?" she says dismissively, when she finally remembers. "You know what they say about OBEs — Other Buggers' Efforts."

Now they are talking about doctors they worked with. "What was that la-di-da woman doctor friend of yours, Helen?" asks Margaret. She squeezes her eyes shut and pats her forehead with her palm. "No good, nothing bloody in there," she says. And all the while she keeps interrupting herself, saying, "You will come back again, won't you?"

I wheel my parents back along the long corridor. Halfway down an elderly resident suddenly steps out of her doorway and blocks our way. She starts singing in a faux Cockney accent, with a surprisingly strong and melodious voice:

> *"Daisy, Daisy, gi' me an answer do,*
> *I'm 'alf crazy over the likes o' you.*
> *It won't be a stylish marriage,*
> *I can't afford a carriage,*
> *But you'll look sweet upon the seat*
> *Of a bicycle made for two."*

Then she steps smartly aside and waves them through, as though seeing them off after a wedding, and my parents wave back to her.

At the end of the corridor, in order to get the chair over the lip of the threshold, I have to heave it up on its back wheels, and they both bob up into the air. Mum shrieks, and Dad roars with laughter, as though they are on a carnival ride. Staff members appear at doorways and windows, smiling and waving too, attracted by the laughter. My parents wave back regally from their double wide; they are having a great time, holding hands as they careen along in an ugly old wheelchair through the shabby corridors of the old folks' home. I make them pose for a photo, and when I examine it later they look surprisingly youthful.

FOR OUR TOUR of the new suburb of Borrowdale Brook, which the locals have already christened Sin City, I drive; Mum navigates. The print in her atlas is so small, she spends most of her time tossing her head, trying to focus the sweet spot of her bifocals. The map is out-dated anyway and still has the old colonial street names. But it's somewhat academic since most of the street signs have been stolen to melt down. And Borrowdale Brook is new, crisscrossed with freshly made roads unmarked on any map. Soon we get lost, but we're in no hurry, so we wend slowly farther north, following our noses.

My parents are clucking in wonder at the dozens of new houses springing up out of the bush: grandiose mansions of marble and glass, with landscaped gardens and sparkling pools. In a country with the world's fastest-shrinking economy, where people are starv-ing, this is voodoo economics at work.

Then the houses end abruptly, and we round a bend to be greeted by a large sign saying POLICE: NO STOPPING! It takes me a moment to realize just how far off course we are—we have blun-dered upon the president's new palace. Ahead are several policemen toting AK-47s. They don't look happy at our arrival.

Driving in a prohibited area can be extremely hazardous in this country. The main road in front of the State House is blocked to traffic from 6:00 p.m. to 6:00 a.m., and forgetful people like us have been shot dead at the roadblocks there—including the son of a for-mer deputy governor of the Bank of England.

"Look old," I tell my parents, "and unthreatening." I keep driv-ing steadily, as the sign commands. To turn around now is to in-crease the risk of being shot, so we continue slowly past Mugabe's new mansion. It is in the final stages of construction, protected from inquisitive gazes like ours by a high wall of sheet metal. But there are gaps through which we can see flashes of a tall pagoda-style roof of azure blue tiles. Newspaper reports say the Serbian-designed mansion is the largest private dwelling in Africa, three stories on a four-acre footprint, within a fifty-acre garden; they tell of twenty-four bedrooms, a bunker, and all the latest communica-tions links so that the government can be run from here.

We proceed under the baleful stare of the policemen. One is noting down our license number on a clipboard. Soldiers perch on the wall farther along. Two of them have rocket-propelled grenade launchers on their shoulders. For the moment, the explosive pods on the end of the barrels are turned skyward. When we round the corner, and they disappear from view, we all exhale.

"Well, that wasn't such a hot idea," says my father unnecessarily.

Mum begins to deny responsibility for the navigational error, but she stutters to a halt as we see what lies ahead — the road comes to a dead end. We are obliged to turn and retrace our route, running the gauntlet of the gunmen again.

As we round the bend in front of the presidential palace, we see that the soldiers have been reinforced by a dozen more. These new ones carry machine guns, and the brass bullets in their bandoliers shimmer with menace as they catch the sun. At least ten weapons are now pointed directly at us.

"Oh, God!" mutters Mum. "We're all going to be shot. I *told* you we should have gotten a new atlas, Dad."

No one is actively signaling for me to stop, so I keep going, very slowly now, staring purposefully ahead. Mum folds her hands in the floral print of her lap, draws her chin down onto her chest, closes her eyes, and waits for the shot. In my rearview mirror, I see Dad's monumental head. He is adopting a different tactic, smiling and waving gaily at the scowling soldiers.

"Don't, Dad!" I hiss without turning. "Don't give that open-palm wave. It's the opposition sign, remember?"

He can't hear me. But the shot never comes, and we drive slowly away in silence, leaving the palace behind as the road climbs steeply out of the valley in a series of sharp bends. Just as we start to relax, a mercury Mercedes Kompressor, a *maBenzi* with smoked windows, appears behind us, its orange sidelights flashing urgently.

"Oh, God, it's the CIO," says Mum, looking around in alarm.

Dad reads the plate: "Echo 834," he says, reverting to wartime radio speak. "That's brand new, right out of the box."

I slow down, and the Merc steams past, overtaking us on the crest of a blind corner. It disappears from sight, and finally we really do exhale. And only then do I allow myself to feel angry — that a pleasant outing can turn into this, leaving my parents shaken and scared. That we are now a people cowed and fearful, vulnerable, disposable.

WE ARE BACK in the grove of new McMansions. The huge houses are cathedrals of kitsch, as badly finished as a Husseini palace. At the bottom of their driveways stand sentry boxes, and in them loll the armed policemen, assigned to guard senior government members, and private security guards, ensuring the safety of the new kleptocratic elite, the robber barons of the bush.

At the bottom of the valley we arrive at the new Borrowdale Brook Shopping Plaza. Here stands Spar Supermarket, just opened, reputed to be the grandest in the country—a temple of plenty in a land of paucity. It's owned by James Mushore, another black classmate from St. George's, who is now a successful local investment banker. My idea is to stock up here with nonperishable standbys so my parents will have enough food to last until I return. So I have come armed with two banded blocks of pink, freshly minted Z$10,000 bearer-bond notes, our new pseudocash, which the government is printing because it has run out of real money. (The bearer bonds have expiration dates on them that the governor of the Zimbabwe Reserve Bank has told us to ignore.) Each banded block totals a million bucks, but that's now only worth about US$160 on the "parallel market."

I walk along sweeping armfuls of tins into the cart, beans and corned beef and tuna, and my mother comes along behind me examining the prices and putting most of them back. She is fierce about rejecting anything imported; buying imported luxuries at a time like this she considers to be appallingly extravagant and vulgar. In the end, I manage to keep about a tenth of what I select, which is still vastly more than they have bought on a single shopping trip for years. My mother marvels at the four shopping bags it fills.

Dusty workers from the surrounding construction sites wander the marble white naves with us, wide-eyed at the largesse, almost all of it beyond their reach even though they are among the lucky few to have jobs. None has a cart or even a basket. They are looking for the very tiniest bottles of cooking oil, but Spar doesn't stock them. Spar is not here for this kind of customer. They will not mix easily with the diplomats, the kleptocrats, the fat cats, none of whom wants to be reminded of the aching poverty around them as they buy gourmet dog food and balsamic vinegar and artichoke hearts, genuine Cuban cigars and champagne.

"Look over here," exclaims my father, and we congregate around a tank with live lobsters in it. "Fancy that!"

Next to us, a construction worker is also ogling the crustaceans, looking at their bound claws, and the way their whiskers twitch as they try to climb the glass walls of their aquatic prison.

"Excuse me," he says to me, "but what are these ones?"

"It's called a lobster."

"Lob-i-ster," he repeats, the new word thick upon his tongue. "And where it is from, this lobister?"

"It comes from far away, from the ocean."

"What do you do with it?"

"You eat it," I explain.

He shakes his head in amazement, that such an animal as this exists, that it has been carried hundreds of miles from the ocean, but mostly, I suspect, that some shopper will spend Z$300,000 — five times his monthly wage — to buy it.

We have decided on a picnic lunch, so we head for the deli counter, where I solicit orders from my parents while using my body to shield the prices from their sight. Our orders are tonged into little plastic containers, themselves a source of remark to my parents, and then we head up Hogerty Hill. At the top, we turn into a side road and pull over under a jacaranda tree, with a view out over the Domboshawa Hills. We open our doors, and my parents dig into their tubs with gusto. Roast veggies and a chicken leg for Mum; sausage rolls and a warm Zambezi lager for Dad. Mum is confused by the pull tab on her Diet Coke, so I open it for her. She has never drunk a soda out of a can before.

Across the valley is a sweeping vista of the commercial farms, all of which are now in the hands of cabinet ministers, judges, generals, and bishops. Directly below is a lush new golf course and luxury gated housing development, mansions sprouting around it — a conclave of looters. My father lets out a low whistle and shakes his head.

On the way home, we pass right by Christchurch, the site of Jain's new grave. I pull in.

"I won't be a minute," I tell my parents, and run out just to say good-bye.

Rodgers, the gardener, whom I have tipped to take special care of the grave, sees me and rushes over to apologize that he hasn't yet compressed the soil around the edges.

"I will do it now, sir," he says, "this very afternoon," and he jogs over to the tool shed and returns with a hoe.

As we drive back, Dad sinks down into his seat and closes his eyes. Despite the violent swerving as I avoid sharply cratered potholes, he dozes. At home, I help him to his bed, and he falls asleep immediately. I gently slide his glasses off and put them on his bedside table.

THE NEXT MORNING, my father summons me into his room. Mum is there, doing her daily ritual of rebandaging his feet.

"Once upon a time, Pete," he begins, "twenty, thirty, forty years ago, I considered that we were among the top ten percent or so of this country, socially, economically. After yesterday, I realize we are nowhere near that now. I mean there are people there with houses worth fifty times what ours is, with three cars each worth a hundred times what ours is."

He winces as Mum pulls off the dressing.

"Do you think there is any room left for an honest white in this country, Pete?"

"I don't," volunteers Mum.

"I consider that we are now like Greek slaves in Rome," says

Dad. "Some of the culture may come through us, but all the power lies with the Roman soldiers."

"I often feel that I'm like a Greek slave," says Mum. "It gives me a thrill, actually. At least we have some use culturally, even though we've been reduced to a subclass. Some people still want to know us."

I worry that yesterday's outing hasn't been such a good idea after all. It's as though, confronted with the new wages of corruption, Dad realizes just how irreversible it is now, that the country he thought he knew, in which he has lived for more than fifty years, has suddenly morphed into this quite separate place, one that he no longer recognizes, one that no longer has a place for him.

TONIGHT, my last night, I finally manage to get my parents out to dinner. I have been trying to do this for weeks now, until Mum takes me to one side and reminds me that since Dad's hijacking he won't go out after dark. They lock themselves down in Fort Godwin at sunset. Tonight I have brokered an exception, a farewell dinner at Amanzi, probably the city's best restaurant.

I've phoned ahead for permission to park up at the kitchen delivery bay, as it's too far for them to walk from the parking lot. At 5:59 p.m. we hobble in—the first customers of the evening. We are seated on the veranda facing the sloping lawns and ponds amid a grove of musasa trees, whose antlerlike branches, covered in lichen and dripping with ropes of vine, are spotlit from below. The waiter lights the large candelabra on our table. My parents struggle to read the menu by candlelight, so I conduct a recitation. Mum orders lamb chops, and Dad the Lebanese meze platter. Two scotch and sodas each, followed by a carafe of Western Cape table wine (Mum has banned locally produced plonk as "blood wine" since some of the Zimbabwean vineyards have been *jambanja*'d), and they are getting quite giggly and loud.

"Are we embarrassing you?" Mum asks hopefully.

I have become the parent, they the teenagers.

On one side of us is a table of African Americans—from Nashville, by the clues in their conversation. Smartly dressed in gorgeous West African national costume, the women tchink with Yoruba bracelets. They are high-spirited and excited to be in Africa and in this beautiful location. I find myself resenting their enjoyment and the flattering reports of this country that they may well carry home. I suppose as viewed from the Sheraton and from Amanzi, and from a chauffeured limousine flush with fuel, this place could still seem like something. I suppose if you hadn't been here before, you might not notice that the economy has halved in size in five years, or that 70 percent of the black middle class has fled.

Halfway through our meal, guests arrive at the table on our other side: the leader of the opposition, Morgan Tsvangirai, no less, and his wife, Susan. They are hosted by an Irish businessman.

Mum says in a stage whisper, "Georgina helped write Susan's speeches, you know."

My father, seated with his back to them, keeps craning around to see if it's really Morgan. The movement induces one of his terrible coughing fits, but he refuses to drink a proffered glass of water to quell it.

They order fried ice cream with toffee sauce, which is followed by Irish coffee, on the house.

"Should Dad really be doing this?" I ask Mum, fearing that he may go into some sort of diabetic shock.

"Hell, you only live once," she says.

I take a contemplative sip of my Irish coffee and, finding it too sweet, push it away. Dad seizes it and tosses it down his throat. He starts making affectionate snorts across the table to Mum, and then waggles his finger in a box elephant to her. She returns the gesture, trumpeting back.

There is stuff I've been planning to say tonight, son-to-parent stuff that I have rehearsed in my head. But it doesn't feel right to do it now. I don't want to puncture the moment. They are young again, flirting with each other, exchanging their own secret elephant calls, oblivious of the great and good around them. For this moment my father is not in the final stages of diabetes; his feet, below the crisp linen tablecloth, are not black and gangrenous; his heart is not weak and irregular; his lungs are not slopping with fluid. They are just a couple in love, and I, I am a spectator, and that is how it should remain.

AS WE GET into the car Dad sobers up enough to become fearful of being carjacked.

"Make sure we're not followed, Pete," he warns me. "Don't go straight home, go around the block first to see if anyone's tailing us."

The streetlights are all out, and it is a tar-dark, moonless night. We drive in silence, and I loop around once, but there are no other cars on the road, not a single one. No one has fuel. Finally, we turn into my parents' road, St. Aubins Walk.

"Nearly there," I say, and I start to pat my pockets for the house keys. But our proximity to home does not relax Dad at all; it is here he was attacked the last time. Here, at his own gate, he now feels most vulnerable.

As we mount the final speed bump, our headlights point skyward for a second, and when the beams descend they illuminate dark moving forms. People are rising from the grass shoulder, many of them, armed with clubs and sticks, their heads shrouded in balaclavas.

"Oh, God!" says Mum. "We're being hijacked again — and there are so *many* of them."

I can't believe this is happening, that I have bullied my parents into coming out at night, brushing aside their fears, just so I can feel like a good son, and now we are going to be robbed. I'm scared and angry, both at the same time.

"Put your foot down," urges Dad, even though St. Aubins Walk is a cul-de-sac.

I rev up the engine, wondering if there's enough room, enough time to do a three-point turn. Then I notice that some of the hijackers are wearing Day-Glo reflective flashes on their backs — not the usual livery of the hijacker—and with a flood of relief I realize this is the local neighborhood watch forming for a night patrol. There must be about thirty of them, black men and women, led by a special officer like Ephraim.

I roll down my window. "*Manheru*," I say in Shona, my voice still a little shaky. "*Tatenda, fambai zvakanaka.*" "Good evening. Thank you, and go well."

They all shout greetings back, and the column of women at the back begin an impromptu dance and a rhythmic chanting and form into a sort of honor guard for us as I get out to unlock the security gate.

I feel like weeping. Weeping at the way Africa does this to you. Just as you're about to dismiss it and walk away, it delivers something so unexpected, so tender. One minute you're scared shitless, the next you're choked with affection. My parents are giddy with relief.

"I hope we didn't embarrass you *too* much tonight," says Mum as I hoist her out of the car. Dad walks very gingerly from chair back to chair back to the front door. I navigate them inside, switch off the lights, lock the doors, and bolt the rape gate behind us. And as I shut my bedroom door, I can hear my mother at my father's bedside. She is singing a gentle lullaby to him.

ON MY LAST MORNING, we sit out on the jasmine patio drinking our tea, overlooked by the hawkers. I blather on about last-minute administrative things, and Dad closes his eyes in apparent concentration, a quirk I have become used to over the years. Then he lowers his forehead onto the white plastic garden table and falls profoundly asleep. It is past his naptime, and his extra medications have taken their toll.

I creep away to say good-bye to the staff. Isaac is already standing patiently at the front gate, ready to let me out. Cheesely, in her school pinafore, is at his side, holding his hand, smiling a dazzling smile. She is about to be wrenched from her good city school and tossed into a dilapidated rural one, without pens or paper or even desks. And soon she will probably stop going to school altogether, and at fourteen she will start having babies and spend her days stooped over in the fields, hoeing.

Isaac and I both know this is the last time we will see each other.

"Good luck farming," I say. "I hope the rains are good."

"Yes," he says. "I hope so too."

I walk back and call Gomo, taking him away from the kitchen, away from his washing and his ironing, away from my parents' ears, into the courtyard. I slip him a block of bright pink Z$10,000 bearer-bond notes, and he flicks a supersonic glance at them, so quick I think I may have imagined it.

"Please look after my parents well."

He cocks his head slightly to one side, a vigilant listener. And to confirm comprehension, he echoes the last part of my sentence in a beautifully soft baritone, with a lilting Shona accent.

"Parents well."

"They will need your help more and more as they get older."

Gomo nods emphatically. "Get older."

"And if there's any problem you must call me in America."

He nods again. "Call you in America."

"The number is by the phone in the hall."

"By the phone in the hall."

"If you're worried about anything, just call me. Anything at all."

"Anything at all."

We shake hands, his still damp with sudsy washing water. I try to complete it the double African way, but he breaks off after one Western-style shake. We are on opposite trajectories of politeness, Gomo and I.

Mum and Dad have now arranged themselves in the hall on the two telephone chairs, waiting for me. For our farewell, Mum has put on her "special dress," a green-striped mail-order dress sent to her by her sister, Honor, in the mideighties and only broken out for special occasions. Dad has donned a crisp blue short-sleeved shirt and gray trousers with cuffs over his *GOIF* slippers.

"Are those *chinos?*" asks Mum, pronouncing the word very deliberately, a foreign land mine to her native tongue.

"Sort of," I say, then realizing that she wants them to be. "Yes, yes, they are chinos."

"See, Dad, I told you. You're wearing *chinos.* They're very fashionable, you know."

My father comes out only as far as the front step. I hug him close, and in my arms he seems suddenly insubstantial. I can feel the crenulated notches of his vertebrae, the fragile runnel of his shoulder blade and the curl of individual ribs—a birdcage in which his labored heart beats with the irregular fluttering of captive wings.

"You stay alive, Dad, OK?"

He nods, and I see his pale blue eyes shimmering behind their tortoiseshell frames.

"I'm coming back soon with the boys, and they want to meet their grandfather, so you just stick around, you hear?"

"OK," he smiles. "I will."

My mother gives me a less tentative hug than usual, though she manages to hold back her own tears. We all do in the end. We have to.

twenty

January 2004

D AD'S FALLEN OUT of bed twice," says Mum when I finally get through to them on the phone one morning in late January, worried because I haven't heard from them for a week.

"Why does he keep falling?" I ask.

"It's because he spends a lot of time sitting on his bed to ease the pain in his feet, and he must have dozed off and fallen. It may also be the effect of new nerve-relaxing drugs. He's broken two pairs of glasses, and grazed his forehead. It looks as though he's been fighting," she says. Dad snorts on the extension.

"He also has chronic diarrhea," says Mum.

"I was just about to e-mail you," Dad says, "but it would have been a one-word e-mail: shits."

Mum doesn't want to daunt Gomo from starting full-time for them, so she has been hand-washing all the soiled laundry herself and can barely keep up. Dad sounds despondent. When Mum gets off the line "to feed the dogs" and leaves the two of us alone, he can think of little to say. "So, the boys have been enjoying the snow," he finally manages, echoing my earlier chirpy report.

I chat on about tobogganing with the kids in Central Park and the Hudson being thick with ice floes. And when I run out of news, he says, "OK, well, good-bye, then." The phone clicks off, and all I can hear is the buzzing of distance. And instead of hanging up, I leave it at my ear, listening to the audio signature of the long line to Africa, something I have listened to much of my adult life. I imagine the lines looping from pole to pole across Harare, with paradise flycatchers and blackeyed bulbuls and masked weavers perched on it as it strings through the jacaranda and musasa trees until it swoops down past the Hindhead hawkers and over our garden, over the aloes and papyrus reeds, the monkey puzzle and Jain's kapok tree and onto the Dutch gables of the house, where my mother is up to her elbows in crappy sheets, and Dad is toppling off his bed, and Gomo is padding quietly about the kitchen.

THE NEXT DAY, I return to our apartment on Riverside Drive, red faced, wet nosed, and steam breathed from playing in the snow with the kids, to find the single red eye of the answering machine blinking.

It is a message from my mother: "Peter, can you call home."

She tells me that Dad has been admitted to the hospital with abdominal pain, probably gallstones. It is nothing too serious, nothing to worry about, she says. But there is a quality to her voice, a sort of damped-down vibrato, that makes me suspicious, so as soon as I hang up I call the Watsons.

"We've been put on our oath to tell you it's just gallstones," Sydney confesses immediately. He was so ill he couldn't go by car to the hospital. Dad, normally allergic to any "fussing," meekly accepted that Mum call a private ambulance. "At the hospital," says Sydney, "he was seen by the Yugoslavian, Mr. Dakovic. He operated on my brother's stomach," she offers brightly. "With good results."

One more in the roster of world conflicts reflected in my father's health care. Over the years, they have all washed up in Zimbabwe:

Sudanese, Ugandans, Congolese, Cubans, Ethiopians, and now a Yugoslav. And it seems entirely fitting, as Dad too is on the run from conflict; they are all refugees there together.

I phone Georgina in London, and an hour later she delivers Dakovic's phone numbers: home, office, clinic, beeper. I start with his home number, and get through after multiple attempts. It is now after 9:00 p.m. in central Africa, and Dakovic sounds a little sleepy. "I'm sorry to bother you at home, I hope I didn't wake you," I say, and he laughs the bitter little laugh of an on-call doctor. "How is he really?" I ask, in what I hope is a cut-the-bullshit way.

"He's a very, very sick man," says Dakovic in a marked Balkan accent. "But I would never operate on him. He is too sick. He would not survive anesthesia." There is a pause on the crackling line, and he adds in a deliberately italicized voice, "Perhaps *sicker* than you realize . . ."

What I want to ask without bluntly blurting it out, as Dakovic well understands, is whether my father is about to die. But we continue to dance around it.

"He is definitely very ill," he says. "Look, I am surgeon, but he has symptoms from heart, blood pressure is low, pulse is fast, he is lacking in oxygen." He pauses to marshal his English. "I see your mother is used to situation where he recovers, but I must admit that this time he is *seriously* ill." The *seriously* is elongated to commandeer the whole sentence. "She asked me, 'When he will be going home?' and I told her, I said, 'Well, let's hope he *is* going home . . . ' " There is another pause while I try to take stock. "If you are in doubt to come, you make reservation on flight now," he says finally.

I hang up and call my mother, and when I eventually reach her, she comes clean immediately, clearly relieved to do so. "He's on a morphine drip," she says. "I've put a 'do not resuscitate' notice on him. But he's fully compos mentis," she adds. "Before he left for the hospital he was still joking as Fiona Watson rummaged his shelves for spare pajamas. 'Look, Mum!' he said. 'There's a *girl* in my closet!' "

After I hang up, I book my flight to Harare. I pack late into the night, and at the top of my suitcase I place my folded black Nehru suit.

I awake at dawn and check my e-mail. There is one from Mum headed "*future plans.*" It says simply, "*please phone home ASAP.*" The time of transmission is Sunday, February 8, just before 4:00 a.m. Eastern Standard Time. I begin dialing immediately but keep getting a hissing recording that tells me that "All international circuits to the country you are calling are busy—please try your call later." On my twelfth attempt, I get through. Mum picks up promptly. She is sitting by the phone waiting for me to wake and make this call.

"How's Dad?"

"Peter, he's gone," she says in a hushed voice.

This is a conversation I have been anticipating and yet it still seems so unexpected.

"Very peacefully," she continues. "We were there, the Watsons and me. He went just before 11:00 a.m., at the end of visiting hour. I had been talking to him, his eyes were open. I was holding his hand and smoothing his forehead the whole time. He was breathing quietly, then he just exhaled and didn't breathe in again."

She sounds exhausted—and relieved.

"He seemed to be with us right until the end. It felt completely natural. As he died, the Salvation Army brass band was playing 'Abide with Me' beneath his window."

My father has died a week short of his eightieth birthday. I sit at my desk, stunned. My younger son, Hugo, arrives at my side and starts humming a manic version of the theme song to "Batman," then he switches midphrase to an equally demented rendition of "Frère Jacques." Sometime in the middle of our winter night, as the wind howled down the Hudson and rattled our windows, he had burrowed into our bed and demanded, "Milk? Milk in a bottle, please!" And in spite of all the importuning of the child-rearing manuals, I had gotten up to get him a bottle, and as I did so I had noticed the red digital readout on the clock radio showing a few minutes to four. Exactly then, a continent away, my father lay dying.

Hugo wanders off, and I sit numbly at my desk, trying to assemble the resolution to phone Georgina and break the news. She is at her daughter's fourth birthday party, and Mum has begged me not to spoil it for her. The phone rings, and I answer to hear the sound of little girls laughing and squealing. Georgina has sensed that something more serious is wrong with Dad than Mum has told her. I start to dissemble, as instructed, but she interrupts. "Don't you lie to me too!" she shouts, trying to make herself heard above the party. "For God's sake, just tell me the truth."

And so I do.

"I'm sorry I tried to lie," I say, after I've told her that Dad is dead. "Mum didn't want the news to ruin Xanthe's party."

"It's my party and I'll cry if I want to," sings Georgina tremulously. She swallows back her tears and tries to compose herself. "I'll tell Xanthe later. I'd better get back to musical chairs."

I put the phone down, and in front of me, the computer screen kicks into screen-saver mode, parading a random medley of photos from my album. They are mostly shots of the kids, but then the screen fills with a black-and-white image of my parents as a young couple at a party. Mum with a broad grin and a dark dress, flared sharply out from her wasp-thin waist; Dad in black dinner jacket with satin lapels. He looks dashing, vital. Alive.

twenty-one

February 2004

O N MY FIRST MORNING back in Africa after my father died, I sit with Mum in the sunroom. "He was still a man, you know, not an invalid, when he died," she says. "At the end he asked me, 'Why am I staying alive? What good am I doing?' And I said to him, 'You stop me from being alone.' "

And she remembers the day of the big fight in the garden, the fight between Isaac and the man with the clubfoot, when Dad hobbled painfully out onto the plastic chair at the front door and sat there with his revolver in his lap, still trying to protect her though he could barely walk himself. Still a man, not an invalid. A man.

MUM TELLS ME that while I was in the air on the way home, she was visited by a delegation of her nurses from the hospital. They bring *chema* with them, an envelope stuffed with cash for funeral expenses, as is the African custom. And my mother accepts it, as she should. They ask if they might pray, and my mother nods. And they get down on their knees on our tatty brown carpet and they pray for practical things: for a safe flight for me and for my mother to be strong. And then they decide to sing, and soon our spartan house is filled with the thrilling swell of four-part harmony as they sing Psalm 46 in Shona, the one that goes, "We will not fear though the earth should change, though the mountains shake in the heart of the sea, though its waters roar and foam, though the mountains tremble with its tumult."

And my mother sits, her knees together, on the edge of our old sofa, the one with the Java print slipcover, tears finally flowing freely down her face. It is all right to weep, for she is among friends.

ON THAT FIRST EVENING in Africa after my father died, it rains. Afterward, my mother and I sit on the veranda listening to the clear, clean call of the Heuglin's robin—always the first in the morning and last at night to sing. The garden is a riot of greens and reds.

"The two colors that your father could not distinguish," she remembers wistfully. "He always complained that there was no color in this garden." I think of his Polish gunners firing at a passing submarine because Kazio Goldfarb couldn't see the red warning flag against the green Scottish hillside. I look around at the vividness of it all, this lush oasis, one that he saw drained of its brightness and its contrast. Maybe this color blindness reflected something—an inner numbing, the result of losing his family to the Holocaust, and of his boyhood exile, losses that prevented him from enjoying things to the full, a filter of fear that strained out the full luster of his life.

The Heuglin's robin pauses to catch its breath, and in its absence the arrow-chested babblers take up their chorus of raucous derision, a vulgar taunting call.

"When Dad was a boy at St. Leonard's before the war, his mother sent him some Polish delicacies, a care package in a box, wrapped in brown paper and tied with string," says Mum. "He saved a piece of that string and carried it around in his pocket for years. He said it was the last contact he had with his mother before she was killed by the Nazis. The last thing that she had actually touched. When he lost the string not very long ago, he was heartbroken.'"

THE NEXT MORNING Mum is all bustling practicality. She opens her diary to make a to-do list. I notice it is a diary of the year 1997, and I wonder if it is not confusing.

"Not at all," she says. "New diaries are exorbitant, so Dad recycled old, unused ones. 1997 had the same days of the week to dates as 2004, until February 29. Then, because this is a leap year, we move on to a 1998 diary." She turns to a new page. "Now, we need to inform people, so they can come to the funeral."

She is determined to muster a good turnout and is diverting all her energy into this. She opens up their Christmas-card book containing the names and addresses of all the friends and acquaintances to whom they send cards. Then she suddenly saddens again.

"You know the last time we sent Christmas cards was two years ago. It got too expensive. A local stamp is going up to Z$2,300. To the UK, it's Z$19,000." She is defiant, not ashamed.

"We are too poor to send Christmas cards," she says, and shakes her head in wonder at this bald fact. "Most of our friends are too."

We're interrupted by a great splash from the other side of the fir trees.

"Abyssinians," says Mum, as though she is identifying a bird species. "It's the Abyssinian children swimming."

"Abyssinians, Mum? They haven't been called that since Mussolini fled!"

"Well, anyway, that's where the Air Ethiopia manager lives. It's like the American South in the aftermath of the Civil War. When people lose everything, your social status is determined by whether you have to turn your swimming pool into a fishpond. All the rest are carpetbaggers."

She goes back to the stiff browned pages of the old Christmas-card book, scanning down her list of antique friends. Many of the names are crossed out because they have died, and most of the rest have their African addresses crossed out and replaced with new ones in England and America, Australia and New Zealand, South Africa and Canada.

Even my mother is surprised, seeing them all listed like this. "So very few of us remain," she says quietly.

There is a honking at the gate — short, long, short, short — Morse code for Linnea, and I go out to let her in. Linnea, like my late sister Jain, is a grade school teacher, and though some years older, in some ways I think Linnea is my mother's substitute for Jain. She has come today, she says, to administer "needle therapy." It doesn't involve injecting drugs; it involves hard-core sewing. The two of them get busy running up a funeral dress for Mum. Soon they both have mouths full of pins.

"I'm not going to wear stockings at the funeral," says Mum defiantly. "It's too hot."

I leave them sewing and go to call my family, to tell them I've arrived safely. Joanna puts Thomas on the line.

"Are you missing me while you're in Africa, Dad?" he asks.

"Yes, I am."

"Do you sleep while you're there?"

"Sleep? Yes, of course. You sleep at night in Africa just like you do in New York, it's just that night here is at a different time —"

"And do you dream?" he asks, cutting short my attempt to explain time zones.

"Yes, sometimes I dream."

"What do you dream about?"

"Well, I dream about you and Hugo and Holly."

"And do you dream about Grandpa, *your* dad?"

"Yes, sometimes I do."

"But he's *dead* now, isn't he?"

"Yes, but you can still dream about people after they're dead."

He pauses. "Mr. Debussy's dead," he says. "But his *music* lives on."

Joanna comes back on the line. "They've been studying Debussy in Mr. Colligan's music class," she explains.

* * *

THERE IS NO FOOD in the house, so I take Mum grocery shopping. At the butcher, as we try to replicate my father's very particular meat order, of dog bones and tiny portions of ham and chopped pork, she suddenly erupts into tears, and the whole shop stills. "Shopping was Dad's job," she wails, and flees.

In our local supermarket, Bon Marché, the black manager beckons us into his cubicle. "I have something for Mr. Godwin," he says, smiling as he reaches under his desk to retrieve a special stash of Schweppes soda water and Indian tonic.

"I'm afraid George passed away last week," says my mother.

The manager looks confused.

"He died," I say. "Mr. Godwin is dead."

The manager is astonished, as though such an event is unthinkable. And then, to his own evident consternation, he begins to cry, and this sets Mum off again.

"I can't believe it," he says, and turns away to hide his tears. "He was here just last week. I wondered where he was when he missed last Saturday, but I thought he'll definitely come on pensioners' discount day, so I saved his soda and tonic . . ."

He loads it into our cart anyway, and we trundle it sadly away. When I look back he has closed the door to his glass cubicle and through it I see he has his head in his hands, crying.

On our return from the shops, Mudiwa arrives on a condolence visit. He had sat with my mother while I was on my long flight over from New York. "Until your own son gets here," he had told her, "think of me as your son."

We discuss the funeral arrangements. It is to be held on Monday, at Christchurch in Borrowdale, the same church where Jain is now buried, where my father bought a plot that afternoon during the Final Push last May, after the surprise offer from Father Bertram. And now Bertram will preside over Dad's funeral too — he is becoming our regular Stygian boatman. Mudiwa will place the funeral notices in the newspaper — but not in the *Herald*, the government paper, which my mother refuses to subsidize.

When he has gone, we start working out the order of the service. Father Bertram has sent us three Bible readings to choose from, and Mum decides on Ecclesiastes 3:1–8, which she hands me. It is that famous passage, "For everything there is a season, and a time for every matter under heaven." But if you read on, beyond the nominated lines, it gets much darker, and it starts to resonate with the cowed country around us, where the populace has been beaten back so many times that now the master only has to so much as reach for his whip for them to skulk off back to their hovels in fear.

> Again I saw all the oppressions that are practiced under the sun. And behold, the tears of the oppressed, and they had no one to comfort them! On the side of their oppressors there was power, and there was no one to comfort them. And I thought the dead who are already dead more fortunate than the living who are still alive. . . .

My father is well out of it.

My mother likes the idea of choosing only hymns with lyrics written by C. F. Alexander, a distant great-aunt, Frances (Fanny, as she was known), who was married to William Alexander, the archbishop of Armagh, primate of all Ireland. It was for her own Sunday school kids that she penned such favorites as "All Things Bright and Beautiful," "Do No Sinful Action," "There Is a Green Hill Far Away," and "Once in Royal David's City." She had a stirring turn of phrase, old Fanny, and most have remained remarkably popular. One, however, "All Things Bright and Beautiful," had needed reworking to make it politically correct, explains my mother. She begins to sing in a clear alto soprano:

> *"The rich man in his castle,*
> *The poor man at the gate,*
> *He made them high or lowly*
> *And ordered their estate."*

"That's the verse that had to be cut," she says. And I could see why. It seems to be calling down divine justification of our earthly class status.

It reminds me of how the old South African president, the last grand defender of apartheid, P. W. Botha—who liked to be called the "*Groot Krokodil*," the "Great Crocodile"—once tried to use the scriptures as a justification for white rule. Addressing nearly three million black Vapostori pilgrims (from the Zion Christian Church sect) at their annual Easter gathering in the Moria Hills north of Pietersburg, he said that the Bible had a clear message for the rulers and those ruled. "Thus we read in Romans 13," he told them, "that every person is subject to the governing authorities. There is no authority but from God."

In the end this invocation of the divine right of presidents wasn't enough to save him, and the *Groot Krokodil* was forced to regurgitate the sun, and to watch his successor, F. W. de Klerk, hand the country over to black rule. And the city of Pietersburg (named after a Boer general) became Polokwane (Place of Safety, in Ndebele).

But things have changed here too. Many of the rich men in their castles are of different hue, though the poor men at the gate are the same, only there are more of them now and they are poorer still.

The phone is ringing regularly with condolence calls. This morning it is Dr. David Parirenyatwa. He is the minister of health, and his father was Zimbabwe's first black doctor, the one after whom the hospital was named. My mother likes him even though he is in the government. She feels he is a technocrat, not an ideologue. But she's worried that coming to the funeral might cause problems for him, as it will be full of opposition stalwarts. Pius Wakatama, Ellah's dad, who is now a firebrand columnist for the last opposition paper, has asked if he may preach.

My former classmate James Mushore, the owner of Borrowdale Brook Spar Supermarket, drops by to say that he might be able to help find a way out of another problem—Georgina's inclusion on a new personae non grata list of a hundred and nineteen "enemies of the state." The minister of information, Professor Jonathan Moyo (widely reviled as a turncoat), is on record as saying that anyone on the list is welcome to return, and that he would arrange convenient accommodation for them at Chikurubi Prison.

But in the end, we decide that Georgina should not come. It is Mum's call, and she is petrified that Georgina will be arrested. This fear, Mum says, will overshadow the funeral for her. So Georgina complies with her wish—cross, frustrated, sad. (In the end James himself has to flee the country two weeks later, accused of exchange-control violations.)

The Walls arrive bearing an elaborately frosted homemade cake. After the Simpsons, they took over at Chimanimani School, where Honest is probably still waiting to be picked up. When we return from seeing them off at the gate, we discover that our deaf Dalmatian has jumped up on the veranda table and eaten their whole cake. He spends the night retching noisily on the lawn.

ON MY THIRD DAY in Africa after my father died, it rains again, in the late afternoon. Before the rain I go to the funeral of a school friend of mine, Andy van der Ruit, an architect, someone I have known all my life, my age to the very month. The funeral is at the Chisipite Girls School, the school Georgina once attended. I sit on a concrete step with Julia, Mudiwa's wife, and as we wait for mourners to file in, she fills me in on the reports of Andy's death. He was taking a presupper nap at about 8:00, she says, when he awoke to see intruders standing at the end of his bed. When he shouted out, one of them pulled a gun from his waistband and shot him point-blank. On hearing the gunshots, Felicity, his wife, tried to press the alarm button to summon the security guards, and the robbers shot her too.

As my father lay dying in hospital, Felicity, newly widowed, lay in the ward next door.

At the wake, the talk is of the other fatal robberies in Harare, of inside jobs by off-duty police officers, of suspects who were allowed to escape from a police van at a traffic light.

At the head of the receiving line, Felicity, a therapist and counselor whom I have also known since my childhood in Chimanimani, sits on a school chair, straight backed and remarkably composed. "Thank you so much for coming," she says, and hugs me.

A bunch of us Chimanimani kids are there, middle-aged now and somewhat broken by what has befallen us, by what we have all seen, the reversal of progress, the shocking decline, the descent into darkness. The anticipated trajectory of our lives has gone horribly awry.

After the wake, I trudge back across the road to our house. It looks painfully shabby. Richard, the replacement gardener, is AWOL, unable to get back from his week off at his tribal home because the buses have no fuel. The driveway is peppered with monumental dog shits—fecal speed bumps for condolence visitors.

As I fiddle with all the padlocks and chains around the gate, I am startled by a hacking cough. It is a black tramp, one of a growing number of scavenging desperadoes, emerging from the cement storm drain outside our house. He is wearing dark strips of filthy rag, and broken, mismatched shoes. Over his bony shoulders he has slung a torn canvas Tyrolean rucksack. His hair is wildly unkempt from sleeping in the open; it is what the Shona call *mufushwa,* hair that has twisted into peppercorn bobbles. He stares at the ground, not bothering to look up as I open the gate. He seems to inhabit a world beyond envy because it is beyond hope.

ON MY SIXTH DAY back in Africa after my father died, thunderheads of cumulus build up, and it rains again. It is President Mugabe's eightieth birthday. He has made it to the hallowed hall of the octogenarian that my father just missed. Reaching eighty in black Zimbabwe is an astonishing achievement—the average life expectancy at birth is now down to thirty-four (from fifty-seven at independence in 1980). Mugabe is well into his third lifespan here.

The power comes on briefly, and we watch his birthday celebrations on ZTV news. Afterward there is a ninety-minute interview entitled "His Excellency Robert Gabriel Mugabe at 80." Of the opposition MDC he says, "The Devil is the Devil—there can never be an occasion to sup with him." And he mentions an earlier attempt on his life by the presidential cook, who, he says, garnished his food with ground glass.

"Was it a plot by Western imperialism?" asks the interviewer.

"I don't think it was Western imperialism," says Mugabe. "Western imperialism is much more thorough than that. I think a witch had spoken to the cook."

"Do you fear for your life?" asks the anchor.

"We remain vigilant, yes," replies Mugabe, slipping unconsciously into the royal plural.

He is asked what his plans are for the future. "In five years, I'll still be here, still boxing," he says, grinning like a lizard and punching his palm. "Still in politics, but retired, obviously." But he soon contradicts this, saying he intends to stay in power "until I am a century old."

My mother is intrigued by the president's use of symbolism. "At the end of two recent speeches," she says, "the camera stays on him as a white-gloved servant brings him a silver tea tray with a silver tea set on it. He pours milk from the silver jug into a delicate bone-china cup and then adds tea from the heavily embossed silver teapot and then the film fades out as he sips from the cup. All this at a time when ordinary folk can't get milk." She stalks over and switches off the set.

ON MY SEVENTH DAY in Africa after my father died, there are heavy showers in the afternoon. But before they hit, I go to the Avenues Clinic where he spent his last day. And there in the parking lot under his window, just as they had the week before, the Salvation Army brass band strikes up under huge black clouds aching with rain. Despite the soggy prestorm heat, the bandsmen and a woman are decked out in their full uniforms — white shirts and jackets and dark blue neckties with the Salvation Army crest, an *S* superimposed over a crucifix, bearing the motto Blood and Fire. In front of them are their tarnished silver music stands, shaped like little harps. The veteran instruments they play — a snare drum, a

316 • PETER GODWIN

couple of cornets, a tenor horn, a baritone, an E tuba, a trombone, and a euphonium—are dented with age and use, but lovingly polished. They reflect in the fleeting shafts of sun, brilliantly but benignly, unlike the brass bullets in the bandoliers of those other soldiers, the president's guards.

Eventually they strike up "Abide with Me," and I remember how Jain and I would sing it during the civil war, when we drove across the Hunyani Bridge, which we were worried might be landmined by guerrillas. We would roll down our windows, hold hands, and bellow it out. Jain's theory was that if you were killed while you were actually singing "Abide with Me," you went straight to heaven.

ON MY FIRST SUNDAY in Africa after my father died, it pours yet again, this time in the early evening. Before the rain begins, we sit at the veranda table and read the condolence notices in the *Standard*. From the playing fields of Oriel Boys School, the Vapostori service is in full throat. I recognize the Shona hymns from singing them with the Vapostori as a boy. At least one soundtrack of childhood has survived.

My mother hands me a letter from Albert Nhamoyebonde, "on behalf of the dormant committee of the Zimbabwe Britain Society," of which he is the chairman. "Hopefully, one day, the Society will become active again," he has written, "and we shall be able to function in more normal circumstances and renew our friendship and cooperation with members and outside colleagues. Meanwhile, we wish you and your family God's comfort and blessing in this sorrowful period."

"Why is it dormant?" I ask Mum.

"Because they were hassled by the police and hounded by the CIO as spies," she says, "and everyone was too afraid to go to meetings as the UK had become the Great Satan."

Richard, the new gardener, has returned now from his enforced leave, and snips frantically at the verdant foliage, which the incessant rain has boosted into a jungle canopy that threatens to choke the house. The Hindhead border is still open to the hawkers and the street beyond. The sights and smells and sounds of Africa's huddled masses are within our castle walls now. The differences between us are diminishing, as we all sink together.

ON THE DAY of my father's funeral, it rains in the morning. Afterward, we get ready to leave for the service. Richard takes his guard post, sitting in a green wheelbarrow in the front drive in the shade of the flame tree. He is armed with an old mahogany truncheon. Mum has read that opportunistic *tsotsis* target houses after scanning the death notices. She says they come on the day of the funeral, assuming that the residents will be conveniently absent.

We are early at Christchurch. My mother is calm now, steeled at the prospect of the frantic bereavement socializing ahead; she has switched into her formidable mode, a combination of ER doctor and chaplain's daughter.

The Watsons arrive when we do, and Manuel Bagorro, the best man at Georgina's wedding, is already there, testing the dusty little upright piano. "Flattering acoustics," he says approvingly.

Halfway down the nave, the baptismal font is full of pink rosebuds. They have been sent by my nine-year-old daughter, Holly, in London. A note attached to them reads: "Grandpa, I'm so sorry I didn't get to spend more time with you."

There is no coffin. It remains at the morgue waiting to be cremated, as my father requested.

The mourners file in and Manuel plays Chopin's nocturnes, some of Dad's favorite pieces of music, that very occasionally he would fire up the old Tempest valve stereo to hear.

Mudiwa roves around, videoing the service for my missing sister. The church, plain and wide, is full of mourners of all races. I sit in the front pew with Mum, who holds her hands together on her lap and wears a fixed half-smile.

Soon I will have to speak, and yet great sobs swell up inside me, pure and angry, grief not just at the loss of my father, but for the loss of it all, the loss of hope. Grief, at our solitude, our transience. Grief too, at my father's alienness, his otherness, his isolation. And looking around the church, I see how we've all been battered by our history, by eight years of war followed by twenty-three years in thrall to a violent and vengeful ruler. Now that Dad is dead, his near-twin, Mugabe, can die too; I am free to wish this without hexing my father.

Tears roll down my face and splash onto my black Nehru suit, and I don't bother to wipe them away. They are welcome. I am crying at last, as I have needed to for so long now, even if it is happening in public. Just as I get a grip, Manuel plays the melancholic opening chords of Fanny Alexander's hymn "There Is a Green Hill Far Away," and it overwhelms my resolve. My mother hands me a tissue, and pats me on the leg, comforting me as I should be comforting her. Robin Watson steps up to the pulpit looking every bit the Anglo-Indian RAF wallah he once was.

And then it is my turn. I am getting used to making tributes to my family now, having done one so recently for Jain. I read a short, moving eulogy sent by Georgina, who, with Xanthe and Holly, is attending a parallel memorial organized by Mum's cousin, Anastasia, at the Russian Orthodox church in Oxford. Then it is time for me to say something.

I find myself describing how it has rained every day since my father's death, sometimes twice in a day, great downpours that have left the earth sodden and the air scrubbed and clear and fresh. And how my father's rain gauge—a bottle green glass cone in a special iron stand on our lawn—has filled right up to its wide mouth, but I can't bear to empty it, measuring his absence in inches of precious rain rather than in hours and days.

And I try to recall him. I recall that he was so straight and honest in his dealings, so allergic to bribery, that it chafed me, that he became poor while all around him lesser men prospered. To recall that even when I began reporting on things that brought them into danger, he never counseled caution, though it was certainly in his nature. To recall that, however mad and sad this place has become, he could never quite bear to leave it. And now he would never have to.

I look up at the congregation for the first time, and I feel my composure slipping. I need to finish up and sit down.

"This morning I phoned home and my five-year-old son came on the line.

" 'Are you having fun in Africa, Dad?' he asked.

" 'Well, I'm a bit sad, actually,' I said, 'because my dad is dead.'

"And he shot back: 'Can't you get a new one?'

" 'No,' I said. 'I can't.'

"Today would have been my father's eightieth birthday. Happy Birthday, Dad. Wherever you are."

AT THE END of the service Manuel plays "Ishe Komberera" variations, a haunting melody he has written himself based on the hymn "God Bless Africa," and we file out into the church hall. The circle of widows, coming together in an age-old ritual to welcome a new member, have all baked, despite the chronic shortage of ingredients, and the trestle tables in the church hall groan under the cakes and sausage rolls and sandwiches.

The large framed fiftieth-wedding anniversary photo of my mother and father surrounded by Dalmatians, touched up in pastels by Jeremy, like a Victorian portrait, stands on a table. Underneath it is a condolence book made by street children with paper from recycled elephant dung. Linnea has used some of her precious gasoline quota to drive out to Doon Estate on the Mutare Road to buy it, and she has sprinkled the tops of the pages with uplifting aphorisms, written in her meticulous teacher's script, and glued little mementos to them too.

A long line of people wishing to offer condolences coils in front of my mother and me.

"You are now part of our extended family," Pius Wakatama tells us.

Maureen Mutasa, one of my father's protégées, who is now in

charge of the Standards Association, and has sons of her own at Cambridge, says, "He made me what I am, he was my mentor, always encouraging me . . ."

Nurse Machire, my mother's head nurse, approaches. The two of them have worked as a tight-knit team for more than a decade, imposing order on the chaos of a waiting room teeming with the sick. She is small and dainty and formidable. She takes me by the elbow and steers me to one side, away from my mother.

"The day after your father died, I went to visit your mother, Peter," she says earnestly. "And I found her all alone there, Peter. *All alone*. Not even a gardener there. Just by *herself*, Peter." Then she bursts into tears of anger. "I don't ever want to find your mother by herself again," she says, and then she hugs me, and we discuss how we can get her son, a qualified mechanic, a visa to work in England.

Looking at the long line, I realize that my mother is not alone, that my parents are loved and accepted, and I realize just how color-blind their society has become. Mugabe has managed to achieve something hitherto so elusive; he has created a real racial unity— not the bogus one portrayed in the beer commercials of the new South Africa, but something more substantial, a hard-won sense of comradeship, a common bond forged in the furnace of resistance to an oppressive rule. I realize just how African my parents have become. That this is their home. That my father really has died at home. That finally, in this most unpromising of places, where he could never be regarded as truly indigenous, finally, he belonged.

twenty-two

February 2004

T HE MORNING AFTER his funeral, as the rain pummels down
outside, we finally start clearing up Dad's things. It hasn't
seemed right to do it until now.

I unlock the door to his room. Mum has left it just as it was
when he went into the hospital. The bedclothes are still rumpled in
his body shape, and the scent of him still clings to them. She has
returned his tortoiseshell glasses to his bedside table, as if he might
come back and need them again. I sit on the end of his hard, narrow
bed, covered with its mustard candlewick bedspread, and look
around.

His *GOIF* slippers are under his bedside table, next to his terry
cloth "stompies." A half-burned mosquito coil nestles on a old
chipped china saucer that bears the coat of arms of the short-lived
Central African Federation: a sable and a leopard holding a shield
with the motto *Magni Esse Mereamur,* "Let Us Be Great," topped
by a fish eagle, wings outstretched. Next to them a W. G. Sebald
book, *The Emigrants,* I had sent him. The bookmark is halfway

through—he had stopped being able to read about three months before he died. Cheap cotton floral curtains sewn by my mother flutter above a thin brown mat. On the table are a long green plastic shoehorn, a candle, a little pewter cup with pills, and a rough pottery mug filled with water and covered by a fly mesh with a border of little collared beads—an old Christmas present from Mavis—to weigh it down, his Nicorette inhaler, tissues, matches. On the walls are four paintings of English country scenes. Hanging on the closet door is his favorite green safari suit shirt, with pleated pockets and epaulets and a threadbare collar. I remember his boast, no new clothes since he retired, three years ago. In the corner stands a massive red fire extinguisher, "The Invincible No. 3," made in Newcastle-Upon-Tyne by George Angus and Co. in 1956. A huge steel piston head from a bulldozer serves as a doorstop. On top of the closet is an old saw and a heavy crowbar.

"What are those for?" I ask Mum.

"He put them there so we could saw and pry our way out of the burglar bars if the house was on fire," she says. "I told him I'd never be strong enough, but he said, 'You wait and see. If there's a fire you'll find the strength.' "

She looks at his rumpled bed. "You know, it was only last year, Dad told me, that he finally started dreaming in English."

I open the closet. On one shelf he has assembled a little hoard of things that are hard to find these days: toothpaste, soap, shampoo, candles, single-malt scotch, and a jar of Willards instant coffee, still sealed, but congealed with age. The sum of Z$5,170 in notes, carefully concealed—amounting to about US$1 at today's exchange rates. Another shelf is entirely overrun by coins, thousands of them in bags, boxes, film canisters. Saved as parking change or tipping money but, by the end, utterly worthless and no longer even in general circulation. A box containing his cuff links, tiepins, armbands for shirtsleeves. Under his hanging safari suits, he has carefully stored his camera equipment in a converted brown schoolboy's suitcase. He has cut the exact shapes of each lens and camera body out of foam rubber, and on the outside he has attached homemade straps for his tripod.

In the bottom of the cupboard sits Dad's gap bag, a permanently packed bag in case they had to leave at very short notice. Hidden under his pullovers in the very top drawer, where you might expect to find contraband or valuables, is a book in Polish. Georgina bought it for him when she learned he was from Poland. He has hidden it out of habit.

And at the back of another shelf, I find an Air Zimbabwe wash bag, full to bulging. I unzip it, and medals spill out onto the red floor. There are three wars' worth of them. My mother's World War II medals; her father's World War I medals; and my father's Zimbabwean Police Reserve medals, his radio unit badges (a pair of tom-toms — the talking drums). And there too I find his old military insignia from World War II, his Polish First Armored Division cap badge and shoulder flashes. But there are no World War II medals for him. Only later, when I write to the British Ministry of Defense, do I receive a package from their Polish Inquiries section out at RAF Northolt in West London. It contains his war record and a box of medals, four of them, nestling in baize-lined boxes (the 1939–45 Star, Defense medal, and France and Germany Star, and War Medal 1939–45, with more to follow from the Polish army). They have been sitting there on a shelf at the Polish section of the Ministry of Defense — all in the name of Kazimierz Jerzy Goldfarb — unclaimed for fifty years.

MUM ASKS ME to take the remains of his medications, all his unused drugs, to the Medicine Chest, the local pharmacy.

"They're so hard to find, and they may help someone else," she says.

As usual, as soon as I get out of the car, I am assailed by hawkers. They're selling mangos, flowers, apples, bananas, tomatoes, onions, but I fend them off politely in Shona.

On my return from the pharmacy, I am nearly at my car when I hear a loud crash and see one of the flower hawkers who lives under our hedge falling hard against a brushed aluminum Pajero. He looks at me, startled, as he slides down the side of the SUV. No one else appears to have seen him. I stride over to find him lying on a bed of his own roses. His white shirt is speckled with red dots where the rose thorns have pierced his flesh. His eyes are rolling into the back of their sockets, his mouth is flecked with foam, he is choking on his tongue. I kneel down and hold his head up. He is having an epileptic fit. I know what I have to do. I have to reach into his mouth and pull his tongue out. But his perfect teeth, white and sharp, glint brilliantly in the sunlight, and I am afraid that he will inadvertently bite me. And I know that nearly 40 percent of Zimbabweans have AIDS.

"Help!" I call, rather feebly, but no one comes. We are hidden between parked Pajeros. He utters another oxygen-starved groan, and I know he has run out of time. So I reach in to pull out his warm wet tongue. And he doesn't bite me. His shivers grow less, and his eyes return to their normal position, and his seizures slowly subside. I sit with this hawker's head in my lap until his eyes focus again, and he looks up at me, confused. And then suddenly his friends and colleagues appear and help him up to the sidewalk.

I am left amid the pile of crushed long-stemmed roses, white ones, peach ones, red ones, custard ones. I find a pair of white roses that are less damaged than the others and peel away the bruised outer petals until the buds look almost passable. I walk slowly back to the car and sit inside in the baking heat for a minute to calm myself. And then I drive home and present the roses to my mother.

"They may be blood roses, remember?" she chides. "You shouldn't have bought them."

"I didn't buy them," I say.

THAT NIGHT, in the face of another gathering storm, the power cuts out again, and so does the water. We light candles, and they give the house an eerie, Gothic feel, while outside the thunder rumbles closer, and the lightning flickers over the eastern townships. Around us are the wilting condolence bouquets, the trumpet-barreled blunderbuss padlocked to its wall mounting, and the luminous white of the steed under my befrocked great-great-great-uncle. Jain's batik lamp shades, browns, yellows, and oranges, flowers and geometric patterns, look alive in the lambent light.

The power cut reduces Mum to tears again. "Dad used to be so prepared," she says, looking around at the strategically placed candles and flashlights and matchboxes, and at the gas light and battery-powered light strip above his armchair.

Then, as she hears the generators growling to life in nearby houses, she becomes infuriated. "Whenever the power cuts out now, those bloody generators kick in," she says bitterly. "It's another world. Bloody fat cats."

Now that the funeral is over, I feel able to reopen the overdue discussion about her future. I am gently but insistently trying to persuade her that it may be time for her to leave. That the country is in free fall, getting poorer and more dangerous. That famine beckons, and with it, real anarchy. That as she gets older she will become more isolated. And when she stops driving she will be stranded. That she will be more vulnerable now that Dad is gone. She listens attentively to the apocalyptic future I am sketching for her.

"Are you finished now?" she asks.

I nod, and she limps over to the bookshelf and shines her flashlight along the rows of spines until she finds the one she wants. She runs her finger down the index and flicks to her desired page. And she reads silently for a moment, her glasses perched on the end of her nose. Then she hands me the book and the flashlight. It is a volume of poems by Rudyard Kipling.

"The first two and the last stanza," she says. "Obviously for my purposes Rome is Britain, and Britain is Africa."

The book is open at a poem entitled "The Roman Centurion's Song (Roman Occupation of Britain, A.D. 300)." By flashlight I begin to read as instructed.

LEGATE, I had the news last night—my cohort ordered home
By ships to Portus Itius and thence by road to Rome.
I've marched the companies aboard, the arms are stowed below;
Now let another take my sword. Command me not to go!

I've served in Britain forty years, from Vectis to the Wall.
I have none other home than this, nor any life at all.
Last night I did not understand, but, now the hour draws near
That calls me to my native land, I feel that land is here. . . .

Legate, I come to you in tears—My cohort ordered home!
I've served in Britain forty years. What should I do in Rome?
Here is my heart, my soul, my mind—the only life I know,
I cannot leave it all behind. Command me not to go!

"Now do you understand?" she asks when I look up.

WE VISIT Margaret at B. S. Leon in the morning. The staff there told us she wasn't well enough to come to the funeral, that she is scared of strangers now. Nothing at all has changed in the three months since our last visit. It feels like someone has pressed a pause button. She sits at the same Formica table with her back to the same window, reading the same magazine, *This England*, issue of Spring '93. It is open at very the same page, at the article entitled "The Spirit of England," and Churchill is still warning his people that "Appeasement is feeding the crocodile, hoping it will eat you last," and imploring that "Nothing can save England if she will not save herself." In her hand is the green plastic flyswatter. The two other elderly ladies still sit silently hunched over on their bed ends, observing us as Mum and I sit on Margaret's bed.

I must tell Margaret that Dad is dead.

"I have some bad news," I begin.

"Oh, yes?" she chirps.

"George has died."

"Oh, dear," she says enviously. "I wish it were me."

Again, like she did last time, she suddenly whips the swat at a fly, and it falls dead to the floor, and I congratulate her.

"I killed twenty-one in a single day once," she repeats, with a hoot of laughter. "Is it true?" she asks. "Is George really dead?"

"Yes, he died last week," I say. "We've already had the funeral."

"I never went to my Derek's funeral either," she says sadly. "I don't even know where he's buried. I miss him so, you know."

Somewhere at the end of the disinfectant-scented corridor a bell tinkles.

"What's that?" she wonders.

"It's the bell for tea, I think," I say.

"Have I had my cup of tea yet? No, I haven't. I think that's my teatime."

She focuses on us again. "Where did he die?"

"The Avenues Clinic," says Mum.

"Lucky bugger," she says. "I wish it were me."

We chat on for a few minutes, then she suddenly tires. She turns her face up for a good-bye kiss, and I lower my lips to her steroid-grizzled cheek.

"When are you coming back?" she asks, suddenly in tears.

"Soon," I lie.

IN THE AFTERNOON, Mum and I sit at our dining table with a lawyer. We are trying to do estate planning in a country with nearly a thousand percent inflation. He tries to explain the situation. Dad's stocks and shares are worth little; most commercial activity here is on life support or winding down. His life insurance policies, several of them, after years of his struggling to pay the premiums, forgoing vacations and treats and even new clothes to keep them up, are almost worthless. In fact, says the lawyer, the policies will cost more in legal fees to wind up than they are actually worth. Mum might as well tear them up. Her doctor's pension is not adjusted to inflation and is almost worthless. The house is her main asset, and that's not worth much these days. Her only other asset is her elderly Mazda car—for as long as she can keep it from being stolen like the last two were.

My plan, in as much as I have one, is to sell the house and buy her a garden apartment in a serviced, gated community elsewhere in Harare, possibly Dandara, which I would subsidize from abroad. I cannot bear to have her ending up like Margaret, alone with a fly-swatter and a nine-year-old magazine, watching pop videos in the cabbage fumes. She still has many friends here, she insists, and she feels too old to start again somewhere else. I know her well enough not to argue. But she agrees that I can arrange for her to go on a short vacation to visit Georgina in London in a few months, if her "good" hip doesn't fail first.

THE WORSLEY-WORSWICKS invite us to supper the next day to help discuss Mum's options. They are still stranded in town while the wovits occupy their farm. John's wife, Paula, has recently quali-fied as a real estate agent, and she knows about various gated com-munities that might be suitable for Mum. But at the last minute, Mum feels too tired, so I go alone.

The Worswicks have changed address again, this time to a short-term rental on the hill behind the British ambassador's resi-dence, which, despite the power cut, is blazing with privately gener-ated security lights. John shows me around his garden, which has a series of ornamental ponds and a planted rain forest. But what he really sees are potential parking places. "If we can get the equip-ment off the farm," he says, lighting up another cigarette, "we could park tractors here; we could get masses of equipment in the space behind the rain forest."

The ornamental ponds are stocked with tame koi, he says. And I remember Meryl, chief inspector of the ZNSPCA, telling me how she saved the koi in one farm pond by convincing the wovits that the fish were highly poisonous. John begins to tap the ground with the sole of his brogue, which, he assures me, will attract them. None comes, so he steps up to the pond and begins tapping his sole on the surface of the dark green water. Still nothing. "They're usually quite forthcoming," he frowns, now wetting his entire shoe in his deter-mination to summon the promised friendly koi. "Actually," he suddenly remembers, "I haven't seen them for a few days. I suspect the gardener may have eaten them."

After supper, we repair for coffee to the living room, most of which John has converted into a fly-tying workshop with a trestle table along one wall. It is covered with thin spools of wire and tufts of various feathers and dozens of small instruments — just like Dad's radio tools. It has a small vise clamped to one edge. Here, with his broad farmer's fingers, John sits nimbly tying the most exquisitely delicate trout-fishing flies. His latest, which he proudly brings over, is the Glorious 12th, an intricate combination of red grouse feathers and klipspringer hair. While I examine the fly, Paula paces impatiently up and down the confines of their suburban kitchen, a caged feline, waiting for the coffee to brew.

Over coffee, John confides JAG's latest attempts to save their farms. Mugabe is preparing new legislation that will retrospectively legalize the farm seizures, without any financial compensation to the evicted farmers, thus voiding all the farmers' present legal challenges.

Now, in what John is careful to present as a backup tactic, he is thinking of suing the British Crown. "Yes," he says, "the Queen. In her capacity as head of the British state, for handing on to us defective title to the land. We've asked a senior barrister in London to prepare us an opinion."

I DRIVE HOME up Enterprise Road to see if they have any fuel yet at the Chisipite service station, as my gauge is on red. The streetlights are dark because of the power cut. Ahead, I see the glowing tip of a pedestrian's cigarette, and I slow up a little and move into the center of the road to avoid a huge pothole. Suddenly men with guns loom. It's a police roadblock. I slam on my brakes. I should have anticipated it; tomorrow is another in a series of less and less effective opposition strikes, and the police always cordon off the city the day before a strike to stop the opposition from moving its supporters around.

Two armed policemen are standing in the middle of the road, across which they have dragged a couple of logs. There are no warning signs, and the policemen themselves wear no reflective armbands or vests. The roadblock is all but invisible, save for the red glow of their cigarettes.

A baby-faced sergeant leans into my window and exhales a beery plume of smoke into the car.

"You should be stopping farther back," he says crossly.

"Your roadblock is very hard to see," I smile.

He ignores me. "License," he says thickly.

I explain that I don't actually have it on me, but I'm happy to go and get it, happy for him to escort me if necessary. His interest is piqued, there is a potential for baksheesh here.

"If you no have license then you have to wait over there until our shift is finished, and then you must go to the police station with me." He pauses for effect. "You have broken the law," he says magisterially. "You will have to pay a fine."

"According to the law," I say genially, "I only have to produce my license at a police station within twenty-four hours of having been so requested."

He looks momentarily disconcerted and then reverts to his script. "Where is your license?" And we do another round. And this time he warns me that I will have to spend the entire night "in the prison cells."

"OK," I say, giving up. "Where would you like me to wait?"

He looks confused again. Our roadblock duet is discordant. I am supposed to be in a hurry, offer a bribe, and be allowed on my way. But no, I am a freak. A white man with time on his hands.

Annoyed now, he motions me to park at the side of the road. I sit there for a few minutes in the inky dark under a tree. Then a bus wheezes up. According to its route window, it is coming in from the tribal area north of Mount Darwin, where Gomo and Richard are from. The policemen order everyone off the bus and instruct the conductors to hand down the mountain of goods on the roof rack.

Down it all comes: wicker cages of chickens, bicycles, dozens of red-and-white-striped jute bags, a hobbled goat, furniture, firewood. The contraband the police are most interested in is cornmeal, the local staple. The government still insists on a monopoly of grain sales. To transport more than five kilograms of it constitutes the crime of black marketeering.

The country is on the verge of a famine, and the United Nations has warned Mugabe that half of the country's twelve million people are now in danger of starvation. But he has spurned offers of more international food aid, saying, "Why do they want to choke us with their food? We have enough." And one of his most senior ministers, Didymus Mutasa, on hearing of the UN famine projection, implied that such a die-off, at least in opposition areas, was actually desirable. "We would be better off with only six million people, with our own people, who supported the liberation struggle," he was reported as saying. "We don't want these extra people."

The policemen confiscate several bags and put them on their growing pile of loot at the side of the road. An old lady my mother's age pleads with them. She has come all the way from the Zambezi Valley to bring this small burlap bag of meal to her grandson, "a young boy just like you," she says, "but he is without a job; he has nothing to eat." The sergeant does not want to be stripped of his badges of office and humanized. He knows that she doesn't have enough for a bribe, so the cornmeal itself will be his bounty.

She is determined not to cry, but two tears well over onto her long lined cheeks. This is not store-bought cornmeal. This is from corn that she has tended from the beginning, that she has plowed and seeded and watered as tiny, tender lime green shoots, and hoed and weeded and harvested and dried and shucked and carried for miles to a grinding mill and paid to have it ground there into powdered meal and carried back home on her head and loaded onto this bus. It has evaded drought and birds and locusts and rats and antelopes and elephants. And just a few miles and a few minutes from its intended beneficiary, it has been wrenched away from her.

This is what this young policeman is casually stealing tonight, all these months and months of work by this old lady. But he is unmoved by her earnest entreaties.

I should sit quietly in my car. I know this woman is beyond my help. But if I don't at least *try*, I will hate myself for it. I will lie awake during New York nights remembering this moment, the look on her face.

I open my door and walk over. "Sergeant?"

He starts at my voice. "Back! Back inside your car!" he says.

"Please, Sergeant, it's such a small bag of mealie meal, please can you let her take it? I can give you *bonsela* . . ." I reach for my wallet. For this I can break my father's ban on bribes.

"*Wena, mukiwa!*" — "You, white man!" he says, furiously fumbling with the press stud of his holster. Realizing how badly I have misread the situation, I start to retreat, my arms out, palms forward, placating. Over his shoulder, I can see that the passengers on the bus, which is repacked and ready to go, are agog. The sergeant has managed to pull out his pistol now and he's waving it at me. "This is not your business. Do not interfere with police matters," he screams.

The bus conductor is fearful of getting caught up in crossfire, and he calls down urgently to the old lady that they are leaving and she must board now or be left behind. So she limps over to the door and hauls herself up on the chipped metal rail, shaking her head in disgust that it has come to this. That young boys, young enough to be her grandsons, would steal the food she has worked for a whole season to grow. As she reaches the top of the stairs, she half turns and looks down at me as I stand there with my hands up, facing the fulminating sergeant. She inclines her head slightly and raises a hand, bestowing on me her acknowledgment. And then she turns and is gone. The conductor hops in after her, bangs on the side, and the bus revs up and accelerates away in a great black belch of diesel fumes.

The sergeant frog-marches me to my car. If I come out again, he says, he will shoot me "for resisting arrest," and he slams my door shut.

I need to call Mum and tell her not to wait up for me. I dial the number on her cell phone, which I have borrowed. It rings and rings and the answering machine message kicks in just as she picks up.

"Hello? Hello?" says Mum.

"This is 490947," says Dad, in his deliberately enunciated voice.

We wait for him to finish his outgoing message, and then I tell her that the Worsley-Worswicks' supper is running late and she should go to bed.

I sit there in the dark, incarcerated in my car, until finally, as the sun rises, the policemen drag the branches off the road and pack up their roadblock. The sergeant saunters over to me. "I'm going off shift now," he says. "I'm too busy to be bothered with you. Go," and he cocks his head in dismissal.

"Thank you so much, Sergeant," I say with a smile he recognizes as false.

"Ah, just *voetsak*," he says. It's an Afrikaans expletive. Like *fuck off*, only worse.

I SIT IN DAD'S STUDY, red eyed from my night at the roadblock, trying to make sense of his files, trying to regularize the bills and accounts so that it will be easy for Mum to administer. Already the study feels like a mausoleum. Lining the pelmets are my maternal grandfather's trophies—for athletics, rowing, swimming, golf. The silver cups and pewter tankards are dusty and tarnished. Dehydrated husks of small spiders are trapped behind the glass of my old school team photos on the wall.

In front of me, the garden is alive with birds. The egret is at its post on the steps of the fishpond, eyeing the murky water intently. Fire finches with jaunty red bellies, and bronze mannikins hop on the surrounding lawn, pecking at the grass seeds. Up in the acacia thorn tree, a trio of purple-crested louries converse raucously, and a group of wood hoopoes with long hooked scarlet beaks sit quietly on a branch of Jain's kapok tree. Around us, the city—in the grip of another strike, this time organized by the trade unions—is quiet.

I toil there for most of the day, and as it starts to get dark I have worked through all the files and come to one last locked drawer. Mum bustles around and finally finds the key. In this last cabinet there are thick albums, half a dozen of them, each dated, covering periods from the early eighties onward. They contain clippings of all the pieces I have ever written, carefully glued down and meticulously cross-referenced. Every review of my books and TV documentaries. Every ad for every book reading. Videos of all my programs. It is a master record of my entire career. My father has been minutely following it, the career he officially hoped I would abandon in favor of "a real job." And the pages show signs of some serious wear and tear. Of having been well thumbed.

"He would come in here some nights and get them all out and just sit here on his own reading through it all," says my mother, who has entered with a mug of chicory for me. "And he would rewatch your old documentaries too. It was almost as though he was seeing the world through your eyes." I struggle to hold back tears.

"He was very proud of you, really," says my mother, putting her hand on my shoulder and squeezing it. "For some reason he found it so difficult to tell you."

I just start to howl, and the egret flaps away up over the burned bougainvillea.

WE ARE STILL WAITING to hear from Keith when Dad's body can be cremated. There is only one crematorium in Harare, the one out at Warren Hills, where Jain was cremated. They are waiting for a delivery of butane gas, he says. Some is expected soon.

But this morning I get a call from the mortuary where Dad's body is stored. Like so many parts of the city, they too are without power. And now they are running out of diesel for their backup generator. They have only enough to last another two days. After that the morgue will rapidly heat up and the corpses will begin to decompose. If we do not claim my father's body by then, they will have no choice but to give it up to the Ministry of Health for burial in the mass grave out past the city limits. Health regulations stipulate this. He is very sorry. These are difficult times.

I put the phone down and sit there in a daze. The one thing that Dad made me promise him was that I would have him cremated and not buried. Why the hell hadn't I paid closer attention? The last thing he'd asked me to do for him, and now I can't deliver it.

I phone Keith and ask him what options I have.

"Well, there's Bulawayo, but I think that's out of order at present," he says. "And it would be tough to get the paperwork done in time."

"And I don't have the fuel to get there," I say miserably.

He pauses. "I suppose you *might* try the Hindus, a couple of whites went that route a while back."

"The Hindus?"

"Yeah, you know, a funeral pyre," he says. "Burn him yourself."

"For Christ's sake, Keith, I can't torch my own father."

"Well, you'll just have to bury him, then."

I page through our old phone book and find a number for the archaically spelled "Hindoo" Society.

"I'm so sorry," says the man who answers in a singsong Indian accent, "but the government has banned all non-Hindus from being burned here. And anyway we are between priests at present. The old one has already left, and we have sent to India for a new one, but he has not arrived yet. In any case, the metal trolley on which the pyre is built is broken. But, listen, I am new here, you should speak to Mr. Patel. Mr. Kiran Patel."

Patel answers his cell phone in what is obviously a bustling shop with voices bargaining in the background and the regular *ker-ching* of a cash register. I put my case to him: that I need to cremate my father before the end of the week, or they will put him in a mass grave. He repeats the ordinance banning pyres for non-Hindus. "I'm sorry," he says. "We can't burn whites."

I plead and plead, repeating that I've come all the way from New York to do this, and that it was my father's dying wish.

Finally his voice softens. "Well, there is *one* way around the ban. As head of the Hindu community, I suppose I have the authority to declare him an honorary Hindu, and then you could go ahead and burn him on our pyre."

"How would you do that?" I ask.

"Well, I would just declare it, and then it would be so," he says.

"Will you do it?"

"You buy me a beer sometime if I come to New York, OK?"

"Absolutely," I say. "Several."

"All right," he says. "What's his name?"

"Godwin, George Godwin."

He clears his throat and asks for quiet in the shop. The hubbub dies down and then in a formal voice he says: "I solemnly declare that your father, George Godwin, is hereby an honorary Hindu."

I thank him profusely.

"You come to our temple and make the arrangements there, OK? And remember my beer sometime in New York?" He laughs and turns back to his shop, where the background *ker-ching*ing has started up once more.

I find Mum in the dining room puzzling over documents.

"Dad is a Hindu now," I tell her.

"What?"

"He's been declared an honorary Hindu so that I can cremate him at their site. Otherwise it's illegal. Only Hindus can be burned there. It's a pyre."

"I've always liked the Hindus," she says, "I think there's a lot to be said for their belief system." And she wanders off to see if she has any books on Hinduism.

It seems oddly appropriate somehow. My father is born a Polish Jew, becomes an English Christian, and is cremated an African Hindu. That's enough shape shifting to impress Dambudzo Marechera's manfish, the *njuzu*.

ROBIN WATSON arrives the next morning in a Nissan pickup truck he is looking after for a farmer from Chinhoyi who's fled the country. Mum doesn't want to come to the Hindu temple, she says, and Mr. Patel has told me that traditionally women here do not attend a funeral.

"We're not going to make you commit suttee, and put you on the pyre too, you know," I try to joke, and she makes a face. "Wait a minute," she says as we get in the truck. She goes inside and re-emerges with a big round Quality Street chocolate tin, decorated in electric shades of mauve and pink, and featuring a grinning soldier embracing a maiden in bustle and bonnet. "To put his ashes in," she says, and waves us off.

We drive down Samora Machel Avenue out to the suburb of Belvedere, in the old days a designated "Indian Area." During World War II, this was one of the main bases of the vast Empire Air Training Scheme, a production line for fighter pilots (and aircrew), most of them from Britain. Here they were out of reach of German bombers, and the climate was perfect for flying. They would take a young man who'd never been behind a joystick, start him off in a Tiger Moth biplane, and a few months and 130 flying hours later, he would have wings sewn on his chest and be on his way to battle the Luftwaffe. After the war, many of those surviving airmen came back to settle here, which is why so many white farmers can fly.

"This was the actual runway," says Robin as we swing onto a very wide, straight paved road, now called Ganges Road. We turn onto Boeing Road and left onto Cessna Drive, right onto Anson, and there before us, like a spaceship that has landed on the veld, are the towering brick tiers of the Hindu Omkar Temple, topped with gold turrets and fluttering red pennants. We park next to it. There are offerings of frangipani petals and grains of rice on its front step. Inside I can see the statue of the Monkey God, Lord Hanumanji, and off to one side, the Elephant God, Lord Ganesha, with his four hands. In his curled trunk he holds a golden lotus blossom. I find myself thinking that in our in extremis sect of postmortem Godwin Hinduism, Lord Ganesha might represent a deification of a box elephant.

At the office I pay a fee of Z$200,000, which includes my license and the wood. Robin backs the pickup against the woodshed, and a gang of laborers appears, herded by an elderly Indian caretaker. The men load a medley of tropical timber, musasa, mopani, eucalyptus, wattle, and some conifers too, fir and cypress. In the background, a piano plinks, as piping voices learn the new national anthem, "Blessed be the Land of Zimbabwe." When the truck is groaning under a great pile of timber, we set off for the burning ground with two of the laborers perched on top of the wood.

From the Hindu temple we drive down Bishop Gaul Avenue, past the fading gold edifice of the Yugoslav-built Sheraton Hotel, and the ZANU-PF party headquarters next door on Rotten Row. "A rather apt address," Robin says. The building, Jongwe House, is topped by a triangular facade, in the center of which stands a rampant crowing cockerel—*jongwe* in Shona—the ruling party's symbol. We turn into Remembrance Drive, past the Mbare single men's hostels, and then into Pioneer Cemetery, the city's oldest graveyard.

At the gatehouse, we pick up a municipality foreman, Tapera. He is a tall, imposing black man dressed in a long-sleeved green shirt, pin-striped gray pleated trousers, and suede desert boots. Tapera escorts us slowly through the vast graveyard, pointing out its different religious precincts: Buddhist, Muslim, Jewish, Catholic, Dutch Reformed, Anglican, Methodist, Presbyterian—all sects are represented among the run-down graves. From time to time we encounter a blue-fatigued laborer slashing away at the tall canopy of elephant grass that threatens to overwhelm the place.

"We have too few people for the upkeep of sixty-five acres," says Tapera as we drive through the Jewish quarter with lichen-covered Stars of David peeking through the tangle of African foliage. It is home to some two thousand Jews; the oldest grave here belongs to David Henry, who died in 1895, aged one year and eight days. Nearby, a mass mausoleum, shaded by the dense dark green crown of a thunder tree, a natal mahogany, contains the bones of white farmers killed in the Mashona Rebellion—the first *Chimurenga*—the following year.

We arrive at the Hindu section, and unload the wood from the truck. Then we start heaving the logs into a large iron crib, which sits on wheels on a railroad track. Tapera explains the science of pyre making as we work. Alternating layers of slower and faster burning wood, our pyre slowly rises until it reaches the top of the sooty crib.

"It used to be, in the old days," says Tapera, "you had to shout to be heard here." He points over at the factories that surround us, as Pioneer Cemetery is in the industrial part of town. "But so many of these factories are shut down now, there is no more noise. No more jobs. It is just quiet."

Overlooking us to the south is Rufaro Stadium, "where our independence ceremonies were held in 1980," he reminds me. "But now it's all gone sour," he says. "We've gone from bread bin to dustbin. Mugabe's persecuting his own people. But our time will come. Every dog has its day."

MY FATHER IS NOW more than an hour late. We sit on a mossy stone bench under a giant fig tree, waiting for him. We have finished the little Chinese thermos of coffee that my mother prepared, and the sandwiches.

Tapera looks up. The motion pleats the base of his shaven skull into an accordion of glistening brown flesh.

"At last," he says. "He is arrived."

The car, long and low and sinister, glides slowly toward us, only the black roof visible above the reef of elephant grass. It passes us and then backs up into position.

Keith jumps out of the passenger side.

"Sorry we're late," he says. "We were stopped at a police roadblock up on Rotten Row. They wanted to check inside. Can you believe it?"

He hands me a clipboard. "Sign here and here."

The driver reaches down to unlatch the tailgate. It opens with a gentle hydraulic sigh. Inside is a steel coffin. Together we slide it out and carry it over to the concrete steps. Keith unlatches the lid to reveal a body tightly bound in a white linen winding-sheet.

"Why don't you take the top," he says.

I ease one hand under the back of my father's head and my other arm under his shoulders, and I give him a last little hug. He is cool and surprisingly soft to my touch. The others arrange themselves along his body, and on Keith's count we lift it out of the coffin.

We shuffle up the concrete stairs that lead to the top of the iron crib. We have woven fresh green branches through its black bars. And on top of the tiers of logs inside it, we have placed a thick bed of pine needles and garnished it with fragrant pine shavings. Upon this bed we lay my father down.

Gently, Tapera lifts Dad's head to place a small eucalyptus log under his neck as a pillow. As he does so the shroud peeks open at a fold, and I get a sudden, shocking glimpse of my father's face. His jaw, grizzled with salt-and-pepper stubble; the little dents on his nose where his glasses rested; his mustache, slightly shaggy and un-kempt now; the lines of his brow relaxed at last in death. And then, as his head settles back, the shroud stretches shut again, and he is gone.

Tapera is staggering up the steps with a heavy musasa log. He places it on top of the body.

"Huuuh." My father exhales one last loud breath with the weight of it.

"It is necessary," Tapera says quietly, "to hold the body down in case . . ." He pauses to think if there is a way to say this delicately. "In case it explodes because of the buildup of the gases." He looks unhappily at the ground. "It happens sometimes, you know."

Keith slides the empty coffin back into the hearse and drives away down the lane, where it is soon swallowed up again by the green gullet of grass.

The old black grave digger, Robert, has his hand in front of me now. His palm is yellow and barnacled with calluses. He is offering me a small Bic lighter made of fluorescent blue plastic.

"It is traditional for the son to light the fire," says Tapera, and he nods me forward.

I stroke my father's brow gently through the shroud, kiss his forehead. Then I flick the lighter. It fires up on my third trembling attempt, and I walk slowly around the base of the trolley, lighting the kindling. It crackles and pops as the flames take hold and shiver up the tower of logs to lick at the linen shroud. Quickly, before the cloth burns away to reveal the scorched flesh beneath, Tapera hands me a long metal T-bar and instructs me to place it against the back of the trolley, while he does the same next to me. We both heave at it. For a moment the trolley remains stuck on its rusty rails. Then it groans into motion and squeaks slowly toward the jaws of the old redbrick kiln a few yards away.

"Sorry it's so difficult," says Tapera, breathing heavily with the effort. "The wheel bearings are shot."

The flaming pyre enters the kiln and lurches to rest against the buffers. Robert, the grave digger, clangs shut the cast-iron doors and pulls down the heavy latch to lock them.

We all squint up into the brilliant blue sky to see if the fire is drawing. A plume of milky smoke flows up from the chimney stack, up through the green and red canopy of the overhanging flame tree.

"She is a good fire," says Tapera. "She burns well."

FIN

ACKNOWLEDGMENTS

As I have made clear in the text, some parts of this book draw on reporting I did in Africa for *National Geographic,* the *New York Times Magazine, Reader's Digest, ForbesLife, Men's Journal,* Channel 4 TV (via Windfall Films), the *Observer* (London), the *Guardian,* and the *Times* (London). I'm grateful for their assignments. The passage on Dambudzo Marechera appeared in a somewhat different form as an introduction I wrote for the Penguin reissue of his novel, *The House of Hunger.*

Without the cloistered retreats of MacDowell and Yaddo, the artists' colonies in New Hampshire and Saratoga Springs, I would still be procrastinating. I acknowledge my debt to them both.

I thank my agent, Andrew Wylie; my editors at Little, Brown, Judy Clain and Marie Salter; and my British editors at Picador, Ursula Doyle and Nicholas Blake. And I am beholden to my wife, Joanna Coles, who has stoically borne my literary preoccupation.

The enormous help provided by my mother, Dr. Helen Godwin, and my sister, Georgina Godwin, has been essential to this book.

Without their contributions, I could never have written it. Which isn't to say they necessarily approve of all that is between these covers. That responsibility is mine and mine alone.

Peter Godwin
New York
2006